The
HIGHWAY
KIND

The
HIGHWAY
KIND

Tales of Fast Cars, Desperate Drivers, and Dark Roads

EDITED BY PATRICK MILLIKIN

MULHOLLAND BOOKS

LITTLE, BROWN AND COMPANY

NEW YORK BOSTON LONDON

Compilation copyright © 2016 by Patrick Millikin

Mulholland Books
Hachette Book Group
1290 Avenue of the Americas, New York, NY 10104
mulhollandbooks.com

First Edition: October 2016

Copyright acknowledgments appear on page 337.

Mulholland Books is an imprint of Little, Brown and Company, a division of Hachette Book Group, Inc. The Mulholland Books name and logo are trademarks of Hachette Book Group, Inc.

Library of Congress Cataloging-in-Publication Data

Millikin, Patrick, editor.
The highway kind : tales of fast cars, desperate drivers, and dark roads :
    original stories by Michael Connelly, George Pelecanos, C. J. Box,
    Diana Gabaldon, Ace Atkins & others / edited by Patrick Millikin.
First edition. | New York : Mulholland Books, 2016.
LCCN 2016017934 | ISBN 978-0-316-39486-4
Detective and mystery stories, American. | Crime—United
    States—Fiction. | Automobiles—Fiction. | Automobile driving—Fiction. |
    Muscle cars—Fiction.
LCC PS648.D4 H54 2016 | DDC 813/.08720806—dc23

10 9 8 7 6 5 4 3 2 1

LSC-C

Printed in the United States of America

CONTENTS

I can only suspect that the lonely man peoples his driving dreams with friends, that the loveless man surrounds himself with lovely loving women, and that children climb through the dreaming of the childless driver.

—John Steinbeck, *Travels with Charley*

Stealing a man's wife, that's nothing, but stealing his car, that's larceny.

—James M. Cain, *The Postman Always Rings Twice*

PREFACE

ON A DRIVE from Phoenix to Colorado Springs recently, I pulled over east of Holbrook, Arizona, where a thin strip of weedy asphalt wound in and out of view. This remnant of Route 66 soon disappeared as it merged with the interstate for several miles, then branched off again to continue its path. As I drove on to the sound of freight cars clanking on the nearby railroad line, the years seemed to slip away and I found myself transported into the country's recent past. For decades, Route 66 connected travelers from the east to the "promised land" of California, serving everyone from Depression-era Okies fleeing the dust bowl to an endless succession of young would-be actresses seduced by the allure of Hollywood. Military convoys utilized it during World War II, and later, in the 1950s and '60s, hell-raising teenagers drag raced hot rods on the two-lane blacktop. The iconic route bore witness to a remarkable period of change and upheaval.

When President Eisenhower signed the Federal Aid Highway Act in 1956, he launched the immense interstate system that would create unprecedented ease of movement around the country. This signaled the demise of Route 66 and other venerable roads and in some ways marked the end of our innocence as motorists. Roads meant everything to the country, and then they meant something else. With high-speed thoroughfares came convenience, but also anonymity and a dramatic rise in interstate crime and accident-related deaths (up until the early 1960s, seat belts remained optional in many vehicles). Postwar prosperity ushered in a golden age of the country's car culture: the middle class was on the rise, gas was cheap, and in Detroit the race was on to create the biggest, the most luxurious, the fastest cars. Americans were going places, and mobility equaled freedom. It is an easy era to romanticize now: a time of sleek, big-finned sedans, when knowing one's way around an engine symbolized masculinity, and owning a car meant a literal sort of empowerment.

We live in a vastly different world today, but many of us still spend significant portions of our lives alone in our cars. Over the years, the automobile has come to represent not just our freedom, but our isolation. For many Americans, driving is the closest we'll get to a meditative state. When we're not checking our e-mail or text-messaging with our friends, we're driving and we're thinking. We silently plot crimes, decide to quit drinking, sneak cigarettes, muster the courage to leave our husbands or wives, binge on fast food at anonymous drive-ins. Our cars facilitate our secret lives.

And perhaps this is because roads remain the most *democratic* of all our institutions. For the moment, anyway, we're free to roam wherever and whenever we wish (if we can afford to do so), and the roads connect us, from the lowliest barrio to the most exclusive neighborhood. Follow a lowered '60s Impala, a Honda minivan, or a new Mercedes S-Class sedan, and you'll likely end up in three very different places, listening to three very different stories.

American crime fiction and cars have been accomplices from the beginning, partly because they both developed during the same time. The classic Western loner became, in urban America, the hard-boiled detective maneuvering down the mean streets in his car. The mythology of the Old West depended on an American wanderlust that nicely translated from the horse to the automobile, and the terse and tough realism defined by Hammett, Chandler, and Cain (among others) has always owed more of a debt to Natty Bumppo and Huck Finn than the British drawing room. At its best, crime fiction in this country remains a kind of outsider art form, providing a street-level view of the American landscape.

Tales of Fast Cars, Desperate Drivers, and Dark Roads is the subtitle for this collection of car-inspired stories, and to be sure, the reader can look forward to equal measures of all three. When I solicited the authors, I kept the guidelines pretty loose in order to encourage as many different approaches as possible. The stories were to be about "cars, driving, and the road." I expected a provocative mix of visceral, plot-driven stories and more outré existential tales; what I didn't expect was the deeply personal, almost confessional tone that many of these stories possess. Ben Winters establishes the mood with his opening salvo about a veteran car salesman and a test drive gone horribly wrong. Willy Vlautin writes the aching tale of a middle-aged housepainter, a Pontiac Le Mans, and a young kid's painful coming of age. George Pelecanos contributes a moving elegy to the Vietnam era, when Mopar was king and young men raced cars in the night. Then there's Diana Gabaldon's inventive reimagining of a notorious real-life Autobahn accident in Nazi Germany as narrated by Dr. Ferdinand Porsche, not to mention Joe Lansdale's unforgettable tale of two kids on the road during the Great Depression. Luis Alberto Urrea rounds out the collection with his surreal story about an old man bent on vengeance, a tricked-out VW bus, and a cartel boss known as El Surfo. These are but a few of the varied treasures to be found herein, so whether you're a gearhead or just someone who digs a good exciting tale, you're in for a wild ride.

Patrick Millikin

The
HIGHWAY
KIND

TEST DRIVE

by Ben H. Winters

I WAS GIVING it to this SOB with both barrels, boy. I tell you—
I was laying it on *thick*.

"This vehicle right here, this is the real thing," I told the
test driver, and I was giving him my usual go-getter grin, my
usual just-us-fellas wink. "Minivan or no minivan, this thing
is the real deal. It *looks* like a dad-mobile. Right? And it is *priced*
like a dad-mobile, especially when you buy it from *us*. But
hey—you feel that? You feel that right there?" The engine
had given a little kick, perfect timing, just as the guy eased it
out of the space. "It doesn't *drive* like any dad-mobile, now,
does it? No, it does not. Pardon my language, sir, but hell no, it
does *not*."

I widened the go-getter grin. I eased back in the shotgun
seat, tugged on the seat belt to get myself a little more breathing
room. The test driver's name was Steve. I hadn't caught the last
name, if he'd offered one, but that didn't matter. I'd get the name
when he signed the contract. A test drive takes all of fifteen
minutes; it would take another forty-five to do the paperwork;

I'd be home with a beer, celebrating my fourth sale of the week, by seven o'clock. I whistled a little through my teeth while Steve maneuvered the 2010 cobalt-blue Honda Odyssey out of the lot and headed west on Admiralty Way along the water.

That's the test drive: the long block down Admiralty, right on Via Marina, another right on Washington, then one more right and you're back on our lot. A quick loop, but plenty of time to get a man to fall in love with the vehicle. But those Odysseys, boy? Especially the 2009s, 2010s, those third-generation Odysseys? Well, I'll tell you something, they really do sell themselves.

"That's a V-six engine in there, three point five liters, and you can feel it, right? I don't care how much tonnage a vehicle is, I really do not. You give me a darn grand piano and you slip this V-six in it, the thing's gonna *drive*."

Steve grunted, the first noise I'd heard from him since we got in the car, but his expression did not change. I knew what I was dealing with here: tough customer, cold fish, not about to let himself get conned by some smooth-talking-salesman type. Et cetera, et cetera. Listen: I've seen 'em all. I was not concerned. I could handle the Steves of the world.

"You're right, my friend. Let's just enjoy. You just drive and enjoy."

He gave me a sidelong glance and I gave him the wink again, the magic wink: *Just you and me out here, pal. Wife's at home. No kiddies.* Just two men talking, and it's men who know what makes a car a *car*. But Steve was not a smiler. His hands were tight on the wheel. He was a little old for a soccer dad, I noticed. His hair was gray at the temples and retreating from his forehead. He drove exactly at the posted limit. His eyes were blue and watery behind thick glasses.

I sighed. I looked out the window, watched the late-day surf rush against the beach. I didn't need this grief, this pain-in-the-ass, late-day closing-time hard-case test drive. I was the manager, wasn't I? I was running the whole show down there at South Marina Honda. I was doing the test drive only because I *liked* to do test drives every now and then. Keep my ear to the ground, if you know what I mean. Keep my dick in the soup. And I seen this fella, this Steve, giving Graham a cold look and heard him saying, *Who do you got who's been around a while?*

That was me. I been around a while.

"Okay, so you just wanna make this right here, when you get through the light. We'll take her around the block, and when we get back, you know what you're gonna say?"

Steve sniffed. "What?"

Miracle of miracles! The man could speak!

"*I'll take it.* You are going to sign the papers and drive home in this gently used 2010 Honda Odyssey. You mark my words."

"We'll see," said Steve, lips tight, teeth clenched. Showing me he was no sucker. Showing me who was the boss in this situation. But he was wrong. I was the boss. I was always the darn boss.

Steve took the turn, kept the thing at an even forty-five, letting cars stream past us on the left.

"So you live right around here in the area, Steve?"

"No."

"No? Oh—here—so hang a right just here, after the light. We're going to go around the block, the long block here. There you go. So where you down from, then? Malibu? Bel Air, maybe?"

I chuckled. This was a joke. The man was not from Bel Air. Not in that bargain-bin windbreaker. Not with that haircut. Steve didn't laugh.

"Folks come down here from all over the city looking for a deal," I told him. "They hear about us, they hear we're the guys that are wheeling and dealing. They hear our ad."

"'When you hear our deals, your *ears* won't believe their *eyes*,'" sang out Steve suddenly, loudly, and I laughed. I slapped my knee.

"Our commercial!" I said. "You've heard it!"

But that was the end of it. My test driver was all done being convivial. His eyes stared straight ahead. His hands stayed at ten and two. And he had this look on his face like... well, I don't know *what* to call it. Whatever he was looking at, it wasn't Washington Boulevard. It wasn't the world around him. He was looking at some memory, this guy, or looking at the future. I don't know. His eyes, though, man. This guy's darn *eyes*.

I mean, look, you always get cuckoo birds out there. Alone in a car with a stranger, driving around in circles, that's just the name of the game. You get people who think a test drive is therapy; people who think it's *The Dating Game;* people who think they're in a confessional booth. One time, poor Graham had a fella who pulled over on the side of Via Marina, asking Graham to suck his ding-a-ling. I liked to rib Graham about that one. *Anything for a sale, Graham,* I liked to say. *Anything for a sale!*

"All right, Steve," I said. "So tell me. Where *are* you from?"

"Indiana," said Steve in that cold, shovel-flat voice of his. "Vincennes, Indiana."

"Huh," I said. "Well." I mean, Indiana? What the hell do you say to *that?* "You're a long way from home."

Steve grunted. The more time I spent sitting next to this guy, the less comfortable I felt, and I gotta tell you, I have a very broad tolerance for strangeness. That's how you get to be manager, you know? That's one of the ways.

"All righty," I said. We passed the Cheesecake Factory. We passed Killer Shrimp. "And how many kids you got?"

"Zero."

Now, *that* pulled me up short. Zero kids was even weirder than Vincennes, Indiana. I have sold a lot of Odysseys over a lot of years, and every one of them was to a parent. Soccer moms and lawn-mower dads, lawn-mower dads and soccer moms. Same as with the Toyota Sienna, same as with, I don't know, the Kia Sedona. You're talking minivans, you're talking young couples, you're talking about hauling the kiddos around, volleyball practice and ballet class and all the rest of it.

"Stepkids?" I ventured, and Steve shook his head tightly, and now I did not know *what* to say. Was I supposed to make some kind of joke here? *So what are you, then, Steve? Scout leader? Child molester?* But I didn't even try it. Not with that look on the man's face, that faraway stare, that death grimace, whatever you want to call it.

Next thing, he blew past the right turn back onto Admiralty.

"Hey—hey, now. That was—*hey!*" I craned around, looked down the roomy interior of the Odyssey and out the back window, watched a string of other cars making the right. I turned to Steve. "You missed it, man. You're gonna have to make a U-turn, just up here—"

But Steve hadn't made any mistakes. No, sir. He stomped on the accelerator, and the V-6 roared.

"Whoa," I said. "Hey!"

His cheeks were pale; his knuckles were tight and white; his eyes stared darkly down the road. The word came to me then, the word I had been feeling around for. The word for that look on the man's face: *purposeful.*

"I *did* have kids, you see," said Steve, and he careened the Odyssey across three lanes toward the entrance to the 405. Horns bleated around us. "But they're dead. They're all dead."

"I will tell you the whole story, Mr. Roegenberger," said Steve. "It won't take long."

That's me, I'm William M. Roegenberger, although I can tell you for a fact that I hadn't told Steve that. I *never* introduced myself with my last name, my last name is just too much of a mouthful for customers to deal with. "I'm Billy" is what I'd said, same as I always said, when we were getting into the Odyssey for the test drive.

But here we were, him calling me by the name I'd never told him, and we were on the 405 barreling northward in the HOV lane, and my tight-lipped test driver had started talking at last and now he would not stop. He gunned that engine and gunned it again, taking the Odyssey up past ninety miles an hour, his hands still driver's-ed correct, leaning forward and talking nonstop.

"We were on the way home from a soccer tournament. This was our car. This exact car. 2010 Honda Odyssey LX. Same color. This *exact same car.*" He lifted one hand off the wheel and made it into a fist, punched the steering wheel three times: *exact…same…car.* Exits for Mar Vista and Bundy Drive flew past outside the window. I looked at them with longing.

"Sean played in a lot of tournaments. That's my boy, Sean.

Thirteen years old. And I don't know if he was the best player in the state, but I do know that this was the highest-scoring middle-school soccer team in the state of Indiana, and I do know that Sean was the best player on that team. By leaps and bounds." He did it again, made a fist and punched the wheel. *Leaps...and...bounds.*

I looked at the odometer. We were inching up toward a hundred and ten. Where were the cops? I thought helplessly. Where were the darn cops? Rousting hard-luck cases for public urination down on Skid Row. Pulling over black guys for busted taillights.

"Now, this particular tournament, this was in Iowa, and this was the first one to take place out of state, you see? He had been to tournaments before with this team, all over Indiana, but this was special, and so we *all* went. Me and Katie, and the girls. Three little girls." He took one hand off the wheel, showed me three fingers: three little girls.

What if I just...jumped out? I mean, really, I was thinking as the minivan bounced and flew, *what would happen if I jerked open the door of the car and rolled out onto the highway?* Well, Christ. I would smash into the road at a thousand miles an hour and my body would burst open and I would be hit by a series of cars and I would die. That's what would happen. I would *die.*

"Steve," I said. "Steve?" But he wasn't listening. He was lost in his story.

"Now, the problem was, Angie did *not* want to come to that tournament. All of seven years old, and with a mind of her own. Lord, did Angie put up a stink about that one. Said she could stay at her friend Kristi's house for the weekend. It was Kristi's birthday, and Angie was gonna miss the whole party, but I said we all had to be there. We all had to support Sean. Even Katie said, 'You know, maybe if she'd rather stay,' but I said *no*. Absolutely not. I said she had to come. I said that. I *made* her."

"Well, you know," I said quietly. "Kids."

"And then, of course, the twins," he said. "Gracie and Lisa. Lisa and Grace."

Steve had to stop talking for a second. A hitch in his voice. A spasm in the tense line of his throat.

What if I punched him? was my next thought. Just smash a hard right into his jaw, bounce his crazy head against the driver's-side window? I formed one hand into a fist. But then what? What? Grab the wheel? Get my feet on the brakes? I had literally never hit a person in my life, and what did I think, I was going to knock this man *unconscious*? Was that even possible?

I let my fist relax. I focused on not vomiting. The car hurtled along the HOV lane, passing Lexuses and Beemers, passing Expeditions and Hummers, roaring past Santa Monica and Culver City, past all of twilight Los Angeles.

"Sean was the star of the tournament, he really was," said Steve when he was able to speak again. "I mean, you know, they don't give an MVP or anything like that, but that boy was the star. Always the star. And then on the way home…on the way home to Indiana…"

Tears were wet in Steve's eyes. I knew what was coming, right? It had to be a wreck. They're driving home, it's late, Steve's eyes drift shut…or there's a sudden storm, Midwestern floodwaters. I was waiting for Steve to tell me about it, about the sudden squall, about the slick of rain on the road, waiting to hear how he lost control…

This was going somewhere bad, I knew that it was, I felt that it was, but there was no escape. There was just the road ahead of us, just us and the empty backseats: two captain's chairs in the middle row, and then the third row behind that. For one crazy second I saw them back there, Sean in his headband and cleats, petulant Angie playing with a plastic pony, the twins strapped into their infant seats…

The Getty Museum glowed white, a castle on the hill above us. We were coming up fast on the Skirball exit.

"Anyway, so, so, Mr. Roegenberger, so we walk back to the car after a quick stop for dinner. A Subway attached to a gas station, just across the state line. It's twilight. It's not even dark. And here we find two men in the process of stealing the minivan. One of them was crouched, you know, crouched under the steering wheel with his wrench and his pliers, working on the wires. And the other one — he's got the gun. He's got it, it's pointing at us. And I said, *It's okay.* I said, *You just go right ahead and take the vehicle.* Because I'm no dummy, Mr. Roegenberger. I'm no fool."

He glanced at me then, and I nodded. "You're no fool," I said. "You're no dummy."

"It's just a car. But see—see—this man was on drugs, you see. You understand? Later on we would find out that he was under the influence of various substances. Bath salts. Have you heard of bath salts, Mr. Roegenberger? Apparently they can make a person behave in unpredictable ways. The other man, he was a professional car thief. But this guy…this man…his name was Vance. Later on we found out his name was Vance."

"Oh," I said. "Vance."

"And he just—well—I don't know. We'll never know,"

Steve whispered. "But he just started shooting and he shot and shot and shot." Steve put his blinker on. He lurched out of the HOV lane, moving rightward. "And everybody died, you see? Just my luck, see? Everybody died. Everybody but me."

He was waiting for me to say something, but what was I supposed to say?

"Well, that's terrible, Steve," I said lamely. "That's just terrible."

"Yes," he said. "Terrible." We took the exit. We flew down the off-ramp, took a hard left up onto Laurel Canyon Drive. "And it's all your fault."

And then we were going up.

Poor Steve slowed the Odyssey just enough to allow for the tight turns and dead-man's curves of Laurel Canyon Drive as it climbs up into the Hollywood Hills. My stomach bobbled and quivered inside me, a ball of liquid, as he whipped the two tons of minivan upward.

"So, hey," I said, keeping my voice as calm and casual as I could. "Steve? There is some kind of misunderstanding here or something. I did not steal your vehicle. That was not my fault, okay? I'm just a guy. I'm just some guy. What happened to you, that's — well, like you said, Steve. It's terrible. But this is not your vehicle."

"Well, of course it's not my vehicle," said Steve. "That Odyssey was impounded by the police. After the crime scene was processed. After all of it. I know this isn't the same car. I'm not an idiot."

A long pause. Just driving, fast up the hill, too fast. Higher and higher. Up and up.

He picked a turn to take off Laurel Canyon, one of the tight little one-lane side roads that wind up yet higher then narrow until they turn into the private driveways of millionaires. Halfway up that small road, he jerked the wheel hard so the car turned all the way to the right, and then he slammed on the brakes.

"Steve?" I said. *"Steve."*

He turned off the car. Carefully, ridiculously, he depressed the rectangular button to turn on the hazards. We were perpendicular to the roadway, lengthwise to two lanes of traffic. The front end of the Odyssey was pushed up against the gates of whatever studio executive's palazzo this was, and the butt end poked very slightly out over the edge of the steep face of the hill. If someone came flying around from the north, they'd smash directly into us. If, on the other hand, someone came up from the south, they'd send us spinning around and off the hill. In the one second it took me to process these particulars, to realize how much peril we were in here, Steve had pulled a small silver gun out of the pocket of his cheap-ass windbreaker. The gun was pointed directly at my face. His expression had not changed.

"Steve…" I said. "Come on. I don't know Vance. I didn't kill your family. I live in California, Steve."

"But you do steal cars."

"I do not!"

He thumbed back the hammer on the gun and said, "You organize the stealing of cars."

"Yes," I said, pulling my body backward, away from the gun. Squirming inside my seat belt.

"Okay. Yes."

"Tell me how it works, Mr. Roegenberger."

I hesitated; gulped for air.

"Talk."

"We—we—get lists from the DMV. On Hope Street. I have a—there's a guy there. I pay him. For existing VINs. Unclaimed VINs. Vehicle numbers."

"I know what VINs are." Steve had undone his seat belt, inched his gun hand closer to me.

"We clone the lists, and then we retag them onto different cars."

"Different cars? *Different* cars? Stolen cars. Stolen from where?"

"From Oregon, Steve. From—I don't know. Idaho. Washington State. Far, far, far from Indiana."

"That doesn't matter," said Steve. "That's not the point."

I lunged for the door and Steve shot me in the hand. I screamed. I writhed in pain while the tip of my finger spouted blood, but all my writhing and screaming made the car rock a little beneath me, so I stopped, afraid of sending us over the edge. I whimpered. I clutched my hand.

Steve spoke. With agonizing slowness, he spoke. "It doesn't matter that it wasn't you, because there was someone like you in Indiana too. Someone that Vance and Vance's friend were working with. I couldn't figure out who that was. But you, you and your friends, you're less careful, I guess."

Graham, I thought while my finger pulsed blood. Fucking Graham!

"But it doesn't matter. It's not you, but it's you. The world is full of you. My state, your state. Everywhere. The world is full of you. Scheming and taking. Grasping. Cheating. Pulling strings, taking shortcuts. And what is at the end of it? Far off at the other end, where you can never see? My family. My boy. My girls. My beautiful girls. Dead in the road."

I didn't want to die. I thought I could hear an engine starting, close by, maybe at the top of the road. Any second a car would come tearing up or come roaring down.

"What do you want, Steve? What do you want?"

"I want my family back."

"I can't do that."

"I know."

He pushed the barrel of the gun into my temple. I gazed out into vast smoggy sprawling twilight Los Angeles and knew it would be the last thing I'd ever see. There was definitely a vehicle coming down the hill; I could hear it clearly now. A gardener, I bet. Done for the day. Gardening truck, flatbed. I could picture it. In another ten seconds it would be on top of us. It would cut the Odyssey in two or send it spiraling over the side of the hill, and it wouldn't matter, not to me, because Steve was going to shoot me first.

But I had to try. I had to keep trying—right? That's what you do?

"Listen, Steve, I'm sorry. I admit it. I'm bad. I see that now. I admit it. Is that what you want? For me to admit it?"

"Admit it? Why would I care if you admitted it?" He gave his head a little shake while he dug the gun tighter into my sweaty forehead. "No, no. I want you to die for it."

I closed my eyes and the city disappeared and I waited. But nothing happened. I tasted the cigarettes and Starlight mints on my breath. I heard the engine of the truck coming down the hill. I felt its rumble in my butt cheeks.

I heard Steve crying. I cracked my eyes open, one at a time, and the gun was still pressed against my skull but Steve's head was lowered and his cheeks were red and wet with tears. His shoulders shook. The gun slowly came down, dragging along my forehead, my cheek, my chin. He was no killer after all. He was just a man, a poor sad man — lawn-mower dad, widowed husband, middle-aged and alone and out of his mind with grief.

And then I heard them and I turned and I saw Sean in the middle row in jersey and cleats, earbuds in, gazing out the window. Angie with her nose in a children's novel, one lock of dirty-blond hair wound around her index finger. The twins in the back, mewling and yelping, the happy little shouts of infancy. The floor of the car was littered with snack crackers and granola crumbs, splattered with spilled juice, the discarded cellophane wrappers of cheese sticks like shed skins beneath the seats.

Angie looked up and gave the small shy smile of a curious kid, and in the center of her forehead was a bullet hole. Sean had two through his chest, and the babies a half a dozen each, a spray of holes in their tiny bodies.

"I am so sorry," I whispered to those kids, to Angie and Sean and the babies. I had opened the shotgun door, and I was half in and half out, saying sorry like saying good-bye, and the children opened their mouths, maybe to forgive me and maybe not, but the horn of the garden truck was blaring by then and it was too late.

POWER WAGON

C. J. Box

A SINGLE HEADLIGHT strobed through a copse of ten-foot willows on the other side of the overgrown horse pasture. Marissa unconsciously laced her fingers over her pregnant belly and said, "Brandon, there's somebody out there."

"What?" Brandon said. He was at the head of an old kitchen table that had once fed a half dozen ranch hands breakfast and dinner. A thick ledger book was open in front of him and Brandon had moved a lamp from the family room next to the table so he could read.

"I said, somebody is out there. A car or something. I saw a headlight."

"Just one?"

"Just one."

Brandon placed his index finger on an entry in the ledger book so he wouldn't lose his place. He looked up.

"Don't get freaked out. It's probably a hunter or somebody who's lost."

"What if they come to the house?"

"I don't know," he said. "I guess we help them out."

"Maybe I should shut off the lights," she said.

"I wouldn't worry about it," he said. "They probably won't even come here. They're probably just passing through."

"But to where?" she asked.

She had a point, he conceded. The old two-track beyond the willows was a private road, part of the ranch, and it led to a series of four vast mountain meadows and the foothills of the Wyoming range. Then it trailed off in the sagebrush.

"I saw it again," she said.

He could tell she was scared even though there really wasn't any reason to be, he thought. But saying "Calm down" or "Don't worry" wouldn't help the situation, he knew. If she was scared, she was scared. She wasn't used to being so isolated—she'd grown up in Chicago and Seattle—and he couldn't blame her.

Brandon found a pencil on the table and starred the entry he was on to mark where he'd stopped and pushed back his chair. The feet of it scraped the old linoleum with a discordant note.

He joined her at the window and put his hand on her shoulder. When he looked out, though, all he could see was utter darkness. He'd forgotten how dark it could be outside when the only ambient light was from stars and the moon. Unfortunately, storm clouds masked both.

"Maybe he's gone," she said, "whoever it was."

A log snapped in the fireplace and in the silent house it sounded like a gunshot. Brandon felt Marissa jump at the sound.

"You're tense," he said.

"Of course I am," she responded. There was anger in her voice. "We're out here in the middle of nowhere without phone or Internet and somebody's out there *driving around*. Trespassing. They probably don't even know we're here, so what are they doing?"

He leaned forward until his nose was a few inches from the glass. He could see snowflakes on the other side. There was enough of a breeze that it was snowing horizontally. The uncut grass in the yard was spotted white, and the horse meadow had turned from dull yellow to gray in the starlight.

Then a willow was illuminated and a lone headlight curled around it. The light lit up the horizontal snow as it ghosted through the brush and the bare cottonwood trees. Snowflakes looked like errant sparks in the beam. The light snow appeared as low-hanging smoke against the stand of willows.

"He's coming this way," she said. She pressed into him.

"I'll take care of it," Brandon said. "I'll see what he wants and send him packing."

She looked up at him with scared eyes and rubbed her belly. He knew she did that when she was nervous. The baby was their first and she was unsure and overprotective about the pregnancy.

During the day, while he'd pored over the records inside, she'd wandered through the house, the corrals, and the out-buildings and had come back and declared the place "officially creepy, like a mausoleum." The only bright spot in her day, she said, was discovering a nest of day-old naked baby mice that she'd brought back to the house in a rusty metal box. She said she wanted to save them if she could figure out how.

Brandon knew baby mice in the house was a bad idea, but

he welcomed the distraction. Marissa was feeling maternal, even about mice.

"Don't forget," he said, "I grew up in this house."

The old man hadn't died at the ranch but at a senior center in Big Piney, population 552, which was eighteen miles away. He'd gone into town for lunch at the center because he never missed it when they served fish and chips and he died after returning to his table from the buffet. He'd slumped forward into his meal. The attendants had to wipe tartar sauce from his cheek before wheeling him into the room where they kept the defibrillator. But it was too late.

Two days later, Brandon's sister, Sally, called him in Denver at the accounting firm where he worked.

"That's impossible," Brandon said when he heard the news. "He was too mean to die."

Sally told Brandon it wasn't a nice thing to say even if it was true.

"He left the ranch to us kids," she said. "I've talked to Will and Trent and of course nobody wants it. But because you're the accountant, we decided you should go up there and inventory everything in the house and outbuildings so we can do a big farm auction. Then we can talk about selling the ranch. Trent thinks McMiller might buy it."

Jake McMiller was the owner of the neighboring ranch and he'd always made it clear he wanted to expand his holdings. The old man had said, "Over my dead body will that son of a bitch get my place."

So…

"Do I get a say in this or is it already decided?" Brandon had asked Sally.

"It's already decided."

"Nothing ever changes, does it?" Brandon asked.

"I guess not," she said, not without sympathy.

Will and Trent were Brandon's older brothers. They were fraternal twins. Both had left home the day they turned eighteen. Will was now a state employee for Wyoming in Cheyenne, and Trent owned a bar in Jackson Hole. Both were divorced and neither had been back to the ranch in over twenty-five years. Sally, the third oldest, had left as well, although she did come in from South Florida to visit the place every few years. After she'd been there, she'd send out a group letter to her brothers confirming the same basic points:

The old man was as mean and bitter as ever.

He was still feuding with his neighbor Jake McMiller in court over water rights and road access.

He was spending way too much time drinking and carousing in town with his hired man Dwayne Pingston, who was a well-known petty criminal.

As far as the old man was concerned, he *had* no sons, and he still planned to will them the ranch in revenge for their leaving it.

The brothers had been so traumatized by their childhood they rarely spoke to each other about it. Sally was the intermediary in all family business because when the brothers talked on the phone or were in the presence of each other, strong, dark feelings came back.

Like the time the old man had left Will and Trent on top of a mountain in the snow because they weren't cutting firewood into the right-size lengths. Or when the old man "slipped" and branded Trent on his left thigh with a red-hot iron.

Or the nightmare night when Will, Trent, Sally, Brandon, and their mother huddled in the front yard in a blinding snowstorm while the old man berated them from the front porch with his rifle out, accusing one or all of them of drinking his Ancient Age bourbon. He knew it, he said, because he'd marked the level in the bottle the night before. He railed at them most of the night while sucking down three-quarters of a quart of Jim Beam he'd hidden in the garage. When he finally passed out, the family had to step over his body on the way back into the house. Brandon still remembered how terrified he was stepping over the old man's legs. He was afraid the man would regain his wits at that moment and pull him down.

The next day, Will and Trent turned eighteen and left before breakfast.

When their mother started complaining of sharp abdominal pains, the old man refused to take her into town to see the doctor he considered a quack. She died two days later of what turned out to be a burst appendix.

When the Department of Family Services people arrived on the ranch after that, the old man pointed at Sally and Brandon and said, "Take 'em. Get 'em out of my hair."

Brandon had not been back to the ranch since that day.

"It's a car with one headlight out," Brandon said to Marissa. "You stay in here and I'll go and deal with it."

"Take a gun," she said.

He started to argue with her but thought better of it. Everyone in Sublette County was armed, so he had to presume the driver of the approaching car was too.

"I wish the phone worked," she said as he strode through the living room to the old man's den.

"Me too," he said.

Apparently, as they'd discovered when they arrived that morning, the old man hadn't paid his phone bill and had never installed a wireless Internet router. The electricity was still on, although Brandon found three months of unpaid bills from the local power co-op. There was no cell service this far out.

Brandon fought back long-buried emotions as he entered the den and flipped on the light. It was exactly as he remembered it: mounted elk and deer heads, black-and-white photos of the old man when he was a young man, shelves of unread books, a lariat and a pair of ancient spurs on the wall. The calendar behind the desk was three years old.

He could see a half a dozen rifles and shotguns behind the glass of the gun cabinet. Pistols inside were hung upside down by pegs through their trigger guards. He recognized a 1911 Colt .45. It was the old man's favorite handgun and he always kept it loaded.

But the cabinet was locked. Brandon was surprised. Since when did the old man lock his gun cabinet? He quickly searched the top of the desk. No keys. He threw open the desk drawers. There was a huge amount of junk crammed into them and he didn't have time to root through it all.

He could break the glass, he thought.

That's when Marissa said, "They're getting out of the car, Brandon. There's a bunch of them." Her tone was panicked.

Brandon took a deep breath to remain calm. He told himself, *Probably hunters or somebody lost.* Certainly it couldn't be locals because everyone in the county knew the old man was gone. He'd cut a wide swath through the psyche of the valley where everyone knew everybody else, and the old-line ranching families — who controlled the politicians, the sheriff, and the land-use decisions — were still royalty.

As he walked to the front door, he smiled at Marissa but he knew it was false bravado. She looked scared and she'd moved behind the couch, as if it would protect her.

He pulled on one of the old man's barn coats that hung from a bent horseshoe near the front door. It smelled like him: stale cigarette smoke, gasoline fumes, cows. The presence of the old man in that coat nearly caused Brandon to tear it off. He shoved aside the impulse and opened the door.

Three — no, *four* people were piling out of a dented white Jeep Cherokee with County 23 plates. So they were local after all, he thought.

The driver, who was standing outside his door waiting for the others, was tall, wiry, and bent over. He looked to be in his seventies and he wore a wide-brimmed cowboy hat and pointed black boots. He saw Brandon and grinned as if they were old friends.

An obese woman grunted from the backseat as she used both hands on the door frame to pull herself out. For a moment her feet stuck straight out of the Cherokee while she rocked back and threw her bulk forward to get out of the car. She had tight orange-yellow curls and wore a massive print dress that looked to be the size of a tent.

Two younger men about Brandon's age joined the wiry

older one while they waited for the fat woman. One of the younger men had a shaved head, a full beard, and tattoos that crawled out of his collar up his neck. The second man looked like a local ranch hand: jeans, boots, Carhartt coat, battered and greasy KING ROPES cap.

Brandon stepped out on the porch and closed the door behind him. He could feel Marissa's eyes on his back through the curtains.

He said, "What can I help you folks with? There's no need for all of you to get out."

The wiry man continued to grin. He said, "You might not remember me, Brandon, but I sure as hell remember you. How you doing, boy?"

Brandon frowned. There was something familiar about the man but whatever it was was inaccessible to him at the moment. So many of his memories had been locked away years before.

"Do I know you?"

"Dwayne Pingston. I remember you when you were yay high," he said, holding his hand palm-down just below his belt buckle. "I don't blame you for not remembering me from those days, but I was close to your old man."

Brandon nodded. Dwayne Pingston.

The Dwayne Pingston who Brandon had discovered butchering a deer out of season in the garage. The Dwayne Pingston who'd lifted Brandon off his feet and hung him by his belt from a nail while he finished deboning the animal.

"This is my lovely wife, Peggy," Pingston said, nodding the brim of his hat to her as she struggled to her feet next to the car and smoothed out her dress.

"My son, Tater," he said and the man in the jeans and ball cap looked up.

"And my buddy Wade," he said, not looking over at the bald man.

"Nice to meet you all," Brandon said. "Now, what can I do for you?"

"I guess you could say I'm here to collect a debt," Pingston said.

Brandon tilted his head. "A debt? You know the old man passed a couple of weeks ago, right?"

"Oh, I heard," Pingston said. "They wouldn't let me out to attend the service, though."

"What kind of debt?" Brandon asked. "I'm officially going through his books now and he didn't leave much of anything."

"Tell you what," Pingston said, moving over to Peggy and sliding his arm around her. "Why don't you invite us inside so we can discuss it? If you haven't noticed, it's snowing right now and it's getting colder by the minute. I nearly forgot how much I didn't miss Big Piney until I stepped outside this morning and the hairs in my nose froze up."

Pingston started to lead Peggy toward the front steps and the two other men fell behind them.

"Hold it," Brandon said. "My wife's inside and we really weren't planning on any company. She's expecting our first baby and now isn't a good time. How about we discuss whatever it is you want to talk about tomorrow in town?"

"I wanted to talk about it with you today," Pingston said, still smiling, still guiding Peggy toward the porch, "but when I called they said the phone was disconnected. So we had to come out in person. I didn't realize Peggy's Jeep had a headlight out. Those are the kinds of maintenance things I used to take care of before they sent me away."

Sent me away, Brandon repeated to himself in his head. *They wouldn't let me out to attend the service.*

"Really," he said. "You folks need to get back in your car and we'll meet tomorrow. How about breakfast or something?"

"Won't work," Pingston said, withdrawing his smile. "I got to hit the road first thing in the morning. I'm only here for the night."

"That's not my problem," Brandon said. "Look, there's going to be a legal process in regard to everything my dad left behind. You need to contact his lawyer about your debt—not me."

Pingston shook his head. "Brandon, you're the one I want to see. We don't need no lawyers in this."

Wade with the shaved head stepped out from in back of Pingston. "Open the door," he said. "Let's get this over with."

His glare sent a chill through Brandon that had nothing to do with the temperature outside. Wade was tall and solid and the bulk of his coat couldn't hide his massive shoulders.

"Give me a minute," Brandon said. "Let me talk to my wife."

"Don't take all day," Pingston said. "It ain't getting any warmer."

Brandon entered the house and shut the door. Marissa was still behind the couch, rubbing her belly almost manically.

"They want—"

"I heard," she said.

"I'm not sure what to do," he said, keeping his voice low.

"Pingston used to work for the old man. My guess is he wants back pay or something like that. Knowing the way my dad was, they probably had some kind of dispute."

"What did he mean, they wouldn't let him out to attend the funeral?"

Brandon shrugged because he didn't want to answer.

"What are you going to do?" she asked, incredulous. "Invite them in?"

"What choice do I have?"

Before she could answer, the front door opened and Tater poked his head in.

"Look, folks, my mom is standing out there in the freezing snow. She's gonna get pneumonia and die if she don't come in here and warm up."

Brandon looked from Marissa to Tater to Marissa. She was saying *No* with her eyes.

"Come on, Mama," Tater said over his shoulder. Then he walked in and stepped aside so Peggy and Pingston could enter, one after the other. They couldn't do it shoulder to shoulder because Peggy was too wide.

"Thank you kindly," she wheezed. Her cheeks were flushed and she labored the four steps it took to reach a recliner, where she settled in with a loud sigh.

Pingston came in behind her and looked around the house. Wade slipped in behind him and shut the door.

"Hasn't changed much," Pingston said, removing his hat and holding it by the brim with both hands in front of him.

"Please," Brandon said, moving from Marissa closer to Pingston. "There's nothing I can do for you. All I can do is make a recommendation to the lawyers on selling the assets and either splitting up the estate or selling it. I couldn't write a check from his account if I wanted to."

Pingston smiled as he nodded his head. "That's just blah-blah-blah to me, Brandon. We don't need lawyers to settle up accounts. We can do this man-to-man."

Brandon didn't know what to say.

Wade had positioned himself in front of the door with his arms crossed over his chest. Tater stood behind Peggy and had opened his coat. Brandon wondered if Tater had a weapon tucked into the back of his Wranglers and had opened his coat to get at it more quickly.

Suddenly, Marissa said to Pingston, "You were in prison, weren't you?" It was an accusation. "You just got out."

Pingston shook his head sadly and looked down at the hat in his hands. "I'm afraid so, ma'am. It isn't something I'm proud of, but I paid my debt to society and now I'm back on the straight and narrow. Peggy here," he said, nodding toward his wife, "waited for me for the past five years. She struggled and it wasn't fair to her. Now I've got to make things right with her and my boy."

"Make things right?" Brandon asked cautiously.

"Now you're gettin' it," Pingston said.

"So how do we make things right?"

"You were in prison with him?" Marissa said to Wade.

"We shared a cell," Wade said. "We got released within a couple of days of each other last week. I'm just here to support my buddy Dwayne."

"Support him," Marissa echoed.

Brandon looked over at his wife and implored her with his eyes to please let him handle things. But she was glaring at Wade.

"You people need to leave this house," she said. "You have no right to be here."

Wade raised his eyebrows and shook his head. Nobody moved.

Peggy asked Marissa, "How far are you along, honey?"

It broke the tension slightly. Brandon looked on.

"Seven and a half months," Marissa said.

"Boy or girl?" Peggy asked Marissa.

"A little boy. Our first."

"Well, God bless you," Peggy said. Her face was strangely blank and it didn't match her words, Brandon thought. "The last thing you need right now is a bunch of stress in your life, I'd bet."

Marissa agreed with a pained smile.

"That's what I thought," Peggy said. "So what I'd suggest to you is to talk to your husband here to get this thing over with. Then we'll all be out of your hair and you can get on with your life. How's that sound?"

As Marissa thought it over, Pingston said to Brandon, "It ain't gonna be as bad as you think. It's going to be downright painless."

Brandon and Marissa exchanged a glance, and Brandon said, "So what is it you want with us?"

"First of all," Pingston said, "I need to tell you a little story. It'll explain why I'm here."

"Go ahead," Marissa said.

"Six years ago this area was booming with oil-field workers. That's before the bottom dropped out of the market. I'm sure you know about that," he said. "Them boys had more money than they knew what to do with and for a short time there were four banks in town. Now we're back to one, as you probably noticed.

"The old man resented the hell out of the oil boom because none of it was on his land. Plus, he didn't like it that a bunch of out-of-staters had moved into the valley and they were acting like big shots. As far as your old man was concerned, they didn't deserve to run the county.

"Well, somebody got clever and hit one of the Brink's trucks after it picked up a bunch of cash at one of those fly-by-night banks they had then. Nobody got killed, but the driver and the guard were pistol-whipped and tied up and the thieves stole all the cash out of the back of the truck. Something like a hundred and seventy-five thousand dollars, if I recall. It was quite the big story in Sublette County: an armed robbery at gunpoint."

"I remember reading something about that," Brandon said. Maybe in one of Sally's letters?

"At the time it happened I'd just told the old man I was quitting the ranch to seek employment in the oil patch," Pingston said. "I thought to myself: *Why should I bust my ass for that mean old bastard when I could get a job driving a truck or delivering tools for twice what I'm making out here?* Peggy deserved a better life and Tater was in junior high at the time. So why should I put up with that old bastard?"

Brandon shrugged.

Pingston continued, "The old man didn't like that. He knew the word was out up and down this valley that he was a bastard to work for and he didn't pay much. So he said he needed help around here and he wouldn't let me quit. He said I had to pay off all this damage he claimed I'd caused when I worked for him—wrecked trucks, cattle that died during the winter, anything he could think up at the time and pin on me. You know how he was," Pingston said.

"I do," Brandon said.

"I told him to shove all that up his ass," Pingston said. "I didn't owe him a damned thing. You can imagine how well he took it. The last I seen of him, he was limping toward this house to get his gun so he could kill me. He was so mad, smoke was coming out of his ears. So I jumped in a ranch truck and beat it toward town. It was that old '48 Dodge Power Wagon that had been here forever. I figured I'd leave it in town for the old man to pick up later."

Pingston paused and looked around the room. Brandon guessed that Wade, Peggy, and Tater were about to hear a story they'd heard many times before even if Brandon and Marissa hadn't.

"The sheriff's department intercepted me before I could even get to Big Piney," Pingston said. "Lights flashing, sirens going, the whole damn deal. The old man must've reported a stolen Power Wagon, and they had me on that. But before I could explain I was fleeing for my life they had me facedown in the dirt and I was being arrested for that armed robbery and for hurting them two Brink's guys."

Pingston lowered his voice now for effect. He said, "The old man said it was me who did that Brink's job. He told the sheriff some bullshit about me being gone the day it happened and that he'd suspected it all along. If you remember the sheriff and the judge here at the time, you know that ranchers like your old man pretty much told them what to do and they did it.

"Supposedly the sheriff found a pistol in my duffel bag in the truck that matched what was used in the armed robbery, but I always suspected he planted it there after the fact. I was in prison in Rawlins at the Wyoming State Pen before I knew what hit me, just because I quit my job here. Your old man put it to me, and hard.

"To make matters worse," Pingston said, "Peggy had to get a job to survive and the only one she could find was at the senior center."

Peggy spoke up. "So two or three times a week I had to ladle the gravy on your old man's lunch and pretend I didn't know what he'd done to my Dwayne," she said. "There he was with that big roll of cash he always kept in his pocket for buying drinks for politicians, but he never missed a free lunch at the senior center with old folks who didn't have two nickels to rub together. I'd look out from behind the counter at your old man holding court with his cronies and think of my Dwayne down in Rawlins surrounded by murderers and rapists."

She turned to Marissa. "Honey, you may think having a child is hard. But what's really hard is putting a fake smile on your face and serving the man who put your husband away."

Wade shifted his weight and sighed. It was obvious he was bored by the story he'd no doubt heard a thousand times before.

Brandon said, "If you're asking me to make you whole out of the proceeds of the ranch, I don't know how I can do it. There are liens on the equipment and the cattle, and the old man hadn't paid any bills in months. He might have always had a roll of cash on him but he didn't use it to pay off his debts. All those people are filing claims and they get their money first when everything gets sold. I sympathize but I just don't know what I can do."

Pingston stared at Brandon for a long time. Finally, he said, "I kind of figured that."

"So why are you here?" Marissa asked, exasperated.

"I want that '48 Power Wagon," Pingston said.

"What?" Brandon asked. A wave of relief flooded through him but he tried hard to conceal it.

"It's a goddamn classic," Wade said.

Pingston nodded and said, "People don't realize what a workhorse that truck was. The greatest ranch vehicle ever made. Three-quarter-ton four-by-four perfected in WW Two. After the war, all the rural ex-GIs wanted one here like they'd used over there. That original ninety-four horse, two-hundred-and-thirty-cubic-inch flathead six wouldn't win no races but it could grind through the snow and mud, over logs, through the brush and willows. It was tough as a damn rock. Big tires, high clearance, a winch on the front. We could load a ton of cargo on that son of a bitch and still drive around other pickups stuck in a bog."

Brandon shook his head, puzzled. "That's what you want?"

Pingston nodded. "Look, I suppose you're thinking that if I restored that beast to its former glory, I could make a lot of money on it and you're right. I've seen where some of 'em sell for seventy thousand or more in cherry condition. But I don't give a crap about that. I want to fix it up and get it running. This one is too damned beat up to ever amount to much."

"Then why do you want it?"

"It means something to me," Pingston said. "That was the truck I drove every damned day I worked on this ranch.

Twelve years, Brandon. I know that truck as intimately as I do Peggy."

Peggy smirked at that. Brandon thought that odd.

Pingston said, "I know when to downshift going up a vertical hill, how to power through six-foot drifts, how to use that winch to pull myself up the side of a damned cliff. If I ever go elk hunting again, that's the vehicle I want to take.

"Plus," Pingston said with a wink, "it's the truck I borrowed to go to town when your old man sent me up the river. I like the idea of that old bastard rolling in his grave knowing I'm riding around in high style in the Power Wagon he owned all his life. It gives me a small measure of satisfaction, if you know what I mean."

Marissa said, "If we give you the truck, will you all go away?"

"That was rude," Peggy said. She folded her thick arms over her bosom.

Brandon said, "I should discuss this with my brothers and sister, you know. We all have a say in how the assets are divided up."

That's when Wade stepped forward and said, "We don't have the time."

Out of the corner of his eye, Brandon saw Marissa tense up and move back.

Brandon said, "If I give it to you, how are you going to get it out of here? I doubt it'll start after all these years. I don't even know if it still has a motor in it—or tires. And I don't even know if it's in the shed out there."

"Oh, we brung a tow rope in the Jeep," Pingston assured him.

Brandon hoped that the Power Wagon was not only in the

shed but also in good enough shape for them to take it away that night. He was still basking in the relief he'd felt at the words *I want that '48 Power Wagon.*

Even if it didn't make any sense. Four people to retrieve a truck? In the snow? At night?

"If it's there, it's yours," he said to Pingston.

Wade grinned and said, "Let's go check it out."

"I'm going too," Tater said.

"No," Pingston said sharply. "You stay here with your mother and Marissa."

And Brandon felt the fear creep back inside.

"Why don't you all come with me?" Brandon asked.

"No," Pingston said sharply. "Peggy don't need to stand around outside in this weather while we mess around with an old truck."

But Brandon heard, *I want my son to stay in here and keep an eye on Marissa so she doesn't try anything.*

When he looked over at his wife, Marissa nodded to him and mouthed, *Go.*

It took a while for Brandon to locate a set of keys in the old man's desk that might open the old shed. While he searched, Wade kept a close eye on him from the door. More than once, Brandon caught Wade glancing toward the gun cabinet.

"Okay," Brandon said when he found a ring of ancient keys. "I can't guarantee anything but one of these might work." None of them were marked or labeled.

"We'll follow you," Wade said, closing in behind Brandon as he left the room.

Brandon pulled on the ranch coat and looked over his shoulder at Marissa. "Back in a minute," he said.

She nodded but her mouth was set tight as if holding in a sob.

Pingston and Wade followed Brandon outside into the snow. It was coming down harder now and the flakes had grown in size and volume.

He led them away from the house toward a massive corrugated-metal shed where the old man kept his working ranch equipment as well as the hulks of old tractors and pickups that no longer ran. The pole light that had once illuminated the ranch yard had long ago burned out, so Brandon had to peer through the snowfall to find the outline of the shed against the snow.

"I told Wade I wasn't sure if I have the right key," Brandon said in Pingston's direction.

Pingston didn't reply.

The shed had a side door but it was clogged with years of weeds that were waist-high, so he figured it hadn't been used in a while. Brandon walked through the snow to the big double garage doors that were closed tight. A rusty chain had been looped through the handles and secured with a padlock.

Brandon bent over and tried one key after another in the lock.

"I need some light," he said. "Did either of you bring a flashlight?"

Instead of answering, Wade extended a lighter in his hand and flicked it on. The flame lit up the old padlock in orange.

The next-to-last key on the ring slid in, and Brandon turned it. Nothing.

"Jerk on it," Pingston said.

Brandon did and it opened. Tiny flakes of rust fell away from the lock into the snow below it. He closed his eyes with relief. Wade reached over his shoulder and pulled the chain free.

"Okay, step aside," Pingston said, reaching forward with both of his hands and grasping the door handles. He groaned as he parted them. The old door mechanism groaned as well.

"Give me a hand here," Pingston said to Wade. The two men wedged themselves into the two-foot opening and each put a shoulder to opposite doors. With a sound like rolling thunder, the doors opened wide.

Brandon watched Pingston walk into the shed and disappear in the dark. A wall of icy air pushed out from the open doors. It was colder inside the shed than outside, Brandon thought. Then a single match fired up in the corner and he saw Pingston's finger toggle a light switch. Above them, two of four bare bulbs came on.

"See, I remembered where the lights were after all this time," Pingston said.

"Good for you," Wade said without enthusiasm. "You figured out how to operate a light switch."

The shed layout was familiar to Brandon and much of it was the same as it had been. Some of the equipment was so old it looked almost medieval in the gloom. Thrashers, tractors, one-ton flatbed trucks without wheels, a square-nosed bulldozer, a faded wooden sheep wagon as old as Wyoming itself, a lifetime of battered pickups. And there, backed against the far sheet-metal wall, was the toothy front grille and split-window windshield of the '48 Power Wagon. It sat high and still on knobby tires, its glass clouded with age, the two headlamps mounted on the high wide fenders looking in the low light like dead eyes.

"Son of a bitch," Pingston said. "There it is."

Wade blew out a sigh of relief.

"How you doin', old girl?" Pingston said to the truck. He approached it and stroked the dust-covered hood. "It looks like the old man backed it in after they arrested me and it hasn't been moved since," he said.

Brandon put his hands on his hips and took a deep breath. He said, "Then I guess my work is done here."

"Not so fast," Wade said, stepping over and placing his hand on Brandon's shoulder. Then to Pingston: "Check it out."

Check out what?

Pingston nodded and opened the front door of the Power Wagon and leaned inside. Brandon was surprised how obedient Pingston had been to the command. Then he realized Wade was actually the one in charge, not Pingston.

"What's he looking for? The keys?" Brandon asked.

"Shut up."

Brandon pursed his lips and waited. He could see Pingston crawl further into the cab and could hear the clinks of metal on metal.

After a long few moments, Pingston pushed himself out and looked to Wade. Pingston's face was drained of color.

"It's not there," he said in a weak voice. "The tools are on the floorboard but the toolbox is gone. The old man must have found it."

Wade closed his eyes and worked his jaw. Brandon felt Wade's hand clamp harder on his shoulder. Then Wade stepped back quickly and kicked Brandon's legs out from under him. He fell hard, half in and half out of the shed.

When Brandon looked up, Wade was crouching over him with a large-caliber snub-nosed pistol in his hand. The muzzle pressed into his forehead.

"Where is it?" Wade asked.

"Where is what?" Brandon said. "I don't have a clue what you're looking for."

"Where. Is. It?" Wade's eyes were bulging and his teeth were clenched.

"Honest to God," Brandon said, "I don't know what you're talking about. I haven't been in this shed for years. I wasn't even sure the Power Wagon was here. I have no idea where the keys are."

He tried to rise up on his elbows but the pressure of the muzzle held him down.

"Fuck the *keys,*" Wade said. He barked at Pingston, *"Look again."*

Pingston practically hurled himself into the cab of the truck. His cowboy boots stuck out and flutter-kicked like he was swimming.

"Don't lie to me or I'll kill you and your wife," Wade said and Brandon didn't doubt it. "Where is it?"

Brandon took a trembling breath. He said, "This is my first day back on this place. I have no idea what you're asking me. I've not been in this shed. You saw how rusty that lock was, Wade. It hasn't been opened in a long time."

Something registered behind Wade's eyes. The pressure of the muzzle eased but he didn't move the gun.

"My old man was in this shed since I was here last. Hell, Dwayne Pingston was in this shed after I left. I don't know what you're looking for. I'm an *accountant,* for God's sake."

Wade appeared to be making his mind up about something. Then his features contorted into a snarl and he withdrew the revolver and hit Brandon in the face with the butt of it. Brandon heard his nose break and felt the hot rush of blood down his cheeks and into his mouth. Wade struck again and Brandon stopped trying to get up.

Wade got off him and Brandon tried to roll to his side but he couldn't move his arms or legs. He was blacking out, but he fought it. For some reason he thought about the fact that the only violence he had ever encountered in his life was here on this ranch. And Marissa was back in the house…

His head flopped so he was facing into the shed. Through a red gauzy curtain, he watched Wade stride toward the Power Wagon with the gun at his side.

And he heard Wade say to Pingston, "You stupid, miserable old son of a bitch. I knew I should have never believed you about anything. You kept me on the hook for years so I'd watch your back inside."

Pingston said, "Wade! Put that down."

Pop. Pop.

Brandon didn't want to wake up, and each time he got close, he faded back. He dreamed of freezing to death because he was.

He groaned and rolled to his side and his head swooned. He threw up on the sleeve of the old man's ranch coat and it steamed in the early-morning light. His limbs were stiff with cold and it hurt to move them. His face throbbed and he didn't know why. When he touched the area above his right ear he could feel a crusty wound that he couldn't recall receiving.

But he was alive.

He gathered his knees under him and pushed himself clumsily to his feet. When a wave of dizziness hit him, he reached out and grabbed the end of the open shed door so he wouldn't fall again.

It took a minute for him to realize where he was and recall what had happened. He staggered toward the Power Wagon, toward the pair of boots that hung out of the open truck door.

Dwayne Pingston was dead and stiff with a bullet hole in his cheek and another in the palm of his hand. No doubt he'd raised it at the last second before Wade pulled the trigger.

Brandon turned and lurched toward the open shed door.

The morning sun was streaming through the east wall of willows, creating gold jail bars across the snow.

The Jeep was gone but Tater's body lay facedown near the tracks. Peggy was splayed out on her back on the front porch, her floral dress hiked up over blue-white thighs. Both had been shot to death.

"Marissa!"

He stepped over Peggy's body like he'd once stepped over the old man. The front door was unlocked and his eyes were wide open and he was breathing fast when he went inside.

His movement and the warmth of the house made his nose bleed again, and it felt like someone was applying a blowtorch to his temple. He could hear his blood pattering on the linoleum.

"Marissa!"

"Oh my God, Brandon, you're alive!" she cried. "I'm in here."

She was in the old man's den.

When he filled the door frame and leaned on it to stay up, she looked up from behind the desk and her face contorted.

"You're hurt," she said. "You look awful."

He didn't want to nod.

Five tiny hairless mice, so new their eyes were still shut, wriggled in a pile of paper scraps on the desk in front of her.

"What are you doing?" he asked.

"Checking on my babies."

It was incomprehensible to him. "What happened?"

She shook her head slowly and said, "When I heard the shots outside I ran upstairs and locked myself in the bathroom. All I could think of was that you were gone and that I'd be raising this boy by myself.

"I heard Tater yell and run out, then Peggy followed him. There were more shots and then I heard a car drive away. I didn't unlock my door and come out until an hour ago. I went outside and saw you lying in the snow and I thought you were gone like the others."

Brandon said, "And the first thing you did after you saw me was check on the mice?"

"They're helpless," she explained. Then he noticed her eyes were unfocused and he determined she was likely in shock. She'd succumbed to her maternal instincts because she didn't know what else to do. His other questions would have to wait. He hoped their baby had no repercussions from her terror and tension throughout the night.

"I'll get the car," he said.

"Can I bring the babies?"

He started to object but thought better of it.

"Sure."

As he turned he heard her say, "There's a towel in the bathroom for your face."

Brandon was shocked at the appearance of the person who looked back at him in the mirror. He had two black eyes, an enormous nose, and his face was crusted with black dried blood. A long tear cut through the skin above his right ear and continued through his scalp.

Wade, he thought. Wade had stood over him after he'd shot Pingston and fired what he'd thought was a kill shot to his head. He'd missed, though, and the bullet had creased his skull.

He *looked* like he should be dead.

When Brandon went outside he saw that Wade had left them a present: all four tires on their minivan were slashed and flat and there was a bullet hole in the grille and a large pool of radiator fluid in the snow.

When he shook his head, it ached.

Then he turned toward the shed.

When he went inside, long-forgotten memories rushed back of observing the old man, Pingston, and various other ranch hands working on equipment, repairing vehicles, and changing out filters, hoses, belts, and oil and other fluids. The old man thought it was a waste of time and money to take his equipment into town for repair so he did it all himself. Those were the days when a man *could* actually fix his own car. And as the men worked, Brandon would hand them the tools they requested.

It had been another world, but one Brandon eased back into. A world where a man was expected to know how a motor worked and how to fix it if necessary.

The battery in the Power Wagon was long dead so he borrowed the battery from his minivan and installed it. The air compressor in the shed sounded like an unmuffled jet engine, but it sufficed to inflate the tires. He filled the Dodge's gas tank from a five-gallon can he found in the corner. Then, recalling a technique the ranch hands had used on especially cold mornings, he took the air filter off the motor and primed the carburetor with a splash of fuel.

Like they were for all ranch vehicles, the keys had been left in the ignition. He opened the choke to full and turned the key and was astonished that the truck roared to life.

The Power Wagon reminded Brandon of a grizzly bear that had emerged from its den. It shook and moaned and seemed to stretch. The shed filled with acrid blue smoke. Pingston had been right when he'd inferred that the old truck was indestructible.

When Brandon eased it out through the doors, he saw Marissa standing open-mouthed on the front porch.

It was a rough ride and Brandon couldn't goose it past thirty-five miles an hour. Blooms of black smoke emerged from the tailpipe. The heater blew dust on their legs when he turned it on. The cab was so high that the ground outside seemed too far down. He felt like a child behind the massive steering wheel.

He'd forgotten what it was like to drive a vehicle without power steering or power brakes. He didn't so much drive it as point it down the road and hold on tight to the steering wheel so the vibration wouldn't shake his teeth loose.

On the way into Big Piney, he glanced over at Marissa, who was holding the box of mice in her lap.

"When did you go into the shed?" he asked. He had to raise his voice over the sound of the motor to be heard.

"Yesterday, after I found the nest of mice."

"How did you get in? The doors were locked."

"The side door wasn't locked. The one with all the weeds? That was open and I went right in."

He nodded and thought about it.

She said, "Are you accusing me of something, Brandon? Your tone is mean."

"I'm sorry," he said, reaching over and patting her thigh. "I'm just confused. There are three dead people back there and my head hurts."

"It was Wade," Marissa said. "Peggy told me after the three of you left. Wade was behind it all."

"I get that. But what were they after?"

Then, before she could answer, he reached into the box of mice and grasped a fistful of the shredded paper. He downshifted because the brakes were shot and he eventually pulled over to the side of the dirt road and stopped the Dodge. The motor banged away but didn't quit running. He could smell hot oil burning somewhere under the hood.

"What is it, Brandon?" she asked.

The strips of paper in his hands were blue and old. But when he pieced them together he could see the words *Trust, Security,* and *Stockman's* printed on them.

He said, "Stockman's Security Trust. That's the bank that got hit years ago. These are bands that held the piles of cash together. Where did you find them, Marissa?"

"I told you," she said. "They were in the nest. I didn't even look at them."

He tried not to raise his voice when he asked, "Where was the nest?"

"It was in the back of this truck. When I found it and realized their mom wasn't around, I looked for something to put them in so I could save them. There was a toolbox under the seat of the truck so I poured all the tools out and put the babies in the box. Brandon, why are you asking me this?"

He sat back. The water tower for Big Piney shimmered in the distance.

"Pingston did that armed robbery and hid the cash somewhere inside the Power Wagon. Probably beneath a fender or taped to the underside. He got pulled over and arrested before he could spend it or hide it somewhere else. And all these years he thought about that money and worried that the old man would find it—which he did."

Marissa seemed to be coming out of shock and she registered surprise.

"Either that," Brandon said, "or my old man was in on the robbery all along and fingered his partner. That way, he could always have a big roll of cash in his pocket even though the ranch was going broke. We may never know how it all went down.

"Pingston told his cell mate Wade about the cash and promised him a cut of it when they got out. I heard Wade say something about protecting Pingston inside and that makes sense. Wade kept Pingston safe so they could both cash out. Only the money wasn't there and Wade thought his old pal had deceived him all along. He went berserk and killed Pingston, then Pingston's family."

Brandon put the truck in gear and turned back onto the road. "We've got to let the sheriff know to look for Peggy's Jeep so they can arrest Wade and send him back to Rawlins."

"Why didn't he kill us and eliminate all the witnesses?" she asked.

"He thought I was dead," Brandon said. "I think maybe he panicked after Peggy and Tater were down and just got the hell out of there. Maybe chasing down a pregnant woman was too much even for Wade."

"Or maybe," she said, "he thought he was stranding me out there to freeze to death without a car, that bastard."

As they entered the town limits of Big Piney, Brandon had to slow down for a dirty pickup that pulled out in front of them. The legs of a massive elk stuck straight up from the bed, and sunlight glinted off the tines of the antlers.

Marissa said, "I can't believe you grew up here."

Brandon patted the steering wheel and said, "We're keeping the Power Wagon. I don't care what my brothers or sister say about it."

"Why?"

"I don't know," he confessed. Then: "Maybe because I got it to run again with my own two hands."

BURNT MATCHES

by Michael Connelly

THE COURTHOUSE ELEVATOR was a sardine can filled with people and the collective breath of desperation and failure. Nobody ever came out a winner in this place. They all rode down in silence and defeat. Like me. I had just taken an all-counts-guilty verdict in a two-week trial in superior court. All that work, all that planning, and I didn't turn a single juror on a single count. My client was going off to jail for a long, long time and there was nothing I could do about it. His case and his appeal would go to somebody else now. And it wouldn't surprise me if they built the appeal around an ineffective-assistance-of-counsel cause. I lost the case. Truly guilty or not, they always blame the lawyer.

I tried to hold my breath in the elevator. I always do and I always fail. It moves so slowly, stopping at almost every floor. Others hoping to escape this place crowd up in the hallway as the doors slide open, the look of one more defeat on their faces when they realize there is no room and they must wait longer.

Finally, we reached the lobby and I pushed my way out

through the trudging bodies. I headed to the exit onto Temple and then started looking for the Lincoln.

I turned right onto Spring—that was where most of the drivers waited—and checked the license plates on the lineup of Lincolns at the curb. There was LEGLWIZ followed by LV2RGUE and LNCNLAW, and then, finally, IWALKEM. They say imitation is the sincerest form of flattery, but sometimes it gets hard to find my ride. This is what happens when they make a movie out of one of the cases you've won. But that victory and the glory of the movie seemed like distant lights on a far-off shore as I walked to my car.

I looked around but Cisco wasn't standing in his usual place on the sidewalk shooting the breeze with the other drivers. That and his not responding to my text telling him I was on my way down should have alerted me that something was wrong but I missed it, like I seemed to be missing everything else. I was thinking about the verdict—an across-the-board wipeout was as much a statement about the lawyer as it was about the defendant. I had some thinking to do and I had already started by the time I opened the rear passenger door and got in.

As I slipped, briefcase in hand, into my customary spot in the rear passenger seat I saw a man sitting on the other side of the car. He moved the aim of a nickel-plated pistol from the back of my driver's head to me.

"Get in," he said. "Close the door."

I put the briefcase down on the floor and raised my hands in a gesture of compliance. No false moves from me.

"Okay, okay, no problem," I said in a voice as calm as I could manage.

The images of the courtroom and the jury forewoman's

dead-eyed stare at me while the clerk read the verdict disappeared quickly. Keeping my eyes on the gunman, I reached out behind me to the door and pulled it closed. I realized as I did so that I recognized the man. I couldn't place him but guessed he was the father or the brother or the husband of one of my violent clients' victims. A face from a courtroom, somebody who had watched me attempt to turn the villain into the victim at his dead or damaged loved one's expense. He couldn't get to the offender because the offender was probably in prison. So he was getting to me.

"Okay," I said. "Now what? What are we doing here?"

The man turned the gun and banged it once on the headrest behind Cisco to get his attention.

"Drive," he said.

"Where to?" Cisco said as he reached forward and started the car.

Dennis "Cisco" Wojciechowski was a very capable investigator and bodyguard. He was driving for me only because a recent surgery on his knee kept him off his Harley and limited his mobility. I was between drivers and he needed to justify his paycheck. He had volunteered and had somehow allowed this man with a gun into the backseat.

"Get on the freeway," the man said. "Go north."

Cisco dropped the car into drive and pulled away from the curb, almost immediately making a U-turn in front of city hall.

"You want to get you and your boss killed quick?" the gunman barked. "Make another move like that."

"You said get on the freeway," Cisco responded. "This way's the freeway."

Cisco didn't have a concealed-carry permit but more often

than not he was carrying something. Usually a Kimber .45 or at least a boot gun. But that was when he was working the streets, chasing down witnesses in some of the rougher neighborhoods in the City of Angels. I had no idea whether he was carrying or not now but I found myself hoping he was. Our abductor's eyes were so intense, they glowed in their sockets. They told me this man was at the end of his line.

The man with the gun turned and looked out the rear window to see if Cisco's maneuver had drawn notice from police or anyone else. Satisfied, he turned his attention back to me and I was ready for it.

"So what can I do for you?" I asked.

"What can you do for me?" he said. "You're asking me that? I'll tell you what — what you can do for me is die. We're heading out to the desert where I'm going to get your driver here to bury your ass in the sand."

Cisco had turned on Temple and taken it to Broadway. The entrance to the northbound 101 Freeway was just a block away.

I said, "Look, sir, I don't know if it was your wife or your daughter who got hurt, but my job is to defend the accused. The system is based on it. Everybody accused of a crime is entitled to a vigorous defense. It's in the Constitution. Your complaint with me is —"

"You dumb shit," the man said. "I don't have any wife or daughter."

And then it hit me — he wasn't a grieving father or husband of a victim. He was a client. I didn't recognize him from a courtroom gallery; I knew him from the defense table. We had sat next to each other through a trial and now I couldn't remember his name or his case to save my life.

"So, another satisfied customer," I said. "You're going to have to tell me who you are. I know I should recognize you, but over the years I've had a lot of clients and a lot of trials. I know you from a trial but I am sorry, I don't remember your name."

I glanced at the rearview and saw Cisco's eyes looking back at me. We were merging onto the 101 heading north, like the man wanted.

"I'm just a burnt match to you," the man said. "That's what you called me."

That didn't help me conjure up the name.

"I never called you that," I said. "What I said was that some of these cases—like yours, I assume—are hopeless. They put me in a position where I'm basically trying to sell burnt matches to the jury. And no one buys burnt matches. So you're here because you blame me for losing your unwinnable case."

"No, man, that's not how it was."

"Yeah, it was. I don't remember your name or your case but I guarantee it was a dog. I told you to take the offer from the DA and you said no. You insisted on a trial even though I told you—I warned you—that we couldn't win and you'd end up with more time. Now tell me that isn't what happened."

The man angrily shifted in his seat and momentarily turned his face from me and looked out the window. It was so unexpected I didn't react. I missed the chance to go for the gun.

Still, it told me two things: one, I was right about the case, and two, he might make the same turn-away move again if I pushed him hard enough. The next time I'd be ready to go for the gun.

We were moving on the 101 at a brisk pace. It was the middle of the day and traffic was light. We had already gotten to

Hollywood. As we passed a green freeway sign announcing the exit to Hollywood Boulevard, the man shook his head.

"Hollywood," he said. "I mean, you fuck up people's lives and what happens? They make a movie about you. Matthew fucking McConaughey. They showed that shit one night at Corcoran. I'm watching it and I hear the lawyer's name and I'm thinking, *That guy's playing my motherfucking lawyer. The guy who fucking put me here.*"

I didn't have many clients that ended up in Corcoran but it still didn't bring the name to mind.

"Are you going to tell me who you are or are we just going to keep playing a guessing game?"

"Oscar Letts."

I recalled the name and soon the general outline of the case came back to me.

"Remember me now?" he asked.

"Yeah," I said. "Felony hit-and-run manslaughter. You were drunk and the lady you hit was the wife of a sheriff's deputy. No, actually, he was a captain."

"I wasn't drunk. I'd had two beers!"

"That's what you said. The bartender they brought into court said different."

"Because she was forced to by the sheriffs—they were going to close her down. I went away for nine years. I had a house and a wife and a kid and I lost it all. You didn't fight for me, Haller, you didn't do shit. You didn't care at all."

"This is ridiculous."

I leaned forward and reached down to my briefcase.

"What the fuck you doing?" Letts said.

He put the muzzle of the gun against my head.

"My computer," I said. "I want to pull up the file."

"Give me the briefcase," Letts said. "I'll get the computer."

I slid the case over the transmission hump to him. He pulled the gun back and brought the case up to his lap. As he flipped the locks one at a time and opened the case I stole another glance at Cisco in the mirror. We held each other's eyes for a long moment. He shook his head slightly. I think he was telling me he didn't bring his gun. I slowly nodded once. I hoped he knew what I was saying: I was going to make a move against this guy and he needed to be ready.

Letts inspected the contents of the briefcase as if thinking he might find a weapon. He then opened the laptop and checked it out before handing it to me.

"The case is almost ten years old," he said. "You're telling me you still have it on your computer?"

"I have conflict-of-interest software," I said. "All my cases are digitized and loaded, so if a name from an old case shows up in a new one, I'll know. Cops or witnesses from old cases come up from time to time. Occasionally even clients."

I went into the software and typed in *Oscar Letts*. His case file immediately opened on the screen. I started scanning the summaries. I was looking for something in particular and soon found it.

"Okay, right here," I said. "Offer of disposition from the DA's office. You were offered a term of four to seven years in exchange for a guilty plea. You turned it down, against my advice. You made me go to trial. You insisted we go to trial. There was no case. We had no defense. You left the bar, you blew through the stop sign, and you hit the captain's wife in the crosswalk. There was nothing I could do. It was burnt matches, but you wouldn't listen. You insisted we take it to a jury and we did and you ended up with nine to fifteen from the judge. Am I missing anything?"

Letts didn't respond. I turned slightly to my left to face him. I slowly closed the laptop and moved my right foot toward the door so I could brace it.

"You were the architect of this," I said. "I remember everything now. You hit her and then you just kept driving while she bled to death in the crosswalk. How was I supposed to sell that to the jury?"

"I didn't just keep going," Letts protested. "I got out. I checked on her. I had no phone. I had to get to a phone and get her help. I made the call, goddamn it!"

"Yeah, well, there was no record of it."

"It was because of him. The captain. He pulled the records because he knew it would make me look bad. And you let him get away with it. You never even fucking called him to the stand."

"I couldn't call him. There was no evidence he did anything. I'm going to put the victim's husband on the stand and go after him with nothing? You should have taken the deal. You would have been out in four and you would still have your life. But don't you fucking dare blame me. You want to shoot somebody, put that gun in your own mouth."

Letts gritted his teeth angrily, pulling back his lips in disgust. I saw the muscles of his neck and shoulders tense. The grip on his gun tightened. He then turned away again, as if finding his bearings before firing the gun at me.

I made my move. Raising the laptop up as a shield, I lunged across the seat and into him; I slammed the laptop into his face just as he turned back toward me. Then I grabbed the top of the gun barrel with one hand, put my other hand over his, and forced the weapon toward the floor. And I yelled as loud as I could, "Cisco, pull over! Get back here!"

I braced my foot against the door and pushed my body into Letts's. He was stronger than I thought, and control of the gun until Cisco could help was the immediate challenge. He tried to pull the weapon's muzzle up and I fought to hold it down. I tried to jam a thumb behind the trigger but Letts cleared the trigger guard and started firing the weapon, two quick shots into the floorboard that made Cisco swerve the car back and forth. The force of the double move threw me off Letts and then right back onto him. He managed to bring the gun up and fired into the seat in front of him.

Cisco was hurled forward into the steering column, and the car went into a clockwise spin. I took one hand off the gun and reached for Letts's door.

"Cisco, the lock!"

Somehow Cisco knew what I meant and managed to hit the electronic lock button. Even with the squealing of sliding tires, I heard the pop of the locks coming up. I grabbed the door handle and yanked it up. Centrifugal force did the rest. The door flew open and Letts was jerked out of the car as if by two unseen hands. I was about to follow him but the car slammed into the guardrail at the side of the freeway. It came to a jolting stop that threw me in the other direction.

I looked over the seat at Cisco. He was leaning forward, one arm up and under his leather coat.

"Cisco, you hit?"

"Fucker got me in the shoulder. Where is he?"

Good question. I turned and looked out the back window of the Lincoln. I recognized that we were in the Cahuenga Pass, where the freeway cuts through the Santa Monica Mountains and enters the San Fernando Valley. We were hard against the railing in the freeway's breakdown lane. There was no sign of Letts at first and then I saw cars in the slow lane swerving to avoid something in the road.

It was him. An opening between cars gave me a glimpse of Letts on the asphalt, crawling and then struggling to his feet. His clothes were ripped and he had a bloody abrasion on the side of his face. He still held the gun, the knuckles on his hand torn open from the skid on the asphalt. Just as he got to his feet, a car coming up behind him swerved out of the lane and crashed into a panel van already occupying the next lane over. The impact propelled the car right back into its original lane and it hit Letts from behind, flipping him up over the car and into the air. He came down in front of another car and was dragged under it as it skidded to a stop and was promptly rear-ended by an SUV.

I scrabbled across the seat to the door behind Cisco and climbed out. Then I went to the front door and opened it. I reached in for my driver.

"You okay?"

"I will be. Where is he?"

"He's down. We don't have to worry about him. It's over."

"Jesus Christ."

"Yeah."

"He came up to the window with a train ticket. Wanted to know how to find Union Station. I tried to tell him and then he pulled the gun."

"Don't worry about it."

"Told me to unlock the back door."

"Well, it's over."

"What about what he said about making the call?"

"What call?"

"That night he said he called for help. You think the sheriff's captain pulled the 911 recording?"

"That was before you worked with me. Saul was my investigator back then. He looked into it, couldn't find anything. Letts said he made the call from a gas station where he borrowed somebody's cell. We never found anybody to back it up. Believe me, we tried. That was the case right there."

"Too bad—if he was telling the truth."

Cisco struggled out of the car and leaned against the side, keeping his hand on his left shoulder.

"Yeah, too bad."

Cisco rubbed his shoulder beneath the jacket. I could see the crimson stain spreading on the white T-shirt he wore under the leather.

"Got me right in the rotator, I think. Probably going to get a new shoulder to go with my new knee."

I didn't answer. I leaned against the car next to him and watched traffic build up behind the accident scene. Pretty soon it would be a parking lot stretching all the way back to downtown.

RUNS GOOD

by Kelly Braffet

CARO MISSED THE bus. She usually did. The last one left the mall at ten and unless she managed to clock out a few minutes early, she inevitably saw it pull away from the curb as she was still running across the parking lot. Tonight, sweaty, heart pounding, feet killing her, she put her headphones on and started walking.

Past the car dealership, on the side of the road near a place that sold outdoor furniture, she came upon a battered white Civic. One side mirror was held on with duct tape and there was a decent-size dent in the bumper. The sign in the window said FOR SALE, $1,000, RUNS GOOD. It was late; she was tired and bitter about missing the bus, which was bright and quick and safe. Too often her life seemed disproportionately inconvenient and annoying, and now, looking at the car, she found her feet slowing, and stopping, until she stood by the side of the road in the cool damp grass as cars roared by on the four-lane next to her.

A thousand dollars. What a big, slippery number that was.

If she managed to squirrel away a hundred a week she could have it in ten weeks (three months-ish, by which time the car probably wouldn't even be there anymore so why was she even bothering to do the math). She put the numbers together in her head, food and electricity and the phone—Margot's SSI almost covered rent—and looked away. She couldn't manage to save fifty dollars a month, let alone a hundred a week. And that wasn't even figuring in insurance and gas. Her last boyfriend had been all worked up about insurance and gas, how much they cost.

But at the same time, she wanted the car. It pulled at her. Having her own car would make everything better. It would mean no more walking by the side of the highway in the middle of the night, no more hauling everything she needed for both of her jobs around in her backpack. The car would mean no wrestling Margot onto the bus for doctors' appointments, no more hikes to the bank to deposit checks. No more having to take *Does he have a car?* into account when a guy asked her out, no more having to take *But he has a car* into account when she didn't want to see him anymore.

Caro was not quite eighteen, but she was smart, and, more than that, she was realistic. She knew that right now, as things stood, she could not have the car.

Someday, she thought—as she always did—*I will look back on this part of my life, and it will be in my past, and I will not have to live it anymore.*

Still, she burned with frustration.

It was not fair.

Caro had applied for a job as a bartender and she would have gotten it, but her fake ID was terrible, and Freddy, the manager, didn't buy it for a second. He said he'd hire her as a waitress, and she needed money so she took the job. She acted more grateful than she was and got good at finding reasons not to be alone in a room with him.

The place was at a new midrange hotel out on the strip outside Pitlorsville, the kind that was supposed to appeal to business travelers, a step above the hot-breakfast-buffet sort of deal in that it had an actual restaurant with an actual bar. Caro didn't think the food was anything special. All the sandwiches came with sauces that were basically mayonnaise with stuff mixed in—Parmesan or garlic or pesto or whatever—and the French fries and bread all came frozen off the Sysco truck. Caro mostly worked the dinner shift, which was normally dead. She usually had one table going at any given time. Two was rare. Three tables left the kitchen in the weeds, even though everything was basically reheated. Her paychecks were minuscule. Her tips were nothing. But after a few weeks, Freddy started giving her bartending shifts, and that was experience she might be able to turn into a real job somewhere else.

The humid air of September gave way to the brisk mulchy wind of October, and still the car sat. Waiting, she thought—for a thousand dollars to fall out of the sky at her feet, for whatever cosmic forces controlled the world to decide she'd been taunted enough, for someone luckier to drive it away. Halloween was coming. November and December were right around the corner. Winter would bring snowstorms and icicles and long hours in the dark predawn, numb hands stuffed into Margot's old mittens, scraping ice off the front steps of the rickety little duplex where they lived, clearing the driveway. (Caro had negotiated that last winter, shoveling the snow in exchange for an embarrassingly small break on the rent.) Winter would bring school closings. Caro didn't like school but it was better than home, better than hours spent curled up under a blanket in the barely heated duplex hiding a book from Margot and forcing herself through it one sentence at a time. Yanking herself, by sheer force of will, into any world other than this one, any room other than one of the three tiny ones she shared with Margot.

The guidance counselor, who thought he knew things, passed her in the hallway one day and said, "Hey, Carolyn! How's your mother?"

She forced a smile and said, "Good." As soon as he was around the corner, one of the other girls said, "God, she even fucks the *guidance* counselors." Caro stared at her until she looked uncomfortable and walked away. The girls at school thought they knew things too.

She took the school bus home with all the other kids who didn't have cars, staring fixedly out the window and ignoring the cacophony around her. At home she found Margot nestled inside a fort she'd made out of the kitchen table by turning it on its side and surrounding it with the chairs, similarly upended. An old afghan was draped across the top, letting light in through its crocheted holes.

Caro wondered if any of the other girls at school had mothers who made blanket forts. She crouched down so she could see Margot sitting inside, cross-legged like a child, her wide eyes staring out of the dappled darkness. She was wearing sweatpants and a hooded sweatshirt—no zippers—and her arms were pulled in close, as if they were cold. "That kind of day?" Caro said.

"Yes," Margot said in her weird, affectless way.

Caro looked around for a plate or a paper towel or some crumbs. "Eat anything?"

"Nothing was out," Margot said.

Caro sighed. "Want me to make you a peanut butter sandwich?"

Margot nodded.

"Okay," Caro said, and stood up. "Cover your ears. I have to open things."

She heard a soft whimper from inside the fort, and then her mother said, "Okay," in a tense, muffled way that Caro knew meant that Margot had clapped both hands over her ears and was curled in a tight defensive ball. "Hands, Carrie?"

Automatically, Caro pulled her sleeves down over her hands. There was an empty pitcher on the counter; with her hands still inside her sleeves, so she didn't touch the metal faucet, she put it in the sink and let the cold water trickle into it. As quickly and quietly as she could, she opened the drawer and took out a knife, opened the cupboard and took out the peanut butter. She had to open another drawer to get the bread and that was the worst one because sometimes it squeaked. Margot squeaked too when she heard it. There was a half a loaf of bread left: seven slices. The peanut butter in the jar was enough for two reasonable sandwiches and one scanty one. Caro made the sandwiches, put all three of them on a plate — she heard Margot yelp with fear as the cabinet door slammed shut — and slid them into Margot's den. Then she took the full pitcher of water from the sink, got a glass down from the cupboard, and crouched down next to the tent again.

Margot still had her ears covered. Her eyes were squeezed

shut too. Caro reached in and tapped her knee. "Margot," she said, and her mother opened her eyes. Caro showed her the pitcher and the glass. "Water's right here, okay?"

"Are you leaving?"

"My shift starts at four."

With one hand, pale and slightly swollen from her meds, Margot pulled the plate in close to her. No other part of her moved. "You have homework?" she said.

"Taking it with me."

"Have you ever read Simone de Beauvoir, Carrie?" Caro shook her head no, and Margot shook her head too. "Shame. I think you'd like her." Her watery eyes, so like and unlike Caro's own, blinked, and she made a sad, wistful noise that was somewhere between a sigh and a breath. "I wish they hadn't gotten to the books. So many good books out there. None of them are safe."

"Do you want to go to the bathroom before I leave?" Caro said instead of responding to that, and Margot did, so Caro opened the bathroom door and turned on all the lights and the taps. She waited outside in the hallway until Margot was done, then went in and flushed the toilet and turned everything off. She washed her own hands too, because they smelled like peanut butter, and then redid her ponytail. By the time she got back into the kitchen, Margot had returned to her fort and there was the steady sound of eating.

"I'm going now," Caro said.

"Have a nice day, sweetie," Margot said. Just like a real mother would.

As always, Caro thought, *It's nighttime,* and as always, she didn't say it.

On the nights she didn't work at the hotel, she worked her old job at the Eat'n Park, in her green polyester jumper and the ribbon-bow earrings she'd bought from the cheerleading squad's latest fund-raiser. School colors: blue and gold. Go, Golden Bears. She didn't know if there was even such a thing as a Golden Bear and she'd never seen a bear of any color in worn-down, suburban Pitlorsville, but there were an awful lot of Golden Bear alums. If she stood there on her aching feet and listened to some fat old dude wax nostalgic about his glory days on the whatever team and smiled as if she cared, it was sometimes worth an extra dollar or two. All of the other waitresses went to school with her and most of them hated her. She had to keep an eye on her order slips or they'd magically migrate to the end of the line, and she had to keep an eye on her bag or it ended up full of ketchup. So, really, the nights at the hotel weren't so bad. At least she got to wear nice clothes and wasn't surrounded by people whose boyfriends she might or might not have slept with.

That night she ended up working the counter in the smoking section, which none of the other girls wanted. A guy in a blue work shirt with sewn-on patches ordered bacon and eggs; he said thanks when she brought them and not much else, but he left her a big tip and a note with his number. *To the prettiest thing I've seen all night. Call me.*

She put the note in her pocket and tried to remember the words on the patches. Was he a cop? A paramedic? A paramedic might be able to help her with Margot sometimes. A cop wouldn't be worth it. A cop would probably call people.

Or maybe the patches had said *Security Guard*. With her luck, they probably had. Out on the highway, the car still waited.

* * *

She worked at the hotel bar a few nights later. Only one customer came in her whole shift; she offered him a table, but he chose to sit at the bar and ordered without looking at the menu. He wore gray slacks and a white button-down shirt. Hair cut recently and conservatively; the watch on his wrist was nice, and the phone he left sitting next to his plate on the bar was glossy and new. He had a friendly face. "You have a turkey club, right?" he said.

"We do," she said.

"All hotel restaurants have to have a turkey club," he said and gave her a tired smile. "I think it's a rule."

She smiled back, because she had to, and put the order in. The cook was on the phone with his girlfriend, arguing. She wondered if the turkey-club guy was a chatter. She didn't always mind chatters—sometimes they tipped well—but she had a lab report to write up for chem.

Her books were spread out behind the bar, which technically they weren't supposed to be, but nobody was going to rat her out tonight. For a while she worked and Turkey Club watched the crawl on CNN and the restaurant was filled with canned music and a companionable non-quiet. The music covered the sound of what's his name fighting with his girlfriend and meant that Caro had to listen closely for the bell that meant Turkey Club's turkey club was ready. When the bell finally rang, she brought the man his food, nodded at the TV, and said, "I can turn that up for you if you want. Or change the station."

He looked around. "Yeah, it doesn't look like anybody will complain. What are you working on?"

"Lab report for chemistry," she said.

"Where do you go to school?" he said.

Somehow she understood that he thought she was in college. When she worked at the hotel she wore all black, with dark lipstick and some fake diamond earrings she'd bought at the drugstore. "Community college," she said. "Nothing fancy."

He nodded. "That's smart. Do a few years at community, transfer to a school with a name, save yourself some money." A dab of mayonnaise stuck to his lip; he wiped it away. "Or just stay at community. There's nothing wrong with community college."

There seemed to be something wrong with the Pitlorsville community college. Caro had never known a single person who'd managed to graduate from it. But she probably just knew the wrong people. "That's my plan. Transferring." And wouldn't that be a lovely plan.

"I was a chemistry major myself," he said.

"Really? What do you do now?"

"I'm in sales."

"That doesn't seem to have much to do with chemistry."

He shrugged. "I never really had the patience for lab work. I just liked mixing things together so they went boom. And the degree got me my first job in pharma." He looked down at his half-eaten sandwich, the fries cooling in a puddle of ketchup. "Which led to the glamorous life you see before you."

"There's nothing you can tell me about glamour," she said, arching an eyebrow. "I work *here*."

Grinning, he said, "Well, it's quiet."

Quiet it certainly was. Turkey Club was her first and last

customer of the night. Freddy, her boss, came in as she was closing up, looked at the posted schedule, and shook his head. "There's no good way to say this," he said, and then he told her that after this week, they were closing the restaurant for dinner. They'd be doing room service instead, splitting those shifts between the two bartenders and whatever hotel staff was available. "If you wanted to, you could work breakfasts," he said. "We're always busy at breakfast."

So was Caro. In English class. For the nine millionth time she wondered if it would be easier to quit school, but as always, something in her balked at the thought. Margot had quit school. Margot thought there were evil elves in the wall monitoring her and Caro's movements through every metal thing or printed word in the house. "I need this job, Freddy," she said.

"And you've got it. For one more shift."

"How generous of you," she said.

He had the decency to look sad. "Just so you know, I hate firing people. And it's not that I don't like you. You're a great kid. You're good with the customers. If there were more of them, this wouldn't even be a question."

She trudged home in the cold. When she passed the car, she didn't even let herself look at it. There was no way. Absolutely no way.

The next night she worked at Eat'n Park. She left at the same time as a girl named Cathy who was in her math class and who had her own car. Cathy didn't offer her a ride home. Caro hadn't expected her to. Even the girls who didn't have a specific reason to hate her stayed away, and she understood why. In high school, being a pariah was like having a communicable disease. And maybe Cathy had a boyfriend too. Caro didn't set out to *steal*. She just took opportunities as they arose. She couldn't afford not to, and it was nice not to feel alone, and all of those girls had loving mommies and doting daddies and there would be other boys for them, other futures.

She thought about blowing off her last shift at the hotel but she couldn't justify it—and besides, what was she going to do instead? Sit at home with Margot and watch her meds not work? So, two days later, she was back in her black shirt and pants, standing behind the bar doing homework. Algebra this time. She'd failed it the year before.

Turkey Club was back too. Staring at a menu, a faint frown on his face. She said, "We have a great turkey club."

He looked up at her and smiled. She could see that he was pleased that she'd remembered him, which was what she'd intended. "I know. I've had it for four meals in a row, except breakfast. What else is good?"

She shrugged. "Chicken Caesar salad?"

He groaned. "Do you know how many chicken Caesar salads I've eaten over the years? Caesar salads, turkey clubs, western omelets. It all tastes the same."

"It all comes off the same truck," Caro said.

"Sometimes, I think one more day on the road is going to break me." He rubbed his face. "I am going to literally turn into a preservative. A living, breathing molecule of BHT."

"There's a pesto-tortellini thing," she said. "Occasionally they put actual prosciutto in it."

He closed the menu. "Sold. One pesto-tortellini thing with occasional actual prosciutto in it, please."

She put in the order and brought him a basket of bread.

"More chemistry?" he said, and at first she thought he was talking about the bread but then he nodded at her books.

"Algebra." She wondered if that was a mistake, if chemistry majors in college didn't have to take algebra. She tried to remember if she'd actually told him she was a chemistry major. Then she decided that it was all too much work on her last day. "I lied to you before. I'm still in high school," she said, feeling faintly reckless. The truth. What a novelty.

His eyes widened. "I would not have thought that."

"It's the makeup. I am a senior, though."

"Big plans for after?"

She thought about saying *Taking care of my schizophrenic mother* — but there was such a thing as too much truth. "Probably what you said. Community college, then transfer."

"It's still a good plan."

"Sure, if I can afford it."

"Is this a good job? It seems like it should be. But I never see anybody here."

"They're closing the restaurant," she said. "This is my last shift."

"Oh," he said, and then, "Oh."

She heard the bell ring from the kitchen. "One pesto thing with occasional prosciutto," she said when she came back, setting the plate down in front of him. "Sorry, though. You didn't get the prosciutto."

"That's a shame," he said.

"They must have run out."

"No," he said, picking up his fork. "About your job."

"It's okay. I have another one."

"She said grimly."

That made her smile. "Well, I didn't say it was a great job."

"I'm surprised your parents let you have two jobs while you're in school," he said. "You must get spectacular grades."

A thousand things were on the tip of Caro's tongue but what came out was "I'm saving up to buy a car."

"Still, two jobs? Is borrowing your mom's car really so bad?"

"Walking is," she said.

He blinked. "Walking. In this weather."

Because the wind was biting and harsh even though it wasn't yet November. Caro shrugged.

"None of your friends can give you a ride?"

She shrugged again. "I get off so late."

"And your parents are okay with all of this."

"Don't make me keep shrugging," she said.

He looked at her for a long moment and then nodded. "Okay," he said. "Life is complicated. Sure."

He ate his pesto thing, said good night, and left the restaurant—presumably to go upstairs. He left her a big tip, but not big enough to make a difference. She fantasized briefly about being that lucky one-in-a-million waitress who got the lucky one-in-a-million tip: five hundred dollars, a thousand. Ten bucks was nice, though. She wouldn't argue with ten bucks.

Finally, her shift was over. She walked out into the lobby, past the potted trees that nobody was supposed to notice were made of plastic. There was a twenty-four-hour coffee station set up near a small sitting area with a couch and a coffee table, but it was right in front of the door, so she couldn't imagine why people would choose to sit there when they had an entire hotel room all to themselves upstairs. Someone was sitting there now, though. It was Turkey Club. He stood up when he saw her.

"I thought you might like a ride," he said.

She felt her back go stiff and her guard go up. "No, thank you."

"It's thirty-eight degrees outside."

"I like the cold."

He sighed and rubbed his eyes. "Yeah. You're probably right. You shouldn't take rides from somebody you barely know. If I had a daughter, I wouldn't want her to do it either. I just thought—it's so cold and so late. I thought I'd offer, is all."

"And I appreciate it," she said briskly, "but no." She was waiting for him to turn around and go away so she'd know he wasn't going to follow her out to the parking lot. He wasn't turning around or going away. He was standing by the couch, chewing his lip.

"Okay," he said suddenly. "Here." He walked over to the front desk. The woman working behind it was there almost every night when Caro left, but they'd never spoken, and Caro didn't know the woman's name. The man took out his wallet. "Here's my driver's license," he said to the woman working the desk, laying the piece of plastic down on the high counter between them. "And here's my business card. See? That's me. Chris Mitchell. Matches my name on the room, right?"

"I guess so," the woman said. She was much older than Caro. Her eyes flicked back and forth between Caro and the man, suspiciously.

"And you already have my license number and my credit card and everything, don't you?"

"Yeah."

He looked at Caro. "So if something happens to you while you're with me, they'll know exactly who I am. Hell," he added, turning to the clerk again, "if I'm not back in an hour, call the cops straight off, okay? Just to be on the safe side."

Caro bit back a smile. He saw. She saw him seeing.

"Let me give you a ride," he said. "That's it. I promise."

She thought about it for another second. "Fine," she said.

The woman behind the desk shook her head.

It really was cold outside and Caro was shivering by the time he turned the engine on. His car was new, like his phone and his haircut. It smelled faintly of coconut and was very clean. There were a few coffee cups on the floor mats and a stack of CDs tucked into the console, but no fast-food wrappers, no dirty shirts balled up in the backseat. "The thing is," he said, turning the heat up, "I wouldn't want my daughter walking around this late at night in this weather either. Where do you live?"

"Why did you say an hour?" she said.

"Because I don't know where you live," he said patiently. "I mean, I'm assuming that if you walk, it's relatively close. But I don't *know* that. I'd like to help you out and all, but I don't actually want to get picked up by the police on suspicion of kidnapping."

"Not to mention the fact that I'm a minor," she said.

He grimaced. "Even more reason for me to get you home safe. Where's home?"

"You know where Main Street is?" He nodded. "Drive down Main Street and then take a left at the junior high."

The car was beginning to warm up. As he pulled out of the hotel parking lot, she saw the streets were almost deserted. To get to Main Street he had to drive by the car, her car—no, not her car, never her car. It was there and gone in a flash of white, which seemed appropriate.

"That's the car I was saving for," she said. "We just drove past it."

"How much do you need?"

"A thousand dollars."

"That's not too bad."

"Might as well be a million."

"How much do you have?"

"Right now? This minute?" She thought for a moment, subtracted the electricity bill, subtracted groceries. "A hundred and fifty."

"That's not much for a girl who works two jobs and lives at home."

"Yeah, well," she said. "I chip in."

"Ah," he said. "Would you like me not to ask any more questions about that?"

"Good instinct." She flipped through his CDs. "So what's your deal? Where do you live?"

"Outside Cleveland."

"Vague."

"I have a nice split-level house and a wife named Lisa."

"Kids?"

"Not unless you count Kermit."

"The frog?"

"The Havanese."

"What's a Havanese?"

"It's the national dog of Cuba."

"Little? Big?"

"Little. Fluffy."

"Yappy?"

"Ours isn't."

"You don't seem like a little-fluffy-dog guy."

"What kind of dog guy do I seem like?"

Caro didn't know much about dogs. "The dog-food-commercial kind. The ones that catch Frisbees."

"Well, Kermit is great, but—yeah, that's more my type," he said. "Lisa has allergies, though."

"How does she feel about you traveling so much?"

He shrugged. "She doesn't love it. But she likes the money. It's the way our life is, that's all. So, does my answering all these questions mean I'm allowed to ask you some?"

"I'm just trying to get to know the stranger who's driving me home," she said. "There's the junior high, up ahead."

He turned. "I'll tell you what," he said. "You've piqued my curiosity. I'll ask. You don't have to answer. You live with your parents?"

"My mom."

"What about your dad?"

"Have you ever heard the term *sperm donor* used in this context?"

"Got it. Your mom doesn't work?"

She didn't answer.

"Two jobs, plus high school," he said. "Don't you get tired?"

"I'm always tired," she said. "Turn right up here."

They drove in silence for a minute or two. Then he said, "I'm guessing your mother has some problems. I don't know what kind. I suppose I don't need to know."

She didn't answer.

"Mind if I get gas?" he said, and he flicked on his turn signal.

He pulled them into a SuperSpeedy, lit almost to daylight and busy even at this time of night. She sat in the warm cocoon of heated air while he filled the tank of his car. Then he leaned in. "I want a doughnut. You want anything?"

"A doughnut sounds good."

He nodded and went inside. She watched as he stopped at the cash machine and then sank back into the plush of the car's interior and pretended this was her life, that she was an adult and she was heading far away from the shabby little duplex instead of to it; this was her car. The man inside was her husband. He had a good job and she had a purse full of credit cards in good standing. When she looked out the window she saw a couple just like the one in her imagination, obviously coming back from a night out somewhere nicer than the hotel restaurant.

"Hello," she said to them through the closed window. "My name is Lisa Mitchell. This is my husband, Chris, and our dog Kermit. He's a Havanese. It's the national dog of Cuba."

The door to the convenience store opened and Chris came out carrying a box, so she shut up before he could see her talking to herself.

Back in the car, he took one doughnut out of the box and handed the rest to her. "All yours."

"I don't need charity doughnuts," she said.

"Charity doughnuts, my ass. They only sold them by the dozen." That was a lie but she let him get away with it. The doughnuts smelled amazing and Margot would eat them, because all she had to do was open the box.

"Thanks," she said.

"You're welcome."

He started the car, and she expected him to put the car in gear and pull out, but instead he just sat and stared back into the SuperSpeedy. His brow was furrowed and his jaw was working slightly, as if he were poking at a sore tooth with his tongue.

"I'm not eighteen yet," she said.

"You mentioned that."

"I know," she said, "but that's why I don't answer questions. Until I'm eighteen, I have to be careful. Anyway, I'm just telling you because I can see you feel sorry for me—things will get better." She spoke with a conviction she didn't entirely feel. Except she had to feel it, because otherwise her feet wouldn't move, her lungs wouldn't expand. "I mean, the ride and the doughnuts—I really do appreciate them. But you don't need to feel sorry for me, is all I'm saying."

"What are you going to do when you turn eighteen?" he said. "Is that what the car is for?"

"Is *what* what the car is for?"

"Well," he said, "if you're eighteen, and you have a car, you can pretty much go anywhere you want. Do anything you want. You don't have to live at home. You don't have to live in Pitlorsville. You could drive to LA, break into show business. Or you could drive to Houston and break into the oil business. We get born into these situations, and you do the best you can with it, but sometimes the best you can do is get the fuck out, you know?"

She thought of the car, gleaming white by the side of the road—the road that stretched on, all the intersections and exits that led from here to places like LA and Houston and Seattle and Des Moines and who the hell even knew where.

"My mom needs me," she said.

"Yeah, well," he said. "Everybody needs something. We don't all get it. You need a car, right?"

He was smiling but the things he said hurt. "What about you?" she said. "What do you need?"

In the semi-light from the SuperSpeedy, she saw him roll his eyes, as if the things he needed were legion, and there was no point in talking about it. "What do I need," he said, almost to himself.

Then he didn't say anything else, and for a moment they sat in silence in the parking lot, the engine the only sound. The silence lasted so long that Caro began to feel nervous. "Are we going to go?" she said.

"Yeah, but—" He turned to look at her. "Maybe we could help each other."

Her guard snapped back up. He must have seen it on her face because right away he said, "No, no. Not that. Don't worry. I could use some help with an errand, is all."

"An errand," she said.

"Really quick. I just need you to run something inside to a friend of mine, at his office."

"What?"

"A package. Not a bomb or anything, I promise."

But not something legal, or he'd do it himself. "You said you work in pharma," she said. "You mean pharmaceuticals? Like drugs?"

"Legitimate medicine. Headquarters in Jersey and everything.

I rep all sorts of things: Antibiotics, boner pills. Statins for high cholesterol."

"Is that what's in the package you want me to run inside to your friend?" she said, a bit dryly. "Antibiotics and boner pills?"

"Not exactly."

"So painkillers."

He looked at her steadily and said, "There's all kinds of pain in the world. Not all of it shows up on an ER scan."

Caro didn't say anything. She was thinking. Once she'd worked at a box office in a movie theater, a corporate chain; the usher had palmed the tickets, and she'd resold them, and they'd split the profits. They made minimum wage there, with no overtime no matter how much they worked. Nobody knew the difference and nobody got hurt. But the couple who lived upstairs in the duplex were on pills, when they could get them, and they were a mess. The cops came all the time and it was a pain; sometimes they wanted statements and Caro had to lie, and then she had to make sure Margot could act sane for a few minutes. Drugs were not movie tickets. She wasn't sure she wanted to get involved in anything having to do with drugs.

"My friend's office has security cameras," he said. "I've already been there once today so it would look weird if I came again after hours. I'll pay you." He gave her a tense smile. "But you kind of have to decide quick. We're running out of time."

"How much?" she said.

"How about five hundred?" he said. "That'd get you a long way to your car."

She shook her head and suddenly realized that she'd made a decision. "For taking something into a building? No. You give me that much money, I can't play stupid when the cops come." The closer a lie was to the truth, the easier it was to pull off. "One hundred."

"Are you sure?" he said. "The cops won't come. I can give you more."

"Ticktock," Caro said, and he laughed, and said, "Okay, fine."

His friend, whoever he was, had an office in a nearby medical complex. The doors were all unlocked, and she could hear a vacuum cleaner in another room. The paper bag felt completely normal in her hands. It could have had a peanut butter sandwich in it, except it was heavy, and it rattled faintly. She opened the door to the office Chris had directed her to go to; it looked like the average doctor's office, with a high counter and computers and chairs to wait in. Down a hallway she found the backmost office, which was too full of a gleaming wood desk. The walls were plastered with framed diplomas. She dropped the bag onto the chair behind the desk, tried not to look at any of the diplomas so she wouldn't know the doctor's name, and left.

"Go okay?" Chris said out in the car.

"You need to take me home," she said. "What's her name at the front desk is going to call the police."

After everything, after all of it, she was still home fifteen minutes earlier than she would have been if she'd walked. When he pulled up to the curb in front of the duplex, he said, "Well, thanks. Don't forget your doughnuts."

She smiled and picked up the box. "There's only two of us. They'll be stale before we finish them."

"Stale doughnuts are still pretty good," he said. She agreed they were, said good-bye, and got out of the car.

Inside the house, Caro saw Margot had left her den and was a huddled lump under the blankets on the couch. "Here, Margot," Caro said. "Take a doughnut."

Margot's hand slipped out from under the blanket, took the doughnut, and receded out of sight. "I love doughnuts," she said, and Caro heard a happy sigh. It had a false, tinny note to it. Like Margot vaguely remembered what a happy sigh sounded like and was doing her best to get there.

Caro took the doughnut box into the kitchen. She set the table and chairs back on their feet and hunted around in the crumbs and muck under the edge of the cabinets for the folded pad of newspaper they used to keep the table level. After she found it, she opened her backpack and brought out her algebra book again. She still had six problems to solve.

Two days later, the last of the doughnuts had turned to rock. "They aren't safe anymore," Margot had said but—as usual— had been unable to articulate why the doughnuts were dangerous or how they had gotten that way. Just like she had been unable to articulate why books were bad, or sunlight, or the sound of the garbage truck that came on Friday mornings. Caro didn't know if Margot herself didn't know or if she just couldn't find the words, but she knew that her mother's terror was real. That it consumed her, that it drove her into dark soft places and, sometimes, into flaming rages of fear. Sometimes when she thought of school ending and the long months and years that came after, Caro herself felt a panicking flutter of fear deep inside her, and the thought that the flutter might be something akin to what Margot felt—the beginnings of it, maybe—kept her awake at night.

Caro took a bite of the stale doughnut. Chris was wrong. Stale doughnuts were actually pretty depressing. She dropped the box in the garbage.

The white paper inside shuffled and shifted. She stopped and looked again.

There was something else in the box.

Something green.

It was December. The sugar cookies Eat'n Park sold were all shaped like Christmas trees instead of smiley faces. Her manager called her up to the front; when Caro got there, he was wearing a scowl. "Somebody to see you," he said. "Outside. Make it quick."

She went out. There was a bench there, for busy Sunday mornings after church when the breakfast crowd overflowed the lobby, but now there was only one woman sitting on it, huddled against the cold and smoking a cigarette. When she looked up at Caro, her face twisted into a sneer.

"Well," the woman said, standing up, "at least you're pretty."

"I don't know who you are," Caro said.

"Oh, don't you?" The woman's voice was cold. "How convenient for you. I'm Lisa Mitchell is who I am. Chris's wife. His *wife*."

"Oh." Caro took a step backward.

"I found your hair all over my husband's car," Lisa Mitchell said. "I found your goddamned lipstick under the seat. You know what I didn't find?" She tossed her cigarette into a snowbank. There was an ashtray right next to her too. "I didn't find *him*. I can't seem to find *him* anywhere."

Caro hadn't lost a lipstick. She had only two, pink for Eat'n Park and red for the hotel, and they were both in her bag. "Look," she said, "I don't know what you think happened—"

"I don't care what happened," Lisa said, her voice low and bitter and vicious. "I traced that son of a bitch here, to that crappy hotel, and the manager there told me you were a lying little tease with a fake ID and that you worked here." Caro felt a surge of anger. But before she could say anything in her own defense, Lisa took a step closer. "God, look at you. You're a child."

This woman was an adult. Adults didn't tackle and spit and pull hair, but Caro's body was wary, ready to fight. Her mind was ice-cold.

Lisa tossed her hair. Her eyes were glittery with tears. "Okay, look. I don't care. Whatever happened, whatever you did—I don't care."

A group of diners was coming across the parking lot. "All right," Caro said.

"All right?" Lisa's face turned red and the tears spilled over and suddenly she was screaming. "Where is he? That lying... *liar*—that—" The words seemed to tangle in her mouth and she tore at her hair with one hand, shaking with rage. "He took all our money. He took our *dog!*"

The entering diners looked askance at the two women and went inside without a word.

"Karma's going to get you," Lisa said. "It's going to get you, hard." She spit on the ground at Caro's feet. So adults did spit. From one of her clenched fists, she threw something right at Caro's face. Caro jerked back and it missed her, but barely. It fell to the frozen sidewalk with a snap and a clatter. Lisa turned on her heel and left. Caro watched her as she stomped across the parking lot, got into a car—it looked like Chris's—and drove away.

Caro stood for a moment, breathing in the deep cold air. When she felt calm again, she reached down and picked up the thing Lisa had thrown at her. The lipstick. The case had cracked with the force of the impact. Not Caro's lipstick. Not Lisa's. Somebody else's.

It was Clinique, though. Caro slipped it into her pocket.

In the restaurant, the manager pulled her aside. "That's it, Caro," he said. "I've had enough."

"I'm a good waitress," Caro said.

"Yeah, but you're a lousy coworker. I've been hearing complaints about you from the other girls for months, and now I'm getting them from the customers too?" He shook his head. "You're out. Go get your stuff. I'll mail your check."

"Fine," Caro said. In the pocket of her green polyester jumper, her fist closed around the lipstick. She thought about throwing it at him. She didn't. It was a good color.

What she did was go into the back room, grab her bag, and walk out the front door and across the icy parking lot to the space under the light where her car sat and waited for her—for her, for tomorrow, for the next day. For infinite possibilities. For anything that might happen.

NIGHT RUN

by Wallace Stroby

LATER, KIRWAN WOULD think about how it started, when he might have stopped it. What he could have done differently. But by then it didn't matter.

He'd just crossed the Georgia/Florida line on I-95, running south, the lights of Jacksonville in the far distance ahead. Two a.m. and his eyes watery, his legs jumpy. The Volvo had nearly three hundred thousand miles on it, and its suspension was shot. Every pothole or patch of uneven blacktop jolted his spine.

Still, he felt himself drifting, eyelids heavy. He'd need to sleep soon but wanted to make it as far south as he could. The meeting at Marco Landscaping, to show them the new brick samples, was at ten a.m., and New Smyrna Beach was still about a hundred miles away. He'd give it another hour on the road, then find a motel.

He thought of Lois Pettimore, Marco's accountant. She'd be at the meeting. The same perfume as always, her blouse open one button too deep, with a glimpse of black lace beneath.

Sometimes in their office he'd notice her watching him, but he never knew how to respond. He'd look away, his face flushed, then flee as soon as he had their order sheets and contracts.

At the last meeting, two weeks ago, she'd handed him an invoice, let her nails brush the back of his wrist. He'd seen then that her wedding band was gone, only a faint white line left where it had been. He wondered if the imminent divorce she always managed to bring up in conversation had gone through.

His right front tire crossed onto the shoulder, hit gravel. The noise and vibration snapped him awake. He sat up straighter and steered back into his lane, the momentary burst of adrenaline clearing his mind. *That was stupid,* he thought, *dangerous. Stay alert.*

Powering down the window to let in the night air, he caught the rotten-egg-and-sulfur smell of the nearby swamp. Trees and wetlands on both sides of the highway here. Even at this hour, the air was warmer than when he'd stopped in Roanoke for dinner eight hours ago.

A car flew by in the far left lane, a blur of taillights as it passed. The speed limit for this stretch of interstate was seventy, and Kirwan kept the Volvo at a safe sixty-five, let the other vehicles pass him.

He turned on the radio, scanned stations. Somewhere south of Charleston, the all-news station he'd been listening to had dissolved into static. Now he got only snatches of rap, country music, preachers. Nothing coming in strong. *Get that satellite radio set up,* he thought. *Do yourself a favor. Or at least get the CD player fixed.*

He drove a thousand miles a week, and sometimes during

thunderstorms he would pick up faraway AM stations, the signal bouncing off the clouds. Once, near Atlanta, he'd gotten a talk station out of Fort Wayne, Indiana, crystal clear for a solid half hour before the storm passed.

No such luck tonight. More static; then, near the end of the dial, someone speaking rapid French. A Haitian station out of Miami. He switched over to FM, finally got a country tune he recognized. He left it there, settled back.

Sometimes at night, when the danger of falling asleep at the wheel was strongest, when he felt himself starting to dream, he'd turn off the headlights, the road going black in front of him. The jolt of adrenaline and panic that followed would wake him up, keep him going for another half hour. He'd leave the lights off for only a few seconds, but it was enough.

There was a guardrail on the right now, and the lane seemed to narrow. He signaled, even though there were no other cars around, started to move into the near left lane, heard the sharp bleat of a horn.

He jerked the Volvo back into the right lane, saw the single headlight to his left. A motorcycle had come out of the blind spot there. Had he missed it in the rearview? Had he even checked the mirror before changing lanes? He wasn't sure.

He turned off the radio, wanted to call out *Sorry*, realized how stupid that would sound. He slowed, waited for the motorcycle to pass. Instead, it came abreast of him, hung there. He could hear the rider shouting. Kirwan kept his eyes forward. He couldn't make out the words, but his face grew hot.

He slowed to fifty-five, but the bike stayed with him. He looked then. It was a big Harley with extended front forks, black all around, dual silver exhausts. The rider had a beard and mustache, wore a leather jacket and jeans with a wallet chain. No helmet.

Kirwan faced front again. *Don't look. It'll just aggravate the situation.*

The biker was still shouting. Kirwan looked in the rearview, hoping to see a vehicle coming up from behind that would force the bike to speed up or pass him. Only darkness back there. They were alone on the road.

The yelling stopped. He chanced a look, saw the biker's right hand leave the throttle and come up, middle finger extended. Kirwan shook his head, faced front again. *Just go,* he thought. *I'm sorry about what happened, but it's over now. Just go.*

The bike surged past him, engine growling, went up two car lengths, and swept into his lane. His headlights lit the back of it, the pale gray Georgia plate, and then the bike slowed and the Volvo was almost on top of it. Kirwan hit the brake, and the Volvo slewed to the right, the front fender inches from the guardrail. The boxed samples in the rear cargo area slid across the floor, bumped into the wall. He straightened the wheel, got centered in the lane once more. The biker twisted around in the headlights, grinning, gave him the finger again, then sped up.

Kirwan felt a rush of anger. Without thinking, he hit the gas, closed the space between them. The motorcycle glided easily back into the left lane, the rider gesturing to Kirwan as if inviting him to pass. When he didn't, the rider looked at him, grinned, and shrugged. A tractor-trailer came up in the far left lane, rumbled past them, disappeared over the rise ahead.

Kirwan knew this part of 95 — no exits for at least another few miles. He could pull over, hope the biker kept going, but there wasn't much shoulder here. It would be dangerous to stop.

The biker slowed until they were even again, then pointed at him. Kirwan tried to ignore him, kept the speedometer at sixty. It was no use speeding up or slowing down. The motorcycle would stay with him. He just had to wait until the biker lost interest, sped off.

More shouting. He started to power up the window, saw the motorcycle ease ahead of him. The biker's right arm flashed out, and something clicked against the windshield, flew off. Kirwan jerked his head back, saw the tiny chip in the glass. A coin, maybe. Something too small to do much damage, but enough to mark the glass, get his attention. The bike slowed, and they were side by side again. Kirwan turned to look at him then and saw the gun.

It was a dark automatic. The biker pointed it at him through the half-open window, not shouting now. The gun was steady.

Kirwan stood on the brake. The Volvo's tires screamed, and its rear end slid to the left, the wagon going into a skid. He panicked, fought the wheel, and pumped the brake, trying to remember what he'd learned — *turn in the direction of the skid. Don't lock the brakes.* The front end of the wagon swung from right to left and back again, headlights illuminating the guardrail, the trees beyond, the roadway, then the guardrail again. The sample boxes thudded into the back of the rear seat.

He steered onto the shoulder, gravel rattling against the undercarriage. He braked steadily, avoiding the guardrail, and the wagon came to a stop, bucked forward slightly, settled back and was still.

A cloud of dust rose in his headlights. He jammed the console gearshift into park, gripped the wheel, tried to slow his breathing. His knuckles were white.

When the dust cleared, he saw the motorcycle. It had pulled onto the shoulder three car lengths ahead. The rider was looking back at him.

Kirwan felt the sharp stab of fear. He waited for the rider to get off, come back toward him, the gun out. For a moment, crazily, he considered shifting back into drive, hitting the gas, plowing into the bike. Decided that's what he would do if the rider came at him with the gun. *Could he do that? Run a man over, maybe kill him?*

But the biker stayed where he was, boots on the gravel, balancing the bike under him. No sign of the gun. Kirwan wondered if he'd imagined it, if his fear and the night had colluded to make him see something that wasn't there. Or had the gun just gone back into wherever he'd pulled it from? Maybe the biker had brought it out only to scare him, make him overreact and oversteer, wreck the Volvo on his own.

The biker watched him as if waiting to see what he would do. Kirwan didn't move, kept his hands tight on the wheel. The biker grinned, faced forward again. He steered back onto the roadway, gave the Harley gas. His taillights climbed the rise and vanished.

Breathe, Kirwan told himself, *breathe.* His neck and shoulders were rigid. He could feel a vessel throb in his left temple. What now? Get off at the next exit, find a town, a police station, report what happened? Even if he did, he had no proof except the chip in the windshield, which could have come from a small rock, a piece of gravel. And the Harley had been moving fast. They'd never catch up with the biker, and what if they did? Down here, like as not, the gun would be legal—if there even was a gun. It would be Kirwan's word against his. No witnesses.

His cell phone was in the console cup holder. He could call 911, give a description of the biker, have the dispatcher alert the highway patrol. But he'd already forgotten the plate number. A *G,* maybe an *X* after that, but that was all he had. And calling it in might mean more questions, a report, hours spent in a station house or trooper barracks. And if they caught the biker, Kirwan would have to face him again, the man who'd pointed a gun at him, nearly run him off the road.

Cars passed. When his breathing was back to normal, he powered the window shut, put on his blinker. He shifted into drive, waited until the road was clear, then steered into the lane, gave the Volvo gas.

He would have to get the alignment checked, the tires as well. The Volvo had lost its grip on the road for a moment, and that had frightened him almost as much as the gun—the sense of powerlessness, of being out of control. He'd find a garage in New Smyrna tomorrow, right after the meeting; he wouldn't put it off. Get the windshield fixed too, before the chip turned into a crack.

Back up to sixty, keeping it steady there. Any cars that came up behind would pass him, give him space. And with every minute, the biker would be farther ahead, farther away from him. Kirwan breathed in deep, then exhaled. He turned the radio back on, the same country station.

After a while, he realized he had to urinate. He tried to ignore it at first, but the pressure in his bladder grew. He didn't want to stop, wanted to keep going, make up the time he'd lost. But now there was a twinge of pain, and he knew he couldn't wait until he found a motel.

There were exits ahead now, motels and mammoth gas stations right off the roadway, their signs raised on poles so they'd be seen from a distance. He took the exit for I-10. At the end of the ramp, signs pointed left and right, logos showing what gas and food were available in either direction, how far they were. It made no difference. The restaurants would be mostly fast-food joints, and some of them would be closed at this hour. If nothing else, he'd top off the tank at a gas station, find a restroom.

He turned right, the road here leading away from the highway. A mile ahead, he saw the lights of a truck stop and diner, a Days Inn adjoining them. He thought about checking in, but it was too early still, and he was wired, wouldn't sleep. He decided to keep driving for a bit longer before he found a place to stay. Then a quick breakfast in the morning and on to New Smyrna. He thought of Lois, her perfume.

He signaled, even though there was no one behind him, pulled into the diner lot. And there, parked alongside an idling tractor-trailer, was the Harley. Kirwan felt his stomach tighten, and for a moment he thought his bladder would let go. He pulled the Volvo beneath a tree on the edge of the lot, out of the light wash from the big pole lamps, killed the engine and headlights.

Half a dozen cars here, and just the one tractor-trailer. Through the big diner windows, he could see people sitting at booths, two men at the counter beyond. No sign of the biker.

Was it the same motorcycle? He looked at it again, unsure

now. It seemed to be black, like the other one, but that might be a trick of the light. It had the same extended front end, and he could see the Harley insignia on the gas tank, so that much was the same. But he couldn't be sure.

Turn around. Get back on the road, then onto the highway. Find another diner or truck stop, another bathroom. Drive away.

Inside the diner, a door swung open, gave a glimpse of a white-tiled hallway, where the restrooms and trucker showers would be. The biker stepped out, went to the counter. He looked older in the bright interior lights, gray in his hair and beard. He spoke to the waitress there, his back to the window.

When he came out the front door, he was carrying a Styrofoam cup of coffee. He spit on the ground, looked around the lot.

Kirwan slid lower in his seat. The biker glanced in his direction, then away. He set the cup atop a metal trash can, put both hands on the small of his back and stretched, then reached inside the jacket. *He's going for the gun.*

The hand came out with a pack of cigarettes. Kirwan wondered again if the gun had been his imagination, his fatigue, his fear.

The biker lit the cigarette with a plastic lighter, put the pack away, blew out smoke. He was standing in the direct light fall from the windows now, and Kirwan could see the glint of a diamond stud in his right ear. He hadn't noticed that before. Was it even the same man?

The biker went over to the Harley, opened the right saddlebag. He crouched, looked inside, moved something around, fastened the flap again. He retrieved his coffee, walked around the bike as if checking for damage, the cup in his left hand.

He looked out at the road for a while, smoking and drinking coffee, then flicked the cigarette away. It landed sparking
on the blacktop. Straddling the bike, he took a last pull at the
cup, pitched it toward the trash can. It fell short, splashed
on the sidewalk, sprayed coffee on the door of an SUV parked
there. Then he rose in the seat, came down hard, kick-started
the engine. It roared into life. The people inside the diner
looked out. He sat back, revved the engine, still in neutral, as
if enjoying the attention. The heavy throb of the exhaust
seemed to fill the night.

He wheeled the Harley around toward the road. Would he
go left, back to the lights of I-95? Or right and farther west into
unbroken darkness? In that direction, I-10 would eventually
take him to Tallahassee, Kirwan knew, but there was a lot of
nothing between here and there, mostly sugarcane and swamp.

Kirwan started his engine. *Drive away,* he thought once
more. *You'll never see him again. Your business, your life, is down the
road. Places you need to be, people to see. Commitments and responsibil-
ities.*

Still, a sourness burned in his stomach. The biker had
laughed about what he'd done, and now he was riding off as if
nothing had happened. He'd laugh again when he told the
story later of how he'd put the fear of death into a middle-aged
man in a station wagon.

The Harley pulled out of the lot, back tire spraying gravel.
He turned right, as Kirwan had somehow known he would.

Headlights off, Kirwan followed.

No lights on this stretch of road, no moon above, but the Harley was easy to follow. Twice, cars coming in the opposite

direction flashed their high beams at Kirwan, letting him know his lights were off. But the biker didn't seem to notice. The Harley kept at a steady speed, didn't try to race ahead, lose him. *He doesn't know I'm here.*

He powered down the window, could hear the deep growl of the Harley's engine. The swamp smell was strong, and a low mist hung over the roadway, was swept under the front tires as he drove. The urge to urinate was gone.

Houses started to pop up, most of them dark. Concrete and stucco, bare yards. The road began to run parallel to a canal, the Harley's headlamp reflected in the water.

Past the houses and into tall sugarcane now. In the Harley's headlamp, Kirwan caught glimpses of dirt roads that ran off the highway. The Harley slowed, as if the rider was watching for an upcoming turn. Kirwan slowed with it. *He's almost there, wherever he's going. You'll lose him. And maybe that's a good thing.*

An intersection ahead, with a blinking yellow light in all four directions. The Harley blew through it without slowing. Kirwan did the same. The road began to curve gradually to the right. Ahead, lit by a single pole light, a concrete bridge spanned the canal.

Pull over. Let him go. Put your headlights on, turn around. You're in the middle of nowhere, and you're losing time. Don't be stupid.

The Harley slowed, rider and machine leaning to the right as they followed the curve of the road. Kirwan floored the gas pedal.

The Volvo leaped forward, faster than he'd expected, closed on the Harley in an instant. The bike had almost reached the bridge when the rider shifted in his seat, looked back, saw him for the first time. Kirwan hit the headlights, gave him the brights, barely thirty feet between them.

The biker was still turned in his seat when the Harley reached the bridge. Kirwan saw it as if in slow motion—the biker looking forward at the last moment, the bike coming in too sharp, the angle wrong. Then the front tire hit the abutment and the rider was catapulted into the darkness, the bike somersaulting after him, end over end, off the bridge and onto the ground below.

Kirwan's foot moved from gas pedal to brake, stomped down hard. The Volvo shimmied as it had before, slewed to the right, the samples thumping into the seat back. The tires squealed, dug in, and the Volvo came to a shuddering stop just short of the bridge.

He reversed onto the shoulder, shifted into park, and listened. All he could hear over his engine noise were crickets. He switched on the hazards. Didn't want another car to come speeding along, rear-end him in the darkness.

He got out, left the door ajar. There were bits of metal and broken glass on the bridge, a single skid mark. He walked up the shoulder, hazards clicking behind him, the headlights throwing his shadow long on the pavement.

At the bridge, he looked down. The ground sloped steeply to the edge of the canal. The bike was about fifteen feet away, had ripped a hole through the foliage. The rear tire was spinning slowly. From somewhere in the darkness came a moan.

He went back to the car, opened the glove box, took out the plastic flashlight, looked at the phone on the console.

Back at the bridge, he switched on the flashlight. The bright narrow beam leaped out, starkly lit the grass below. Torn-up earth down there. The bike had tumbled at least once before coming to rest in the trees.

He aimed the light toward it. It lay on its right side, the forks bent back and twisted, the front tire gone. The left saddlebag had been thrown open and its contents—clothes mostly—littered the grass. The air smelled of gasoline.

The moaning again. He picked his way carefully down the slope, shoes sinking in the damp earth. Playing the light along the edge of the canal, he followed the noise.

The biker lay on a wide flat stone below the bridge. He was on his left side, and there was blood on his face. Kirwan walked toward him, watching where he put his feet, not wanting to slip and fall.

The biker's right boot was scraping uselessly against the stone. His left boot was missing, and the leg there was bent at a right angle away from his body. He'd dragged himself onto the rock, left a smear of dark blood and mud on the stone to mark his passage.

Kirwan shone the light in his face. The biker raised his right hand, let it fall. His left arm was trapped beneath him.

The gun. Watch for the gun.

He came closer. The biker was hyperventilating like a wounded animal, chest rising and falling. His left eye was swollen shut. He raised his arm again, weakly.

He doesn't recognize me. Doesn't know what happened.

Kirwan came closer, shone the light up and down the biker's body, then around it. No gun.

"Help…help me." The voice was a hoarse whisper. In the darkness, something splashed in the canal, swam away.

Kirwan squatted. "You don't know who I am, do you?"

The biker tried to shift onto his back, gasped.

"Remember me?" Kirwan said.

He turned the flashlight toward himself, holding it low so the biker could see his face. The good eye narrowed into a squint. He shook his head.

A big leather wallet was on the ground a few feet away, had come free from its chain. Kirwan tucked the flashlight in his armpit, picked up the wallet, unsnapped and opened it. In one pocket were three hundred-dollar bills and six twenties. In another was a laminated Georgia driver's license with the biker's picture. His name was Miles Hanson, and he was sixty-one years old.

Hanson coughed, and Kirwan looked back at him. The biker raised his head, spit a blot of blood onto the stone. "Keep it, man…it's all yours. Just help me." The voice still weak.

Kirwan closed the wallet, set it on a rock.

"Hurry up, man. I think I got something broken inside."

"My cell phone's in the car. I'll call 911."

He started up the slope, then stopped, looked back down. Hanson was watching him. He saw the glimmer of the diamond stud, remembered the grin, the middle finger, the chip in the windshield.

He went back down the slope, set the flashlight in the grass.

"What are you doing?" Hanson said.

Kirwan crouched, gripped the back of the man's leather jacket with both hands. Hanson swatted at him with his good arm, but there was nothing behind it. Kirwan took a breath, straightened up so as not to pull a muscle, then jerked the jacket up, pushed, and tumbled Hanson face-first into the canal.

Kirwan couldn't tell how deep the water was. Hanson splashed once, went under. He floundered there, got his head above the surface for a moment, gulped air, then went under again.

Kirwan found a stone the size of a basketball beside the canal, lifted it high, then dropped it into the water where he'd last seen Hanson's head. Water spattered his pants.

He dusted off his hands, picked up the flashlight, and shone it down into the water. Hanson was a shadow just below the surface, not moving. A dark red cloud bloomed in the stagnant water, then dissipated.

He stood there for a while, watching to make sure there were no bubbles. Then he went back to where he'd dropped the wallet, took out the bills, and folded them into his shirt pocket. He kicked the wallet into the canal, then stepped out onto the flat rock, unzipped, and urinated into the water, a long stream that caught the light from the bridge, the pressure in his bladder finally easing.

When he was done, he zipped up, walked back to where the bike lay. It ticked as it cooled in the night air. Strewn on the grass were a pair of jeans, dark T-shirts, a sleeveless denim jacket. An insignia on the back read WHISKEY JOKERS DAYTONA BEACH above an embroidered patch of a diving eagle, claws out.

He reached into the open saddlebag, rooted deeper through more clothes. And there, at the bottom of the bag in a flat pancake holster, was the gun.

He drew it out, looked at it. At some point, maybe at the diner, Hanson must have holstered it in the saddlebag. But this gun was a revolver, and the one he'd seen had been an automatic. Or had it? Was this a second gun?

He went around to the other side of the bike, stepping over torn foliage. Using a pair of T-shirts to protect his hands, he took hold of the frame. It was still warm. He grunted, lifted, vines pulling at the ruined front end. The bike rose and then fell on its other side. The gasoline smell grew stronger.

He got the flashlight, opened the other saddlebag. More clothes, a full carton of cigarettes—Marlboro Reds—and a lidded cardboard box about half the size of a hardback book. No gun.

He opened the box, saw tissue paper. He peeled it back and in the middle was a cheap cloth doll—a cartoonish Mexican with a sombrero and poncho playing guitar, his floppy hands sewn to the cloth instrument.

Was this what he'd been checking in the saddlebag? A gift for a child? Then Kirwan squeezed the doll, felt the unyielding lump inside.

He turned it over, lifted the cloth flap of the poncho. Stitches ran up the back of the doll, thick ones, a darker color than the material. He tucked the flashlight under his arm again, pulled at the stitches until they were loose. The back of the doll came apart at the seam, revealing more tissue paper packed around a metal cigar tube. He unscrewed the top of the tube and pulled out a tightly rolled plastic bag. He poked a finger in, teased out part of the clear bag. Inside was a thick off-white powder, caked and compressed.

He pushed it back into the tube, screwed on the top. He put the tube in his pants pocket and tossed the doll out into the water.

He picked up the holstered gun, walked back up the slope to the Volvo, the road still empty in both directions. The yellow light blinked in the distance. The Volvo's hazards clicked, insects flittering in the headlights. A breeze came through, moved the sugarcane on the other side of the road.

He opened the Volvo's tailgate, pushed aside the sample boxes to get at the spare-tire compartment. He lifted the panel, pried up the spare, and put the tube and gun under it, then let the tire drop back into place. He closed the panel, shut the tailgate.

Back behind the wheel, he put away the flashlight, shut the glove box, gave a last look at the cell phone.

He reversed onto the road, swung a U-turn, headed back the way he'd come. He was calm inside, centered, for the first time that night. At the intersection, he turned the radio back on.

After a while, he began to feel sleepy again, a pleasant drifting. He looked at his watch. If he kept going, he could push through to New Smyrna by three thirty or so, find a motel, get five or six hours' sleep before the meeting. It would be enough. Maybe he'd ask Lois out to dinner that night, divorce or no.

He had two free days after that. He could stay down there, figure out what exactly was in that tube, what it might be worth. There didn't seem to be much of it, whatever it was. Maybe it was just a sample for some larger deal to be made later.

Rain began to spot the windshield, thick heavy drops. He turned on the wipers. They thumped slowly, and on their second arc, he saw that the chip in the windshield was gone. He touched a thumb to where it had been. Nothing there now, the glass unblemished. One less thing to take care of, at least.

He was humming along to the music by the time he reached the on-ramp for 95. What had happened had happened. There was no going back. Not now, not ever. The road and the night were his.

WHAT YOU WERE FIGHTING FOR

by James Sallis

I WAS TEN the year he showed up in Waycross. It was uncommonly dry that year, I remember, even for us, no rain for weeks, grass gone brown and crisp as bacon, birds gathering at shallow pools of water out back of the garage where Mister Lonnie, a trustee from the jail, washed cars. And where he let me help, all the while talking about growing up in the shacks down in Niggertown, bringing up four kids on what he made doing whatever piecemeal work he could find, rabbit stew and fried squirrel back when he was a kid himself.

I'd gone round front to fetch some rags we'd left drying on the waste bin out there and saw him pull in. Cars like that — provided you knew what to look for, and I knew, even then — didn't show up in those parts. Some rare soul had taken Mr. Whitebread's sweet-tempered tabby and turned it to mountain lion. The driver got out. He left the door open, engine not so much idling as taking deep, slow breaths, and stood in the shadow of the water tower looking around.

I grew up in the shade of that tower myself. There wasn't

any water in it anymore, not for a long time, it was as baked and broiled as the desert that stretched all around us. A few painted-on letters, an *A*, part of a *Y*, an *R*, remained of the town's name.

I could see Daddy inside, in the window over the work-bench. Didn't take long before the door screeched in its frame and he came out. "Help you?" Daddy said. The two of them shook hands.

The man glanced my way and smiled.

"You get on back to your business, boy," Daddy told me. I walked around the side of the garage to where I wouldn't be seen.

"She's not handling or sounding dead on. And the timing's a hair off. Think you could have a look?"

"Glad to. Strictly cash and carry, though. That a problem?"

"Never."

"I'll open the bay, you pull 'er in."

"Yes, sir."

"Garrulous as ever, I see."

I went on around back, wondering about that last remark. Not too long after, Mister Lonnie finished up and headed home to his cell. They never locked it, and he had it all comfy in there, a bedspread from Woolworth's, pictures torn from magazines on the wall. You live in a box, he said, it might as well be a *nice* box. I went inside to the office, which was really just a corner with cinder blocks stacked up to make a wall along one side. Daddy's desk looked like it had been used for artillery practice. The chair did its best to throw you every time you shifted in it.

I was supposed to be studying but what I was doing was

reading a book called *The Killer Inside Me* for the third or fourth time. I'd snitched it out of a car Daddy worked on, where it had slipped down between the seats.

Everyone assumed I'd follow in my father's footsteps, work at the tire factory, maybe, or with luck and a long stubborn climb uphill become, like he had, a mechanic. No one called kids special back in those days. We got called lots of things, but special wasn't among them. This was before I found out why normal things were so hard for me, why I always had to push when others didn't.

They got to it, both their heads under the hood, wrenches and sockets going in, coming out. Every few pages I'd look through the holes in the cinder blocks. Half an hour later Daddy said the man didn't need him and he had other cars to see to. So the visitor went on working as Daddy moved along to a '62 Caddy.

After a while the visitor climbed in the car, started it, revved the engine hard, let it spin down, revved it again. Got back under the hood and not long after that said he could use some help. Said would it be okay to ask me and Daddy grunted okay. "Boy's name is Leonard."

"You mind coming down here to give me a hand with this engine, Leonard?" the man said.

I was at a good part of the book, the part where Lou Ford talks about his childhood and what he did with the house-keeper, but the book would always be there waiting. When I went over, the man shook my hand like I was grown and helped me climb in.

"I'm setting the timing now," he said. "When I tell you, I need for you to rev the engine." He held up the timing light. "I'll be using this to—"

I nodded just as Daddy said, "He knows."

To reach the accelerator I had to slide as far forward in the seat as I could, right onto the edge of it, and stretch my leg out straight. I revved when he said, waited as he rotated the distributor, revved again. Once more and we were done.

"What do you think?" the man asked Daddy.

"Sounding good."

"Always good to have good help."

"Even for a loner, yeah."

The man looked back at me. "Maybe we should take a ride, make sure everything's tight."

"Or take a couple of beers and let the boy get to his work."

Daddy snagged two bottles from the cooler. Condensation came off them and made tiny footprints on the floor. I was supposed to be doing extra homework per my teachers, but what was boring and obvious the first time around didn't get any better with age. Lou and the housekeeper were glad to have me back.

Daddy and the man sat quietly, sipping their beers, looking out the bay door where heat rose in waves, turning the world wonky.

"Kind of a surprise, seeing you here." That was Daddy, not given to talk much at all and never one for hyperbole.

"Both of us."

Some more quiet leaned back against the wall waiting.

"Still in the same line of work?"

"Not anymore, no."

"Glad to hear that. Never thought you were cut out for it."

"Thing is, I didn't seem to be cut out for much else."

"Except driving."

"Except driving." Our visitor motioned with his bottle, a swing that took in the car, the rack, the tools he'd put back where they came from. "Appreciate this."

"Any time. So, where are you headed?"

"Thought I might go down to Mexico."

"And do what?"

"More of the same, I guess."

"The same being what?"

Things wound down then. The quiet that had been leaning against the wall earlier came back. They finished their beers. Daddy stood and said he figured it to be time to get on home, asked the man if he planned on heading out now the car was looking good. "You could stay a while, you know," Daddy said.

"Nowhere I have to be."

"Don't guess you have a place…"

"Car's fine."

"That your preference?"

"It's what I'm used to."

"You want, you can pull in out back, then. Plenty of privacy. Nothing but the arroyo and scrub trees all the way to the highway."

Daddy raised the rattling bay doors and the visitor pulled out, drove around. We put the day's used rags in the barrel, threw sawdust on the floor and swept up, swabbed the sink and toilet, everything in place and ready to hit the ground running tomorrow morn. Daddy locked up the Caddy and swung a tarp over it. Said while he finished up I should go be sure the man didn't need anything else.

He had the driver's door open, the seat kicked back, and he was lying there with eyes open. Propped on the dash, a transistor radio the size of a pack of cigarettes, the kind I'd seen in movies, played something in equal parts shrill and percussive.

"Daddy says to tell you the diner over on Mulberry's open till nine and the food's edible if you're hungry enough."

"Don't eat a lot these days."

He held a beer bottle in his left hand, down on his thigh. The beer must have been warm since it wasn't sweating. Crickets had started up their songs for the night. You'd catch movement out the corner of your eye but when you looked you couldn't see them. The sun was sinking in its slot.

"Saw the book in your pocket earlier," he said, "wondered what you're reading," and when I showed him he said he liked those too, even had a friend out in California that wrote a few. Everything about California is damn cool, I was convinced of that back then, so I asked a lot of questions. He told me about the Hispanic neighborhood he'd lived in. Billboards in Spanish, murals on walls, bright colors. Stalls and street food and festivals.

Years later I lived out there in a neighborhood just like that before I had to come back to take care of Daddy. It all started with him pronouncing words wrong. *Holdover* would be "*hol'*over," or *noise* somehow turn to "nose." No one thought much about it at first, but before long he was losing words completely. His mouth would open, and you'd watch his eyes searching for them, but the words just weren't there.

"Everyone says we get them coming up the arroyo," I said, "illegals, I mean."

"My friend? Wrote those books? He says we're all illegals."

Daddy came around to collect me then. Standing by the kitchen counter, we had a supper of fried bologna, sliced tomatoes, and leftover dirty rice. This was Daddy's night to go dancing with Eleanor, *dancing* being a code word we both pretended I didn't understand.

That night a storm moved toward us like Godzilla advancing on poor Tokyo, but nothing came of it, a scatter of raindrops. I gave up trying to sleep and was out on the back porch watching lightning flash behind the clouds when Daddy pulled the truck in.

"You're supposed to be in bed, young man," he said.

"Yes, sir."

We watched as lightning came again. A gust of wind shoved one of the lawn chairs to the edge of the patio where it tottered, hung on till the last moment, and overturned.

"Beautiful, isn't it?" Daddy said. "Most people never get to see skies like that."

Even then I'd have chosen *powerful, mysterious, angry, promise unfulfilled.* Daddy said *beautiful.*

It turned out that neither of us could sleep that night. We weren't getting the benefits of the weather, but it had a hold on us: restlessness, aches, unease. When for the second time we found ourselves in the kitchen, Daddy decided we might as well head down to the garage, something we'd done before on occasion. We'd go down, I'd read, he'd work and putter or mess about, we'd come back and sleep a few hours.

A dark gray Buick sat outside the garage. This is two in the morning, mind you, and the passenger door is hanging open. What the hell, Daddy said, and pulled in behind. No lights inside the garage. No one around that we can see. We were climbing out of the car when the visitor showed up, not from behind the garage where we'd expect, but yards to the right, walking the rim of the arroyo.

"You know you have coyotes down there?" he said. "Lot of them."

"Coyotes, snakes, you name it. And a car up here that ain't supposed to be."

"They won't be coming back for it."

"What am I going to see when I look under that hood?" Daddy glanced at the arroyo. "And down there?"

"About what you'd expect under the hood. Down there, there won't be much left."

"So it's *not* just more of the same. I'd heard stories."

"I'm sorry to bring this on you—I didn't know. It's taken care of."

Daddy and the man stood looking at one another. "I was never here," the man said. "*They* were never here." He went around to the back. Minutes later, his car pulled out, eased past us, and was gone.

"We'd best get this General Motors piece of crap inside and get started tearing it down," Daddy said.

We all kill the past in our own way. Some slit its throat, some let it die of neglect.

Last week I began a list of species that have become extinct. What started it was reading about a baby elephant that wouldn't leave its mother's side when hunters killed her and died itself of starvation. I found out that 90 percent of all things that ever lived on earth are extinct, maybe more. As many as two hundred species pass away between Monday's sunrise and Tuesday's.

I do wonder: What if I'd not been born as I was, what if I'd been back a bit in line and not out front, what if the things they'd told us about that place had a grain of truth? Don't do that much, but it happens.

"When the sun is overhead, the shadows disappear," my physical therapist back in rehab said. Okay, they do. But only briefly.

And: "At least you knew what you were fighting for." Sure I did. Absolutely. We steer our course by homilies and reductive narratives, then wonder that so many of us are lost.

A few weeks ago I made a day trip to Waycross. The water tower is gone, just one leg and half another still standing. It's a ghost town now, nothing but weightless memories tumbling along the streets. I pulled in by what used to be my father's garage, got my chair out and hauled myself into it, rolled with the memories down the streets, then round back to where our visitor had parked all those years ago. Nothing much has changed with the arroyo.

You always hear people talking about *I saw this, I read this, I did this, and it changed my life.*

Sure it did.

Thing is, I'd forgotten all about the visitor and what happened that night, and the only reason I remember now is because of this movie I saw.

I'd rolled the chair in at the end of an aisle only to be met with a barrage of smart-ass remarks about blocking their view from a brace of twenty-somethings, so I was concentrating on not tearing their heads off and didn't pay much attention to the beginning of the movie, but then a scene where a simple heist goes stupid bad grabbed my attention and I just kind of fell through the screen.

The movie's about a man who works as a stunt driver by

day and drives for criminals at night. Things start going wrong, then go wronger, pile up on him and pile up more until finally, halfway to a clear, cool morning, he bleeds to death from stab wounds in a Mexican bar. "There were so many other killings, so many other bodies," he says in voice-over near the end, his own and the movie's.

After lights came on, I sat in the theater till the cleaning crew, who'd been waiting patiently at the back with brooms and a trash can on rollers, came on in and got to work. I was remembering the car, his mention of Mexico, some of the conversation between my father and him.

I'm pretty sure it was him, his story—our visitor, my father's old friend or coworker or accomplice or whatever the hell he was. I think that explains something.

I wish I knew what.

THE TRIPLE BLACK 'CUDA

by George Pelecanos

OF THE TWO of us, my brother, Ted, was the good one. I know my father felt that way, though he didn't say it in my presence, at least not while Ted was alive. He didn't have to say it, because I knew. Being second place in my father's eyes was something I struggled with for a long time. I'm still carrying it, and I'm damn near sixty years old.

I grew up in a mostly white, leaning-to-ethnic neighborhood. Polish and Russian Jews, Italians, Greeks, Irish Catholics, and a smattering of Protestants. No blacks or Spanish. Only a few of our fathers wore ties to work, but they all worked, and if the marriages were unhappy, as surely many of them were, most of the homes remained unbroken.

Pop was an auto mechanic at an Esso station a half mile from our house. He woke up early and read the newspaper, front to back, every morning before making sure we got off to school. Then he was on his feet all day, bent over, working under hoods in a to-the-bone cold garage. Which is why he already had arthritis and hip problems in his forties. At night he sat in his recliner, drank beer, smoked Viceroys, and read paperback novels. People assumed he wasn't smart and paid him little attention until they needed him to work on their cars. Then he was their hero.

When I was still in high school, in the early seventies, Ted, who was three years my senior, enlisted in the Marine Corps and did a tour in Nam. The ground campaign was winding down, so the risk factor was not as high as it had been a few years earlier. It was a rite-of-passage thing for him. Also, our father had fought in the Pacific, and Ted knew that by serving he would make Pop proud. Pop was not a supporter of the war, or Nixon, but he thought even less of hippies and the protest movement, and gave Ted his blessing.

I was pissed off when Ted left for boot camp. I had never lived without him, and I felt that he had deserted me. Also, in the back of my mind, I knew that joining the Corps was another feather in his cap, something that my father would talk about with pride to his friends. Though I loved my brother, at that point in time I resented him a little bit too. I'm not proud of that, but there it is.

Ted had kept my wild streak in line when he was home, but when he headed overseas I went unchecked. I don't mean to suggest that I was like those guys in my high school who carried knives and beat up weaklings. Most of those cretins dropped out before graduation, died on the highway, entered the penal system, or became career military and were never heard from again. That wasn't me. But I did like to fight. Maybe because I was undersized, and I felt like I had something to prove. Whatever the reason, anger was my dominant mood. My fantasies, more often than not, involved violence rather than sex. How do I explain it? I was a boy and the wires inside my head were scrambled. I didn't know whether to shit or go blind. On top of that I liked fast cars.

Muscle cars were the big ticket then. I coveted a maroon, 350 square-block Nova that I'd had my eye on all through high school. A graduating senior was selling it before he went into the Coast Guard, but with nothing in my pocket I couldn't make it work. There was a Vega GT going cheap at a used lot over the city line, and the dealer was offering a loan, but a Vega GT was a girl's idea of a muscle car, and there was the matter of the color: canary yellow, for Christ's sake, with white interior. The sight of it would have drawn laughs from my gearhead crowd. So I settled for a '68 pea-green-over-pea-green Dart with the legendary Slant 6 engine. My father, a diehard Mopar man, approved. An old lady on our street who was blind as Stevie Wonder sold it to me for much less than it was worth and let me pay on it monthly. It was a good, dependable vehicle, but dependable was not what I wanted. A guy's dick should get hard when he gets under the wheel of his first car. Driving that Dart was like taking your sister to the prom.

To pour salt on my wound, my brother was soon to own one of the coolest rides on the street. How that came about shouldn't be much of a surprise, as cars were always passing through my father's garage. When he saw one that was cherry, and he knew, he'd sometimes make an offer to the owner, mostly for grins. That's what happened when the '70 Barracuda pulled in for an oil change. Ted was about to come home from his thirteen-month tour, and Pop wanted to do something special for him upon his return. My father used some of Mom's life-insurance money and his own savings to buy the car.

With the 1970 E-body Barracuda, Plymouth had introduced a new-platform vehicle meant to compete with the
Mustang and Camaro. Through '69, the Barracuda had basically been a glorified version of the Valiant, but in '70 its look
was completely redesigned and made available in all varieties
of muscle. The car my father bought for Ted was a customized
383 with a four-barrel Edelbrock carb, dual-exhaust, a Slick
Shift, console-mount automatic transmission, and after-market
Cragar mags. It wasn't the 440 Six Pack, the holy grail for
enthusiasts, but it was plenty fast. And though it was offered in
period-popular neon-bright hues like Lime Light, Curious
Yellow, and In-Violet, this one's color scheme was strong and
classic: black body, black interior, black vinyl roof. Triple
black.

I was a senior in high school and working as a full-service
pump jockey at my father's gas station when Ted returned
from Nam. His wasn't a hero's welcome, exactly, but where we
lived there was none of the spitting-on-veterans thing you've
heard about. Toward the end of the war most Americans had
begun to understand that the young men who'd served in
Vietnam were not at fault for the darker aspects of the conflict
but, rather, were victims of it. It's not like Ted had committed
any atrocities. To my knowledge, he hadn't even fired his M16
after basic training. But he'd served his country, and he was a
Marine, and in my neighborhood that meant something.

My father owned a slate-blue Belvedere with a 318 engine
and a posi-rear. The day Ted came back we took Pop's car to
the airport, picked up my brother, had lunch at our town's
Greek diner, and drove back over to our street. Ted almost
cried when he saw the 'Cuda parked in the driveway. "It's for

you, son," my father said. Ted was still in uniform and it's hard to forget the way he looked, tall and handsome, and how he hugged our father, the way they *held* each other, on the sidewalk that day outside our house. I wasn't jealous. I only wanted my father to look at me with admiration, the way he looked at Ted. I just didn't know what to do to make that happen.

Ted moved into his old room and settled in. He registered for the upcoming semester at our community college, a couple of classes to ease into it, and got a job as a salesman at a store that sold high-end audio equipment, which was something of a craze at the time. He had always had an interest in electronics, loved rock music, and had bought a tube-amp stereo when he was overseas, so the gig was in his wheelhouse. Despite the fact that he was somewhat introverted and not a guy you'd think could talk someone into it, Ted seemed to like the job.

When Ted wasn't working or in his room listening to records, he was washing, polishing, checking the fluids, or driving his 'Cuda. He was rarely alone. He'd had a girlfriend, Francesca, since tenth grade, and they'd survived the usual infidelities (him with Southeast Asian whores, her with a couple of local guys) during his deployment. Francesca took care of her invalid father and worked in the box office of a single-screen movie theater up at the shopping plaza, so she was frequently occupied. When she wasn't riding next to Ted, I was in the shotgun bucket beside him. Since he'd returned, we'd gotten pretty tight.

The summer after I graduated was a good one. Gerald Ford, a decent man, had stepped in as president, the war had ended, and a kind of calm was in the air. I wasn't going on to college, but I had worked hard to earn a high-school diploma, and I felt as if I had accomplished something. Pop told me that I could shadow him in the garage, and if I took the courses offered to Esso employees, I could eventually become a certified mechanic. Also, I was going around with an older girl named Diane, who had been graced with raven-black hair, lively green eyes, and curves. She was patient, taught me how to last, and showed me what a woman liked. We saw each other a couple times a week, and when we didn't, she never asked why. I was relaxed and free.

Ted and I liked to motor around town at night. In our state, the drinking age had been lowered to eighteen because of the war, so I was legal. We'd ride with open cans of Schlitz between our legs, the windows down, Ted's hand cigaretted and resting on his side-view mirror, the deck playing Allman Brothers, Robin Trower, Johnny and Edgar Winter, Deep Purple, and Zeppelin. Ted used all three speeds of the automatic, as the Slick Shift was engineered to prevent accidental slippage into reverse or neutral when moving up the ladder. My father kept the 'Cuda tuned just right, and Ted knew how to drive it. I clearly remember the feel of those nights, the wind warm in my face and hair, the streetlights dancing like fireflies off the buffed black hood of the Plymouth, the smell of Ted's cigarettes, Johnny Winter's "It's My Own Fault" on the stereo. And always, under the music, the rumble of the 'Cuda's dual pipes.

There was a quiet road about five miles north of our town where the suburbs turned to country, a straight quarter-mile strip of two-lane without traffic lights. That was where the kids in our crowd congregated and raced. Ted and I ended up there one night in August and ran into the Mahoney brothers, who were standing around a '68 cream-over-red AMX, looking to drag someone. Walter Mahoney, the oldest and toughest of the brothers, owned the car.

The Mahoneys were Irish Catholic, just like us. We went to the same church and had known one another all our lives.

Ted pulled alongside them and let the engine run so they could hear it. He was looking to cop an ounce of weed. The Mahoneys sold pot and always had the best shit. Ted was smoking regularly since he'd come back to the world, and I had fallen in love with it too.

Walter stepped forward. The middle brother, a spent-head named Jason, came with him. Mike, the quiet one, hung back. Walter was built in the shoulders and chest. His hair looked home-cut and it was military short. Jason's hair was long and receding, and he wore a bushy Vandyke beard. Though not yet twenty, he would soon be bald. Mike had long curls, which furthered the impression that he was soft. They were all wearing Levi's, patched in places, and pocket T-shirts with Marlboro hard packs wedged in the pockets. Walter was smoking a cigarette now. He hit it down to the filter and kind of flipped it off his fingers as he approached. A flip, not a flick. Walter had perfected the move.

"Ted and his trip-black 'Cuda," said Walter.

"What's good, Walter?" said Ted.

Walter bent down into the window frame, looked at me, and smiled in a way that no guy likes. "Hi, Ricky."

No one called me Ricky, not even my mom when I was a kid.

Ted said to Walter, "You holdin'?"

"I could be," said Walter. "What are you looking for?"

"An O-Z," said my brother.

"I have it at the house," said Walter. "Columbian. Price went up. It's fifty this time."

"For an ounce? *Shit.*"

"I can get you some Mexican if you want a headache. This is primo. You'll trip, Tedward."

"Kind of rich for my blood."

Walter looked at Jason, who smiled in his way that said *serial killer.* Girls walked backward when Jason entered a room.

The kid brother, Mike, lit a cigarette and stared at his shoes, a pair of saddle-colored stacks that I'd seen in the window of the Hanover store in the shopping plaza.

"Tell you what," said Walter. "You can have the ounce for nothin' if your 'Cuda can take my AMX in the quarter-mile."

"What if I lose?"

"You owe me double. A hundred."

"So you want me to race with your Rambler."

No one called the AMX a Rambler or considered it one. AMC had replaced the ultra-vanilla Rambler badge years ago and was making pretty good cars now. Ramblers were slow and boring. Ramblers were for guys who only stuck the head in when they fucked their wives.

"Can you handle it?" said Walter.

"When?" said Ted.

"Right now."

Ted shrugged. "Pull it over to the line."

"Ricky might want to get out," said Walter, "so you're not carrying the extra freight. 'Course, he don't weigh but a hundred pounds."

I reckon I was around one thirty-five then, but the comment cut me, just as it was meant to.

"Rick's my copilot," said Ted. "He can stay."

Walter and his brothers walked away.

"Fuckin' slopes," said Ted, and shook his head.

The Mahoney brothers had an Irish last name but slanted eyes. Their father, retired army, had been stationed in occupied Japan after the Big One and had brought home a bride.

The crowd, standing around their Chevys, Fords, and Mopars, sensed an imminent race and shifted their attention to our cars. Walter got into the driver's bucket of his ride and cooked the ignition. It was a 390 four-barrel with a four-speed BorgWarner stick and Go Package trim: Magnum 500 wheels and hood stripes. Like the Vette, it was a two-seat American muscle car.

We pulled up to the starting line, drawn in chalk on the road. The end point was a street sign by a utility house a quarter mile ahead. No one worried about oncoming traffic. Few used this road at night.

A peroxide blonde named Helen stood between our cars and raised her arms, just like that girl in the James Dean movie had done. We'd all seen that flick on TV.

"Strap in, Rick," said my brother, and I pulled the seat belt across my lap and clicked it home. Ted had pulled the shifter down into first and gripped it. He stared straight ahead. He didn't once look over at Walter Mahoney, who was revving the AMX.

Robin Trower's "Daydream" was playing from Ted's eight-track deck. I remember that to this day. Trower was making love to his Strat, going into his delta-to-the-universe, blues-drenched final solo as Helen dropped her arms and we came off the line in a rush that pinned me back against my seat. Ted punched the accelerator as he upshifted into second and left rubber on the street. He didn't fishtail and kept us straight. For a moment I saw the AMX in my side vision, a blurred steel sheet of cream, and as we hit third it was gone, I mean *disappeared,* and we were in a black tunnel of speed. My heart thumped in my chest as I felt my smile go ear to ear. We crossed the plane of the street sign and it was over. Ted was a wheel artist. He had it.

We turned around in the parking lot of the utility house. When we came back onto the road, Walter was idling and waiting. We went nose to asshole beside him.

"You caught second pretty good," said Walter. His tone was flat.

"I did get it," said Ted. "When can I pick up that weed?"

"Come by the house tomorrow, in the afternoon."

"See you then."

"War hero," said Walter under his breath as he pulled away.

Ted and I drove home. I thought that was the end of it.

The Mahoneys lived in their parents' brick rambler on a street lined with them. Late in the afternoon the day after the race, we went around the back of the house, where the property graded down. Jason's Harley, outfitted with ape hangers, was on its kickstand there. We entered the open back door and walked through a laundry and storage room to a large finished basement. This was the Mahoney brothers' lair.

Walter was seated on a torn-up couch beside Jason, who was spooning ice cream directly out of a tub. There was chocolate dripping in his Vandyke. The youngest, Mike, was seated in a chair that was as shredded as the couch, staring at a cigarette between his fingers as if it held meaning. A fog of pot smoke hung in the air, and Uriah Heep, hard rock for burnouts, played from a compact stereo set in a corner of the room. A purple bong was on a cable-spool table beside an upturned shoebox cover that held a bunch of weed.

Ranger, their shepherd mix, got up on all fours and growled at us as we entered the room. The brothers had been blowing pot smoke in Ranger's face since he was a puppy, which had made him the opposite of mellow. Cannabis had done the dog no favors.

"Ted the man," said Walter by way of greeting, and added, "You too, Ricky."

Ranger, still growling, edged toward us and bared his teeth.

"You got my ounce?" said Ted.

"Do a couple of bongs with us first," said Walter.

"Yeah, sit a minute," said Jason.

"Put that fucked-up animal away and we will," said Ted.

Walter got up off the couch, chuckling, and said, "Ranger, come." The dog followed Walter to the stairs and with the command of "Up," he went to the second floor. We heard a door open, then the Mahoneys' mother yelling something fast in Japanese, and the same door slamming shut.

"She wants us to turn the music down," said Walter.

"Fuck her," said Jason.

I looked around the room. Behind the couch, in the center, was a clean wrestling mat with nothing on it. Against the walls, several terrariums held tarantulas and poisonous snakes. A half-deflated blowup doll with a big O mouth had been tossed in a corner. There was a Super 8 projector facing a wall-hung white sheet on which the brothers projected porn: young teens and dog-on-girl action were among the favorites. Down here, no stone of degeneracy had been left unturned. Mr. and Mrs. Mahoney, who rarely ventured into the basement, had lost control of their own house.

Ted sat on the couch and I took a chair near Mike. He didn't acknowledge me. I couldn't figure out if Mike was retarded or shy.

Walter squeezed himself onto the couch between Ted and Jason. He picked up the shoebox top and shook it like a miner panning for gold. The seeds became separated from the bush and buds. Walter filled the bowl, handed the bong to Ted, and fired it up. Ted let the bong's tube get cloudy, took his finger off its hole, inhaled a shotgun of smoke, held it in his lungs, and coughed it out. The bong went around to each of us and soon we were all high. Ted and the others lit cigarettes.

Jason got up, put on an Aerosmith record, and dropped the needle on the third track.

"This jam is bad as *shit*," said Jason. "Dream On" came fully into the room.

"You like the stereo?" said Walter to my brother.

"It's okay," said Ted, without enthusiasm. They owned a Soundesign compact system with horn speakers. The sound was treble dominant. It wasn't even okay. It was one step up from a clock radio. Ted was being charitable but he wasn't the type to lie.

"I guess you'd know," said Walter. "On account of you're like a manager of that Audio *Chalet*."

Some guys got quiet when they were up on weed. Walter became more aggressive.

"I'm just a salesman," said Ted patiently. "It's called the Audio House."

"Ze Audio *Haus*," said Jason with a German accent, laughing at his own illogical joke, then digging his spoon into the tub of chocolate ice cream.

"Ricky, you should get a job up there too," said Walter. "But, wait, you're working at your old man's station, right?"

"Uh-huh," I said.

"Rick's pumping ethyl," said Jason, and now he and Walter both laughed.

"Nah, Ricky's pumping that little Jewish girl," said Walter. "Diane Finkelstein or whatever her Hebe name is. Ain't that right, Ricky?"

"It's Finkle," I said. Warmth came to my face.

"Aw, look at him," said Jason. "You made Ricky mad."

"Lay off him," said Ted.

"Okay," said Walter. "How's Francesca?"

"She's fine," said Ted.

"You two are hot and heavy again," said Walter. "That's nice. I guess she got it all out of her system while you were over there in Nam, keeping America safe."

"What's that mean?" said Ted.

"Nothin'," said Walter, then winked at Jason.

Ted let it go. No one said anything for a while after that. The song built up a head of steam and Jason, his eyes closed soulfully, began to sing along. It was the part at the end where Steven Tyler repeats the title over and over in a scream. When it finished, Jason got up and took the tonearm off the record and now it was silent in the room.

"I'll take that ounce," said Ted.

"Wrestle me," said Walter.

"What?"

"*Wrestle* me for the ounce."

"I already won it. We raced for it last night."

"If you beat me, I'll give you *two* ounces for nothin'."

"I'll just take the one," said Ted.

"Chickenshit."

"Say what?"

"Big Marine," said Walter. "What, they let faggots into the Corps now?"

A look back in time is in order now. In our day and where we came from, when you got called a faggot, it didn't mean homosexual, exactly. It meant you were a pussy, a coward, and a weakling. It meant you had to fight. On top of that, Walter had implied that other Marines were that way too. And Walter had said all of this in front of me, the kid brother. It was too much for Ted to walk away from or ignore.

"All right," said Ted.

We stood up from our seats at once. Even Mike. There was a physical contest about to happen. We were young men, and the promise of it jacked us up.

The group moved to the mat, marked with a circle in the middle. I assumed that Walter had boosted it from our high school, where he had wrestled his senior year, without distinction, in the 160 weight class.

"I'll ref," said Jason, and he made a thumb-up, thumb-down gesture with his hand to Walter. "Top or bottom?"

"Bottom," said Walter, and he got down on all fours on the mat.

Ted glanced over at me and wiggled his eyebrows, as if to

assure me it was all a game, and then he dropped to the mat and took the dominant position over Walter. Both of them looked up at Jason, who had raised his hand.

"What about a clock?" I said.

"No clock," said Jason, his eyes pink and his pupils dilated, chocolate ice cream staining his beard. "A pin ends it. Go!"

Jason dropped his hand in a slashing movement and Walter immediately scooted onto his ass. Ted tried to hold him but Walter broke free and got up on his feet.

"Escape," said Jason, and he held up one finger.

Ted had gotten to a standing position and he and Walter faced off. Walter's legs were bent and he was moving his hands in a circular motion. Ted was standing straight. I knew little about wrestling, but I sensed that Ted's stance made him vulnerable. He'd made a mistake.

"Shoot him, Walter," said Jason, and Walter went in low on my brother, wrapped his arms around his thighs, and lifted him up off his feet. Walter then drove Ted hard down into the mat. Ted turned onto his stomach to avoid the near fall and pin. Walter straddled him and remained in control.

"Takedown," said Jason. "Two points."

Walter clamped his thighs around Ted's legs and put one hand on his upper back; with his other hand he grabbed the biceps of Ted's right arm and pushed up on it like he was raising a pump arm on a well. Ted's face was crushed into the mat and I heard him grunt.

"Stop," I said.

Walter pushed harder. I saw Ted's face contort in pain.

I shouted at Ted and told him to tap out.

Ted didn't do it. Walter, his face a distorted mask of concentration, pushed the arm to its limit and then wrenched it violently to the left. We all heard something tear free.

Walter stood up, sweaty, his eyes wide with excitement. Jason slapped him five. Mike, sickened, looked away.

I went to Ted, whose arm had dropped but was hanging at an impossible angle to his shoulder. I helped him to his knees and then got him up on his feet. He was in great pain. "You broke his fucking arm," I said. "You happy now, Walter?"

"He's all right," said Walter. "It just needs to be reset or somethin'. Right, Ted?"

Ted didn't answer. Walter and Jason went back to the couch without another word. When we left the house through the basement door, we could hear their brain-damaged dog barking maniacally from up on the second floor.

I drove Ted's 'Cuda to the hospital, Ted in the bucket beside me. Walter was right. Ted's arm wasn't broken. It had been dislocated. It just needed to be reset.

Things happened very quickly after that.

In the ER, Ted mentioned that he had been feeling dizzy lately and that he had been running a low-grade fever off and on for the past few weeks. The doctor on duty did a blood test and saw something he didn't like. Our family physician referred Ted to an oncologist, who, after further lab work, determined that my brother was in the advanced stages of non-Hodgkin's lymphoma. He had cancer.

Ted died three months later in the bedroom we'd shared since childhood. The details of his illness and rapid decline are too painful for me to recall on these pages. We buried him next to our mother in the Catholic cemetery on the grounds of our church.

I don't remember how it got into the head of my father that it was Walter Mahoney who had triggered the cancer in my brother. The doctors never implied that a dislocated shoulder could cause cancer, and there is no medical evidence that I know of to suggest that this could be the case. But my father believed it, and, because I loved and respected him, I began to believe it too.

The allegation got around the community and for many it became fact. Maybe I fueled the rumor, I don't know. Walter Mahoney, the lowlife, had killed Ted Donnelly, a clean-cut, standup guy who had done the right thing and served his country during an unpopular war. It quickly got pretty bad for Walter, a guy few people had liked to begin with. He was even shunned by the car crowd who were his peers. Eventually, he moved out of his parents' house and left the neighborhood. But his absence didn't do a thing to take my father's mind off Ted.

Pop began to put a shot of whiskey next to his beer in the evenings. It took hold of him and he leaned on it. He turned into someone else virtually overnight. He knew what was happening to him, but he wouldn't or couldn't stop.

The house became a place I dreaded to enter. I moved out of my old bedroom to a smaller room in the basement. Pop had parked and tarped the 'Cuda in our driveway, so even the exterior of our home was a cold reminder of Ted's demise.

In the year that followed my brother's death, my father quit his job at the Esso station, and I took his place as a certified mechanic in the garage. There were other changes. I unloaded my Dart and bought a clean-line '71 Fury GT with a 440 under the hood. I filled out, and between that and the pressure and responsibility of living with my father, my face aged and grew hard.

I'd talked to one of Walter's ex–running buddies and learned that Walter had moved to an apartment building over in the neighboring county. He worked in a body shop and was still driving the AMX. Once again, my fantasies turned to violence.

One night I came home to find my father passed out on the floor. His head was cut from where he'd hit it on the edge of the coffee table. He was snoring. I shook him and helped him up. He glanced around the living room as if he'd woken up in a strange place. His eyes were jittery when he finally looked my way.

"It's me, Pop. Rick."

"You," he said. "*You.* Why did this happen to Ted and not you?"

My heart sank. But he needed my help.

"Dad, you're sick."

"What?"

"I'm going to help you," I said. "I'm going to fix it."

My father stared at me and shook his head. He knew me well.

I drove over to the local pub. I needed a beer. The fact is, I'd been drinking heavily for some time too.

After a few I settled up and drove over the county line. It wasn't but five miles from our neighborhood. The area had been largely white and blue collar up until the late sixties, but minorities had moved in, and in less than ten years the whites had bolted and left it to the blacks and the Spanish.

I parked in the lot of the Gardens building, which, despite

its name, was neither a low-rise structure nor one surrounded by greenery. It was an eight-story concrete box with balconies holding bicycles and rusty chairs and tables. Walter's AMX was not in the lot. I decided to wait.

He pulled up late that night, locked his car, and walked to the glass-doored entrance of the building. He was heavier and his hair was long and looked unwashed. He walked unsteadily, with a slight sway. It didn't occur to me then that he had been broken by Ted's death too.

I got out of my car, trailed him to the entrance, and looked inside the lobby. Walter pushed on a door near a single elevator and stepped inside. I followed.

The lobby had no desk or security. The door Walter had entered led to the stairwell. A sign on the elevator said that it was temporarily out of service due to repairs. On the mailbox slots on the opposite wall I saw the name Mahoney. Walter lived on the fourth floor.

I drove home, checked on Pop, and went to bed. I couldn't sleep. I was thinking of my father and how I could help him find some kind of peace.

For the next three nights I sat outside the Gardens and watched Walter Mahoney come home from whatever watering hole he frequented. The pattern was the same. He'd return intoxicated after our county's last call, park and lock the AMX, and stagger-walk into his building, where he'd take the stairs to the fourth floor.

On the third night I gave him a ten-minute lead, then followed his route. The stairwell, at that hour, was deserted. Its steps were concrete. There were blind corners on each landing where a man could hide and wait. If I could surprise Walter, come up behind him and move fast, I'd throw him down the stairs. Maybe that would break his neck. If it didn't, he'd still be too hurt to retaliate. I could crush his skull with a heavy-duty wrench or a ballpeen hammer. That would finish him.

The elevator wouldn't be under repair for much longer. If I was going to do it, I had to do it the following night.

My father came by the gas station the next morning. I was in the bay, gunning the lug nuts off an Olds 88 that was up on the lift, when he walked in.

"Rick," he said. "Can I speak to you a minute?"

"Sure." I wiped my hands off on a shop rag and went to him.

"I'm sorry about the other night," my father said. "What I said to you. I was disoriented. I didn't mean it. I don't know what I'd do if something happened to you."

"It's okay, Pop."

"I haven't been the best father to you, I know."

"It's *okay.*"

"There's something else."

"What?"

"You can't fix this, Rick. You can't." He put his hand on my shoulder and squeezed it. "I know what you're capable of. And I want you to forget it. I want you to stop. Walter Mahoney's parents love him too. I don't want them to go through what I'm going through now. Do you understand me, Rick?"

"Dad."

"*Do* you?" he said.

"Yes."

"Okay." My father nodded at the 88. "What are you doing to that Oldsmobile?"

"Pads and rotors."

"Better get to it, then. I'll see you tonight."

I hadn't thought about Mr. and Mrs. Mahoney. I hadn't thought any of it through, not really. I was still a kid.

Pop was right about one thing. I couldn't fix him.

One day I came home from work and Ted's Barracuda was no longer in the driveway. My father had gotten rid of it. When I walked into the house, he was dead drunk in his recliner. A cigarette was still in his fingers, burned down to the filter.

My father passed in 1979, and I sold the house shortly thereafter.

You wake up one day, and you're old.

Recently, I went back to the old neighborhood and drove its streets. Today, many of the homes are owned by Hispanics, Ethiopians, Arabs, Indians, and Pakis. The new immigrants. Same kinds of folks I grew up with, only with darker skin. It's a cycle.

The parents of the Mahoney brothers are gone now, the home long since sold. Back in the '80s, Jason Mahoney, fried on PCP, dropped his Harley on the highway and got run over by an eighteen-wheeler. Near his mangled corpse, on the median strip, was a spiked Prussian Army helmet that he wore when he rode his bike. Jason was stupid till the end.

Mike Mahoney, the quiet brother, moved to the country, where he raised a family and worked as an electrician. I looked him up on Facebook. In his photos, he's smiling, surrounded by his wife, grown children, and dogs. He did all right.

My own journey has not been predictable, but then, whose is? I worked as a mechanic in my twenties, got married and divorced, struggled with substance abuse, and kicked it. Met a woman in rehab who has been my wife for almost thirty years. Had a son. Somewhere in there I noticed that the guys who were selling water pumps and mufflers to me were driving Cadillacs and Lincolns, so I opened up an auto-parts store, then three more, and within a decade I was bought out by a chain that came to town. By most standards, I'm a wealthy man.

These days, I can afford to buy any car I want, but nothing floats my boat. The rice burners all look alike, and the modern American muscle cars are weak imitations of the more striking originals. I drive a Dodge pickup truck. My father, a Mopar man, would approve.

Jane and I had always wanted to see New Orleans, and about six months ago we went down to check it out. We were staying at the Hampton Inn on the edge of the warehouse district. One afternoon I wandered by the convention center while my wife was shopping up on Magazine Street. There's a huge warehouse nearby where they store the Mardi Gras floats, and there they were having one of those classic-car auctions you see on TV. I walked in.

They were bringing the cars out one by one, with fanfare, before the bidding started. The way they played it up, with music and showgirls and all that, it was like the lions and Christians were coming out into the Colosseum in ancient Rome. I watched it for a while standing next to a guy about my age, said his name was Dan. He was still beside me when they rolled out a '70 'Cuda: black body, black interior, black vinyl roof. Triple black. The announcer said it was a 383.

"The four-forty can go for close to a mill," said Dan. "This one here might fetch a couple hundred grand, at least, if it's straight."

"It's a beauty," I said.

"I always thought the Barracuda from that era had four headlights. This one's got only two."

"This is a '70," I said. "Plymouth only put the four headlights on the '71s."

"You know your cars."

"I used to," I said.

I thought about getting closer to see if the car was Ted's. Surely there was a chain of title. For a hot second, I considered bidding on it and, if I got it, giving the 'Cuda to my son. But that moment passed.

My son doesn't own a car. No interest. He didn't even get his license until he was in his early twenties. He rides a bicycle and uses Uber. I don't understand a young man who doesn't want the freedom and thrill of having his own vehicle, but there are many things about him that I don't understand.

You get to an age, you feel like you don't belong here anymore. But I'm *not* here. The young man I've described to you is gone. I'm not the same person I was so many years ago. Not even close.

Take Walter Mahoney. It scares me now to think that I came so very close to murdering him. If I could talk to Walter again, I'd tell him that it's okay. He was a confused kid, just like me. He was reckless, just like me. He got in a wrestling match with Ted, and he hurt him, but he didn't make Ted sick. I'd tell him that, with the death of his brother Jason, we had something in common now. If I were to spend some time with

Walter again, we might even become friends. But that will never happen. Walter ended up homeless and alcoholic. He's been gone many years. His body was found one January morning, frozen on the street.

My mom and Ted both died of cancer. It runs in my family, so odds are I'm next. When it happens, I'll join Pop, and my mother, and Ted. Walter too. Not in heaven or anything like that. I don't believe in fairy tales.

I'm saying, when I go, we'll all be in the same place: buried in the Catholic cemetery by our church in the neighborhood where I came up, a long time ago. When cars were loud, fast, and beautiful, and we raced them in the night.

FOGMEISTER

by Diana Gabaldon

HE WAS MY *friend. It was my car.*

I had to know.

January 28, 1938, was a cold day. Cold, clear, and dry. Ironic, really—two drivers famous for their skill in bad weather, and that day the Autobahn was dry as a bone, the air clear as a bell. The German Nazi Motorsports Guild arranged to close part of the Autobahn for the speed-record trials; the officials from Mercedes-Benz and the Auto Union each chose a straight kilometer—the ground for their duel—and marked them off. If you stood at the Auto Union starting line, you could see the bridge in the distance.

Rudolf Caracciola was driving for Mercedes. They called him Der Regenmeister, the Rain Master. Great on wet pavement, complete control.

Bernd Rosemeyer could drive in any weather conditions, but to see him come hurtling alone out of a bank of fog, the distant whine of the invisible pack behind him, was a sight to lift the hairs on your neck.

The day before, it had been raining and hazy, but not on the twenty-eighth. A perfect day for this clash of German titans. The Auto Union—and the 1937 Rekordwagen based on my Type C Grand Prix car—had come out of the Recordwoche in October covered in glory and bursting with pride. Bernie set fifteen world and international records that week. Mercedes wanted some of them back.

The Stromlinienwagen, we called it—the Streamliner. I designed it, a new, beautiful, flowing shape for the Grand Prix. It passed out of my hands when my contract with Auto Union expired at the end of 1937, but I created it. It was my car.

> Stromlinienwagen 6.5 L
> Design Note 14.32 [Dr. Porsche]
> Engine capacity to be enlarged to 6.5 liters through a 78 mm bore (75 mm in original 6.1 engine). New pistons, liners, and heads to be machined.*

---

* See Workshop Specifications Number 633–639 and Materials List Number 55A, 55B, 55C, and 62A.

Each company chose its own stretch of road. These were record-speed runs, not a race. The Auto Union's first run was southbound, a straight shot through woodland and under a bridge. The speed recorded was very respectable, but not greater than Bernie's record in the six-liter Streamliner in October. Run two, northbound, took place twenty minutes later. Again, good speed—perhaps a record, but very, very close to Caracciola's time. Someone in the press reported that

Auto Union officials were dubious about another run but that Rosemeyer was willing to try again.

Three times was one too many. I bought every paper available, but most articles reporting the accident talked only about the death of a hero of the Reich and not about how—or why—that death had happened. The *Frankfurter Zeitung,* the local daily, had a few details. There was no doubt, the journalist wrote, that a wind gust triggered the "wide-open" skid to the left. "After having hit a picket in the grass median, the car went on again, back on the concrete track, as one can see from the black marks."

I flipped through the other accounts—no one else mentioned a picket in the grass. The *Kurhessische Landeszeitung* had a quote from a first-aid man who had come to the site of the wreck. The journalist described this gentleman as "quite shocked"—and no wonder, I thought—but he gave it as his opinion that there were two gusts of wind. The first, he said, had forced the car onto the grass median; the second had triggered the deadly skid to the right, after the car was already back on the concrete.

This was nonsense; wind blowing strongly in opposite directions at virtually the same moment for the entire run, which must have taken less than ten seconds? "Do these people even read what they write?" I muttered to myself.

Neueste Zeitung...this was more interesting. Whoever had written the article—there was no name—talked about the airflow, the drag. He got everything else wrong—the direction of the run, which wheels were which in the wreck—but he was right when he said that the longitudinal stability is worsened by an increase in front drag. That means that any side force—as from, for instance, a gust of wind—has a stronger impact at higher speed. Wind that wouldn't even be felt in a passenger car could—maybe—push a racing car right off the track.

"On this event," the author had written, "not even a master like Rosemeyer managed to win over the forces of nature."

I folded up the newspapers into tidy squares and stuffed them into the kindling basket by the stove. It was a cold day today too, and the stove in my sitting room was glowing hot.

Bernie had lost, all right—but was it the forces of nature, some failure of his own famous skill... or some defect in the car?

What had they done to my car!?

Stromlinienwagen 6.5 L

Design Note 67.33A Retention and Placement of Water Radiator

Even though the water radiator has no function, having been supplanted by ice cooling, the radiator itself must be retained at the front of the car in order to balance the weight of the ice tank. (See also Design Notes 80x–93x, on fairings required by altered center of gravity.)

I was still thinking about it in the morning.

There were only two eyewitnesses, according to the reports, both of them officials of the timekeeping team. These men were at the end of the measured course and thus closest to the accident.

Only two eyewitnesses? I doubted that very much. A record run was not a race, so there wouldn't have been a crowd, but surely there would have been a good number of people present. The car's crew, naturally—although they wouldn't have been at the end of the course, they would have seen *something*. A crew chief and the eight mechanics of a race crew, certainly. Maybe a backup driver. Officials from Auto Union, definitely. Which men would those have been? I wondered. Again—probably not located near the actual crash, but every eye would have been fixed on that car for every second of the run.

I'd read the two "official" eyewitness accounts in the newspapers: Otto Geyer and Carlo Weidmann. I'd talked to many newspaper journalists on many occasions. I had yet to read a single interview of myself without errors, and certainly never one that included everything I'd said. I didn't know Geyer, but I'd met Weidmann a few times. I pulled out my watch; nearly 3:00 p.m. Perhaps Carlo Weidmann would like to have a cup of coffee. Perhaps *mit schnapps*—it was a cold day, after all.

> Design Note 55.12 Fairings
> Fairings to be adjusted so that junction with side-paneling is minimal, ideally less than 2 mm. Fairings to be tapered, with a thickness of five cm at the apex of each fairing, tapering outward to 8 cm at point of attachment. Attachment: bolts at intervals of 15 cm.
> See Workshop Order 143/7 for bolt sizing.

"Oh my God." Weidmann took a large swallow of his drink—he'd chosen calvados to accompany his coffee—and coughed hard. "Oh God. You know how it is when there's a bad wreck, you know it occurs so fast, you can't have seen anything, really, and at the same time it seems to move so slowly, like it's—it's happening like an ordinary thing, just in its own time, but it's you that's frozen, so slow that you can't do anything?"

I did know, and nodded. The heat of the coffee was making my nose run; I dabbed it with my napkin.

"The car did skid, though? You saw it?"

"Oh yes." He'd flushed from the coughing but now went a little pale. "Yes, definitely. It was just before the Morfelden clearing—before the bridge, you know? That bridge…He moved to the right, there, I'm sure of it—maybe because of the wind that was coming from the right—but the car's left wheels, they went off the concrete, into the grass of the median." He glanced at me. "We're sure of that; the wheel marks were plain in the grass, when we looked…afterward."

He reached for the calvados.

"A good half meter into the grass. I saw the skid and thought, *Oh God* but still hoped he'd pull out." He took a drink. "At that point, the bridge was only four hundred meters or so away. He knew, he saw, he was doing anything he could to try to save himself, countersteering, braking—there were marks—trying to aim through the bridge."

He stopped and pressed his lips hard together.

"He didn't make it," I finished for him, quietly. He shook his head and drained his glass.

"So young," he whispered.

Design Note 22.3—Air intake plate [Dr. Porsche]

The air intake vents should be increased from three to seven, and the foot pedal shortened and rotated approximately five degrees in a clockwise direction for quicker response. Maintain present size of plate until further measurement. [See further note for discussion of spring.]

I couldn't find Otto Geyer; he'd gone to Munich, I was told, to visit relatives. But in the process of looking for him, I discovered that the pieces of the wreck had been taken to a garage in Darmstadt, close to where the accident had happened.

I drove there, filled with equal parts dread and curiosity. When I introduced myself, the proprietor of the garage raised his eyebrows in respect and ushered me at once to the end bay, its sliding door discreetly closed and fastened with a padlock.

"Here, Herr Doktor Porsche," he said, beckoning me to the side of the building, where a door gave access. "The lady came just a little while ago."

"The lady?"

"Frau Rosemeyer, *ja,*" he said, and opened the door for me.

The last thing I had expected was to meet the grieving widow over what was, in effect, Bernd's coffin, and I entered with some diffidence. Elly Beinhorn — she seldom called herself Frau Rosemeyer — turned when I came in, her eyebrows raising with surprise.

"Ferdinand," she said. Then she smiled, a little sadly. "Of course — you would need to see it too." She stepped back, a hand sweeping low to invite me to look at what lay on the stained concrete under the glare of a big work light overhead.

"It" was what was left of the 6.5 L 1938 Stromlinienwagen. Or the "Death Car," as the newspapers all too accurately called it. There was no visible blood, but the crumpled metal and exploded tires bore eloquent witness to that accuracy.

The Streamliner's dismembered parts were laid out on the ground like sections of a slaughtered, crudely butchered beast. The garage smelled of racing fuel. I loved that smell, but now I imagined the scent of blood mixed in and started to take shallow breaths.

Elly came up bravely to my side but then faltered a little, not quite reaching for my arm.

"I — I don't think…"

I took her hand and tucked it into the crook of my elbow.

"It's all right," I said. "He didn't die in the car, you know."

She'd been holding her breath; she let it go with a sigh like a punctured inner tube.

"You're sure of that?" she asked, and swallowed. She'd been thinking the same things I had; how could she not have been?

"I'm sure," I said, and consciously took a good, deep breath. "He was thrown free." He had been; that much I knew.

The cockpit was enclosed. Normally, it took tools, time, and more than one mechanic to get a driver out. It had taken a fraction of a second for Bernie to be thrown free as the car burst apart. They found him in the grass, lying very peacefully there, his cloth helmet still fastened, not a mark on him (or so they said. You can't trust public reports of anything, especially anything the chancellor takes a special interest in).

My assurance seemed to relieve her, and she let go of my arm and went forward, squatting down to look at the detached fairing, lying nearly paired beside the rest of the wreckage. A side panel lay just beyond, the metal hideously crumpled at one end, and nearby a big, solid metal chest.

"The ice tank?" she said, pointing her chin at the chest. "Bernie told me about it."

"Yes." I squatted myself, with much less grace, and ran a hand over the tank. It hadn't broken open but was very battered.

The car had flipped, then, at least once…the ice tank had replaced the water-filled radiator in function, but not in position, I saw—they'd left the radiator in the front. I could see the fastenings where it had been, and shattered pieces of grille still set in the braces.

The fairings were detached—I saw that the bolts had been too short; half of them had pulled out completely. But what did that matter, as this had clearly happened as a result of the impact with the bridge.

"Do you think they did it?" Elly turned to me, sudden as a stooping hawk.

"Who?" I asked weakly. And, belatedly: "Did what?"

The corner of her mouth twitched, but it wasn't a smile.

"You saw the photos, didn't you? The ones at the beginning."

I had, and the memory of the images was still enough to make the hairs rise on my shoulders. The lovely shape of my car, the original, had been altered, the sides straightened and raised into massive fairings. The news photos had shown it— the skin of the car, the side panel, was warped, distorted over the left side. It hurt me to see it. The air wasn't flowing smoothly at all. Two seconds in and something was happening.

"Them," she said, lowering her voice, thank God, as she jerked her head toward the door, where two brown-shirted men were smoking. Her driver, I supposed, and one of the omnipresent minders; I'd seen such pairs before. I knew she didn't mean these men specifically but what they represented: the Nazi Party and its control.

"Them? But why?" I was honestly bewildered. Bernie had no use for politics—anybody's politics—and neither did Elly. (Elly had little use for anybody's opinions, period. I suppose that a certain disregard for what people think is useful to an adventuress—though it likely works better if the adventuress is beautiful. But then, what doesn't?)

That disregard didn't keep her from being aware of what people thought, though. She gave me a quick, assessing look from the corner of her eye before focusing on the wreckage.

"They've taken over the funeral," she said, her voice carefully neutral. "I said I wanted it to be only us, just our families. But Herr Trotter—from the Reich; he does their promotional information—assured me he has it 'under control.'" There was a brief burst of laughter from the men at the door, some response to a joke quickly stifled as they recalled where they were. She didn't look around, but her shoulders stiffened.

"So it's to be a state occasion," she said in the same neutral tone. "Limousines—Mercedes, I expect—and a band. With—"

"A band? At a funeral?" I risked a quick glance over my shoulder, but the men were paying no attention to us.

"With banners flying," she went on, "and speeches at the graveside." Her face was stiff with distaste. "A full SS state funeral, with Hitler's own honor guard. Now, whether the SS chooses to pay for it...that's maybe something else."

"Ah," I said. My Nazi Party number was 567,902; Auto Union arranged for it, the membership a guise of respectability. Partial compensation for my unfortunate heredity. Bernie's number was 403,201. He'd laughed when I told him about mine and pulled his card out of his wallet to show me. It was folded in quarters and he'd apparently been picking his teeth with it.

The corners of Elly's nostrils had gone white.

"Hitler's hero," she said as if to herself. "They call him— called him—that. You've seen the newspapers?"

I'd seen them; the photographs, I thought she meant. The run. The wreckage. There were a few photos, but not enough.

"When did you first meet Bernie?" I asked, just for something to say, to distract her. They hadn't been married long, barely eighteen months.

She made a little hiccup of a laugh.

"You were there. In Brno, the Grand Prix three years ago."

"Oh," I said. I had no memory of her being at the Czechoslovakian Grand Prix that year—but at a race, I had no eyes for anything but the cars.

"You?" she said, swallowing. "When did you meet him?"

"Oh, that same year—but earlier. When he came to try out as a test driver." I smiled despite myself. "Did he ever tell you about it? All the others came wearing overalls, but Bernie came to drive in his best suit. When the director asked him why, he said he thought it was an important occasion—he should wear the best thing he had."

This time the sound she made was much less a laugh.

"No, he didn't tell me. But he wouldn't, you know; he didn't ever look back—" The last of the word vanished with a small gulp.

She wasn't the kind of woman to whom you would offer gestures of affection without a specific invitation, but I was old enough to be her father, and while my grief could never equal hers, she knew it was genuine. I made a slight reaching motion— she turned slightly toward me—and then she came into my arms and I felt the heat of her face and her tears through my shirt. I patted her back, very gingerly. I could feel her breasts against me too; very large and hard with milk, and for the first time I remembered that she had a baby, no more than two months old.

That made my own eyes sting. The badness of the loss and the thought that at least there was that much left of Bernie — he'd told me they called the baby Bernd Jr.

Neither one of us was the sort to weep in public, though, and she stepped back, turning her face away.

"Let's look," she said.

It was obvious what had caused the wreck — impact with the central pillar of a concrete bridge (what in God's name had made them choose a run with a bridge in it?). Much less obvious was what had caused Bernie to lose control and crash into it.

Elly was an aviatrix; she understood airflow, and together we knelt and turned things over, tracing crumpled metal with our fingers, murmuring possibilities.

"Turbulence?" she said at one point, lifting the edge of the side panel. "I read one account that speculated that it was turbulence caused by the forest. 'Turbulence is unpredictable in a forest,'" she quoted. "'The racecourse ran through dense forest on either side.' A Venturi effect?"

I creased my brow at that and looked at the wreckage, but reluctantly shook my head.

"I can't see how that could be. I haven't seen the course, but I've seen woodland. Too much irregularity — and to develop such an effect in a run of less than ten seconds?"

"Ridiculous," she agreed. "But speaking of airflow — it has to have been that, don't you think?" She spoke with complete confidence, not admitting any possibility that Bernie could have failed in any way.

If I didn't, I wouldn't be here, I thought, but I obligingly got up and came to kneel beside her over a round steel plate — the air-intake regulator. It was battered, a little bent. There were seven air-intake ports, as I'd specified in my design notes— but all of them had been welded shut.

"That would be a lot of help," I muttered. "Do you see the foot pedal?"

"Over there, I think. Is this it?" She reached and handed it to me. They hadn't shortened it, but that didn't matter, as with the intake ports all permanently closed, the driver couldn't regulate the airflow with the pedal anyway. Was this evidence of some tampering, though? I didn't see how it could be—the ports had been sealed with a welding torch; a solid, professional job. No one could have abstracted the plate, made that alteration, and put it back without someone on the crew— probably everyone—noticing. And there *were* plausible reasons why Auto Union might have done that, depending on the results of their own wind-tunnel tests.

It was getting dark outside, and the sighs of the two men near the door were becoming louder. At last we got to our feet and stood, not wanting simply to walk away.

"I'll speak to some people," I said. "At Auto Union."

She nodded. "So will I. I know the crew; they'll talk to me."

We shook hands, very formally, and I walked behind her, away from the wreckage.

Design Note 43.21: Heat Shield
The heat shield is to be placed behind the cockpit, between the driver and the rear axles, which support the ice tank and the fuel tank. Height, 1.1 m, width .87 m. Insulated construction, multiple layers of wood and felt.
Workshop ref. 209/13.

* * *

Bernd grew up on a motorcycle. I always thought that's what made him such a good race driver: he didn't have any sort of preconception as to what a car could do or what the limits might be.

The limits…those were my province. The province of the designer, and the engineer, and finally of the workmen who built the car to our specifications. If Bernie hadn't made a mistake, then someone else had.

I took the train to Zwickau. It was a journey I'd made many times, but there was no sense of déjà vu about it. The train carriage was unheated but crowded, and the condensed breath of the passengers ran in trickles down the windows, smearing the landscape of Saxony. And I carried a weight of anxiety that I'd never had previously, not even before the trials of a new design.

A long journey, but I'd started early, and it was just past two o'clock when the taxi delivered me to the Auto Union premises. These were in the old Horch works, a sprawling brickyard ringed with buildings. It was a weekday and the place was bustling with workers, messengers, trucks bringing in piles of rubber tires and sheet steel, the big trailers for shipping cars clustered outside the plant like a herd of skeletal cows.

I felt the strong pull of the workshops, wanted to wander in and see what was happening, smell the hot solder and the rubber and the metal that was my favorite perfume. Maybe later, I told myself, and instead headed for the white-brick building that housed the main offices.

It was only a couple of months since I had worked here regularly, and the receptionist's face lit up with pleasure at seeing me.

"Herr Doktor Porsche!" he said. "How nice it is to see you again! I didn't know there was a meeting today—shall I bring you a coffee?"

I would at that point have sold at least a small part of my soul for hot coffee, but reluctantly, I shook my head.

"*Danke,* Reinhart. It's not a meeting. I only wanted to see Dr. Eberan for half an hour. Just to go over some technical things about the Stromlinienwagen."

His face sobered at that.

"Such a terrible thing," he said, and shook his head. "Poor Rosemeyer. We couldn't believe it—but we never believe it, do we, and yet we know it happens, it must happen in this business, *nein?*"

"It does, alas," I said. "Can you see if Herr Doktor Eberan is available?" I had thought about sending a telegram to make an appointment but decided against it. I didn't want Eberan to think about it ahead of time and told myself that if he wasn't in, I would just poke around, maybe ask some questions of the other Auto Union officials—and the engineers. Eberan's own car was in the yard, though—a big twelve-cylinder Daimler, dove gray and glossy, with a grille that looked like it was about to eat you alive.

Reinhart gestured me to a chair and disappeared. I didn't sit, though; I hovered in the doorway, looking down the long, dim corridor. The day outside was rainy, and the patches of light that fell into the corridor from the open doors were pale and insubstantial. It seemed I was a ghost myself, recognizing all the things I saw, knowing them intimately, and yet feeling detached.

I'd worked with Robert for many months; we got along, we worked quite well together—yet we'd never become friends.

Part of it was caste; I was a Czech, while his family had been Austrian nobility. They had still been using the name von Eberhorst in his childhood, and one doesn't forget things like that. I had more than once thought that his dislike of working under me had a lot to do with my departure from Auto Union — though the parting itself was reasonably amicable. And then again, he was an ambitious man. He had his own thoughts on design.

Which was what was bothering me now.

Reinhart flickered into sight at the far end of the hallway, and I ducked back into his tiny office to be discovered looking out of the window when he came in, full of apologies, to tell me that Herr Doktor Eberan was called away, had just left for a meeting in Stuttgart. He would be desolated to hear—

"That's all right, Reinhart," I interrupted, and patted his shoulder.

So, plan B. The engineering department was in the same building; I'd need to wait a bit. Teatime was three o'clock; everyone would be going to the canteen and I could slip into the building by the rear entrance, and — with luck — have half an hour alone in the closet that held the files of design notes, plans, and records.

In the meantime, I decided that I might as well stroll by the workshops and see whether anyone I knew was around.

There wasn't much going on. Only two bays were busy; I didn't know the men in the first one, but I spotted Dieter Pfizen in the second, with a half-assembled twelve-cylinder head on a stand in front of him.

"So, Dieter, what have you got?" He looked up, surprised at my voice, but smiled.

"Herr Doktor Porsche!" He stepped back, gesturing at the motor. "Nothing much, yet. Checking the oil flow." There was a strong smell of the kerosene used for cleaning, and I saw small golden dribbles of motor oil on the stand.

We chatted about small things for a bit, but I knew the memory of the accident hung heavy over Auto Union, and the moment I mentioned Bernd's name, Dieter's face clouded. He was a big man who didn't hide his feelings.

"It should never have happened! Never," he said vehemently, shaking his head. "They rushed it, everybody knew. Didn't want to risk Mercedes scooping up the record without even a challenge — not now."

I nodded. The competition between the two companies had risen markedly with Hitler's decision to develop a great German motor industry and his splitting the development money between Mercedes and Auto Union. That split, both companies knew, could be a lot less even next time.

"Rushed, though..." I said, striving for a casual tone. "Surely you wouldn't have let the Streamliner go out with loose wheels and missing bolts?" I thought of those fairings, lying on the ground by themselves.

He snorted at my joke.

"No. But you talk to Ludwig, see what he says about it." Ludwig Sebastien was Bernd's crew chief; he would certainly have been there. "Better yet, talk to Horst Hasse."

"And who's that?" I knew Ludwig well, but not Hasse.

Dieter rubbed the back of his hand across his face, smudging his cheek with grease.

"One of the second-rank drivers. He's the one who drove

the car for a shakedown after the wind-tunnel tests. If there *were* wind-tunnel tests," he added, narrowing his eyes.

"What?" I said, startled. He snorted again, and shrugged.

"Oh, I'm sure there were. But maybe not the way you'd have done them, *mein herr.*"

I spent another quarter of an hour with him, but having said as much as he had, he drew back and became vague, saying only that it had been Christmastime, half the staff not working, short days…and a rush. Things had been done in a rush.

Eventually we shook hands and I took my leave, smelling pleasantly of metal shavings and fresh oil.

I felt like a fool, peering to and fro as I stepped in through the rear door, but no one was in sight, though I could hear voices in the building, conversations in the canteen down the hall. I knew engineers, though, and sure enough, their room was deserted, all of them gone off like a horde of locusts in search of tea and *baumkuchen*.

The file closet was nearly as large as the main room but very well organized, the cabinets and plan shelves labeled. I found the drawer and shelf I wanted—but not a lot more. Eberan's original design notes were there; I flipped through them quickly, but they told me little else than had the shattered remains of the Streamliner. My own preliminary notes for the car, the ones I'd made last year, before leaving—those were there as well, though shuffled together in an untidy roll bound with twine. But there were no operating notes. No results of wind-tunnel tests. No notes on the shakedown drive Dieter had mentioned.

The muffled voices changed their tone; the conversation was breaking up. I closed the drawer as quietly as I could and left by the rear door before anyone could emerge from the canteen and see me.

Eberan's Daimler was still parked in the yard, its grille gleaming in the rain.

TELEGRAM
FROM: E BEINHORN
TO: F PORSCHE

MECHANIC SAYS HE HEARD EXPLOSION NEAR END OF RUN STOP ASK FURTHER QUERY STOP

My wife came in, a plate of rösti and eggs in her hand, and peered over my shoulder.

"An explosion?" she asked, putting the plate down. I shook my head and folded up the yellow paper.

"I don't think so, no." The possibility had sparked for a moment in my mind, but I could not forget the vivid picture of the wreckage; I had dreamed about it all night long.

You might think that the marks of explosion would be lost, masked by the damage—but not to the eye of someone who had built cars and who had seen many wrecks before. Elly was right; it couldn't have been the tires—they hadn't blown out. I thought the probable explanation—if in fact the mechanic *had* heard anything—was that the heavy air-intake plate had struck the pavement with a bang, dropped as the frame twisted.

Still…there was that uneasy suggestion, left by Elly's question: *Do you think they did it?*

The next question, of course, was still "Why?" But the fact that she had asked that gave me an uncomfortable notion of why. Neither she nor Bernie liked politics—Bernie openly laughed at the Nazi Party's pretensions and ceremonial carrying-on. I didn't think he would have been fool enough to come right out and denounce them; I didn't think he cared that much, for one thing. Bernie really only cared about motors. And Elly, to be sure.

I got up, ignoring the remainder of my eggs, and fetched a sheet of paper from the secretary. I wrote:

FROM: F PORSCHE
TO: E BEINHORN
UNLIKELY BUT WILL ASK STOP

I folded it in half, gave it to our maid, and asked her to take it to the telegraph office as soon as she had time.

"And where are you going?" Aloisa demanded, looking from the overcoat on my arm to my half-devoured eggs and back.

"To find a young man named Horst Hasse," I said, and I leaned over to kiss her good-bye.

I went first to visit Ludwig Sebastien, who lived nearby. He confirmed my thoughts about the air-intake plate, had no idea as to the cause of the crash—or at least none he chose to share with me, though his gaze slipped a little to the side as he said it—but he did tell me where to find Horst Hasse; he lived in Stuttgart, fortunately, though in one of the less desirable districts, in a small flat over a *bierstube* owned by his parents.

Hasse was actually in the *bierstube* when I arrived, having lunch. He turned out to be a fair-haired young man, short, slightly built, and with a tendency to breathe through his mouth. An Aryan, if a puny one.

"Herr Doktor Porsche!" he said, blue eyes going very round at the sight of me. "I didn't—I—such an honor!" He seized the hand I offered him and shook it forcefully. "Herr Sebastien said you wanted to talk to me, but I didn't believe him, I thought he was playing tricks again, he's always playing tricks to make people look foolish, so I—"

"*Danke,*" I said, trying to get a word in edgewise. He hadn't let go of my hand, so I tightened my own grip and took a step forward, forcing him to back up into the *bierstube*. I had a quick look round—drivers tended to congregate, and something was telling me it was better if nobody saw him talking to me. There were a couple of stocky men in caps that looked like truck drivers, and a few surly-looking youths crouched over a table in the corner—these turned and gave me suspicious looks, but I saw no sign of recognition on their smooth young faces.

"So good of you to talk with me," I said, smiling at Hasse with what I hoped was reassurance. "Let me buy you a drink."

We settled at last in a corner with our beers. There was no point in trying to set him at his ease with casual chat; I wasn't about to offer him a job, which was probably the only possibility occupying his mind at the moment, and the instant I mentioned the accident, any sense of ease would fly right out the window.

"I wanted to ask you a little bit about the Streamliner—the new one, you know."

His face fell a bit—he *had* been hoping for a job offer, and I was sorry for his disappointment.

"But…you must know a lot more than I do, Herr Doktor?"

"I know the Type C I designed for Auto Union last year, yes…but they changed some things, of course, for the new model." I took a swallow of beer; it was bock, strong and malty, and made me feel a little steadier; I hadn't eaten since breakfast.

"Yes, I suppose so." Hasse looked dubious. "But I wouldn't know about that—shouldn't you—" He was about to ask me why I hadn't gone to Eberan with my questions. I interrupted him.

"Yes, of course I know what changes were made on paper." I smiled, dabbing at my mustache with a napkin. "I've seen the notes." *Well, some of them…*

"I was wondering how the car handled. There are things only a driver would notice, you know that—and I was just thinking after I heard about Bernd…well, I know that you drove on the trials, and I wondered whether you'd noticed any small thing while you were driving…"

The strangest expressions were crossing his face, and I actually stopped talking, watching him. There was sadness when I mentioned Bernd, and he lifted a hand briefly, as though to make the sign of the cross, but he stopped abruptly as his thoughts caught up, and wariness flashed in his eyes, succeeded almost instantly by recognizable fear. He licked his lips and pushed back his chair, making the legs scrape on the floor, loud enough that the louts in the corner looked at us.

"I can't—I'm not allowed—I mean, I shouldn't talk about the trials, Herr Doktor," he said, the words tripping over each other. "I had to, I mean…" He groped for the next word, then stopped and bit his lip. My heart began to beat faster. I reached out and put a restraining hand on his arm, leaning toward him.

"You knew Bernd," I said softly. "He was your friend." I felt safe in saying so; Bernd was everyone's friend. I squeezed his arm lightly. "He was my friend too. I only want to know, because you know, if it was something I did wrong in the design, something I should have foreseen…don't you see? I worry that it was my fault."

There was enough truth in this to touch him. He stared at me for a long moment, then swallowed convulsively and nodded once, then twice.

"I understand, Herr Doktor," he said, and took a deep breath, then looked furtively around the room.

"I signed an affidavit," he said, leaning close to me and speaking low and fast. "They made me say there were no problems, the new body had better stability, that it drove like it was on rails. But—" His lower lip was red and moist from being bitten, but he bit it again. "It was true, what I said—but the only time I drove it was a shakedown, a few days before the accident, an easy run; my orders were not to go above four thousand revs in fourth gear—and there was hardly any wind at all." He stopped to breathe, making up his mind whether to go on.

"Please," I whispered, looking into his eyes. They were pale blue, and full of tears.

"The wind-tunnel measurements—" he blurted. "I wasn't there, but I heard them talking, Herr Eberan and Herr Weber, two days later, on the track before the shakedown. They were arguing—they said the rear lift was lower than the earlier Streamliner's, much lower."

That jolted me. A lower rear lift was good for drag reduction, but with a center of pressure too close to the center of gravity—and that's just what they had, with the ice tank's positioning—low rear lift is a recipe for longitudinal instability.

I forced myself to let go of Hasse's arm and sat back a little, nodding and trying to look only grave and concerned, but I could feel my pulse beating in my ears.

"I see. Did they check for sidewind?" They must have…

Hasse nodded, feeling a little better now.

"It wasn't good, but Weber was telling Herr Eberan that because of the time pressure and it being Christmas, they hadn't been able to be very thorough. They were checking the wind at the track before I started—there really wasn't any, and I was glad about that, having heard them talk. I could tell they were—maybe not worried, exactly, but very cautious."

So they knew. They knew before the record run that the car was unstable—and they didn't test it in real racing conditions. Wind-tunnel data will tell you only so much, and a shakedown cruise will tell you only that the wheels don't fall off and the wiring is good.

They knew. And they went ahead and took the chance, because there wasn't time, and they didn't want to risk looking unready. Didn't want to lose face in front of the Mercedes. Didn't want to risk the chancellor's birthday gift.

"I see," I repeated mechanically. I took a deep breath of my own, and took my hand off his arm.

"I see," I said again. *"Danke."*

DESIGN NOTE 33: Stromlinienwagen 6.5 L
Radiator
The radiator is inactive, as it is supplanted by ice cooling. It should be equal in weight to the ice tank, however, so may be partially filled with water in order to achieve this. Hoses must therefore be detached and sealed.

It was late afternoon when I left the *bierstube,* and dark was already rising in the streets. Too late to visit Elly, I thought, making the excuse to myself. In fact, I needed some time alone before I spoke with her.

So now I knew why Eberan wouldn't talk to me. I could have taken a taxi—it was a long way home and it was beginning to rain—but I needed to walk, needed something physical to keep the rising anger in my belly under control.

"Schweine," I muttered under my breath, *"bastards,"* the words coming out in spurts of white, torn away by the wind. Wind. Unstable in a sidewind. The air vents, the ice tank, the shifted center of gravity, the downdraft, the sealed air intake…and they *knew.* They cut corners, they ignored all the testing protocols, they rushed things—and they killed Bernd Rosemeyer. For the sake of their pride.

I was trembling with rage, the handle of my cane slippery in my fist. I kept seeing the warped side panel, the air-vent plate, the torn-off fairings. A car caroming off the bridge, somersaulting twice, shedding pieces…and the smell of spilled fuel, the car's blood sharp in the wind. And Bernie, lying dead in the grass.

After a time, my blood cooled—it had to; I was soaked to the skin and shivering, my shoes squashing with every step

and the cold water welling between my toes. My thoughts
began to drift back to Elly. Should I tell her? And—perhaps
more important—what might she do if I did?

Go to Eberan and demand an admission of carelessness,
insist on his guilt and demand reparation for herself and little
Bernd? What reparation was possible for the loss of her husband, of a man like Bernd? I felt the loss of him myself like a
salted wound, a slow agony. For her...

More likely, I thought, she would go to the newspapers and
denounce Auto Union and Eberan in public. I was already
shivering, but that thought made me tremble. It would be a
huge scandal—and it was clear to me that this was exactly
what Auto Union feared, the reason why they had concealed
their tests (and the lack of them), why they'd had poor little
Hasse sign his affidavit.

Exposure might destroy Auto Union—and while I was
furious at them for what they'd done, I didn't want that. There
were too many people employed there, too many wonderful
things that had been done; I couldn't bear the thought of it all
being discredited, lost in a furor of accusation and scandal.

And it might destroy Elly too. Scandal was a double-edged
sword, and Eberan would fight back—maybe attempt to
blame Bernd for the accident.

Ludwig had told me only one thing that I hadn't learned or
heard already: when they'd prepared for the third run, the run
they weren't sure was necessary, there had been some fuss
about the wind, which had increased. And Bernd, smiling, had
waved off the crew's mixed concerns and suggestions, saying,
"Don't worry; I can figure it out on my own."

I can figure it out on my own. Those words could be twisted, taken as arrogance—I gave a small puff of a laugh; Bernie *was* arrogant, with the perfect confidence of a man who would walk off a cliff because he knows he can fly. But they could say all kinds of things about him, try to destroy his reputation... and if they did that, what would happen to Elly? If she and Bernie were no longer the hero and heroine of the Reich?

She was a woman of deep feelings, and certainly impulsive. But at the same time, she had a cool head; at the age of twenty-two, she'd crashed her plane in the Sahara, survived the crash, been rescued by a group of Tuareg tribesmen, and talked them into escorting her across the desert to Timbuktu—and eventually got word of her plight to the French authorities, who sent a two-seater airplane to collect her. In a way, she had the same arrogance that Bernie had had; they were well matched. But she had a child now.

I was freezing, shaking now with the cold, my toenails burning. Home was in sight, the tall pale blue building on Mariannenstrasse, its white window boxes winter bare. Home, the glowing stove, food. And sleep. I needed to sleep before I went to talk to Elly.

DESIGN NOTE 10.1 Stromlinienwagen 6.5 L [Dr. Porsche]
Body
Slight alteration to the 6.0 L body. See drawing (attached).

I rose late the next morning, both because I was tired—I still ached from the long walk and the shivering—and because I didn't want to go down until Aloisa had left to do her shopping. She'd been in bed when I came home, and while she'd turned to me, murmuring concern at my frigid skin and taking me to the comfort of her warm bosom, she'd been too much asleep to ask me where I'd been. One look at my face in the morning light, though...

I raised my chin, scraping the razor carefully up the side of my neck. I looked haunted in the mirror, eyes half sunk in my head.

After a little cheese toasted on bread and some coffee, I felt better. Sometime in the night, my mind had made itself up. Elly was Bernie's wife; she deserved to know what I knew. What she chose to do about it was up to her, and I would help her, no matter what she decided to do.

Her apartment was on Bergstrasse, a wide pleasant street lined with well-kept town houses with a small park nearby. The trees were black and bleak, but the weather had cleared and the sky was a hard pale blue.

The door was answered by a girl in an apron who bobbed an old-fashioned curtsy to me. That made me smile, and the wariness with which she'd eyed me—*I must look very bad*, I thought—melted enough for her to answer my request for Frau Rosemeyer.

"She went to the park," the girl said, pointing over my shoulder. "I said it was too cold for the baby, but she said he was wrapped up like a strudel and it would be all right." A touch of disapproval in her voice, but clearly no one could argue with Elly if her mind was made up. With a small qualm, I bowed to her in thanks and went down the steps to the park.

I had crossed the street and was walking toward the gate when I saw a black car pull up before the house—one of the older classic Horch twelve-cylinders. I paused long enough to see a chauffeur in uniform get out and reach into the car for a basket ornamented with ribbons. He stopped for a moment as someone in the car said something to him, then nodded and bounded up the steps

The park was surrounded by a black iron palisade, and the gate was locked. I caught a flash of color through the trees, though, movement on the far side of the park, and I walked hastily around it, hoping to catch her.

The rattle of wheels on gravel led me to her; she was pushing a pram slowly along a path, head bent in thought. It was the maroon of the pram I had glimpsed through the trees; she wore a black coat and scarf, and her eyes, when she looked up at my greeting, were the color of the winter sky.

She bent over the pram to check that the child was covered, then came over to the fence where I was.

"Ferdinand. Do you want to come inside?" she asked. "You can walk round and I'll meet you at the gate—or perhaps it's better to go back to the house?"

"No, no," I said. "Here will be fine, if you're not too cold?" No possibility of being overheard here.

She shook her head with a sort of indifference.

I grasped the iron railings with both hands—I'd thought to wear gloves, fortunately—and told her, as briefly as I could, what I'd found out and what Hasse had told me.

She listened, head bent so I could see only her mouth and chin under the curve of the hat she wore. The lips pressed tight at some points, relaxed at others, but the chin stayed strong. When I stopped speaking, she didn't move. I waited for what seemed a long time, my hands growing colder.

"Elly," I said at last, quietly. "You don't need to decide now. What to do, I mean—if…if you want to do anything," I added quickly. "Just…know I will stand by you."

She did look up at that and met my eyes directly. They were red-rimmed and tired, but not weeping, and the strong features of her face were carved deep with sorrow. But that chin was still strong.

"Ferdie," she said softly and reached out to touch my gloved hand, very briefly. "Thank you. You are our friend, our good friend, and I'm grateful to you. Some people say it's better not to know too much, but I've never thought so."

She paused, but I could tell she wasn't through, and I waited. On the far side of the park, I heard the throb of a twelve-cylinder motor; the big car that had stopped at her house was pulling away.

"You had a visitor," I said, nodding toward the fading sound. "Someone brought you a fancy basket."

That made her lips compress again and for the first time, a small light came into her eyes—not a pleasant light, though. She made a little snorting sound and tossed her head.

"Them," she said. "He's not been dead a month, and the courtship begins. There are half a dozen at least, and more to come, I'm sure."

That shocked me for a moment. I hadn't thought of it. But of course, a young widow, and a famous one, a person valuable for her fame…I was sufficiently taken aback by the situation that I missed what she said next.

"*Bitte?*" I said, and she looked at me sharp, like a governess.

"I said I won't do anything," she repeated. She saw my face, and her expression relaxed. "I'm grateful to know, Ferdinand— and so grateful for your friendship. But…" She stopped for a moment and looked at me with great penetration, as though she could see through me to the row of town houses behind me.

She turned round to the pram and bent, fumbled among the blankets, came out with a handbag. This she opened and took out a piece of paper, which she handed to me through the bars.

It was an envelope, folded in half. I spread it out; it was addressed to Bernd Rosemeyer et Ux—*et uxor;* that meant "and wife"—and the address in the upper corner was of the Chase Morgan Bank, New York City. The envelope was empty, and I looked up at her, bewildered.

She took a deep breath and let it out in a white wisp.

"We went to America last year, Bernie and I."

"Yes?"

"We opened a bank account in New York while we were there." She nodded at the envelope and waited for me to grasp the implication, which took only a moment.

"Oh," I said, realization hitting me like a blow in the stomach. They'd meant—maybe—to emigrate. To move to America. Leave Germany.

"Oh," she echoed with a mild irony. "Yes." She nodded again at the empty envelope. "The bank sends us a statement of the account each month. That one arrived a few days ago. I didn't feel up to doing anything about it, so I left it on the little desk in my bedroom. Yesterday, I found some energy at last, and began to tidy things up a little. That was still on the desk—but it was open, and empty."

I took hold of the iron railing with my free hand and felt the cold spread through my body.

"Your bedroom," I said. "Your maid…"

"No. I don't let her go in there. And—" She took the envelope from me and, with one brisk movement, tucked it back in her bag. "Why would she take such a thing?"

Who would? Someone who recognized that that paper was a statement of intent as well as money and had taken it as evidence.

"One of your—your suitors?" I managed.

"Perhaps. Maybe one of their minders; the suitors"—her mouth twisted at the word—"the ones who belong to the party always bring at least one, maybe two or three men with them. Like a knight in the old times, coming with squires to show how important he is."

She'd meant that as a wry joke, and I smiled a little in response. It was true; all the high-ranking Nazis trailed retinues in their wake.

"Don't worry about me, Ferdinand." She leaned forward, her eyes intense, and wrapped her own bare hand around my gloved one where it grasped the fence. "They won't harm me, and they can't force me to marry. But I have family here…" Her other hand rose, gesturing to the world outside the palisades. "My parents, my brother, my grandmother…and of course…" She glanced over her shoulder at the pram and its snug bundle. The child—quite invisible—wore a woolly knit cap with an enormous red bobble on it that trembled in the slight wind.

"If I left—" Another deep breath. "Well. There's nothing to leave for, is there? Not without Bernie." She closed her eyes briefly, then opened them.

"But if I were to go to the newspapers, if you and I were to tell what you've found out—it might damage Eberan and the others…God damn their souls!" she burst out. She stood with her fists clenched, trembling. I said nothing, and after a moment, she got hold of herself again.

"It might," she said, her words clipped off like bits of wire. "But it might damage me and my family a lot more. The newspapers accusing me of betraying Germany, planning to leave, making up stories. Auto Union has a relationship with the Reich; they wouldn't suffer me to slander them. Or you."

There was a long silent moment between us. I coughed and bowed my head.

"You're right," I said quietly. "If you should change your mind, though..."

"I won't," she said, and she reached for the handle of the pram. "Bernie never looked back—I won't either."

She put both hands on the handle and pulled the pram to turn it, to head to her house. She looked at me then, one last time, her eyes now dark in the shadow of her hat.

"But that doesn't mean I will ever forget. I won't do that either, Ferdie. Good-bye."

I stayed there for some time, long after she had disappeared; I heard the clang of the gate on the other side of the park.

I knew enough.

It was my car. And Bernie was my friend.

Author's Note: This story is really a piece of historical narrative rather than historical fiction. The events are factual, taken from primary sources of the time and from analyses published after the accident. The technical details are taken mostly from Aldo Zano's thorough analysis of the record attempt and the Stromlinienwagen's engineering details. Most of the people mentioned are real people, and their backgrounds, positions, and relationships are drawn from biographical accounts. Only the inquiries undertaken by Dr. Porsche and Elly Beinhorn are fictional. I am deeply indebted to Doug Watkins, both for the original suggestion for the story and for the research material that gave it its bones.

WHIPPERWILL AND BACK

By Patterson Hood

CHARLIE ALWAYS DROVE way too fast. The car was overpowered and rusted, and the road twisted and wound through red-clay foothills and pine thickets. Lester was slouched down in the passenger seat, rolling a joint with one hand while exclaiming and gesturing wildly with the other. They both had Milwaukee's Best cans between their legs as the car tried to hang on to every curve. There was a cooler with a bunch more Milwaukee's Best cans on some ice just behind the driver's seat and every so often Lester and Charlie would throw their empties out the window, Charlie would say, "Lester, grab another Beast," and Lester would grab two more, open them, and light another joint. It could have been just any Thursday night, or any other night, for that matter. With one difference.

"I ain't heard Dale lately. Think we ought to check on him?"

Lester's question didn't seem to register with Charlie at first and he just kept on driving. Perhaps he didn't hear him, as Thin Lizzy's *Live and Dangerous* was blasting really loud from the Craig PowerPlay eight-track, that part where "Cowboy

Song" runs straight into "The Boys Are Back in Town," which normally Lester would know better than to interrupt. It had been a couple of hours since they had left the Zippy Mart and initially everything had gone fairly smooth. They were friendly with Dale. Not best buds or nothing, but he always had good dope and would let them shoplift if no one else was in the store and only occasionally asked for a kickback. He was stuck way out of town and he didn't really know anybody out there and it got lonely and spooky whenever he had to pull that seven-to-three shift, so he was generally glad to see Lester and Charlie come in, even if it was just to steal something. Dale would call the cops thirty or so minutes later and say some "colored kid" had driven off with some gas, might have shoplifted too. Then he'd describe a customer from earlier in the evening. This was before they installed cameras everywhere, back when you could get away with stuff like that.

The Chevy Chevelle SS was nearly ten years old and was pretty much ragged out. It had originally been a dark metallic green but now had oxidized to a color somewhere between piss and rust. It burned oil and leaked some too, needed new tires, and Charlie had to pump the brakes a little before every stop sign. The stereo was the only thing fully working on it and it had seen better days. Charlie had only a few tapes, but they all were what the ad on TV referred to as Freedom Rock and he usually ended up playing Thin Lizzy anyway so it didn't matter.

Charlie was small-framed but strong with muscular arms and close-cropped dark curly hair. He had a chipped front tooth and the blackest of eyes but he always looked like he was smiling or about to.

Lester was slightly taller and much skinnier than Charlie. He had greasy hair, fair skin, and peach fuzz on his upper lip like a boy five years younger. His ragged jeans were slightly too big for his thin frame, and his Willie Nelson T-shirt was faded. He was more or less a permanent part of Charlie's passenger seat, staring out the windshield and as agreeable as a dog. Charlie could always count on Lester for a yes vote to whatever he suggested, and Lester could always count on Charlie to drive and have a cooler full of beer and some weed. Maybe even a little blow. What the hell else was there to do?

Charlie had bought his Chevelle secondhand from the mama of its original owner, Jimmy Ray, who had died in the passenger seat of a buddy's Camaro in a crash a few years earlier. Jimmy Ray's mama liked Charlie since he'd helped put out her aunt's kitchen fire, and she couldn't stand looking at that car anymore. She practically gave it to him just to get it out of the driveway. It was still in pretty good shape when Charlie got it, but being a Chevy, its door handles kept coming off and the roof liner kept falling down and the suspension had become mushy and the steering loose. But it always started when he turned the square key. It would flat-out shit and git, as they say, and that big 396 had the greatest low-rumble sound in the world. It guzzled gas, which by 1979 had become a little expensive after the oil embargo, and the fuel gauge didn't work anymore so Charlie had to keep it topped off, but he loved that car more than anything in the world and always talked about what a classic it would someday be and how he was going to one day get the cash to fix it up to showroom condition and keep it that way. Besides, Charlie could get rubber from twenty miles an hour, and once he'd gotten it up to a hundred and twenty-five going across the Natchez Trace Bridge. He named it Jimmy Ray after its late original owner and he and Lester liked nothing better than hauling ass down some backcountry roads with the windows down and the stereo blasting and the wet summer air blowing through their hair.

"Think we should check on Dale?" Lester asked again.

They pulled over to the side of the Gunwaleford Road and Charlie handed Lester the oval key and he got out and opened up the trunk. Dale was lying in there amid the spare tire and some clutter. He was tied up with a hankie loosened at his mouth like a gag that no one had bothered to tighten. His eyes were rolled back in his head and he appeared to be dead.

"Oh shit, Charlie," Lester just kept saying over and over.

Charlie got out and stood next to Lester, staring into the trunk but not saying a thing as Lester started stammering the way he always did when he got excited or scared.

After a while Charlie closed the trunk and got back in. Lester was still standing outside carrying on about Dale's not breathing until finally Charlie yelled for him to get the fuck back in the car. Once Lester got in, Charlie pulled out slowly and carefully began driving toward Whipperwill.

Charlie had been driving drunk for over a decade without getting so much as a scratch on the car's paint job. He had a survival instinct that made him drive more carefully the drunker he became. An innate ability to always land on his feet in whatever situation. As a kid he had started literally playing with fire and at one point nearly burned down his junior high school, but even then he was able to squeak out without actually getting caught. Then, a few years later, he figured out how to turn his pyromania into an asset, becoming the youngest guy at the Tuscumbia Volunteer Fire Department and exhibiting a fearlessness that made him a hero and earned him a grudging respect from everyone on the civil-service boards of the two-county area.

Once, when he was in his early twenties, Charlie got them to lower him down from a fire ladder on a rope into the middle of the inferno that totally destroyed a local car dealership, Chris Blake Pontiac. Just Charlie and the fire hose amid the smoke, heat, and chaos. He fought his way from the middle of hell to the sidewalk outside. The building collapsed anyway, only moments later, in fact, but Charlie's reputation was made as a fearless motherfucker who could be counted on to do whatever crazy shit that was asked and not expect anything in return but maybe a blind eye turned from the way he'd chosen to live his life. He usually didn't hurt anybody, or at least not in a way that would call for paperwork and questions being asked, so Charlie was all right.

Charlie was able to parlay his good graces with the local law enforcement into a sweet job running errands, mostly carrying beer and money, for the various bootleggers that were so prominent in the area. The Tennessee Valley was all dry back in those days. To buy legal beer you had to drive up to the Tennessee state line, and to get liquor you had to drive an hour each way to Savannah, Tennessee, or Minor Hill. This opened the doors for a slew of bootleggers to sell beer and liquor, at a greatly inflated price, to the general populace. Enough palms were greased with enough cash for the cops to not ask questions and as long as nothing happened that brought undo attention to the situation or required extra paperwork for the cops, no one was arrested, much less prosecuted or convicted.

Lester never finished school or got around to taking his GED but he could roll a perfect joint with one hand and never questioned Charlie's authority over him. If Charlie was crazy, Lester was a little bit crazier. Charlie's impulses seemed to form a straight line between where he was and where he wanted to be whereas Lester's seemed to be based on whatever whim he thought of at any given time, sometimes likely to be inspired by something he saw in a movie or on TV. It was Charlie who first suggested robbing the Zippy Mart where Dale worked. Lester didn't have a job or any money of his own and Charlie thought it'd be nice for Lester to pull a little more weight for once. It was Lester who thought it would be a better idea if they tied Dale up and put him in the trunk. They would take him out to Whipperwill and leave him there with enough of the take in his pocket that he wouldn't feel compelled to turn them in.

When they pulled up to the store, only Dale's car was in the parking lot. They could see him standing behind the counter, leaning on the cigarette rack and watching something on the TV. Lester began filling up Jimmy Ray's tank and Charlie went inside. By the time Lester went in, Charlie was holding a bag full of money. He and Dale were both laughing about something. There was way more money than expected in the register since the day-shift lady had had a doctor's appointment and had to leave early without doing the deposit. Dale had already been there since midafternoon and was bored and itchy so he was kinda glad to see them.

It was surprisingly easy for Charlie to talk Dale into letting them tie him up and put him in the trunk. Charlie promised to cut him in on the take and said they'd make it look convincing. Boys like Dale and Lester looked up to guys like Charlie.

They took the money, some smokes, a tank of gas, and some beef jerky and left with the lights still on and door unlocked. The Zippy Mart was out past Barton, near the Mississippi line, and probably one of the most remote convenience stores in the state. Dale had been begging his boss to have a second person work the late shift with him for ages but the asshole was too cheap to do so. A previous employee of the late shift had been shot in the head. They'd found him tied up in the office the next morning, blood all over the place. It was in all of the papers. The guy that did it was on death row but that didn't bring anybody back. Dale figured that getting into Charlie's trunk would be a way for him to pick up a little extra dough and maybe it would teach his boss a lesson.

All was smooth until they got to Whipperwill, which was where kids would go back then to show off their fearlessness by jumping off the cliffs into the Tennessee River. Some of the higher bluffs were probably forty feet or more, and you could break your neck if you landed wrong, or you could hit a log or one of the rocks that jutted out. About once every couple of years some teenager would get killed or paralyzed, which only seemed to make it more attractive to young rednecks who felt they were invincible and had something to prove. The trail from the road to the cliffs was littered with beer cans and used rubbers. Every so often the cops would crack down on it and police the place, but times were hard and they couldn't really spare the manpower to actually shut it down, and besides, many of the cops themselves had come of age jumping off those cliffs and banging little redneck girls in those woods. Usually it would empty out by midnight or so, especially during the week, but on this night it was still unexpectedly crowded so they decided to keep driving around for a while, with Dale still tied up in the trunk. They would head up to the Line and get some more beer, then double back in a little while after it emptied out. Then it sort of slipped their minds.

Dale was most certainly alive when they got to Whipperwill the first time but now he appeared to be otherwise. Neither one of them were doctors, but Dale was unresponsive and didn't appear to be breathing. Lester couldn't find a pulse and started panicking and stuttering that way he would always do when he got nervous. Charlie just stood there, expressionless, casually lighting a cigarette and kind of staring off into space for a bit, then he closed the trunk and put the oval key in his pocket and got back in the car.

When Jimmy Ray started up, Lester got in and shut the door. "Emerald" was playing loud on the eight-track and Charlie drove slow and carefully toward Whipperwill. He figured they would be back at the cliffs in about ten more minutes.

Lester sat in the passenger seat rolling the joint and drinking another Beast. He was trying to calm his nerves but was shaking so bad he was spilling the weed, which was mostly seeds and stems anyway, onto his lap. He didn't want Charlie, who always seemed so cool no matter what the situation, to see him so unnerved. He tried to think happier thoughts, but his mind kept returning to his time in reform school and being raped in the shower when he was fourteen and pretty much weekly afterward until he eventually found a sort of sad acceptance of his situation and to how alone he had been and how he'd never really had any friends until Charlie took him under his wing a couple of years after Lester was released. He downed his Beast and opened another. He was officially drunk now, but still shaking. He wished he had something harder.

Both of them were what folks around there referred to as poor white trash. Opportunities were few and far between in this part of the country even in the best of times, and the late seventies were far from that. So much of the local economy was built around the Ford plant, and now, better-built and more economical Toyotas and Datsuns were what was selling, and Ford was saying they were gonna close down the local operation in a couple of years. That factory was where boys who wouldn't be going to college could find decent-paying work, and if Ford wasn't hiring, no one else was about to take up the slack. Weed and illegal liquor were about the only steady jobs left that guys like that could count on.

They pulled up to Whipperwill and sure enough it had emptied out. It was an especially dark night with clouds obscuring what little moon there was. It was hot and muggy and no sign of a breeze at all. Just a dark stillness that added another level of creepy to the situation. Charlie turned off the engine, put the square key in his pocket, walked around to the trunk, and opened it with the oval key. Dale lay there, still and lifeless. Charlie leaned in and untied the ropes that were binding his hands, noting that he was still warm, perhaps from the heat of the exhaust pipe being so close to the trunk.

"Wh-wh-why'd you untie him?"

Charlie was trying not to be annoyed with him.

"If we leave him tied up, there'll be too many questions. We don't want anybody saying *kidnap*. We need to keep this simple so the cops don't have to work too hard. We just need them to think he did something stupid, panicked, and jumped off the cliff."

"Wh-wh-wh-wh-what about his car?"

"I'm still trying to figure that one out. You want to keep stuttering all night or you want to help me lift this heavy fucker out of my trunk? Oh, and get your gun."

Lester reached under the passenger seat and pulled out a loaded snub-nose Colt Cobra .38 that had belonged to his older brother before he died. It was bundled up in a dirty towel, which Lester unwrapped. He stood there for a moment staring down at it but Charlie reached out for it and Lester handed it over to him without a moment's thought.

Charlie nonchalantly said, "You never know," as he stuck the gun in the back pocket of his jeans.

They then heaved Dale out of the trunk, pulled him into some brush, and closed the trunk. Charlie put the oval key into his pocket. Then he stuffed the gun down the waistband of Dale's jeans.

"I c-c-c-can't go back to jail."

"Goddamn it, Lester, I can't hear myself think. Dale got in over his head and died. Dead happens all the time."

They began pulling Dale through the grass and brush and down the trail to the cliffs of Whipperwill. He wasn't a big guy, but he was bigger than either of them and the deadweight made him seem heavier than they would have thought. By the time they got to the cliffs, they were both panting and covered with sweat. Up there, with the river wide below them, there was a slight breeze that would have felt good if either had been in the mood to notice.

Charlie got behind Dale and lifted him up by his under-arms. "I want you to hit him a couple of times. We need to make this look like he put up a little bit of a fight."

This might not have made sense to Lester if he'd thought about it, but Lester never questioned anything Charlie said so he hit Dale twice, very hard, in the face. Blood spattered from his nose and lips, and Lester cut his knuckle on one of Dale's teeth.

Lester stood there, holding his sore knuckles and looking down. "Fuck," he said, without a trace of stammer. Tears welled up in his eyes and he felt very much like vomiting. When he looked up, Charlie had Lester's gun in Dale's hand pointed straight at him. It took Lester a few moments to figure out what was going on. Lester tried to make eye contact with Charlie but he was staring at his chest without any hint of expression. Lester opened his mouth to say something but nothing came out but his last breath.

The shot rang loud, echoing down the river. It hit him straight in the heart and Lester fell over dead in the clearing. The gun dropped onto the ground and then Charlie dragged Dale to the edge of the cliff and hoisted him up and over. He heard a faint splash, then walked over to make sure Lester was dead.

Lester was lying there, his Willie Nelson T-shirt soaked in blood and a trickle coming out of his mouth. His eyes were staring straight up and Charlie turned him over. He pulled Lester's wallet from his back pocket and took most of the money out of it, then put the wallet back. He put the oval key in Lester's front pocket. He would miss Lester's company but now wasn't the moment to be getting sentimental. He would walk back to his house and in the morning call the police and report his car missing.

Charlie didn't waste any time. The last thing he needed was for someone to see him out there. He took smokes and his personal effects out of the car, stuck the Thin Lizzy tape in his back pocket, and put the square key in the ignition. He knew it would seem strange for Lester to have stolen Charlie's car like that, but the cops knew he had always been trouble and no one would want to pull Charlie any deeper into it than necessary. White-trash boys were always killing each other around here and with everyone neatly dead, there wouldn't be too much paperwork, no messy trials or investigations.

Charlie began walking back toward town. It would take him a couple of hours and he would need to stay off of the main roads and not be seen. He would have plenty of time before the sun came up, and no one would discover the bodies until later the next day. If everything went smoothly, he could get home, get a little sleep, and report his car missing early the next morning. He often left the key in the ignition because no one would steal a piece of shit like Jimmy Ray anyways. He never locked his doors because he didn't want anyone breaking his windows looking for drugs. The cops would just figure that Lester went a little crazy, took the car, robbed Dale and the Zippy Mart, and then it all went wrong and they killed each other. Charlie had never much been one for making plans or working things through in advance, but he'd always been able to think on his feet, and, so far at least, he'd always been able to get through whatever landed in his path. Some folks just survive, no matter what. As Charlie walked down the road, his mind cleared and it all seemed to make sense and he relaxed, knowing he wasn't going to get into much trouble. This was all goddamned Lester's fault anyway, as it was his dumb idea to put Dale in the trunk in the first place.

The walk was slow but peaceful. The night was dark and way too quiet but since it was now getting really late it was starting to cool down a little. The lack of moonlight made him less likely to be seen walking alone in the night. Every so often he'd hear a car coming or see headlights and he'd step off the road into some woods. He'd hear the whoosh of the car going by or maybe a song from the stereo blasting, then see the honeysuckle glowing red from the taillights. When the coast was clear, Charlie would step back onto the road and resume his walk.

It was still dark when Charlie got into town, the only light coming from a billboard for the latest wet/dry referendum that was coming up this fall. Every so often they would bring it up for another vote and the local churches would come out in force, buying up TV and billboard ads to make sure that legal sales weren't allowed. The churches profited from this as tithes were always high during election season and it was easy to stir up the old folks with tales of all of the drunken debauchery that would ensue if liquor were ever legal there. The package stores and honky-tonks up at the Tennessee state line, or the Line, as everyone called it, would get into the action, donating tons of money to the bigger churches, as legal sales down there would wipe out their business. The bootleggers and the redneck mafia that controlled them would also get into the action, as everyone wanted to protect the status quo.

As Charlie got to his neighborhood, the sky was taking on the first glimmers of light and echoing with sounds of the morning birds. Charlie's stomach was rumbling and he realized that he hadn't really eaten anything since a late lunch the day before and now his buzz was diminished and fast being replaced with the first pangs of what would surely be a terrible hangover. It had been a long night and Charlie was pretty exhausted but wired from all of the excitement. His mind started playing tricks on him. What if Dale wasn't really dead at all and was just unconscious from the carbon monoxide in the trunk? Maybe all of this was some kind of fever dream or overreaction. His mind was racing and he knew he needed a beer, maybe a joint, to try to turn it all down so he could get some shut-eye before having to deal with cops and questions. He always dreaded dealing with the police and had to make sure that he kept his story straight, but knew that it would all work out okay. They all thought he was some kind of hero. He knew how to be cool in the fire.

Folks were always saying that Lester would end up dead somewhere anyway. Charlie could feel himself becoming resigned to the notion. Some dudes just don't make it. Getting all weepy wasn't gonna bring him back now. Just bad breaks. Dale too. Charlie and Dale weren't really buds, but he'd always liked him okay. You meet those guys along the way. You have some good times, then you move on. Life gets tough sometimes. It was always rough around those parts.

As he rounded the curve to his house, there was Jimmy Ray parked, just there under the streetlight in front of his house like he always left it. The 1970 redesigned Chevelle SS had such beautiful lines. She needed a lot of work but he'd get around to it one of these days.

Charlie stood there for a bit, taking it in. His mind slowed and he was suddenly totally calm and relaxed. He felt like he was out of his body, looking down and seeing the whole scene, as if in a movie. His mind felt strangely rational and deliberate, the way he would get when he started those fires that made him a hero. The way a hunter feels as he draws a bead on his kill.

The air had developed a slight chill now and he thought he could smell a faint trace of smoke in the pines. The cooler was still in the back and the hood was still warm. He noticed that the square GM key was not in the ignition. He wondered what, if anything, might be in the trunk and wished he had the oval key to check.

Charlie's house was dark and still but his door was standing wide open. He lit a cigarette and inhaled deeply, threw the match down on the ground, and walked toward the front porch.

DRIVING TO GERONIMO'S GRAVE

by Joe R. Lansdale

We ought never to do wrong when people are looking.

—Mark Twain

I HADN'T EVEN been good and awake for five minutes when Mama came in and said, "Chauncey, you got to drive on up to Fort Sill, Oklahoma, and pick up your uncle Smat."

I was still sitting on the bed, waking up, wearing my night-dress, trying to figure which foot went into what shoe, when she come in and said that. She had her dark hair pushed up on her head and held in place with a checkered scarf.

"Why would I drive to Oklahoma and pick up Uncle Smat?"

"Well, I got a letter from some folks got his body, and you need to bring it back so we can bury it. This Mrs. Wentworth said they were gonna leave it in the chicken house if nobody comes for it. I wrote her back and posted the letter already telling her you're coming."

"Uncle Smat's dead?" I said.

"We wouldn't want to bury him otherwise," Mama said, "though it took a lot longer for him to get dead than I would have figured, way he honky-tonked and fooled around with disreputable folks. Someone knifed him. Stuck him like a pig at one of them drinking places, I figure."

"I ain't never driven nowhere except around town," I said. "I don't even know which way is Oklahoma."

"North," Mama said.

"Well, I knew that much," I said.

"Start in that direction and watch for signs," she said. "I'm sure there are some. I got your breakfast ready, and I'll pack you some lunch and give you their address, and you can be off."

Now this was all a fine good morning, me hardly knowing who Uncle Smat was, and Mama not really caring that much about him, Smat being my dead daddy's brother. She had cared about Daddy plenty, though, and she had what you could call family obligation toward Uncle Smat. As I got dressed she talked.

"It isn't right to leave a man, even a man you don't know so well, lying out in a chicken house with chickens to peck on him. And there's all that chicken mess too. I dreamed last night a chicken snake crawled over him."

I put on a clean work shirt and overalls and some socks that was sewed up in the heels and toes, put on and tied my shoes, slapped some hair oil on my head, and combed my hair in a little piece of mirror I had on the dresser.

Next, I packed a tow sack with some clothes and a few odds and ends I might need. I had a toothbrush and a small jar of baking soda and salt for tooth wash. Mama was one of the few in our family who had all her teeth, and she claimed that was because she used a brush made from hair bristles and she used that soda and salt. I believed her, and both me and my sister followed her practice.

Mama had some sourdough bread, and she gave that to me, and she filled a couple of my dad's old canteens with water, put a blanket and some other goods together for me. I loaded them in another good-size tow sack and carried it out to the Ford and put the bag inside the turtle hull.

In the kitchen, I washed up in the dishpan, toweled off, and sat down to breakfast, a half a dozen fried eggs, biscuits, and a pitcher of buttermilk. I poured a glass of milk and drank it, and then I poured another and ate along with drinking the milk.

Mama, who had already eaten, sat at the far end of the table and looked at me.

"You drive careful, now, and you might want to stop somewhere and pick some flowers."

"I'm picking him up, not attending his funeral," I said.

"He might be a bit stinky, him lying in a chicken coop and being dead," Mama said. "So I'm thinking the flowers might contribute to a more pleasant trip. Oh, I tell you what. I got some cheap perfume I don't never use, so you can take that with you and pour it on him, you need to."

I was chewing on a biscuit when she said this.

I finished chewing fast as I could, said, "Now wait a minute. I just got to thinking on this good. I'm picking him up in the car, and that means he's going to go in the backseat, and I see how he could have grown a mite ripe, but Mama, are you telling me he ain't going to be in a coffin or nothing?"

"The letter said he was lying out in the chicken coop,

where he'd been living with the chickens, having to only pay a quarter a week and feed the chickens to be there, and one morning they came out to see why he hadn't gathered the eggs and brought them up—that also being part of his job for staying in the coop—and they found him out there, colder than a wedge in winter. He'd been stabbed, and he had managed to get back to the coop, where he bled out. Just died quietly out there with their chickens. They didn't know what to do with him at first, but they found a letter he had from his brother; that would be your father"—she added that like I couldn't figure it out on my own—"and there was an address on it, so they wrote us."

"They didn't move the body?"

"Didn't know what to do with it. They said in the letter they had sewed a burial shroud you can put him in; it's a kind of bag."

"I have to pour perfume on him, put him in a bag, and drive him home in the backseat of the car?"

"Reckon that's about the size of it. I don't know no one else would bother to go get him."

"Do I have to? Thinking on it more, I'm not sure it's such a good idea."

"'Course you got to go. They're expecting you."

"Write them a letter and tell them I ain't coming. They can maybe bury him out by the chicken coop or something."

"That's a mean thing to say."

"I didn't hardly know him," I said, "certainly not enough to perfume him, bag him up, and drive him home."

"You don't have to have known him all that well, he's family."

My little sister, Terri, came in then. She was twelve and had her hair cut straight across in front and short in back. She had on overalls with a work shirt and work boots. She almost looked like a boy. She said, "I was thinking I ought to go with you."

"You was thinking that, huh," I said.

"It might not be such a bad idea," Mama said. "She can read the map."

"I can read a map," I said.

"Not while you're driving," Mama said.

"I can pull over."

"This way, though," Mama said, "you can save some serious time, having her read it and point out things."

"He's been dead for near two weeks or so. I don't know how much pressure there is on me to get there."

"Longer you wait, the more he stinks," Terri said.

"She has a point," Mama said.

"Ain't they supposed to report a dead body? Them people found him, I mean? Ain't it against the law to just leave a dead fella lying around?"

"They done us a favor, Uncle Smat being family and all," Mama said. "They could have just left him, or buried him out there with the chickens."

"I wish they had," I said. "I made that suggestion, remember?"

"This way we can bury him in the cemetery where your daddy is buried," Mama said. "That's what your daddy would have wanted."

She knew I wasn't going to say anything bad that had to do with Daddy in any manner, shape, or form. I thought that was a low blow, but Mama, as they say, knew her chickens. She knew where I was the weakest.

"All right, then," I said, "I'm going to get him. But that car of ours has been driven hard and might not be much for a long trip. The clutch hangs sometimes when you press on it."

"That's a chance you have to take for family," Mama said.

I grumbled something, but I knew by then I was going.

"I'm going too," Terri said.

"Oh hell, come on, then," I said.

"Watch your cussing," Mama said. "Daddy wouldn't like that either."

"All he did was cuss," I said.

"Yeah, but he didn't want you to," she said.

"I think I'm gonna cuss," I said. "My figuring is, Daddy would have wanted me to be good at it, and that takes practice."

"I ain't forgot how to whip your ass with a switch," Mama said.

Now it was figured by Mama that it would take us two days to get to the Wentworths' house and chicken coop if we drove fast and didn't stop to see the sights and such, and then two days back. As we got started out early morning, we had a pretty good jump on the first day.

The clutch hung a few times but seemed mostly to be cooperating, and I ground the gears only now and again, but that was my fault, not the car's, though in the five years we had owned it, it had been worked like a stolen mule. Daddy drove that car all over the place looking for spots of work. His last job had been for the WPA, and we seen men working those jobs as we drove along, digging out bar ditches and building walls for what I reckoned would be schools or some such. Daddy used to say it was mostly busywork, but it paid real money, and real money spent just fine.

Terri had the map in her lap, and from time to time she'd look at it, say, "You're doing all right."

"Of course I am," I said. "This is the only highway to Marvel Creek. When we need the map is when we get off the main road and onto them little routes back in there."

"It's good to make sure you don't get veered," Terri said.

"I ain't getting veered," I said.

"Way I figure it, it's gonna take three days to get there, or most near a full three days, not two like Mama said."

"You figured that, did you?"

"I reckoned in the miles and how fast the car is going, if that speedometer is right, and then I put some math to it, and I come up with three days. I got an A in math."

"Since it's the summer, I reckon you've done forgot what math you learned," I said.

"I remember. Three days at this pace is right, and this is about as fast as you ought to go. Slowing wouldn't hurt a little. As it is, we blowed a tire, they wouldn't find nothing but our clothes in some bushes alongside the road, and they'd be full of shit."

End of that day we come near the Oklahoma border. It was starting to get dark, so I pulled us over and down a little path, and we parked under a tree for the night. We had some egg sandwiches Mama had made, and we ate them. They had gotten kind of soggy, but it was that or wishful thinking, so we ate them and drank some water from the canteens.

We threw a blanket on the ground and laid down on that and looked up through the tree limbs at the stars.

"Ever wonder what's out there?" Terri said.

"I read this book once, about this fella went to Mars. And there was some green creatures there with four arms."

"No joke?"

"No joke."

"Must have been a good book."

"It was," I said. "And there was four-armed white apes, and regular-looking people too, only they were red-skinned."

"Did they have four arms too?"

"No. They were like us, except for the red skin."

"That's not as good," Terri said. "I'd like to have had me four arms, if I was one of them, and otherwise looked regular."

"You wouldn't look regular with four arms," I said.

"I could stand it," Terri said. "I could pick up a lot of things at once."

When we woke up the next morning, my back hurt considerable. I had stretched the blanket out on an acorn, and it had stuck me all night. I come awake a few times during the night and was going to pull back the blanket and move it, but I was too darn tired to move. In the morning, though, I wished I had. I felt like I had been shot with an arrow right above my belt line.

Terri, however, was as chipper as if she had good sense. She had some boiled eggs in the package Mama had ended up giving her after it was decided she was going, and we had one apiece for breakfast and some more canteen water.

After wrapping up the blanket, we climbed back in the car and started out again, drove on across the line and into Oklahoma, going over the Red River, which wasn't really all that much of a river. At that time of the year, at least where we crossed, it wasn't hardly no more than a muddy trickle, though as we went over the bridge, I could see down a distance to where it was wider and deeper-looking.

We come to a little town called Hootie Hoot, which seemed to me to be a bad name for most anything, and there was one gas pump outside a little store there, and by the door going into the store was a sign that said they was looking for a tire-and-rim man. We could see the gas in the big jug on top of the pump, so we knew there was plenty, and we pulled up to it. Couple other stations we had passed were out of gas.

After we had sat there awhile, an old man with bushy white hair wearing overalls so faded they was near white as his hair came out of the station. He had a big red nose and looked like he had just got out of bed. We stood outside the car while he filled the tank.

"They say the Depression has done turned around," he said. "But if it did, it darn sure didn't turn in this direction."

"No, sir," I said.

"Ain't you a little young to be out driving the roads?" he said.

"Not that young," I said.

He eyed me some. "I guess not. You children on an errand?"

"We are," I said. "We're going to pick up my uncle Smat."

"Family outing?"

"You could say that."

"So we will," he said.

"We might want something from the store too," I said.

"All right, then," he said.

Me and Terri went inside, and he hung up the gas nozzle and trailed after us.

I didn't have a lot of money, a few dollars Mama had given me for gas and such, but I didn't want another soggy egg sandwich or a boiled egg. I bought some Vienna sausages, some sardines, and a box of crackers, and splurged on Coca-Colas for the two of us. I got some shelled and salted peanuts to pour into the Coca-Colas, bought four slices of bread, two cuts of bologna, and two fat cuts of rat cheese. The smell of that cheese made me seriously hungry; it was right smart in aroma, and my nose hairs tingled.

We paid up, and I pulled the car away from the pump and on around beside the store. We sat on the bumper and made us a sandwich from the bread, bologna, and cheese. It was a lot better than those soggy egg sandwiches Mama had made us, and though we had two more of them, they had reached a point where I considered them turned, and I planned on throwing them out on the road before we left.

That's when a ragged-looking fellow come up the road to the store and stopped when he seen us. He beat the dust off the shoulders and sides of his blue suit coat. His gray hat looked as if a goat had bitten a hunk out of the front of it. The suit he was wearing had been nice at one time, but it was worn shiny in spots and hung on him like a circus tent. His shoe toes flapped when he walked like they were trying to talk. He said, "I hate to bother you children, but I ain't ate in a couple days, nothing solid anyway, and was wondering you got something to spare?"

"We got some egg sandwiches," Terri said. "You can have both of them."

"That would be right nice," said the ragged man.

He came over smiling. Up close, he looked as if he had been boiled in dirt, his skin was so dusty from walking along the road. One of his nose holes was smaller than the other. I hadn't never seen nobody like that before. It wouldn't have been all that noticeable, but he had a way of tilting his head back when he talked.

Terri gave him the sandwiches. He opened up the paper they was in, laid them on the hood of our car, took hold of one, and started to wolf it down. When he had it about ate, he said, "That egg tastes a mite rubbery. You ain't got nothing to wash it down?"

"We could run you a bath if you want, and maybe we could polish your shoes for you," Terri said. "But we ain't got nothing to wash down that free sandwich."

The dusty man narrowed his eyes at Terri, then gathered himself.

"I didn't mean to sound ungrateful," he said.

"I don't think you give a damn one way or the other," Terri said.

"Look here," I said. "I got the last of this Coca-Cola; you don't mind drinking after me, you can have that. It's got a few peanuts in it."

He took the Coca-Cola and swigged some. "Listen here, could you spare a few other things, some clothes, some more food? I could give you a check."

"A check?" Terri said. "What would it be good for?"

The man gave her a look that was considerably less pleasant than a moment ago.

"We don't want no check," Terri said. "If we had something to sell, and we don't, we'd want cash money."

"Well, I ain't got no cash money."

"There you are, then," Terri said. "A check ain't nothing but a piece of paper with your name on it."

"It represents money in the bank," said the man.

"It don't represent money we can see, though," Terri said.

"That's all right," I said. "Here, you take this dollar and go in there and buy you something with it. That's my last dollar."

It wasn't my last dollar, but when I pulled it out of my pocket, way he stared at it made me nervous.

"I'll take it," he said. He started walking toward the store. After a few steps, he paused and looked back at us. "You was right not to take no check from me, baby girl. It wouldn't have been worth the paper it was written on. And let me tell you something. You ought to save up and buy yourself a dress and some hair bows, a dab of makeup, maybe take a year or two of charm lessons."

He went on in the store, and I hustled us up, bringing what was left of our sandwiches with us and getting into the car.

"Why you in such a hurry?" Terri said as I drove away.

"Something about that fella bothers me," I said. "I think he's trouble."

"I don't know how much trouble he is," Terri said, "but I darn sure had him figured on that check. As for a dress and hair bows, he can kiss my ass. I wish him and all fools like him would die."

"You can't wish for all fools to die, Terri. That ain't right."

Terri pursed her lips. "I guess you're right. All them fools died, I'd be pretty lonely."

We went about twenty miles before the motor steamed up and I had to pull the Ford over. I picked a spot where there was a wide place in the road and stopped there and got out and put the hood up and looked under it like I knew what was going on. And I did, a little. I had developed an interest in cars, same as Daddy. He liked to work on them and said if he wasn't a farmer he'd like to fix engines. I used to go with him when he went outside to put water in the radiator and mess with the motor. Still, I wasn't what you'd call a mechanic.

"You done run it too long without checking the water," Terri said.

I gave her a hard look. "If you weren't here, I don't know what I'd think was wrong with it."

I got a rag out of the turtle hull, got some of our canteen water, and, using the rag, unscrewed the radiator lid. I had Terri stand back, on account of when I poured the water in, some hot, wet spray boiled up. Radiator was bone dry.

We got enough water in the car to keep going, but now we were out of water to drink. We poked along until I saw a creek running alongside the road and off into the woods. We pulled down a tight trail with trees on both sides, got out, and refilled the canteens from a clear and fast-running part of the creek. The water tasted cold and clean. I used the canteens to finish filling the radiator, and then we filled them for us to drink. I decided to take notice of this spot in case we needed it on the way back. While I was contemplating, Terri picked up a rock and zinged it sidearm into a tree and a red bird fell out of it and hit the ground.

"You see that," she said. "Killed it with one shot."

"Damn it, Terri. Wasn't no cause for that."

"I just wanted to."

"You don't kill things you don't eat. Daddy taught you that."

"I guess we could eat it."

"No. We're not eating any red birds. And don't you never kill another."

"All right," she said. "I didn't really know I'd hit it. But I'm pretty good with rocks. You know Gyp Martin? Well, he called me a little bitch the other day, and I hit him with a rock so hard it knocked him cold out."

"No it didn't."

"Yes it did. Sharon Miller was with me and seen it."

"Terri. You got to quit with the rocks. I mean, well, I give you this. That was a good shot. I don't know if I can even throw that far."

"I'd be surprised if you could," she said. "It's a natural talent for a rare few, but then you got to develop it."

We got to where we were going about dark that day.

"I thought you said three days," I said. "We made it in two, way Mama said."

"Guess I figured in too many stops and maybe a cow crossing the road or something."

"You did that, did you?"

"I was thinking you'd want to stop and see the sights, even though you said you didn't."

"What sights?"

"That turned out to be the problem. No sights."

"Terri, you are full of it, and I don't just mean hot wind."

The property was off the road, up in the woods, and not quite on top of a hill. We could see the house as we drove up the dirt drive. It was big but looked as if it might slip off the hill at any moment and tumble down on us. It was even more weathered than our home place. The outhouse out back was in better shape than where they lived.

As we come the rest of the way up the hill, we saw there were hog pens out to the side with fat black-and-white hogs in them. Behind that we could see a sizable run of henhouses. I had expected just one little henhouse, but these houses were plentiful and had enough chicken wire around them you could have used it to fence in Rhode Island.

I parked the Ford and we went up and knocked on the door. A man came to the door and looked at us through the screen. Then he came out on the porch. He had the appearance of someone that had been thrown off a train. His clothes were dirty and his hat was mashed in front. His body seemed about forty, but his face looked about eighty. He was missing all his teeth and had his jaw packed with tobacco. I figured he took that tobacco out, his face would collapse.

"Who are you?" he said and spit tobacco juice into a dry flower bed.

"The usual greeting is hello," Terri said.

I said, "Watch this, sir." And I gave Terri a kick in the leg.

"She had that coming," he said.

Terri hopped off the porch and leaped around yipping while I said, "We got a letter from your missus, and if we got the right place, our uncle Smat is in your chicken house."

"You're in the right place. When she quits hopping, step around to the side, start up toward the chicken houses, and you'll smell him. He ain't actually up in a henhouse no more. A goddang old dog got in there and got to him, dragged him through a hole in the fence, on up over the hill there, into them trees. But you can smell him strong enough, you'd think he was riding on your back. You'll find him."

"You didn't have to kick me," Terri said.

"I got a bit of a thrill out of it," said Mr. Wentworth. "I thought maybe you was a kangaroo."

Terri glared at him.

A woman wiping her hands with a dish towel and looking a lot neater than the man came to the door and stepped out on the porch.

"You take these kids to their uncle," she said to Mr. Wentworth.

"They can smell him," he said.

"You take them out there. I'll go with you."

She threw the dish towel inside the door, said, "But I got something you'll need."

Mrs. Wentworth went in the house and came out with a jar of VapoRub and had us dab a good wad under our noses so as to limit the smell of Uncle Smat. I was beginning to get a bit weak on the whole idea of a Christian burial for a man I'd never seen and by all accounts wasn't worth the water it'd take to put him out if he was on fire.

Dabbed up, the four of us started around the house and up the higher part of the hill. We passed the chicken coops, and this gave Mrs. Wentworth a moment for a bit of historical background concerning their time with Uncle Smat.

"He walked up one day and said he needed some work, most anything, so he could eat. So we put him out there chopping firewood, which he did a fair job of. We let him sleep in one of the coops that didn't have a lot of chickens in it. We couldn't have some unknown fella sleeping in the house. Next day he wanted more work, and so he ended up staying and taking care of the chickens, a job at which he was passable. Then one night he come up on the porch a-banging on the door, drunk as Cooter Brown. We wouldn't let him in and told him to go on out to the coop and sleep it off."

Mr. Wentworth picked up the story there. "Next morning he didn't come down to the back porch for his biscuits, so I went up and found him dead. He'd been knifed. I guess maybe he wasn't drunk after all."

"He was drunk, all right," Mrs. Wentworth said. "That might have killed some of the pain for him. Fact was, I don't know I'd ever heard anyone drunk as he was that was able to stand. I went through his clothes, and he had some serious money on him, and I won't lie to you, we took that as payment for his room and board."

"You robbed a dead man for sleeping in your chicken coop?" Terri said. "Why didn't you just take his shoes too?"

Mr. Wentworth cleared his throat. "Well, they *was* the same size as mine, and he didn't need them."

Wentworth lifted a foot and showed us a brown brogan.

"Them toes was real scuffed up," Mrs. Wentworth said, "so I put some VapoRub on them, rubbed it in good, and put a solid shine on them, took out some of that roughness."

"Damn," Terri said, looking down at the shoes on Mr. Wentworth's feet. "You did take his shoes."

"You're talking like a gun moll," Mrs. Wentworth said to Terri.

"I'm talking like someone whose uncle was robbed of money and shoes, that's how I'm talking," Terri said.

"It's all right," I said. "Let's see him."

As we walked along, Mr. Wentworth said, "When I come to look in on his body yesterday, he wasn't in the coop, but the coop was broke open, and something had dragged him off. It was either a pack of dogs or coyotes. They dragged him up there a ways and chewed off one of his feet. They got a toe off the other foot."

Terri looked at me. I gently shook my head.

Top of the hill near a line of woods, we seen his body. The smell was so strong, that VapoRub might as well have been water. I ain't never smelled nothing that bad in all my life. If at the bottom of the hill it had been strong as a bull, at the top it was a bull elephant.

Uncle Smat wasn't a sight for sore eyes, but he damn sure made the eyes sore. He was up next to a line of woods, half in a feed bag. It was over his head and tied around his waist with twine. His legs stuck out, and his pants legs was all ripped from animals dragging him out of the coop and on up where he lay. One foot, as Mr. Wentworth had said, was gnawed off, and Mr. Wentworth was right about that missing toe on the other foot; the big toe, if you're curious.

"So the man dies, you put a bag over his head and leave him with the chickens and write us a letter?" Terri said.

Mr. Wentworth nodded.

"Yeah," Terri said. "I guess there ain't no use denying any of that."

"It's been too hot for digging, and thing is we don't know him. We found his name and your address on a letter in his billfold, and we wrote your family. We figured we'd leave the rest to his kin."

I went over and untied the twine around his waist and

pulled the bag off his head. Uncle Smat was not a pretty man, but I recognized the family nose. His eyes was full of ants and worms and such. His stomach was bloated up with gas.

"He's all yours," Mr. Wentworth said.

"Oh," said Mrs. Wentworth. "I guess you ought to have his hat. I put it on the back porch and put corn in it for the squirrels. I like squirrels. Oh, one more thing. He had a car, but the night he died, he didn't bring it back with him. He come on foot or someone dropped him off. Didn't want you to think we took his car."

"Just his billfold and what was in it," Terri said.

"Yeah," Mrs. Wentworth said, "just that."

In the car, Uncle Smat lying in the backseat, tucked completely inside a big burlap bag, we started out. I had paid a quarter for the used jar of VapoRub, which was far too much but at the time seemed a necessity. I poured Mama's perfume over him, but if it knocked back the smell any, I couldn't tell it. We drove through the night with the windows down and the car overflowing with the aroma of Uncle Smat. Terri hung out of her window like a dog.

"Oh, Baby Jesus," she said. "This here is awful."

I was driving and leaning out my window as much as was reasonable and still be able to drive. The air was helping a little, but there wasn't nothing that could defeat that smell short of six feet of dirt or the bottom of the deep blue sea.

The Ford's headlights was cutting a path through the night, and I felt we were making pretty good time, and then I seen the smoke from under the hood. It was the radiator again.

I pulled over where the road widened against the trees and

parked. I got the hood up and looked at the radiator. It was really steaming. I knew then it had a hole in it. I decided it was a small hole, and if I could keep water in the radiator and not drive like John Dillinger in a getaway car, I might make it home.

With the car not moving, Uncle Smat's stink had taken on a power that was beyond that of Hercules.

"Oh, hell." Terri was in the woods throwing up and calling out. "I holler calf rope. You win, Uncle Smat. Lord have mercy on all His children, especially me."

I used most of our water to fill the radiator and was going to call Terri up from the woods when the wind changed and the smell hit me tenfold. It was like I was in that bag with Uncle Smat.

Terri was coming up the hill. I said, "You're right. We can't keep going on like this. Uncle Smat deserves a burial."

"We ain't got no shovel," Terri said.

This was an accurate observation.

"Then he deserves a ditch and some Christian words said over him."

"I'm all for that ditch, but we ain't got no preacher neither."

"Damn it," I said.

"I say we just put him in a ditch and go on to the house," Terri said.

"That ain't right," I said.

"No, but it sure would be a mite less smelly."

We packed our noses with VapoRub, dragged Uncle Smat out of the car by the bag he was in, and pulled him down a hill that dropped off into the woods. The bag ripped on a stob. Uncle

Smat came out of the bag and rolled down the hill, caught up on a fallen tree branch, and stopped rolling. I could see that Uncle Smat's coat had ripped open. The lining was fish-belly white in the pale moonlight.

"Ah, hell," Terri said. "Can't believe that bag was holding back the smell that much. Oh heavens, that is nastier than a family of skunks rolled up in cow shit."

I was yanking the branch away from under Uncle Smat so he could roll the rest of the way down when Terri said, "Hey, Chauncey. Something fell out of his coat."

I looked at what she had picked up. It was a folded piece of paper.

Dark as it was, we went up to the car and I turned on the headlights, stood in front of them, and looked at the paper. It had some lines on it, a drawing of some tombstones, and the words *Fort Sill* and *Geronimo's grave* written on it. There was a dollar sign drawn on one of the tombstones.

"It was in his coat," Terri said.

"Probably stitched up in the lining."

"He must have had a reason for hiding it," Terri said.

"If he hadn't, the Wentworths would have found it."

"What you think it is?"

"A map."

"To what?"

"You see what I see," I said. "Where do you think?"

"Geronimo's grave?"

"Domino," I said.

"I ain't going there," she said.

"Me neither. We're going home. Remember, Terri. The

hogs ate him. Nobody is going to believe the chickens did it. It would take them too long."

Back with Uncle Smat, I finally managed to pull the branch aside that was holding him, and as there was a deep, damp sump hole at the bottom of the hill between two trees, I gave him a bit of a boost with my foot and he rolled down into it. One of his legs stuck out, and it was the one with the chewed-off foot. I scrambled down and bent his leg a little and got it into the sump, and then I tossed the ripped bag over him and kicked some dirt in on top of that, but it was like trying to fill in the ocean with a pile of sand, a spoon, and good intentions.

"Hell with it," Terri said.

"Maybe we can come back for him later," I said.

"Ha," Terri said. "I say we stick to that story about how the Wentworths' hogs got to him and ate him."

"I can live with that," I said.

"Mostly I can live with him being out of the car," Terri said.

"It ain't much of a Christian burial," I said.

Terri inched closer to the sump hole, put her hand over her heart, said, "Jesus loves you...Let's go."

We drove with all the windows down, trying to clear out memories of Uncle Smat. When we got to the Red River and was about to cross, the car got hot again and I had to pull over. We didn't have any more water, other than a bit for drinking, so I decided wasn't no choice but for me to take the canteens and go down the hill and under the bridge and dip some out of the river.

Terri stayed with the car. When I came back up the hill with the full canteens, sitting there on the hood with Terri was the ragged man we had seen the other day. He was sitting there casual-like with his hand clutched in the collar of Terri's shirt, and the moonlight gleamed on a knife blade he had in his hand, resting it on his thigh.

"There he is," the man said. "Good to see you and Miss Smartass again."

I placed the canteens gently on the ground and picked up a stick lying by the side of the road and started walking toward him. "Let go of her," I said, "or I'll smack you a good one."

He held up the hand with the knife in it.

"I wouldn't do that, boy. You do, I might have to cut her before you get to me. Cut her good and deep. You want that, boy?"

I shook my head.

"Put down that limb, then."

I dropped it.

"Come over here," the man said.

"Don't do it," Terri said.

"You shut up," the man said.

I came over. He got down off the car and dragged Terri off of it and flung her on the road.

"I'm gonna need this car," he said.

"All right," I said.

"First, you're gonna put water in it, and then you're going to drive me."

"You don't need me," I said. "I'll give you the keys."

"Now, this here is embarrassing, but I can't drive. Never learned."

"Just put your foot on the gas and turn the wheel a little and stomp on the brake when you want to stop."

"I tried to drive once and ran off in a creek. I ain't driving. You are. The girl can stay here."

"All right," I said.

"I ain't staying," she said. "He needs me to read the map and such."

"I ain't going the same place you was going," the man said.

"Where are you going?" I said.

"Back the way you come," he said.

He reached in his coat pocket and pulled out the folded sheet of paper I had left lying on the front seat. He pointed at the map.

"I'm going here to see where my partner hid the bank money."

Damn you, Uncle Smat. I said, "You mean that dollar sign means real money."

"Real paper money," he said.

After I put water in the radiator, the man sent me back down to get more water while he stayed with Terri. I didn't have no choice but to do what he wanted. Next thing I knew I was turning the car around and heading back the way we had come.

"It stinks in here," said the man.

I was at the wheel; he was beside me, his knife hand lying against his thigh. Terri was in the backseat.

"You ought to be back here," Terri said. "I think I'm going to be sick."

"Be sick out the window," said the man.

"So you and Uncle Smat were partners?" I said.

"Guess you could say that. Ain't this just the peachiest coincidence that ever happened? You coming along, him being your uncle, and me being his partner."

"I think you stabbed your partner," Terri said.

"There is that," said the man. "We had what you might call a falling-out on account we split up after we hit the bank and he didn't do like he said he would. Let me tell you, that was one sweet job. I had a gun then. I wish I had it now. We come out of the bank in Lawton with the cash, and the gun went off and I shot a lady. Not on purpose. Bullet ricocheted off a wall or something. Did a bounce and hit her right between the eyes. Went through a sack of groceries she was carrying and bounced off a can in the bag or something, hit right and betwixt."

I didn't believe his story, but I didn't bring this to his attention.

"So Smat, he decides we ought to split up, to divide the heat on us, so to speak, and he was going to give me a map to where he hid the money. He said he'd hid it in haste but had made a map, and when things cooled, we could go get our money."

Terri leaned over the seat.

"So he come and told you he had a map for you, and he was right with you, and he didn't give it to you?"

"Get your nose back before I cut it off," the man said, and he showed her the knife. Terri sat back in the seat.

"All right, here it is," he said. "It wasn't no bank job at all. We robbed a big dice game in Lawton. One, that was against the law, but the law was there playing dice. This was a big game and there were all these mighty players there from

Texas and Oklahoma, Arkansas, Louisiana, I think Kansas. Hot arms, they were. Illegal money earned in ways that didn't get the taxes paid. This was a big gathering, and the money was going into a big dice game and there was going to be some big winners. We were just there as small potatoes, me and Smat. Kind of bodyguards for a couple of fellas. And then it come to me and Smat we ought to rob the dice game. It wasn't that smart an idea, them knowing us and all, but it was a lot of money. Right close to a million dollars. Can you imagine? You added up every dollar I've ever made sticking up banks and robbing from folks here and there and what I might make robbing in the future, it ain't anywhere near that. Me and Smat decided right then and there we was going to take the piles of money heaped on the floor and head out. We pulled our guns and took it. That woman I shot, it wasn't no damn accident. She started yelling at us, and I can't stand screeching, so I shot her. It was a good shot."

"Yeah," Terri said. "How far away were you from her?"

"I don't know."

"I bet you was right up near her. I bet it wasn't no great shot at all."

"Terri," I said. "Quiet."

"Yeah, Terri," the man said. "Quiet.

"Well, we robbed them, made a run for it in Smat's car, and then we hid out. Smat, after a few days, he begins to think he's done shit in the frying pan. Starts saying we got to give it back, like they were gonna forgive and forget, like we brung a lost cat home. We hid the money near Geronimo's grave one night, took some shovels up there in the dark and buried it by an oak tree. There ain't nobody guards that place. There ain't even a gate. It was a lot of money and in a big tin canister—and I mean big. A million dollars in bills is heavier than you'd think. We took about ten thousand and split that for living money, but the rest we left there so if we got caught by cops for other things we'd done, we wouldn't have all that big loot on us. If we went to jail, when we got out, there'd be a lot of money waiting. Right then, though, we didn't plan on being caught. That was just a backup idea. We were going to wait until the heat died down, go back and get it. But Smat, he got to thinking that, considering who we robbed, the heat wasn't going to die down. He reckoned they'd start coming after us and keep coming, and that worried him sick. It didn't do me no good to think about it either, but I didn't like what he wanted to do. He was planning on making a map and mailing it to them so they could come get the money. He showed me the map. We had driven to Nebraska, where we was hiding out. He was gonna send them the map with an apology, just keep moving, hoping they'd say, 'Well, we got our money, so let's forget it.' He thought he could go on then and live his life, go back to small stickups or some such, and steal from people who would forget it. But them boys at that dice game, I tell you, they aren't forgetters. With a million dollars, I tell him, we can go off to Mexico and live clear and good the rest of our lives. You can buy a señorita down there cheaper than a chicken. Or so I'm told. Shit, them boys were gonna forget it like they would forget their mamas. Wasn't going to happen."

"Yeah," Terri said. "I'd be mad, I was them. I can hold a grudge."

"Damn right," the man said. "What I told Smat. Mama Johnson didn't raise no idiots."

"I guess that's a matter of opinion, Mr. Johnson," Terri said.

"I swear, girl, I'm gonna cut you from gut to gill if you don't hush up."

Terri went silent. I glanced at her in the mirror. She was smiling. Sometimes Terri worried me.

"Thing was, I couldn't let him mail that map, now, could I? So we had this little scuffle and he got the better of me by means of some underhanded tricks and took off with the car, left me stranded but not outsmarted. You see, I knew he had a gal he had been seeing up near Lawton, and the money was around there, so I figured he'd go back. He might mail that map, and he might not. Finding the map in your car when I come up on missy here, that was real sweet. I knew then you knew Smat, and that he was the uncle you were going to see."

"Did Uncle Smat ever mention us?" I said.

"No," Johnson said. "I hitched my way back to Oklahoma, went up to where we buried the money one night, had me a shovel and all, but I didn't use it. Wasn't nothing but a big hole under that tree. Smat had the money. I thought, *Damn him.* He pulled it out of that hole on account of me. I didn't know if he reckoned to give the bad boys a new map with the new location of the money or if he took it with him, deciding he wasn't going to give it back at all. Now he could keep it and not have to split it, which might have been his plan all along. I was down in the dumps, I tell you."

Terri was leaning over the seat now, having forgotten all about Johnson's harsh warning and the knife.

"Sure you were," she said. "That's a bitter pill to swallow."

"Ain't it?" Johnson said.

"I'd have been really put out," Terri said.

"I was put out, all right. I was thinking, I caught up with him, I'd yank all his teeth out with pliers. One by one, and slow."

"He wouldn't have liked that," she said.

"No, he wouldn't. But like I said, I knew he liked a gal in Oklahoma, and I'd met her, and he was as moony over her as a calf is over its mother, though it wasn't motherly designs he had."

"It wouldn't be that, no, not that," Terri said.

I thought, *How does Terri know this stuff? Or does she just sound like she knows?*

"I got me a tow sack of goods I bought with some of that money I had, made my way to her house, and hid out in the woods across the road from her place. I lived off canned beans and beer for two or three days, sleeping on the dirt like a damn dog, getting eat up by chiggers and ticks, but he didn't come by. I didn't know where he was staying, but it wasn't with her. I was out of beer and on my last can of beans and was about to call in the dogs on my plans when I seen him pull up in front of her house. He got out of his car, and, let me tell you, he looked rough, like he'd been living under someone's porch. He went inside the house, and I hid in the back floorboard of his car. When he come out and drove off, I leaped up behind him and put my knife to his throat, which was all I had, having lost my gun in a craps game on the way back to Oklahoma. I had some good adventures along the way. If you two are alive later, I'll tell you about them."

Considering Johnson was telling us everything but what kind of hair oil he used, I figured he wouldn't want us around later. We knew too much.

"So there I was with my knife to his throat, and you know what he did?"

"How would we?" Terri said.

"He drove that car into a tree. I mean hard. It knocked me winded, and the next thing I know I'm crawling out through the back where the rear windshield busted out, and then I'm falling on the ground. I realize I'm still holding the knife. When I got up, there was Smat, just wandering around like a chicken with its head cut off. I yelled at him about the money, and he just looked at me and seemed drunk as a skunk, which I know he ain't. I say, 'Smat. You tell me where that money is, or I'm going to cut you a place to leak out of.' He says to me, 'I ain't got no mice.'"

"Mice?" Terri said.

"I'm sure that's what he said. Anyway, I got mad and stabbed him. I'm what my mama used to call real goddamn impulsive. Next thing we're struggling around, and he falls, and I fall, and I bang my head on the side of the car, and when I wake up I'm on my back looking at stars. I got up and seen Smat had done took off. So I went looking for him high and low, thinking I'd got a good knife thrust or two on him, and he'd be dead thereabouts. But he wasn't. So I went wandering around for a few days, thumbed a ride back to Texas, knowing Smat knew a fellow just over the river. But Smat wasn't there. I cut that guy good to find out if he knew anything about where Smat was, but I killed him for nothing. He didn't know shit. I went wandering for a couple more days, and then I seen you two at that station. Ain't that something? Ain't life funny?"

"Makes me laugh," Terri said.

"I wandered a couple more days, finally caught a ride from

a farmer and was dropped off at the Red River bridge, and when I got to the other side, what do I see but your car and this little fart outside of it, and I think, *Where's that boy? He's gonna drive me.* Then I seen the map on the seat and knew you knew Smat and knew he hadn't mailed any map at all, 'cause there was the same one he'd drawn. I figured you knew where he was, that he'd been in your car, and then the rest of it you can put together."

Before Terri could say anything, I said, "He ain't alive no more, but before he died he said he done that map to trick you so you'd think he was letting go of the loot, but he came back for it. He moved it, all right, but it's still in the same place, buried right behind Geronimo's grave. You missed it."

He studied me a moment to see if there was truth in what I said, and he saw truth where there wasn't any, which goes to prove if I want to lie, I can do it. So we got our bearings and headed out in the direction of Geronimo's grave after stopping at a station for gas and at a general store across the street from it to buy a shovel and some rope. Johnson gave me some money and I went in and bought the goods. Johnson sat in the backseat with Terri to make sure I didn't talk to anyone at the station or the store. He kept the knife close to her.

At the store I was supposed to ask how far it was to Fort Sill, where Geronimo was buried, and I did. When I told Johnson how far it was, he figured we could drive through the night and be there early morning, before or just about the time the sun came up.

It started raining that afternoon, and it was a steady rain, but we drove on, the wipers beating at the water on the windshield.

Johnson said, "Every time it rains, someone says, 'The farmers need it.' I don't give a hang about the farmers. Papa raised hogs and chickens and grew corn and such, and he spent a lot of time beating my ass with a plow line. To hell with the farmers and their rain. I hope their lands blow away. I can eat pork or beef or chicken or a squirrel. I don't care about the farmers. The farmers can go to hell."

"If I'm reading you right, you don't seem to like farmers," Terri said.

"That's funny," Johnson said. "You're gonna funny yourself to death."

Johnson sat quiet after that and didn't say another word until we came close to Fort Sill. Now, it's supposed to be a fort and all that, but the graveyard wasn't really protected at all. We parked up near it, Johnson grabbed the shovel and coiled the rope over his shoulder, and we all trudged into the grave-yard, the rain beating down on us so hard we could barely see. We fumbled around in the dark awhile, but Johnson, having been there before, found Geronimo's grave easy enough. A blind man could have found it. There was a monument there. It was made of cemented stones, and it was tall and thin at the top, wide at the bottom. There was a marker that said GERON-IMO. On the grave itself were pieces of glass and bones and stones that folks had put there as some kind of tribute. The sun was rising and the rain had slackened, but we could see it had beat down the dirt at the back of the grave, behind the pile of rocks that served as Geronimo's marker, and damn if we couldn't see a tin box down in a hole there. The rain had opened the soft dirt up so you could see it clearly as the sun broke over the trees in the graveyard.

I thought, *Uncle Smat, you ol' dog, you.* He had done exactly what I was pretending he did. The box really was there. Uncle Smat figured hiding it right near where it had been before would fool Johnson, and it would have, had I not told a lie that turned out to be the truth. Uncle Smat might actually have meant to mail that map but then he got stabbed, went off his bean, somehow ended up back at the chicken coop where he'd been staying, and died of the stabbing.

Johnson handed me the shovel, said, "Dig it the rest of the way out."

"What happens to us then?"

"You drive me out of here. I can't carry that on my back, and I can't drive. Later, I tie you up with the rope somewhere where you can be found alongside the road."

"What if no one comes along?" Terri said.

"That's not my problem," Johnson said.

I scraped some dirt off the box with the shovel, and then I got down in the hole to dig. Water ran over the tops of my shoes and soaked my socks and feet. I widened the hole and worked with the shovel until I pried the box loose from the mud. I slipped the rope under the box and fastened it around the top with a loop knot. I climbed out of the hole to help pull the box up. Me and Terri had to do the pulling. Johnson stood there with his big knife watching us.

When we got it up and out of the hole, he took the shovel from me, told us to stand back, and then used the tip of the shovel to try and force open the lid. This took some considerable work, and while he was at it, Terri stepped around beside Geronimo's grave.

Johnson stopped and said to Terri, "Don't think I ain't watching you, girlie."

Terri quit inching along.

Johnson got the box open and looked inside. I could see what the sunlight was shining on, same as him. A lot of greenbacks.

"Ain't that fine-looking," Johnson said.

"Hey, Johnson, you stack of shit," Terri said.

Johnson jerked his head in her direction, and it was then I realized Terri had stooped down and got a rock, and she threw it. It was like the day she killed that bird. Her aim was true. It smote Johnson on the forehead, knocking off his hat, and he sort of went up on his toes and fell back, flat as a board, right by that hole we had just dug.

I looked down at Johnson. He had a big red welt on his forehead, and it was already starting to swell into a good-size knot.

"Girlie, my ass," Terri said as she came up.

I bent down and took hold of his wrist but didn't feel a pulse.

"Terri, I think you done killed him."

"I was trying to. Did you hear the way it sounded when it hit him?"

"Like a gunshot," I said.

"That's for sure," she said. "Let's get this money."

"What?"

"The money. Let's get it and put it in the car and drive it home with us."

"A million dollars? Show up at the house without Uncle Smat and with a large tin box full of money?"

"Here's the way I see it," Terri said. "Uncle Smat has left enough of himself in the car it ought to satisfy Mama that it was best we didn't bring the rest of him home, his stink being more than enough. And this money might further soothe Mama's disappointment about us not hauling him back."

"We just pushed him in a sump hole and left him," I said.

"Really want to go pick him up on the way home?"

I shook my head, looked down at the box. It had handles on either side. I bent over and took one of them, and Terri took the other. We carried the money to the car and put it in the backseat floorboard.

It was good and light by then, and I figured it might be best to leave without drawing a lot of attention to ourselves or to the dead body up by Geronimo's grave. I let the car roll downhill before starting it, and when we were going pretty fast, Terri said, "Oh, goddamn it."

She was looking over the seat, and I glanced in the rearview mirror, and there was Johnson. He wasn't dead at all. He was running after us, nearly on us, his arms flapping like a scarecrow's coat sleeves in the wind. He grabbed onto the back-door handle and got a foot on the running board. I could see his teeth were bared and he had the knife in his free hand and he was waving it about.

I jerked the car hard to the right and when I did, the car slid on the gravel road, and Johnson went way out, his feet flying in the air, him having one hand on the door handle, and then I heard a screeching sound as that handle came loose of the car and Johnson was whipped out across the road and into some trees.

"Damn it to hell," Terri said. "He done bent up in a way you don't bend."

I glanced behind me. I could see he was hung up in a low-growing tree with his back broken over a limb so far, he looked like a wet blanket thrown over it. That rock might not have killed him, but I was certain being slung across the road and into a tree and having his back snapped had certainly done it.

The motor hummed, and away we went.

It took us another two days to get home on account of having to stop more and more for the radiator, and by the time we pulled up in the yard, the car was steaming like a teakettle.

We sat in the car for a while, watching all that steam tumbling out from under the hood. I said, "I think the car is ruined."

"We can buy a bunch of cars with what's in that box."

"Terri, is taking that money the right thing to do?"

"You mean like Sunday-school right? Probably not. But that money is ill-gotten gains, as they say in the pulp magazines. It was Uncle Smat and Johnson stole it, not us. Took it from bigger crooks than they were. We didn't take any good people's money. We didn't rob no banks. We just carried home money bad people had had and were using for bad reasons. We'll do better with it. Mama's always saying how she'd like to have a new car and a house, live somewhere out west, and have some clothes that wasn't patched. I think a rich widow and her two fine-looking children can make out quite well in the west with that kind of money, don't you?"

"How do we explain the money?"

"Say Uncle Smat left us an inheritance that he earned by mining or some such kind of thing. Oil is good. We can say it was oil."

"And if she doesn't believe that?"

"We just stay stuck to that lie until it sounds good."

I let that thought drift about. "You know what, Terri?"

"What's that?"

"I think a widow and her two fine-looking children could live well on that much money. I really think they could."

HANNAH MARTINEZ

by Sara Gran

THE BODY WAS put together from different parts—the door was one color and the hood was another and the bumpers were from an '82. The Cadillac was pulled over by the side of a busy road where a big NO STOPPING sign was posted. A woman stood next to the car waving her arms. She looked pretty desperate. No one pulled over.

I didn't pull over either. I had somewhere to go. Someone was waiting for me.

But a few blocks later I made a right and then another right and went a few blocks and made another right. The woman was still there. She was trying to make eye contact with people as they drove by, still waving her arms around. I pulled over about ten feet in front of her and put on my hazards and walked back to her. It was about a hundred degrees.

"Thank God you stopped," she said. She was around fifty-something. Maybe sixty. Her voice was cracking and her hands shook. She was scared, I guessed—out by the side of the road alone. Her hair was white and tied up in a bun.

"Take it easy," I said. "Let's sit down on the curb. Try to relax."

"I know," she said.

We went and we sat on the curb next to her car. She took a few breaths and I put a hand on her arm and she seemed to feel a little better.

After a few minutes she said, "I don't know what happened. I was just trying to get to my hotel. It's down there. Just down the street. All the lights on the dash went on and it just stopped."

I figured she'd run out of oil or gas but I was no expert. I said I would drive her to her hotel. She hemmed and hawed a little but I told her I had nowhere to go anyway, which wasn't true, and finally she agreed. We left a note on the car. She'd just have to hope the Cadillac would still be there when she arranged for a tow.

She got in the car and I put the air on. We drove for a while. Turned out the hotel was actually all the way at the other side of the valley. She said her name was Hannah Martinez. She said she'd been a dancer, which I believed because of how straight her back was, and that she was in town for a job doing outfits for the girls in "a little revue." She said she was also a musician and she'd written a song that was a big hit in Germany about seventeen years ago.

"Boy, I tell you," she said. "Those were some good years. We ate well."

I didn't know if it was true, but so what? What did I know about hit songs in Germany? Everyone had the right to the story they want, I supposed. So what if maybe things happened a little different in real life. Who was keeping score?

Finally, after close to an hour, we got where she was going. It was a motel way over almost in the next county. Nearby were a bunch of places that fixed dents and hubcaps and engines, which I figured was kind of ironic.

She thanked me a bunch of times and I could tell she meant it. I told her it was nothing. When I got home there was a big fuss and no one believed where I'd been. They were a bunch of clowns. That whole crowd was good for nothing. They all said it sounded like a story — about the costumes and the hit song in Germany. Well, I got news for you, kids, I told them, everything interesting sounds like a story. That's life. A bunch of stories. If you think you know what's true and what isn't, good for you.

Before she got out of the car, in the dark of the parking lot, where she wouldn't see what I was doing, I stuck a couple of dollars in her purse and a prayer card I'd been carrying around with me for a while. Saint Francis.

Not long after that, I came across that exact car for sale. Hannah Martinez's actual car. They'd painted it and fixed it all up, but I recognized the burn marks, and they'd left on the '82 bumpers. It was for sale at a used-car place in Van Nuys. I was buying a car for no reason at all, if you can believe that. Things seemed so great then. I'd just married my second husband and he was making good money, really good money. I had a little Japanese car I'd never liked so he says, Well, let's go trade it in. I mean, I was trading it in for another used car, but still.

There was Hannah Martinez's car, for sale in the lot.

"That's the car," I told my husband. "I've always loved that car."

He bought it for me on the spot. I had them check it out again, on account of the breakdown, but the best anyone could figure, it must've run out of gas. Then after I bought it, I took it to my own mechanic for another look, and he said everything seemed fine. Even complimented me on getting it for such a good price.

I kept the Cadillac when we divorced. It was the only thing we had left that was worth anything. I'd pawned my engagement ring and my wedding ring a few months back. Sold all my pricey clothes, the jewelry, the nice things for the house he'd bought for me. That made it easy to leave. Didn't even have to worry about the rings.

After that, things were hard for a couple of years. I sold the Cadillac eventually and replaced it with a series of inferior cars: lower-quality American models and fourth-hand imports. I always kicked myself for it because I knew I'd never get a chance at a car like that again. But life takes you where it takes you, and you need money when you need it, not next week.

I did serve a little time here and there, for kiting checks, shoplifting, vice. I tried to make ends meet—around the West, mostly. I spent some more time in Southern California; when that became too hot I headed up to Portland. That was one city I didn't care for. I like the sunshine. I did okay there money-wise but one day I'd had enough rain and I got in my car and I drove and drove and drove until a couple days later I was in Tucson. Found work in Tucson and had a good thing for a while there. A very nice setup. That resulted in my first real lockup. Women's prison isn't so bad, not if you're a grown woman. The kids fuss and fight but they leave the rest of us out of it. Other women aren't too bad. Never had such a perfect thing as Tucson again. That was a once-in-a-lifetime deal.

After I got out I just couldn't manage to settle down again. Nothing seemed to fit. I'd think I was settling down in one place and then one night I wouldn't be able to sleep and my blood would be rushing through me and I'd get in my car and drive, and I wouldn't stop until I was someplace new.

In Dallas I was in the newspaper because I caused a traffic accident when I stopped short to let a family of ducks cross the street. About six cars played a little bumper-bump but no one was hurt. No one's car was wrecked. They took me to court for vehicular something-or-other, but then a bunch of nature ladies showed up in court to say how I'd done the right thing trying to save the ducks. Everyone had a lot of fun with it and the judge let me off after the nature ladies convinced him. They even put a little thing in the paper — "Duck Lady Has Day in Court."

But then a few days later, who knows what happened, but there was another little bit in the paper: "Duck Lady California Con Girl!" Someone even said the judge should reconsider in light of who I was. So then the paper went to the nature ladies to see what they thought and boy, was I surprised — not one of them had a bad word to say. One woman even said that considering my "background," what I'd done was even better than it had seemed. I don't know why but I just couldn't believe it. I couldn't get over how nice that was. Even if it was kind of a silly thing to say, she'd meant it to be nice. Just imagine if everyone thought like that. By then I was in Galveston, which suited me much better. I liked that part of the country, all around the Gulf there. Easy to live down there. Easier, at least.

I married my third husband in Sarasota, Florida. He was associated with a group called Quest for Wisdom. They were okay, the Quest people. I never got into it; there was a lot of health food and things like that. No smoking. The best part of our marriage was when he was with them. Then when they all fell apart, the Quest people, that was when he got mean.

Eight years later and I was back on the road again. I bought a good car, a Ford, that I was very fond of. Back then, Ford had a bad rap. All the better for me. I got a good price on the car, and I took it with me when I left.

I drove around the South for a while trying to get something going work-wise, money-wise, happening-wise, but didn't have much luck. I wasn't young anymore. Money was harder to come by every year.

After a year and a few more days in lockup, this time for simple larceny, I eventually found myself back in Southern California. I hadn't been there in many years and it didn't seem very different at all. Just more crowded. That same big sun.

I had arranged to stay with an old acquaintance but when that fell through on account of another friend getting involved and making a problem, I had nowhere to go.

I drove around awhile thinking about what I ought to do. I always loved to drive. That's always been my best friend. I started before they even gave me a license. As long as I had a car I was okay. I certainly prefer a bed, and I don't mind flying first class, but you don't need any of that. All you need is a car that runs and a full tank. Then the world really is yours. You can go anywhere you want, driving that car. You got gas in your tank and the car runs, you can be anyone. You can make the story up as you go.

So I'm driving and driving and after a while I see a motel. I need a place to stay and it looks okay, but as I pull into the parking lot, it begins to look familiar, and after I get out and start heading to the front desk, I realize, *Well, fuck me. This is the place. This is the same fucking place.*

So I go to the desk and I tell him I want a room, cash, just tonight for now, we'll worry about tomorrow tomorrow. He gets the paperwork out and says, "Sure. What's your name?"

So I say, "Well," I say, "I guess it's Hannah Martinez."

APACHE YOUTH

by Ace Atkins

JAMMED UP IN traffic on the 405, Jeff's sister turned to him and said, "You really need to get your shit together."

"I like your husband's Bronco," Jeff said. "If I made a million, it would be exactly the kind of vintage ride I'd buy."

"He doesn't have a million yet," she said. "It's a talent-holding deal, not a series. You know how much money he'd be making if he wasn't tied to the network? He just turned down a guest spot on *NCIS: New Orleans.*"

"He do all this refurb himself?" Jeff said, touching the leather wheel of the Ford. The near-perfect smoothness of the dash. "Damn. Or did he pay someone?"

Jeff's sister snorted, crossed her arms over her new and improved boobs, and slunk down lower in the passenger seat. The Bronco was a beauty. Completely restored, show quality, coated in metallic gray paint, and given a brand-new Cleveland 321 engine with dual exhaust and header. The truck was jacked up with a Pro Comp lift kit, Pro Comp wheels, and big, chunky Goodrich tires.

"LA hasn't been good for you," she said. "What you came here for, you haven't found. You can't live your life jacking into free Wi-Fi at Starbucks or holding down the corner booth at Bob's Big Boy. You're going to be forty this year."

"Correction," Jeff said, "forty-two."

"Jesus," his sister said. "There's more to life than all this shit. I don't know how you do it. You're better than this place."

The traffic hadn't moved ten yards in thirty minutes. The old truck seemed to be on the verge of redlining it, blowing a radiator hose and stranding them until well into the night. Jeff played with the radio, searching for some music that would never be found in the city anymore. He was in the mood for Gram Parsons, The Flying Burrito Brothers, something like that.

"I love you," his sister said. "Go. Go, run free."

Jeff began to hum the John Barry theme from *Born Free*.

"Nothing changes," she said.

"Hey," Jeff said. "Holy crap. I'm doing my best."

"I know," his little sister said. "I know. But maybe this isn't the town to sell literature? You've told two show runners they were illiterate, soulless morons."

Jeff shrugged. "One of them called my modern take on *Anna Karenina* 'Baywatch with Guns.'"

The red Hummer in front of him started to move, and the Bronco rolled. It seemed like the start of a really slow and sad parade. Jeff pointed with his right index finger, steering with his left hand. Ten miles per hour.

"I think I have an idea," she said.

When she finished talking, Jeff turned to her and said, "That's not an idea. That's an errand."

* * *

Five days later, Jeff drove the 1970 Bronco out of LA and long into the Arizona desert on Interstate 10.

He took off the truck's bikini top, tied a blue bandanna on his head, and cranked up the Eagles. He wasn't really into the Eagles but enjoyed them ironically with all the cactus and sagebrush whizzing past.

At Phoenix, he took Arizona State Route 87 north to Payson, where he turned east onto the 260, but sometime after midnight, right around Show Low, he took a wrong turn and ended up not knowing what was up or down, north or south. A billboard promised big winners and comfortable beds.

It was late. What the hell? He followed the pointy arrows.

Nine hours later, Jeff lay by the pool of the Hon-Dah Resort and Casino reading an old paperback, Louis L'Amour's *Hondo*. The cover showed a white man knocked on his back throwing over an Indian brave wielding a spear.

"Kill the Indian," a young girl said. "Save the man."

She'd snuck up him. "Excuse me?" Jeff asked.

"That's what they told us after they rounded us up," she said. "Forced into boarding schools in the East. Don't believe what the white men have to say, the brave cavalry and cowboys. The American genocide of the Indian was much admired by Adolf Hitler."

"It's just a book."

"A racist book," she said. "Don't let anyone else see you reading it here."

The girl was very pretty and very Native American. She had dark skin, black eyes, and high cheekbones. Her hair was past her shoulders, slick, black, and shiny. A beaded choker wrapped her throat while she wore a resort uniform of a navy golf shirt and tiny khaki shorts. "Would you like to order something or just keep drinking cheap beer?"

"A club sandwich would be nice," Jeff said. "On wheat if you have it. But no bacon."

She wrote it down and looked back to him. "How'd you get here?" she said. "Or did you get lost?"

"Just passing through," Jeff said, trying to sound like a cowboy.

"Really?"

"Okay," he said. "I took a wrong turn."

Jeff wore his aviator sunglasses on top of his head. He had three tattoos on his forearm: the words *Carpe Diem,* the Chinese characters for strength, and the head of a grinning *Cuckoo's Nest*–era Jack Nicholson.

"Lost in the White Mountains," she said. "Just where are you trying to get?"

"St. Louis," Jeff said, pointing to the other side of the purplish mountains. "I started off in LA."

"The rez is a long way from where you're headed."

"Hmm," he said. "Maybe I'm supposed to be here."

"It's because of the movie," she said. "*Fort Apache?* Subconsciously, you want to be John Wayne, like all white people."

"Or play blackjack," Jeff said. "Or hit that world-famous buffet. You have nice signs. Very colorful. Did you grow up here?"

"Yes," she said. "I'm White Mountain Apache. On the rez my whole life."

"How old are you?"

"Tomorrow is the final day of my coming-of-age cere-mony," she said, not really answering. "That's when I will become a woman."

"Why aren't you there now?" Jeff said.

"I'm covering my sister's shift," she said. "She has a hang-over. Too hot by the pool."

Jeff nodded, squinting into the sun.

"At dawn I will be blessed and dusted with pollen. It rep-resents my emergence from the womb. Would you like fries or fruit with that?"

"Fruit," he said. "And some sparkling water."

The deal had been for Jeff to drive his movie-star brother-in-law's beloved Bronco to St. Louis. The brother-in-law was shooting a werewolf-cop show there, *The Arch,* and really missed his truck. He told Jeff he'd give him a thousand bucks plus expenses to bring it out. Jeff hadn't published a novel in five years, not since his supposedly bold debut, *West of the World,* about a suicidal hedge-fund manager who learned about life through surfing. His latest failure was trying to bring a minise-ries to HBO about the life of silent-film comedian Fatty Arbuckle. He was shut out for months despite attending pitches in period clothes. Driving for cash sounded good.

The whole way from LA, Jeff had kept the soft top down and hadn't touched the AC, liking all that hot wind through the des-ert, sweating through his V-neck T-shirt. As soon as he'd hit the desert, Jeff started to drink beer from his Yeti cooler, a gift from Winona Ryder's half sister, and had run through two packs of Marlboros. The mountains were different. Cool, almost chilly.

At first, he believed stopping off at the casino had been a

stroke of luck. The girl had been right. He loved that movie. Henry Fonda. John Wayne. One of John Ford's very best. But within three hours of getting a room at the hotel, long after he'd left the pool, Jeff had lost all of his pocket money and drained his ATM card. He got to his room, thinking they might decline his debit card, and called the brother-in-law to tell him that he was stuck at an Apache reservation in Arizona.

"How much did you lose?"

"Don't ask."

"I have to go," he said. "Do you know it takes two hours to get me back into the werewolf suit? After they put on the head and face, I can't speak. I have to loop all the dialogue."

"Money?"

"That's your problem," the brother-in-law said. "Did you ever hear anything about Fatty?"

"HBO passed," Jeff said. "They called Roscoe's weight issue off-putting and said that the sex I'd written in the script was grotesque even for them. Come on, man. Just this one time."

"Too many times."

Jeff hung up, took the elevator down to the casino floor, the world buzzing, whirling, blinking, and twirling while he headed back out to the parking lot and the Bronco. The young Native girl from the pool was there, leaning against the shiny hood and smoking a cigarette. "I heard you lost big," she said.

"Isn't there more action going on here than just me?"

"Maybe." The young girl tossed the cigarette down and ground it out with the heel of a clean white tennis shoe. "But I know how you can make it back."

"Okay."

"Ever fight an Indian?"

Lots of Apache had come in for the next day's ceremonies, parking their battered pickup trucks in crooked rows up on a dusty hill. It was night and cooler than he expected for Arizona. The air warmed up as the bonfire crackled to life. A boxing ring had been set up in a clearing in the tall pines, a row of metal folding chairs for old people and Indian leaders who wore suits with their straw cowboy hats.

"Okay, white man," a leathery old man said. "You ready?"

They wanted him to wrestle a girl, a grand champion by the name Faby Apache. Jeff was told Faby wasn't a true Apache, just a professional from Mexico who liked the costumes. She was big, taller and broader than Jeff, wore a singlet made of buckskin, and stuck feathers in her hair. When she saw him before the match, she started to laugh.

"All my debt is gone if I beat her?"

"All your debt is gone if you stay in the ring for just one round," the old man said. "We'll even give you back the money you lost in the casino. Faby's a role model to our young women here. Did you know tomorrow is the last day of the puberty trials?"

"I thought it was called a coming-of-age ceremony."

"It has the same meaning," the old man said. "I am a medicine man. We take the girl through her four steps of life, from infant, to child, to adolescent, and on to womanhood, and we prepare her for the final passage, death. It's a very good time for us. Especially the men who just watch."

"What do the girls have to do?"

"We put pollen all over their bodies, and then we smear clay in their faces and make them run."

"How far?"

"Not far," the medicine man said. If Jeff were writing a

script, he'd cast Chief Dan George as the old man, although he was pretty sure Chief Dan George had died about thirty years ago. He'd just type out *Resembles Chief Dan George.* The smart people would get it. If they didn't understand him, those kid readers at CAA, then screw them.

Jeff stood up, bare to the waist in handmade Japanese blue jeans and no shoes. He let the old man put a navy cavalry hat on his head, and he told him to march to the ring. He felt like a poor man's version of Billy Jack.

"One piece of advice," the medicine man said.

Jeff looked at him.

"Protect your nuts," he said. "Faby usually heads straight for them."

EXT.   WHITE MOUNTAIN RANGE
APACHE RITUAL   NIGHT

A handsome young man is led into the ring by the chief of the tribe. He's introduced as LT. THURSDAY while Apaches boo and throw bottles at him. A muscled woman warrior follows, hands held high, to the shouts and cheers of fans. She walks to each corner of the ring and pumps her fist to the crowd. Jagged purplish mountains surround them on each side. Somewhere in the distance, a drum begins to beat.

CHIEF

The cavalry has returned once again to
burn our village, rape our women, and

scatter us to the wind. Their leader is a
man twisted with lust and hate. Lieu-
tenant Thursday.

THURSDAY

Come on, man. Jesus Christ.

More beer bottles flow onto the stage, break apart, and
scatter across the canvas. A young Native man hops up
and knocks off the bottles with a push broom. He gives a
thumbs-up to the chief. A beer bottle narrowly misses
Thursday's head.

CHIEF

There is but one hope for your people. A
girl, now a woman, who has the strength
of many warriors. She is Faby Apache.

The crowd goes crazy. Little girls hold up hand-painted
signs. Old women begin to cry. Young men watch the gor-
geous warrior as she paces the ring, side to side, like a
caged tiger.

THURSDAY

(Leaning in to whisper to the chief)
This is all an act, right? Just part of the
show?

CHIEF

Sure. If you say so.

Jeff met many Apaches that night; one even handed him an
ice pack for his head. They offered him Mexican beer from
coolers in the backs of their pickup trucks and warm shots of
mescal. He accepted, although he felt bad about drinking with
Native Americans. He'd read countless stories in the *New York
Times* about drug and alcohol abuse among indigenous peoples. But his head hurt a lot. It wasn't from the beer bottle that
had hit him between the eyes; it was from Faby Apache using
one of her signature moves (although Jeff didn't know it was
famous until after he'd come to), the Hurricanrana, in which
the wrestler wrapped her legs around her opponent's neck and
drove him headfirst into the mat.

Faby Apache was beautiful, muscular, and very strong.
But it hadn't been pleasant to be caught between her thighs
and hammered to the ground. He accepted the mescal as a
reward.

"I hear you have an old Bronco," said a young man introduced as Lorenzo. He looked to be very drunk and dangerous.
He had long black hair and lots of ragged tattoos and kept on
telling Jeff that the feds wanted to send him back to jail. His
T-shirt shilled for a band called Eyes Set to Kill.

"Thank you for the drink."

"Can you give me a ride?" he said. "It's a very pretty truck.
Faith told me about it."

"Who's she?"

"The girl who brought you the cheap beer at the pool,"

Lorenzo said. "And the club sandwich on wheat toast. No bacon."

"She's very pretty."

"Yeah?" Lorenzo said. "She's fourteen, dipshit."

"Oh."

"And my little sister."

Lorenzo wanted to take the Bronco through the piney hills at night. Jeff worried the car would get muddy, that something might break, that he might bust a tire or, God forbid, twist the frame. "What the hell do you have a four-wheel drive for if you don't use it? Are you some kind of pussy?" Lorenzo asked.

"I'm no pussy," Jeff said and agreed to let him drive the Bronco. He'd drunk half a bottle of mescal. He told Lorenzo he wanted to eat the worm but Lorenzo told him there was no worm in that bottle. Lorenzo drove with two other men in the backseat and made Jeff run shoeless behind them, trailing the Bronco like a dog. They told him this was a rite of passage for all Apaches: if he followed the Road of Trials, he would be their blood brother. Jeff thought maybe he might sell the story, a first-person account, to *Outside* or maybe *Men's Journal.* "How Mescal Turned to Apache Blood."

Jeff was a runner, knew the Hollywood Hills as well as a coyote, but after a couple miles or maybe a hundred, he stopped, bent at the waist, and tried to catch his breath. The moon above them was huge, painting the pine trees silver. Damn, he wished he had a pen. He'd write down that description and use it in a novel sometime. *Shining silvery pines. "No más,"* Jeff said.

One of the Apaches, a laughing, grinning teen, tossed a Dos Equis bottle at him. It missed by a mile and shattered against a rock.

"What's next?" Jeff said.

"You look at my sister?" Lorenzo asked.

"No."

"I like your Bronco," he said. "How much?"

"It's not mine."

"Everything is for sale."

"My brother-in-law bought it in Malibu," Jeff said. "And he'd never sell it. He loves this truck more than my sister. Okay? So what's next?"

Lorenzo turned around in the driver's seat, lighting up a cigarette, smoke coming from his nostrils. "What are you talking about?"

"The Road of Trials," Jeff said. "The Native American way. Joseph Campbell and all that shit."

"Oh, man," Lorenzo said. "I almost forgot. We were just bullshitting you, man. Come on. Get in the truck, we'll drive you back to the casino. Just don't look at Faith again."

"He owes us for the beer," one of the men said. "Beer costs money."

"And the mescal," said the other. "He drank most of the bottle."

"I like this Bronco," Lorenzo said, driving fast, hitting ravines and rocks, feeling the custom wheel in his hands. Jeff had to hold on to the roll bar or he'd fall out into the endless trees. "I dreamed of this night the whole time I was in jail," Lorenzo said. "I knew it would come."

Jeff played blackjack in the casino most of the next day. The casino paid him out chips for what he'd lost and gave him a voucher for a full buffet breakfast. Lorenzo and his two boys said Jeff owed them fifty bucks. They said they'd come back for it at noon and he'd better have it or else. Lorenzo said he needed cash to provide refreshments for his family. Tonight, Faith would dance for ten hours without interruption. Only through a test of strength, endurance, and character would she truly become a woman. No one should go hungry waiting for all that mess.

Head in hands, Jeff kept losing. Lorenzo took a seat next to him. He had on a T-shirt that showed Geronimo and his boys. It said *Homeland Security — Fighting Terrorism Since 1492.*

"You know my sister can't smile for two days."

"I know how she feels."

"Where are you from?" Lorenzo said.

"I told you," he said. "California."

"Is that where you learned to gamble?"

Jeff stared at him.

"I didn't play cards until I went to jail," Lorenzo said. "Lots of time to learn there."

"I worked my way through grad school playing poker," Jeff said. "That's how I got my MFA and published my book."

Jeff doubled down. The dealer snatched up the cards and the last of his chips.

"You lost again?" Lorenzo said. "Damn, man. It's like you are cursed or something."

"Don't worry about me," Jeff said. "I'll pay you."

"I don't worry," Lorenzo said. "We'll just take the Bronco."

"Over fifty bucks?" Jeff asked. "C'mon. Right."

Lorenzo didn't smile, seeming to be thinking on something new. "The most important thing is that Faith choose the right medicine woman," he said, cigarette hanging from his mouth.

"Me and the boys built her a sacred teepee and later we'll burn it down. I guess there's not much else I can do for her now."

"I'll get you your money."

Lorenzo nodded and scooped up the keys to the Bronco. "You better."

"It's not that I don't believe you," Jeff's brother-in-law said. "It just sounds all so fantastic."

"As fantastic as you in a werewolf suit solving crimes?"

"I don't solve crimes as the werewolf," he said. "The detective turns into a werewolf only when there's danger or he feels threatened. He can't think rationally when he's the werewolf. Come on, man. You're the writer. You know how this shit works."

"I have to stay on the rez again tonight."

"Until the puberty dance is over?"

"Yes," Jeff said. "Exactly. And if I can win just one hand, I'll go back to poker. Blackjack isn't working for me."

"You know that truck is in a chop shop in south Phoenix right now," Jeff's brother-in-law said. "Or have you really lost your mind this time? Not just faked a complete mental breakdown like when you wanted to go to India."

"They want me at the bonfire tonight," Jeff said. "They promise I don't have to pay for the mescal and beer. That tonight it's on them. I'm a real invited guest of the tribe."

"I'm so glad for you, Jeff," the brother-in-law said. "Next time, call your sister instead of me. I don't have time for this crap."

Jeff walked to the bonfire at twilight, sat down on his butt, and watched the dance of the mountain gods, shirtless men wearing black hoods and what looked to be tall candlesticks on their heads jumping around and chanting to a ceaseless drum. Soon, a bunch of girls in white buckskin began to dance, moving around the fire, their faces painted a bright white, ornate necklaces jangling from their necks. Faith, one of them, pretended not to see him.

"It will stay on the woman's mind her whole life," said the medicine man. He'd snuck up on him. It was the same old man who'd prepped him to wrestle Faby Apache. The one who looked a lot like Chief Dan George. Hoffman had been so damn good in that movie.

"What about the boys?" Jeff said. "What do you do for them?"

"There's not a ceremony like this for boys," the medicine man said. "A boy is like a lost dog. He must find his own way."

"How's that?"

"We all have our own path, our own journey to manhood," he said. "I served in the Marine Corps."

Jeff took another drink of the mescal, still looking to the bottom of the bottle for the worm but not finding it. "No shit?"

"Two tours of Vietnam," said the medicine man. "That sucked big-time. The ladies understand ceremony. Boys this age only want to fondle themselves and get drunk."

Faith came to Jeff later, her face painted white, dried mud from chin to below her eyes. She spoke with tight skin and a stoic face, having to be stoic because of the whole no-smiling rule. In bare feet, Jeff had let her inside the small casino hotel room where the AC unit hummed and hummed. She wore white buckskin and feathers in her hair. Her black eyes were very large and dark. She was hopped up, excited with energy, talking so fast Jeff had trouble following. "I want to give you something."

"Why is your face white?"

"To represent the White-Painted Woman," she said. "In

the morning, after dancing all night, I will run around the sacred basket four times and wipe the clay and mashed corn from my face. The giant teepee my brothers built will fall and burn and then I'll be a woman."

Jeff nodded. "Sure."

The girl took his hand and pressed it to her chest. "Do you feel this?"

"Yes," Jeff said. "Yes, I do."

"I am almost a woman."

"I'm more than twice your age," Jeff said. "I can't accept what you want to give me. They could put me in jail. It's wrong. Your brother would murder me."

The girl with the white-painted face narrowed her eyes and shook her head. Beads around Faith's neck clinked softly. She smelled like clay and cornmeal.

"Maybe in a few years," Jeff said. "Maybe if I get my movie produced. It's still being optioned by David Schwimmer. He was Ross on *Friends*. He wants to produce, direct, and star in it. I don't think he's ideal for the part. But I buy him as the trader. He talks smart and fast."

"What you feel is my heart," Faith said. "Not my boob. And my gift isn't my womanhood. You know I'm not a woman until the morning?"

"Oh," Jeff said. "Of course."

"I must get back," she said. "I am to be imbued with the spirit of Changing Woman. Changing Woman is powerful. She has the ability to heal the sick, help the weak-minded. People have come from all over the rez to be touched by the spirit of Changing Woman."

"That's good," he said. "Right?"

She touched Jeff's head and held it in both hands. "But you will accept my gift," she said. "Won't you?"

"Sure," he said. "Why not?"

Faith opened her right hand and showed him the Bronco keys in her palm. "You should run. The truck is parked by the great teepee. As it falls, my brother will be with it. Go."

"And when does it fall?"

"Not long after the medicine man shows his painted hand to the rising star."

"And when exactly is that?"

"I think about nine o'clock."

Jeff couldn't sleep. After a few hours of lying in the dark hotel room, he pulled on his blue jeans and V-neck T-shirt by American Apparel, gathered his things, and walked to the big fire a half mile away from the casino. He sat on a fallen tree and watched the women, young and old, painted and bare-faced, dance around the giant bonfire. Faby Apache was there but no longer dressed as a warrior. Now she had on a plain blue dress, cowboy boots, and a glittery ball cap.

Sparks kicked up into the starry night. The dance was more of a shuffle with closed eyes, a movement with little direction or aim other than to keep moving, keep chanting. No one stopped. The energy was ceaseless.

Men played drums and chanted at the women: *Keep moving. Keep going.* Some of them wore ceremonial dress, others black cowboy hats with colorful beads. One skinny guy wore a Captain America T-shirt with the sleeves cut off. The medicine man made big pronouncements in Apache that Jeff didn't understand. More sparks flew up into the purplish sky.

When two jacked-up trucks drove off from the ceremony, Jeff spotted the parked Bronco and sighed. A white coat of dust had spread over the dented hood. The windshield wipers had cleared off a sliver from the glass, enough to see a little road. Faith continued to dance around the teepee. She did not see him or look anywhere but at the path before her. *Move, move, more. Keep dancing. Keep breathing.* The fire cast a wide slice of light and kicked up white smoke. The women kept up a hobbling kind of dance, moving from side to side with the rhythm of the chanting men. On the page, Jeff hoped it might actually go like this:

```
EXT.   WHITE MOUNTAIN RANGE
PUBERTY CEREMONY   MORNING


A giant morning sun rising over the impoverishment of
the rez. THE MAN hands FAITH SPOTTED EAGLE the
keys to the vintage truck. With the keys, she could escape
the rez, the poverty and drug abuse (assuming there was
drug abuse), and ride away with a greater understanding
of the world. The world was wide open; the future was
fun. The girl was hot. The desert was hotter.


                    JEFF


I want you to have it. Keep the Bronco.
You are now a woman.


Faith Spotted Eagle hugs the Man hard as she wipes the
clay from her face and dirt from her eyes. She can see!
```

FAITH

It's all clear now. I won't forget you.

The Man kisses Faith on the cheek. A brotherly kiss. She looks at him, holds his hands tight, and looks as if she wants to say more. We see the Man toss his travel bag over his shoulder and walk to the rising sun over the mountains.

In real time, Lorenzo slid off the dented hood of the Bronco, took a swig of mescal, and offered Jeff his middle finger. He looked tall and wavy through the haze of the bonfire, the smoke making him seem hard and important. The women kept on dancing, circling around and around. The morning light had gone from black to gray, a yellow swath of sunlight coming up over the mountains.

Several Apache men gathered, including Lorenzo, and walked toward the teepee. Lorenzo carried a metal gas can. The girls stopped dancing, and a large old woman handed Faith a red hand towel. A basket was set away from the teepee and the girls began to run for it as the men doused the teepee with gas. The fire was lit as the girls rushed toward the basket, running round and round, four times, nearly tripping, one falling to her knees with exhaustion.

Faith ran toward a group of old women with fat arms spread wide, wiping the white clay and cornmeal from her face and dust from her eyes. She nodded toward Jeff, and Jeff ran for the Bronco.

He jumped into the seat, slipped the keys into the ignition, and tried to crank the engine. It sputtered and failed and sputtered and failed.

Lorenzo looked up from the flames and falling beams. He spit in the dirt and yelled something to his boys and they turned for the Bronco. Jeff tried the engine again. Lorenzo pointed and yelled, running hard. Arms pumping. In the narrow slice of windshield, Jeff lost sight of the man until he was ten yards away.

Jeff slammed his fist on the wheel as Faby Apache let out a Mexican war cry and tackled Lorenzo to the ground. She pressed his face into the dirt and held the man's head between her thighs. Her muscled chest and arms shone with sweat. She looked across the way to Jeff, mouthed the word *Go!*

Jeff tried the ignition again and the twin pipes growled and joined up with the chanting mountain spirits. All of the girls had found the old women; they were embracing. He smelled the burning wood and corn on the hot morning wind. The sun rose high in the east over a ribbon of blacktop leading away from the rez.

Faith walked down the highway, moving the opposite direction, coated in the white buckskin, her arms disappearing into the buckskin shirt, her face washed clean of the clay. The logs of the teepee fell into a big heap behind them.

She continued to walk, eyes not leaving her path, but this time smiling. A little.

A necklace of mescal seeds dangled from his rearview mirror. Jeff stopped only twice on the way to St. Louis.

THE TWO FALCONS

by Gary Phillips

Present — Four Days Ago

Evening and two men sat slouched on a pleather and chrome couch. They had their legs up on the Goodwill-purchased coffee table and one of the men was barefoot, revealing a little toe missing from one of his feet. Laminated onto the table's surface were numerous baseball trading cards covering various eras. There were several empty beer cans on the thick lacquer as well as a family-size bag of barbecue chips they'd been munching from steadily. The chips rested on two cards of the stolen-base king Maury Wills. The elder of the two men, the one with the missing toe, was an uncle of sorts to the other one via a long-dissolved marriage. He'd bought the chips and beer on sale at Vons.

A corner lamp threw off weak light in the tidy living room as the two were entertained by a program on the flat-screen before them. It was one of those fact-based efforts that revisited historic and modern-day crimes through conjecture and on-screen re-creations. The men shared a joint while a segment unfolded on the television.

"Get your hands up and nobody will get hurt!" the man wearing a Hulk mask yelled as he underscored his command by firing rounds from his MAC-10 into the bank's ceiling.

"Whatever happened to him?" the younger man asked the man he still called uncle, referring to the robber re-created on the program.

The older one shook his head side to side, pulling on the joint. "Not sure. I know they never found that money he ganked. Eight hundred grand."

"Jimmy Moore liked to live large and dangerously," a bass voice informed the viewers. There was a montage of the actor playing Moore in prison as the narration continued.

"Inside, the former police officer was able to avoid confrontations with prison gangs, as he did the bulk of his time away from the general population. Indeed, he was something of a model prisoner who read, played chess now and then, and generally kept to himself. Moore never applied for parole because he never once gave a hint as to where he'd hidden the bank-job loot."

The prison images gave way to a 1964 Falcon Squire station wagon with the fake wood trim on its flanks and rear drop gate. The car drove along a scenic mountain highway as the narrator continued, "When James Moore got out of jail after serving nearly nine years, he was secretly followed by law enforcement, who believed he'd soon try to retrieve his ill-gotten. But Moore seemed to have anticipated this. He moved around from town to town, taking menial jobs such as washing dishes or doing janitorial work."

The uncle cocked his head, remembering something, as the Falcon on the screen crested a rise, the sun low on the horizon.

"Authorities believe that he never retrieved the money, but they ultimately would lose track of Moore near Amarillo, Texas. He was last seen driving the restored Falcon station wagon that had belonged to his mother."

"That's like your ex's wagon," the uncle remarked as the Ford went over the rise and the program faded out to a commercial. He grabbed some potato chips.

"It sure is," said the young man, having finished the joint.

The older man glared at him, a handful of chips hanging before his mouth. "It might be more than that."

"What?" his nephew said.

"That Falcon," his uncle muttered. He sat back, staring off, slowly eating one chip at a time as an idea assembled itself.

1989

Overhead, the police chopper veered left from the northwest and swung back by the row of modest homes on Fifty-First Street between Main and Woodlawn in South Central LA. Its powerful searchlight cut through the warm, humid night, fixing on one specific house as the helicopter maintained a tight pattern above the dwelling with peeling stucco. Starkly shadowed forms moved just beyond the cone of the aircraft's high-intensity beam. There were knots of people anticipating the rock-house raid, including the Secret Service, uniformed officers in riot gear, and several reporters from local TV news, the *Los Angeles Times,* and the *Herald Examiner.* The *Sentinel,* the black newsweekly, hadn't been invited. Too often they'd been critical of the LAPD and the tactics they employed in this community.

Police chief Daryl Gates jutted his jaw as he stood in his full regalia next to former First Lady Nancy Reagan. While he forced himself to keep his mind on the events happening before him, he couldn't help but consider how clips from tonight might be woven into his first commercial should he announce his bid for the governor's chair. He'd come a long way since he'd started out as Chief William Parker's driver in the fifties. A long way indeed, the creator of SWAT reflected as the six-ton armored "mobile entry device," as the vehicle was euphemistically known, goosed up the curb on its big tires and rumbled across the house's dried lawn, churning up turf in its wake.

"This is how we will cleanse our more disadvantaged neighborhoods of the scourge of drugs," Gates said, nodding at Mrs. Reagan, who minutes before had been hunkered down with the chief in an RV parked nearby where they'd nibbled on fresh fruit salad with kiwi—she loved that fruit. The word had come via the two-way and as Gates went over his notes, she adjusted her makeup before they stepped out. *The Establishment* was plastered in flowing script alongside the RV they'd walked away from to make news this night.

"We will return this community to its citizens, and take it out of the grip of the handkerchief-headed gang members and dope slingers glorified in this trash, this rap music misguiding the young people."

A fourteen-foot-long steel battering ram extended from

the front of the armored vehicle, which was called the batter-ram in the community. There was a turret atop the squat four-wheeled, tank-like conveyance. A police officer's head poked out of the turret in shock helmet and goggles. He pointed forward like General Patton at El Alamein. The machine climbed and destroyed the porch's wooden steps, also taking out a low concrete wall. Photos were snapped and video cameras rolled.

More officers were positioned out behind the house in case the occupants tried to bolt and spoil the show. Under a ratty plastic tarp at the end of the driveway leading to the detached garage was an old Falcon Squire station wagon that hadn't moved in years. It sat on its rims. Back out front, the square, thick steel plate at the end of the battering-ram shaft was driven into the metal security screen door. The door buckled and puckered loose on its rust-covered hinges. There was more snapping of pictures and oohs and aahs from the gathered.

Inside the house, Debra Hastings stood in the tidy living room, hands on her hips, shaking her head from side to side. "Oh, these motherfuckers," she lamented. Light from the tele-vision crews' cameras shone through the half-open curtains along with spill from the copter's search beam. Sweat glistened on her smooth forehead.

The armored vehicle backed up some and as the driver revved the diesel engine, the rear tires spun momentarily, then gained purchase and traction. The batterram surged for-ward again with urgency. This time the security screen and the regular door behind it gave, along with a good portion of one side of the house and the picture window, which also had security bars on it. Debra Hastings was all about safety. That's why she'd participated in the neighborhood-watch program sponsored by the LAPD. This and other details would be revealed later after her successful suit brought by the ACLU and the coverage by the media.

But right then, those outside witnessed the rending as hunks of stucco wall and the tar paper, chicken wire, and wood slats underneath broke away and glass burst from the windows. Into the breach rushed the police with batons and heavy mag flashlights in hand, barking orders. Several officers carried ten-pound sledgehammers.

"Down! Get down on the ground! Don't move, don't you fuckin' move a muscle! Who's back there? Kitchen, clear the kitchen…move, move, move!"

Soon four men and two women were marched out of the home with their hands cuffed behind their backs. One of the men was elderly and another had been in his boxers. But Gates had given orders to let the suspects at least get pants on, as he'd previously been lambasted for having his officers parade the arrested around in their skivvies and this was deemed humiliating. Each was made to kneel on the lawn, even the old man. Inside, plaster and lathe walls constructed in the 1930s were busted into by the sledgehammers, and furniture was destroyed in the pursuit of drug contraband.

"Clearly," Gates said into the glare of camera lights, microphones held before his grim face, "we've made another dint in the battle to save South Central. By taking down this known rock house from where large quantities of crack cocaine and misery originated, we've made a difference tonight." He turned his head toward Mrs. Reagan.

She blinked rapidly as if unclear on where she should focus her attention among the numerous camera lenses, but the former actress rallied and said, "I saw people on the floor, rooms that were unfurnished...all very depressing," she intoned mournfully.

Chief Gates added, "We thought she ought to see it for herself and she did. She is a very courageous woman."

It would be reported in a follow-up piece in the *Times* that in addition to a handful of cassette tapes found in what was a homemade recording studio, complete with squares of foam padding tacked to the walls in a back bedroom, an ounce of rock cocaine had been confiscated from the home along with a half-smoked marijuana cigarette.

Debra Hastings looked up from where her face had been pushed down onto the yellowed, scratchy grass. "These motherfuckers," she muttered again.

Present

Sandra "Pebbles" Hastings ascended amid a scruff of wilted ice plants toward the hilltop parking lot. Post her morning shred, though a cold sun resided in the steel gray sky, she'd partially unzipped her wetsuit and tied the arms around her waist, her sports top underneath. She carried her surfboard under an arm, happy to have had a good session in her spot here between Manhattan Beach and El Segundo. Nearing the parking lot, she frowned at the sight of a man bent over the door lock of her boss little '64 Falcon station wagon. She gaped not only because someone was trying to rip off her car but because the dude looked familiar.

"Shit, Scotty, what the hell are you doing?" she called out, dropping her board and running.

"Goddamn it," swore Scott Waid. Quickly he produced a gun, bringing the caramel-hued surfer to a halt.

"Keep back, Pebbles," her former boyfriend warned.

"The fuck, man?" Her hands rose and fell back to her sides.

"Just stay where you are, I don't want to have to hurt you."

"Gee, thanks, Scotty. You just want to steal my car is all." A car he helped her restore, she didn't add.

Alternately glancing at her and at the silver pick shaped like a surgeon's scalpel inserted in the car's lock, he got the door unlatched. He hurriedly transferred the tool to his gun hand. As this required a moment of adjustment, Hastings used the opportunity to cover the distance between them. Waid leveled his gun hand again, the tool falling away. Hastings launched her body in the air sideways and slammed against his torso. They both dropped onto the makeshift parking lot, Hastings on top.

"Bastard," she swore, throwing a punch at his face, which he evaded. Her knuckles scraped against gravel and he gut-punched her, which made her wince. Waid rolled, leveraging her body off of his. Like he was swimming across the gravel, Waid went toward his gun. But the woman had recovered quickly and scrambled as well, then straddled his back.

"What are you doing, Scotty?" she seethed, landing a solid blow to the back of his head. Exhaling, he puffed gravel dust.

"Get the fuck off me, Sandra." This time instead of turning his body he got on all fours and bucked like a stallion. She got her arms around his neck. But Waid was tall, muscular in the shoulders and chest, and got to his feet with her attached. He tried to straighten but she reared back; they toppled against the car and slid part of the way down.

"Hey, Pebbles, what going on?" a new voice rang out. "I'm guessing this ain't what you and your friend here call foreplay."

"Shit," Waid said while simultaneously flipping his ex over his shoulder like a GI Joe in those cartoons he watched as a kid.

It was her turn to exhale hard as she landed on her butt on the gravel.

Waid had the gun again, an old-fashioned snub-nose, and showed it to the newcomer, a blond man, also a surfer, with a goatee and in swim trunks despite the chilly morning. Hastings sat on the ground, making a face at her former squeeze.

"Sorry, but it be's like that sometimes." He got in the Falcon station wagon and rolled down the window, keeping the gun pointed at the two while he jammed his pick into the ignition switch. Two cranks, and the rebuilt, retrofitted small-block V-8 caught and purred like a sewing machine. He put the three-speed clutch in reverse and backed up. He then righted the car and drove off as the sun got warmer.

The blond surfer, Joaquin Ryan, helped Hastings to her feet. "What was that all about?"

"Fuck if I know but I damn sure intend to find out," she vowed.

1997

She was heavy in the hips and this only increased his ardor. He had a tumbler of scotch in one hand and his erect member in the other, flagpole proper sticking out of his boxers. As he sipped, slowly working his shaft as well, the woman in lacy underwear swayed closer. Over the JVC boom box, Biggie Smalls's singsong voice rapped "Mo Money, Mo Problems."

"We gonna party good, baby," she said, legs apart, working her hand inside her leopard-spotted panties and fingering herself.

"That's right," he said, careful not to drink too much. No misfiring for him today, no sir.

She stopped in front of where he sat in the corduroy-covered recliner with its thinning armrests. He rocked gently on the chair's squeaky ball bearings, mesmerized by the considerable breasts before his face. It seemed to him they were barely restrained by the sheer material of her bra. She replaced her hand for his around his stiffening johnson and with her other hand stuck her moist index finger in his mouth. He suckled it joyously and murmured with pleasure and she smiled knowingly. Behind him the shades had been pulled down to half-mast. The second-story windows overlooked a street in harsh afternoon sun of similar modest dingbat apartments like this one in Lennox. Those panes made their own humming as a jet approached Los Angeles International Airport not too far away. The shadow of the plane moved across his Falcon station wagon parked at the curb. The car's body had several dents, the fake wood trim was badly faded, and a slab of roughly sanded Bondo was smeared across a rear panel.

The woman unhooked her bra and twirled it around her head, gyrating her substantial hips.

"Yee-hah," he enthused, wetting his lips and watching her freed breasts jiggle and shake.

She then flung the garment onto the floor where the man had placed his drink.

"Give me those titties, girl," he implored. The man reached up and caressed her breasts and playfully bit on her wonderful, large, erect brown nipples as she leaned over him. He put his head between those marvelous sweaty mounds and worked it back and forth while she took them in hand and pressed the flesh on the sides of his face.

He sat back, gasping. She went to her knees, pushing his farther apart. "I'm going to suck you dry," she promised and he was as giddy as a mosquito in a nudist colony. The man closed his eyes as she expertly worked her tongue on his tip.

"Oh, good sweet God." Jimmy Moore shuddered, causing the recliner to wobble. Underneath the chair, he'd tucked away his badge clipped to his belt holster with his gun in it.

She took him deeper in her mouth, building a rhythm matching the new song's bass beats as Biggie rapped, "Dress up like ladies and burn them with dirty three-eighties" on "Niggas Bleed" on the CD. There was also a cassette tape in the machine. It was not engaged. Later today she would turn it on once she got him coked up and bragging like he liked to do. Then she would have the recording function turned on, but of course only she would be aware of this.

Present

"No, haven't seen him around, Pebbles. Fact, haven't seen Scotty for months, really."

"Well, okay, thanks, Carlos."

"I thought you two were quits anyway."

"We are. But something's come up." She realized that made

it sound like she just found out she had an STD or was pregnant but whatever. Through a gap of the rear sliding door, she could see part of the tarp covering Carlos's classic customized Honda Civic. He was a gearhead, a tuner, who street-raced his whip for money and prestige. She turned and started walking out of Furutani and Sons body shop on Marine in Gardena, a city in what was called the South Bay of LA County. She'd leaned her bike against the wall near the archway leading inside. She put on her helmet, checked her watch, and biked over to El Camino College, where she was a part-time tech in the environmental biology lab on campus. Today was grunt-work day, which included cleaning the lizard habitat and recalibrating instruments such as the atomic absorption spectrometer. This suited her just fine as she could do this work from muscle memory and ponder where to find Scott Waid. She'd gleefully pictured beating him with the aluminum bat she used on her softball team until he told her why he'd stolen her ride.

"Where's that sweet sled of yours, Pebbles?" Dr. Renku Murakama asked her at work. He was a fit surfing biologist in his midfifties who ran the lab and taught at the school.

Hastings was cleaning the glass terrarium of an iguana named Butch who was currently resting on the back of her neck and shoulders. She told Murakama what happened.

"Why didn't you call the cops?"

"What are they gonna do, Ren? Finding my wagon isn't going to be a priority with them." Too, she wanted the satisfaction of solving this matter herself.

"He put a gat on you, homey."

"Yeah, an old-school revolver out of one of those ancient

cop shows you like to watch." She stared off into space. Butch flicked his forked tongue, watching a fly buzz around.

"What?" Murakama said.

"The gun," she answered. "I've seen it before. Better, I've got an idea where that mufa took my car."

"Yeah, where?"

The house was on a narrow street less than three miles from the Hollywood Park Casino, which had nothing to do with Tinseltown. Its official address was on Century Boulevard in Inglewood, a working- to middle-class municipality of changing demographics, as the urban expression went. The area had been majority black and was now majority Latino, though black folks were still most of the local electeds. Scott Waid's Uncle Ro had a modest but well-cared-for home with an old maple tree out front. The tree offered shade under its boughs, rich with gold and green leaves spread like large petrified butterflies. Roland Weathers used to frequent the racetrack where now only the casino was left. He was something of a sporting man who had made money as a boxing promoter, nightclub owner, and gambler, among other ways. He'd even gotten into the top one hundred of the World Series of Poker twice.

"It's got to be in here, nephew," Weathers said as he loosened the rocker panel on the passenger side of the Falcon. "She'd put money out on the street for information as to where this short was." The two men and the car they were disassembling were in the backyard on the driveway where it ended at a detached garage. Two good-size toolboxes were open and tools were strewn about on the cracked, oil-stained concrete.

Waid had his hands on his hips, looking at the rear bench

seat they'd removed from the car. The neoprene covering had been carefully pulled back and the stuffing was exposed. "Maybe I shouldn't have let you talk me into this. Pebbles is gonna kill me."

Weathers made a sound in his throat as he used a penlight to look into the cavity he'd exposed. "The payday we're gonna see on this, you can buy her two of these wagons tricked out however she wants 'em."

"Oh, these motherfuckers," a female voice groused.

"Shit," Weathers cursed.

Pebbles Hastings stood inside the back gate, which they'd left open. Her aunt Debra Hastings was with her. The two women were unarmed but they had little fear of being shot by the men. Both had been here before and the niece recalled seeing the snub-nose that belonged to Uncle Ro. He'd once been married to a second cousin of her aunt.

"Baby, when we bust them greedy fools, they'll come clean. Or I'll knock some sense into that Ro's head," Debra Hastings had said.

"I know how this looks…" Weathers began, hands in front of him.

"I know exactly how it looks, sucka," Debra Hastings said, pointing at him. "You two figured you'd be slick and beat Pebbles out of whatever reward or lost treasure map you geniuses angled to find in this car."

"I wouldn't have used the gun on Peebles," Waid said. "It was just for scare."

"Shut up," the aunt said, moving forward.

"Yes, ma'am."

Debra Hastings stopped before Weathers, who wore overalls.

"After all this time, you suddenly believe that bullshit about the Hauler?"

"Who?" her niece said, something familiar tickling a corner of her memory.

"It was on the other night on *Astonishing Mysteries,* Dee," Weathers said pleadingly.

"I oughta slap the shit out of you, Ro. You two simple Negroes were smoking weed and watching that show when you thought this brilliant idea up, weren't you?"

Waid looked chagrined. "They showed the car. You know, on the what you call it, the re-creation."

"Of all the stupid," she began.

"Who are you talking about?" Pebbles Hastings asked.

"Hauler Kershaw," her aunt answered, exasperated.

That elicited a tingle of familiarity. "The football player."

"Yeah," her aunt drawled.

The younger Hastings snapped her fingers. "You two were a couple in high school."

Her aunt sighed. "Aw, shit, here we go."

1998

Hauler Kershaw: "I told you guys, I'm not gonna hurt anybody."

Police Detective Tim Guidry: "We know that, Hauler. We know that. We just want you to pull the car over."

On television screens across the Southland and the rest of the country, millions of viewers watched in real time as the LAPD did what was later dubbed the first ever little-old-lady chase through the tony neighborhoods of Los Angeles.

Black-and-whites on his tail, Fenton "Hauler" Kershaw was driving his mint silver-gray 1967 Jaguar XKE through the winding roads of Brentwood. Unerringly, akin to his actions in his previous career as a Super Bowl–winning running back dodging defenders, Kershaw evaded the numerous dead-end streets and cul-de-sacs of the area with seeming ease.

An LAPD helicopter and two others from competing news outlets followed the Jag on its roundabout course while in-studio news hosts supplied the hyperbolic narrative. They knew that Kershaw was talking with a police negotiator. He had both hands free to drive and shift as he was using the then fairly recent Bluetooth device, which the talking heads made sure to mention for the enthralled afternoon viewers. Activity stopped at numerous workplaces throughout the city as people gathered in lunchrooms or offices to watch the chase. Kershaw had been a well-paid and well-exposed pitchman for the Bluetooth device. Later, after his capture and trial, after his stabbing death during a prison riot had spawned multiple conspiracy theories, a transcript of the communications during the slow-motion chase was released.

> **Guidry:** Hey, man, it's Tim again. You're getting close, huh? Hello? I'm losing you. Hauler, you still there? Hello? Hauler, you still there? Come on, man, talk to me. Hello? Hello? Hauler? Hello! Hello, don't freeze me out, man... We can resolve this. We're almost at the goal line, right?

The transcript noted in parentheses that the phone cut off and the negotiator redialed.

Guidry: This is Tim again.

Kershaw: Oh, hi, Tim—

Guidry: Are you going up there, Hauler? What do you want to do? I know you're not running.

Kershaw: I just need to clear my head is all, Tim.

Guidry: I know you do, man, but you got everybody scared.

Kershaw: I just want to get to my house, Tim. You know what I'm saying? I just want to walk through my front door and lay my head down in my own bed. You hear what I'm saying?

Present

Before the sun went down, they strung up four mechanic's lights to see. As uncle and nephew put the Falcon back together, having essentially removed only the interior fixtures, niece and aunt sat on upended milk crates talking.

"When Hauler died in prison in '04, there had already been plenty about how the cops had framed him for his girlfriend's murder because of his brother." Debra sipped from a can of beer. "Or that, what's his name, Brody Deets had done it because she'd left him for Hauler."

"He's an actor, Aunt Deb. And a second-rate one at that."

She spread her arms, holding on to her beer. "I know, but us colored folk think all them white folks in the public eye congregate together plotting on us, so you know." She snickered.

Her niece chuckled too.

"Really, this mess started the night of that raid before you were born."

The younger Hastings knew the story. Her aunt and members of the extended family were living in a house in South Central in the late eighties. This was during the time of the infamous—at least in black neighborhoods—administration of police chief Daryl Gates. That night the cops tore down the door and tore up the house—a home that wasn't a rental and just happened to belong to a great-grandmother of Pebbles Hastings. The family subsequently sued the department and settled out of court for a sizable sum.

"How do you mean?" she asked.

Her aunt took another sip. "Jerome was doing his rap tapes then, selling them all over town and at swap meets. Back then NWA, Toddy Tee with his 'Batterram' song, they was all hot and had started like that so he caught some of that wave." She winked at Pebbles. "See how I threw in that surfer reference?"

"Uh-huh," her niece said, smiling.

"Okay, that night the cops bust him with less than an ounce of crack, which he didn't indulge but used as, you know, bribes to get his tapes played at certain clubs like the one Ro had, the Crimson Lounge. Anyway, they also grabbed some of his tapes, thinking the lyrics contained secret code among gang shot-callers."

"Who would be stupid enough to believe that?" the younger Hastings said.

"That's what the cops testified to in court during the suit. But it was just Jerome's raps on the tapes, at least when he had hold of them."

"What do you mean?"

"The tapes supposedly disappeared from the evidence lockup at the Seventy-Seventh Division, where there were several renegade members of the CRASH unit. Dudes who were robbing the drug dealers they busted, framing suspects consorting with prostitutes, and on and on."

Her aunt paused. The niece knew that the now disbanded anti-gang initiative had been the Community Resources Against Street Hoodlums.

"When Jerome started to get a name in the rap game, he became friends with one of those CRASH dudes who liked to bling-bling, an undercover cop who got all caught up in being a gangster his damn self, Jimmy Moore."

"He did time, right?"

"A bank robbery. He'd been dating one of the tellers. The money was never recovered and he disappeared when he got out, having done his full stretch 'cause he never said boo about where the take was." She looked over at the two men. "That's what y'all saw on the mystery show, wasn't it? That he was last seen in his mother's Falcon wagon."

Waid said, "Yeah," as he and Weathers bolted the rear bench seat into place using socket wrenches.

His uncle remained quiet but when the Falcon was brought up on that show, this being the first time he'd heard of a connection to the wagon and Moore, he'd recalled years before hearing from a chick he knew from back in the day when he ran the lounge. She was a party-girl type, always working an angle. She'd been looking for a car but hadn't said what kind. But on *Astonishing Mysteries* they'd re-created a scene with the woman and Moore, a connection Weathers didn't know about till then as well.

"See, that's what I'm sayin'," her aunt commented, "this stuff has all gotten twisted up over the years. The facts have been thrown out in favor of the ghost stories. Hauler's family did own a Falcon wagon like this one here. But this is not that car. This one used to belong to the retired gardener, Tyler Dircks, who died." He'd been the elderly man renting a room in the house on Fifty-First Street.

Four years ago when Pebbles Hastings was going out with Scott Waid, they'd asked her aunt about the Falcon. Waid was something of a shadetree mechanic and the niece was also handy with tools.

Another thread of memory flitted through her niece's mind. "Wasn't there some kind of thing between this crooked cop and Hauler Kershaw?"

"Not exactly," her aunt said. "But the cop who talked to Hauler that day they were trailing him through Brentwood, he'd been partners with Jimmy Moore at one point."

"Another rumor being he'd been in on the robbery?"

"Right."

"Was he?"

"Shit if I know, Pebbles," she said, irritated. "But who knows what other crazy conspiracies that TV show is going to spawn about the missing money or the secret to Hauler's death."

Down south, the sea-level temperature rose in the Pacific off the coasts of Peru and Ecuador, while the trade winds weakened where they normally swirled with strength. These elements signaled specific shifts in the climate patterns in the atmosphere. This in turn would result in the winter storms that usually bestowed heavy rains on the jungles of Central

America and southern Mexico being pushed further north, into Southern California. This El Niño effect portended a wet winter in drought-stricken LA. But currently, as the weeks of weather built up, in the South Bay on a humid fall evening, tipsy patrons drank craft beers in sports bars, pretty girls in stylish shoes checked out their gear in nightclub mirrors, and traffic was light on this stretch of Pacific Coast Highway where swaying palm fronds made their *whisk-whisk* sound in the air.

Pebbles Hastings had the windows rolled down in her Falcon station wagon as she cruised PCH. Against a backdrop of waves swelling and crashing, Sharon Jones and the Dap Kings did their version of "Goldfinger" on the aftermarket CD unit. A hot wind blew through the car's interior and warmed her skin as she came to a stoplight. A familiar-sounding engine rumbled and she looked left and up a hill to the access road that paralleled the highway. There, gliding past the guardrail, was another Falcon station wagon she was pretty sure was the same year as hers. This vehicle too had the wood-style side panels and sport rims not dissimilar to the kind Hastings had on her vehicle. She frowned while the car went along and disappeared from view around a bend. She didn't get a good look at the broad-shouldered driver and considered trying to follow it.

But she quickly discarded that idea and instead stopped in at a bar and got a vodka gimlet, which she drank slowly, contemplatively.

THE KILL SWITCH

by Willy Vlautin

THE HOUSE HAD three stories and was on the National Register but the people who owned it, professors at a university, and their two teenage kids seemed to be hoarders. Eddie Wilkens, a forty-two-year-old housepainter, was standing on a ladder above a small alcove deck on the second floor scraping paint when Houston called to him from below. Eddie waved, set his scraper on the deck's railing, and climbed down.

Houston, a fifty-three-year-old alcoholic, was thin and small in stature with greased-back gray hair. "Man, I don't know about this place," he said when Eddie got down to the ground. "The entire yard is covered in dog shit and it's all around the base of the house too. I've never seen so much. And then when I was walking around near the garage, I found a pair of men's underwear and a half-eaten sandwich sitting on top of it."

Eddie nodded, took a cigarette from his shirt pocket, and lit it. He spoke quietly. "Where I am on the second floor, in the alcove, there are McDonald's bags everywhere, and clothes sitting out, and stacks of moldy books. And on the railing there's what I think is a bloody tampon half wrapped in toilet paper."

Houston laughed and pointed to Eddie's cigarette.

Eddie gave him one from his pack along with a lighter. "When I went inside to get the third-story windows open I saw a plate with a half-eaten steak and green beans sitting on the stairs. It was covered in mold and ants were all over it. And if they want to go upstairs, they have to climb over it 'cause there's stacks of books and papers everywhere else."

Smoke came from Houston's mouth and again he laughed.

Eddie leaned against the house. "I bid this job on a Friday night. I always bid bad on Fridays. I barely looked around. I didn't want it; I could feel something was off so I just doubled the price and forgot about it. And then, shit, they took it anyway." He sighed. "Well, we'll take over the yard from here on out. We can't be stepping in dog shit, rotten sandwiches, and underwear for a month."

Houston nodded and they went back to work. They filled four black plastic garbage bags with trash and shit and then took lunch. When they came back they went up the ladders again and scraped. It was August and hot and the afternoon passed slowly. From the twenty-four-footer, Eddie lit a cigarette and looked out at the neighborhood. He could see his white van with WILKENS PAINTING COMPANY on the side and, past it, the tops of a dozen houses. He gazed out farther, across two streets, and made out a derelict-looking Pontiac Le Mans. It was red with a white top. He'd always liked those cars and decided when the day ended he'd walk over and see it. He finished his cigarette and went back to work.

Houston was on the other side of the house on a sixteen-footer, scraping. He was scared of heights and wouldn't go any higher. He kept in the shade and worked steadily until Eddie came into view.

"It's five thirty," Eddie yelled. "Let's call it."

Houston nodded and came down. They locked the four ladders together and left them next to the house. They swept the old caulk and paint chips from the tarps, folded them, and set their tools in the garage. They both had cigarettes in their mouths when they walked from the house. In front of the work van Eddie took a twenty-dollar bill from his wallet and handed it to Houston.

Houston had been paid in increments for three years. Twenty dollars a day four days a week, and eighty dollars on Fridays. Once a month they'd stop by the post office and Eddie would buy money orders for Houston's phone bill, electric bill, gas bill, and rent. He'd put them in envelopes and mail them off. Their next stop was the bank, where Houston put the rest of his money in a safe-deposit box. A box he could get to only on business days during office hours.

They had worked together for nine years with only two major lapses. The first was when Houston's mother died and he traveled back to Wyoming to clean out her apartment. He told Eddie he would be gone a week and then went missing for five months. When he came back he was drinking a fifth a day and living in his car. The second time he just quit showing up. He didn't answer his phone and wouldn't answer his door. He fell into a three-month-long drunk and ended up losing his place and his car and living on the street. When Eddie finally found him, he was holed up near the river in an old camping tent. He let Houston live in his basement, got him back on his feet, and gave him startup money for an apartment.

Houston bummed another cigarette, got in his car, and left. Eddie finished his and walked down the two streets to the Le Mans. The car sat covered in dust and there was a large dent in the front right panel above the wheel well. The paint was faded and oxidized. A half a dozen spider cracks appeared along both sides of the car where bad Bondo patches had been attempted. The rims were cheap, aftermarket, and two of the tires were flat. The top wasn't vinyl but metal painted white. It was oxidized also. He figured it to be a '68 or '69.

He took a small spiral notepad from his back pocket and wrote, *I'd be interested in buying this car. I have cash. Eddie Wilkens.* He left his number, put the note under the windshield wiper, walked back to his van, and drove home.

In the carport he found the kid, Russell, waiting on a lawn chair near the back door. The boy was eleven but looked much younger. He was small, had brown hair, and his ears were too big for his head, and even at that age he was getting picked on at school. He wore jeans, a red T-shirt, and black tennis shoes. He lived in the house next door with his grandmother, mother, and older half brother, Curtis.

"Where did you work today?" he asked timidly.

"We're on the new job now," said Eddie and opened the back door to his house. He yelled for Early, and an old black mutt got down from the couch and hobbled outside.

Russell went to the dog and began to pet it. "You're done with the lady who had the orange fish?"

"We finished that on Friday."

"Did she like the paint job?"

Eddie said, "Yep. She paid us and made us those cookies I gave you. Remember?"

The boy kept petting the dog. He nodded. "I remember now. So you don't have any brushes for me to clean?"

"Not today," said Eddie. "We're scraping all week."

"That's the worst part of the job, isn't it?"

"It is."

"Did you eat dinner before you got home?"

"No," Eddie said. "Your mom's not around?"

Russell shook his head.

"What about your grandma?"

He shrugged his shoulders.

"Let me look at you," said Eddie.

Russell smiled suddenly and stood up.

"Yep, I was right," he said. "You look hungry."

Russell laughed. "That's what Monica used to say."

Eddie nodded.

"Monica's not coming back?"

"I don't think so," said Eddie.

"Why?"

"It's a long story," Eddie said and bent down and put his hand on the dog. "I know she misses you, though. She told me that the last time I talked to her. Anyway, you want something to eat?"

"I'm hungry if you're hungry," said the boy.

Eddie reached into his shirt pocket, took a cigarette from the pack, and lit it. "Get your bike and tell your grandma you're going to the store. I'll make a list. You go shopping and I'll cook. Deal?"

The boy nodded and went back through the gate. He returned five minutes later pushing a bike with two flat tires. He leaned it against the house, opened Eddie's back door, and walked up the steps into the kitchen. "I think Curtis let the air out of the tires...I can't find the pump," he said softly. His face was red and wet with tears.

Eddie took a drink of beer. "Why would he let the air out of your tires?"

"I don't know," Russell replied.

Eddie finished the grocery list, put out his cigarette, and stood up. "We'll use the compressor in the garage. And remember, you can always leave your bike here if you want to protect it." He handed the boy the list, forty dollars, and the old backpack he had Russell use to carry the groceries in. They went outside; Eddie unlocked the garage, turned on the compressor, and filled the bike tires.

A week scraping on ladders passed. When he could, Eddie looked over the two streets to the Le Mans. He wasn't sure why exactly, but he began to want it. Each day after work he looked to see his note still there and untouched. When there was a night rain in the middle of the week and his note became illegible, he left another. But no one called. When Friday came and they'd finished for the day, he went to the houses around the car. He knocked on doors and asked if anyone knew who owned it, but no one did.

He and Houston worked a half day on Saturday and when they were done, they spread out and knocked on doors farther down the neighborhood and finally Houston met the person who owned the car. It was a man who lived on a busier street a block away. Houston told Eddie which house and left.

The man was in his early twenties and let Eddie inside. The front room had dozens of drawings taped to the walls. They were pen-and-ink and all of them had women in bondage outfits and positions. The women were beautiful but always bound. They didn't appear to be either happy or upset by it; they were just there.

The man was skinny with shaved-short dark hair. He looked anemic and pale and he stood stooped over.

"The guy I work with said you own the Le Mans."

The man nodded.

"You interested in selling it?"

"I might be," he said. "But I ain't broke enough to sell it right now."

"Does it run?"

"It did at one time but I don't know if it still does. A friend of mine said it's not good to start a car with flat tires so I haven't tried in a while."

Eddie glanced around the room. "You drew these?"

The man nodded.

"That's a lot of work."

"Yeah," he replied.

Eddie looked at the man. "You have the title for the car?"

"Yeah," he said.

"Well, I'd like to buy if you ever want to sell it."

"Let me think about it."

"You mind if we swap numbers?"

"Sure," the man said and Eddie began writing his number in the small spiral notebook he kept in his back pocket.

He and Houston had primed the house and were finishing two days of filling and caulking when Eddie's phone rang and the man with the Le Mans told him his rent was due and he didn't have the cash to cover it. He would sell the car to Eddie right then if he had the money.

"Well, how much do you want for it?" Eddie asked while caulking a window.

"How about four hundred?" the man said.

"I gotta go to the bank. I'll be over in an hour," he said and hung up. He got down from the ladder and told Houston the news.

"Don't do it," warned Houston. "You don't even know if it has an engine, do you?"

"No," Eddie replied.

"Then you're nuts." Houston put his caulk gun in a water bucket and wiped his hands with a wet rag.

"It's just one of those things," Eddie said and lit a cigarette. "I'm at the point where I'd pay two grand even if the tranny was shot, the engine was gone, and it didn't have a title. I don't know why exactly, but I just have to have it now."

Houston bummed a cigarette from Eddie. "Even if it does run you'll spend more than two grand fixing it up," he said.

"I know."

"Paint jobs are a lot of money."

"I know that too."

"Old cars are like bad women," said Houston. "They're fun at first but they break down a lot and take your money little by little. For me it's all right when it's little by little, but then always, eventually, they hit you with the big bill. But by then you've already put so much time and money into them it's hard to quit. So you pay up and then it starts all over again."

"I know all that," Eddie said and laughed. "But it'll give me something to do at night."

Houston nodded. "The last car I gave a shit about ruined me. A 1965 Mercury Cougar."

"I like those," said Eddie.

"I did too, but I was downtown, on Broadway, going up the hill when she cut out on me. The car was so damn heavy I couldn't push it and I couldn't back up 'cause there was too much traffic. It was rush hour. And then the cops came." He threw the wet rag in the bucket of water and combed his hair back with a small black comb he kept in his pocket. "They helped me, all right. They saw I was drunk and took me to jail and impounded the car."

"What happened to the Cougar?"

"I didn't give a fuck then and I don't give a fuck now. It was dead to me after that day. The way I look at it, any car that breaks down on me when I'm drunk or in a traffic jam is no longer my car. I give no second chances. I hoped they crushed the shit out of it and melted it into bedpans." Houston stopped and took a long drag off the cigarette. "It was a great-looking car, though. I spent three grand on the paint job alone. White with silver sparkles. Man, it was something else."

Eddie parked the work van in front of the Le Mans. Houston sat in the passenger seat and listened to the radio while Eddie walked to the owner's house.

"I only have a couple minutes," the man said when he answered. He was dressed in an Applebee's work shirt.

"Here's the four hundred," Eddie said and gave it to him.

The man counted it and handed Eddie the signed-over title and two keys. They shook hands and Eddie walked back to the van and got in.

"You get it?" asked Houston.

Eddie smiled and waved the title at him. He started the van and took a small air compressor he kept in a milk crate, plugged it into the cigarette lighter, and went out the back to the Le Mans. The driver's-side door opened and he looked in. It smelled of dust and mold, and the front seat was in worse shape than he'd thought, as was the floor carpet. But the backseat was decent and so was the dash. He opened the trunk to find eight old car batteries sitting on a piece of cardboard.

"Why you think there's so many in there?" asked Houston, who was now watching from the sidewalk.

"I don't know," said Eddie and shut the trunk. He lit a cigarette and opened the hood.

"At least it has an engine," said Houston.

Eddie looked it over. A tired-looking 350 covered in dust and oil and rust.

"You going to try and start it?"

Eddie shook his head. "I have a tow rope. I was thinking you could tow me in the van to my place. After that I'll take you back to your car and set you free."

Houston nodded and Eddie shut the hood. All four tires were nearly bald but they held air and Eddie hooked the tow rope from the van to the front of the Le Mans. With blue painter's tape he spelled out IN TOW on the back windshield, and Houston put the van in low and towed him out of the neighborhood. They went the four miles to Eddie's house and parked on the street.

Russell must have been waiting on the lawn chair in Eddie's backyard when he heard the van because he came out front and walked across the lawn to see Eddie get out of the Le Mans.

"Why are you in that car?" he asked.

"I just bought it," said Eddie.

"You just bought a car?"

Eddie nodded. "You think you can steer? We need to get it into the carport."

Russell nodded. "This is really your car?"

"It is," he said. "Now get in and steer and we'll push it up."

The boy got in the driver's seat and held on to the wheel while Eddie and Houston pushed it from the street into the carport.

"Does it go fast?" the boy asked when he got out.

Houston laughed.

"I don't even know if it runs," said Eddie.

"But you bought it anyway?"

"It looks cool, doesn't it?"

"If you like dents and Bondo, it looks cool," Houston said.

"I like it," the boy said.

Eddie looked at Houston. "See, I told you Russell had taste."

Houston again laughed.

"Will you make it run?" Russell asked.

"Eventually," Eddie said and that set off Houston laughing again.

The next evening Russell sat in the lawn chair next to the dog while Eddie worked. He took the eight batteries from the trunk and set them in a row at the back of the carport. He took the best-looking one from them, put it on a charger, removed the one from under the hood, and put that on another charger. He checked the fluids. The oil was full but the transmission was empty. He wrote a note to get a transmission filter kit and fluid, a fuel filter, oil, and an oil filter. The top radiator hose was bulging and covered with duct tape and would also need to be replaced.

"Do you think it's going to be fast?" asked Russell.

"Probably not unless I put a new engine in it."

"Are you going to put a new engine in it?"

"Nah, I don't care about going fast. Even when I was your age, I didn't. I'll get it running, though."

"Are you going to paint it?"

"Nope," Eddie said. "I'm going to keep the dents. You might think I'm crazy but I like dents. I'll get the front seat reupholstered, new carpet set in, and I'll put in a good stereo. It'll be nice inside when I'm driving around but I don't want to be one of those guys who has a meltdown if a bird shits on the hood."

"I can wash it if you want," the boy said.

Eddie laughed. "I like the way you think, but it probably hasn't been washed in years. It'll be a hard job."

"I can get it clean," the boy said.

"Well, I'll pay you twice what I do for the van 'cause it's going to take you a while. Maybe tomorrow you could come over and let Early out. I have to do a couple bids in the west hills after work so I won't be home until later."

"I can feed Early too, if you want."

"I'd appreciate that," Eddie said. "If you want to wash the car, please do, but don't feel like you have to. I'll put the house key under the front seat of the Le Mans. But don't tell your brother you have it and don't let him in the house, okay?"

"I won't," the boy said. "I don't tell him anything ever."

The next evening Eddie parked the van in the carport. As

he got out, he noticed four of the batteries from the Le Mans were gone. Russell's bike was still leaned against the garage and nothing else was taken. He set down a bag from the Auto Zone, opened the back door, and let the dog out. He took a beer from the fridge, unlocked the garage, and got to work. He changed the oil, replaced the top radiator hose and the fuel filter, and then took one of the charged batteries and set it back in the Le Mans. He put two gallons of new gas in the tank, primed the carburetor, and got in the driver's seat. He put the key in the ignition and the engine caught on the third try and idled smoothly. He got back out and checked for leaks, but there were none. As he stood watching, his gate opened and Russell walked slowly toward him.

"I missed you starting it," the boy said.

"It wasn't much," said Eddie. "I just put a little gas in it and *bam*. I got lucky. She's an old engine but she sounds pretty good."

"I think she sounds good too," he said and went to sit down in the lawn chair but it clearly pained him to do so.

"You're hurt?" asked Eddie.

Russell looked at him and tears welled in his eyes.

"Curtis?"

Russell nodded.

"Did you tell your grandmother and your mom?"

Russell nodded vaguely.

"Do you want me to talk to him?"

Russell shook his head.

"Where's your mom?"

"She's at work."

"Where's Curtis?"

"I don't know."

"You think you need a doctor?"

"No," Russell said quietly.

Eddie paused for a time and took a cigarette from a pack on the hood of the car.

"You did a good job washing the car."

"I couldn't get the hood," the boy said.

"Don't worry about the hood. I'll get it. I'm going to change the tranny filter and if that does the trick and the transmission works, we'll take her for a little spin. Maybe go get pizza." He lit the cigarette, inhaled deeply, and blew the smoke out. "But you don't like pizza, do you?"

"Pizza's my favorite," the boy said and smiled.

"Are you sure?"

"I'm sure," he said.

"I thought you didn't like pizza."

"You know pizza's my favorite," he said and laughed.

"But I got a question to ask you first, Russell. Do you know anything about the missing batteries?"

Tears welled suddenly in the boy's eyes. He tried to speak but couldn't.

"It's all right," said Eddie. "I'm not mad at you. It's just that four of the batteries are missing."

Russell began sobbing.

Eddie went to him and patted him gently on the shoulder. "We'll talk about it later. I'm gonna put this thing up on blocks, change out the tranny filter, and see if we can get it to move."

Russell brought him two beers and a new pack of cigarettes before Eddie finished. He then started the car and put it in reverse, and the car went in reverse. He put it in forward and it went forward.

"We're getting lucky," said Eddie. "The tranny's all right and the engine's all right. I'm going to do one more thing and then we'll take her for a spin."

"What are you going to do?"

"I'm putting in a kill switch."

"What's that?" asked the boy.

Eddie showed him a small electrical switch. "I'll set it up so you'll just hit this switch and the car won't start. It's for safety. These old cars are easy as shit to steal. My brother had his van stolen once; I had a Dodge Dart stolen twice, and I had an old Ford pickup stolen too. That one cost me. I had a lot of tools in it. After that, I started putting in kill switches."

"Then they can't steal it?"

"Not unless they tow it or figure out where the switch is," said Eddie. He spliced the coil wire and ran two wires from each side of it through a hole he'd drilled below the glove box. He lay on his back on the floor of the passenger side connecting the wires to the switch he had hidden there. Russell leaned over the backseat and watched until Eddie finished.

"I think we're done now," he said and sat up. He started the car and then hit the kill switch and the engine stopped. He looked at Russell and smiled. "Now call your mom and tell her we're going to get pizza, okay?"

Russell crawled out over the front seat and walked back to his house. He came back two minutes later while Eddie was cleaning up in the kitchen sink.

"I can go," he said.

"You called her?"

Russell nodded.

"You ever waxed a car?"

Russell shook his head.

"Waxing a car is one of my least favorite things to do. My dad used to make me wax his car, and if I didn't do it right he'd be an asshole about it for a week. So I won't wax my own car. I just won't. But if I call your mom and she says she didn't talk to you, I'm going to make you wax the Le Mans, all right?"

Russell looked at the ground but didn't say anything.

"All right?"

The boy nodded slowly.

Eddie called Russell's mother, spoke to her for a minute, and hung up.

"You shouldn't lie," said Eddie and lit a cigarette. "Lying is a bad habit and no one likes liars. Your mom says you never called. Is she lying or are you?"

"But she doesn't care," the boy told him. "She said she doesn't care what I do as long as I'm home when she gets home."

Eddie looked at Russell. "That might be the case, but that's not the problem. The problem is that you lied to me. We're friends and you lied to me. I know you know about the batteries too. And you wouldn't even tell me about that. It doesn't look good. It looks like you're a bad kid. Now, I know you're not bad but you gotta start acting like a man once in a while and not like a little dude."

Russell began crying.

Eddie took a drink of beer. "I'm going to ask you one question, Russell. Did you call your mom?"

"No," he whispered.

Eddie smiled. "See, it ain't so bad telling the truth."

The boy looked at him with tears streaming down his face. "Do you want me to leave now?"

"Nah," Eddie said. "You got to lighten up. We have work to do. We have to give this thing a test drive and then we gotta eat pizza."

Russell wiped his face and said, "I told you she doesn't care."

"That's not the point," Eddie said and laughed. "Jesus, you can be one hardheaded son of a bitch sometimes."

The Le Mans front end was the problem. It was loose and drifty. The car needed new tie-rods, an alignment, tires and rims, and he'd have to give it a brake job. But it ran and the transmission seemed to be switching gears when it was supposed to. They drove around the industrial side of town for nearly an hour. They passed the horse track and drove along the river. They had the windows down and Russell hung his arm out the side. Eddie took them to a pizza parlor, they ate dinner, and afterward Russell played video games while Eddie drank beer and worked on bids in the corner of the half-empty restaurant.

The next morning Eddie found a can of car wax in the garage and set it on the hood of the Le Mans next to a handful of rags and a note saying *Read the instructions on the can before you do anything. The money is for lunch. I'll pay you for the waxing after you do it.* Underneath the can he set ten dollars.

He went back to the garage and found a quart of old blue oil paint on a shelf. He opened it, stirred it for a long time, and then painted each of the four remaining battery handles. He drove to the job site and parked. The body of the house was finished and now the best part of the job was beginning. They were painting trim. The customers wanted three different colors and it meant two extra days of work. He took his best exterior brushes from his toolbox, his job-site radio, and headed up the drive. He unlocked the ladders and set them up.

He waited an hour before he began calling Houston from the top of the ladder, but Houston didn't answer. At lunch he drove to Houston's apartment to find him in his underwear. The TV was playing behind him. Inside the apartment was dark with the curtains drawn, and Houston was pale and sick and coughed as he stood in the doorway.

"Jesus," Eddie said, smiling. "What happened to you?"

"I'm not sure," said Houston quietly.

"Where did you get the money?"

"A guy I used to know invited me to his house. He was having a party and there was a bottle of Maker's. I took it and sat out on his porch and that's all I remember."

"You drank the whole thing?"

"I don't know."

"It was nice of you to call and tell me you weren't coming in."

Houston ran his hands through his hair. "I set my alarm but I guess I didn't hear it."

"I don't hear it now," Eddie said.

"I must have shut it off somehow."

"Does the TV turn on by itself?"

Houston sighed. "Goddamn it, Eddie."

"Don't get mad at me."

"I couldn't get out of bed, all right? I've been shitting my guts out all morning and I'm sick."

Eddie laughed. "All you fucking guys lie. All you have to do is call and say, 'I got loaded last night and I'm a scumbag pussy and can't get out of bed on a hangover.'"

Houston shook his head and leaned against the doorjamb.

"Get your clothes on," said Eddie. "We'll eat lunch and then you're going to work."

"I don't know if I can."

"I don't give a shit if you puke all over their lawn; they sure as fuck won't notice. Get dressed."

Houston nodded and began looking for his clothes.

Eddie drove them to a Greek diner and they sat in the back, in the bar, and he ordered Houston a beer.

"Drink it," said Eddie, "and then eat lunch. We'll buy you a six-pack on the way to the job site. I don't want any shaky lines today."

"I don't know if I can eat," Houston whined.

"Try a grilled cheese and some soup, you sorry sack of shit," Eddie said. "And if you complain one more time I'll make you buy."

Houston nodded; the beer came and he drank it. He ordered another. They ate lunch, stopped at a mini-mart for a six-pack, and then went back to work. Houston threw up twice but kept at it and the beer finally settled him and he got through the day.

That evening Eddie parked the van in the carport. He took out a bucket holding the dirty brushes in water. He passed the Le Mans and when he did he saw that the rest of the old batteries were gone. He walked to the back door, let the dog out, grabbed a beer from the refrigerator, and sat on a lawn chair and smoked a cigarette. The old dog wandered around the yard and then came back to him and sat by his feet.

Russell came through the gate minutes later. He walked hunched over and Eddie realized just how small the boy was, how thin his legs and arms were. As Russell got closer, Eddie looked at the boy's hands and could see blue paint on them.

Russell stopped ten feet away. "I waxed the car," he said.

"You did a good job," Eddie replied. "It's hard, isn't it?"

"It wasn't that hard, but I couldn't get the hood."

"I'll get the hood," said Eddie.

"Do you need the brushes done?" the boy asked.

"There's five in the bucket. The big one, the three-inch, is pretty trashed so don't worry about it too much."

The boy moved toward the bucket.

"Why don't you come over here and say hey to Early before you get to work?"

But Russell wouldn't come closer to Eddie or the dog.

Eddie looked at him. "Can I ask you a question?"

The boy nodded.

"Why do you have blue paint on your hands?"

Tears fell down the boy's face.

"You can't always cry, man…Get me a beer and yourself a Coke and then come over here and sit."

Russell nodded and went into the house. He came out with two cans and sat across from Eddie.

"I bet you tried like a mother to wash that paint off your hands."

Russell nodded.

"But it wouldn't come off?"

"No."

"That's 'cause it's oil paint. I'll get you some thinner. You have to use thinner with oil."

"I didn't mean to steal them, Eddie. I didn't. Curtis made me."

"Why?"

"He takes them somewhere and they give him money for them."

"Is Curtis home?"

Russell shook his head. "I told him you were my friend and that he shouldn't take them. But...but then he made me take them." Tears again filled his eyes. "You have to believe me, Eddie. I didn't want to take them but he made me." The boy pulled up his shirt and his small chest was black and blue.

Eddie took a drink off the beer and lit a cigarette. His face didn't change. He said quietly, "Follow me to the garage and we'll get the paint off your hands and then you're going to wash my brushes. After that we'll get something to eat. Are you hungry?"

"I am if you are," the boy said.

"Good. You get the brushes done and we'll get a quick bite to eat. I have some errands to do tonight so we'll just get tacos."

"From Alberto's Truck?"

"Sure, we'll go there if you want."

"I want to go there if you want to go there."

Eddie laughed.

"I was worried you'd never like me again," Russell whispered.

"It's your brother who's in trouble," Eddie said and put out his cigarette. "Not you. How old is he again?"

"Fifteen."

Eddie nodded, got up, and waved to Russell to follow him. The blue paint came off the boy's hands with a rag full of thinner and then Eddie sent him to the basement with the bucket of dirty brushes to clean. When he could see the light in the basement go on he went next door to Russell's home. The side door was open and he called out and the old woman, Russell's grandmother, yelled from a back room for him to come inside.

It was a home she had lived in for thirty-five years. Her husband, Des, worked as a truck driver and had kept his shop, lawn, and house clean and well maintained. Eddie and Des had gotten along well, but two years back Des had had a heart attack and passed on. The old woman fell apart after that and her only daughter, Connie, moved in with Russell and Curtis.

The kitchen was nothing but dirty dishes, pans, and garbage. In the living room, clothes were thrown about everywhere and the TV was on. An Xbox sat on a small coffee table next to soda cans, candy-bar wrappers, and fast-food bags.

The old woman sat in her room in a recliner reading a book with the help of a magnifier. She was frail for seventy years old. She had long gray hair that came down to her chest. She wore a bathrobe and slippers. The room was stale and hot and smelled of urine. Both the windows in the room were closed. There was a hot plate with a teapot on it and a stack of Cup-a-Soups on her dresser.

"How you been?" he asked.

"Hello, Eddie," she said.

"What are you reading?"

"A murder mystery."

"Are you still watching *Days of Our Lives*?"

The old woman shook her head.

"No Bo and Hope?"

"I don't like going outside my room."

"Because of Curtis?"

"Curtis and Connie."

"Curtis's not around?"

She shook her head.

"You eating enough?"

"I don't have much of an appetite anymore."

"It's hot in here. Do you want your windows open?"

She nodded.

Eddie went to them. They were both old weighted windows. It took him a while but he got them open and fresh air came into the room.

Houston was in his underwear when Eddie beat on his door two hours later. He was drinking off a forty-ounce bottle of Olde English and came to the door carrying it.

"I thought you said nine?"

"It's eight forty-five," Eddie said. "I don't see how you can drink that shit."

"I like malt liquor."

"Get dressed and let's go."

"And you say you're buying?"

Eddie nodded and lit a cigarette. He went to Houston's fridge, took a can of Coors from it, opened it, and sat down on the couch and waited for him to dress.

They drove to a strip bar called the Little Fox where a half dozen men watched a woman dancing naked. Behind them were five men playing video poker machines and two more sitting at the bar. The bartender was a sixty-year-old black woman and Eddie bought two beers from her, got ten singles, and handed the money and a beer to Houston. Houston went to the front and sat while Eddie stood in the back at the bar. He watched the woman dance to two more songs, ordered another beer, and then Connie came to the stage.

She was a forty-year-old alcoholic with dyed-red hair and large sagging breasts. Even from where he stood, he could see her body was beginning to go. She danced three songs and toward the end of the third, Eddie went to the front and sat. He placed a five-dollar bill down and when the song finished and she went to take it, he said, "You got a minute to talk?"

She nodded and told him she'd come out and find him.

Another woman came onstage and Eddie grabbed Houston and they sat at a small table in the back of the bar.

"Just remember what she says," Eddie said. "She's enough trouble that I don't want to have a conversation with her when I'm alone."

Houston had his eyes on the woman dancing. "You'll buy another round, won't you?"

"I'll buy you a six-pack on the way home. We're gonna get out of here the second she and I quit talking."

Houston rubbed his hands together and smiled. "But I'll need another beer if I'm gonna just sit here and listen."

Eddie took five dollars from his wallet and gave it to him. Houston got another beer and then Connie came out in an Asian robe and black high-heeled shoes.

"What's going on?" she asked and sat at the table.

Eddie told her about the batteries, about Russell's chest and the beatings that Curtis had been giving him.

"I can't control him," she said hopelessly. "How do you think I feel? No one ever asks how I feel living with him. His father won't do a goddamn thing and hasn't paid child support since he was three."

Eddie lit a cigarette. "I know you got a tough deal. I just

want to let you know that if he steals any more of my stuff, I'm gonna call the cops on him."

"You shouldn't be leaving your stuff out there," she said and looked out to the stage.

"What about Russell?" he asked.

"What about him?"

"He's getting the shit beat out of him by his brother."

"Who didn't get the shit beat out of them as a kid? And why you spend so much time with him anyway? What's in it for you?"

Eddie finished his beer and stood. "I'll tell you this: If Curtis steals anything more from me I'll call the cops and I'll press charges. And you let him know if he beats up Russell anymore, I'll go to Child Services and I'll fuck up both your lives."

Eddie walked across the road and disappeared into a mini-mart and then came back carrying a six-pack of beer. He got in the driver's seat and handed the beer to Houston. "I gotta say, I didn't think she'd start crying. I thought she'd jump down my throat when I said the Child Services bit."

"She ain't as tough as she thinks she is," said Houston.

"Was she on something?"

"Heroin, I bet."

"You think so?" Eddie asked.

"My ex-wife couldn't quit that shit," Houston said. "I can tell pretty easy."

Eddie sighed.

Houston opened one of the cans of beer. "You know, I even ironed this shirt. I thought I might have a shot with her. I could move in next door. I'd kick out Curtis. And then Russell and the old lady would move in with you, and suddenly I'd about have my own place. I'd be set."

Eddie laughed and started the van.

The house on the National Register was done and he and Houston packed up the ladders and did the last walk-through and Eddie received the final check. They drove to the next house, a west hills home, a money house, and unloaded their gear and left it on the side of the garage. Eddie deposited the check, gave Houston his eighty-dollar weekend allotment, dropped him back at his car, and drove home.

When he got there, the Le Mans was gone.

He let Early out and opened a beer. He smoked a cigarette, finished the can, and called the police. When he hung up he walked next door to find the side door open again. He called inside and the old woman again yelled from her room. She was sitting in the same chair in a housecoat reading a book. She hadn't seen Russell or Curtis.

The police came an hour later and Eddie filled out a report. Afterward he sat outside and drank beer and barbecued chicken. He cooked beans, made a salad, ate, and then smoked more cigarettes and drank more beer and worked on a bid down the street from the National Register house. After that he went to bed.

His phone woke him at midnight. The police had found his car. It was left in the middle of an intersection downtown. They had apprehended four people and his car had been towed to a police impound lot. He hung up the phone and went back to bed.

He woke early the next morning to let his dog out and saw

Russell sitting on the lawn chair. His face was beat up. Both his eyes were black, and his little nose was swollen.

Eddie told him to come inside and wait in the kitchen. He went to his bedroom and dressed. When he came out, Russell was on the kitchen floor petting Early.

"Can you still chew with your face that beat up?"

The boy nodded.

"I'll make pancakes," Eddie said. "You want bacon with them?"

Russell again nodded.

Eddie started the coffee and bacon and fed Early. The boy sat at the kitchen table and remained silent as Eddie made the pancakes and then set the food on plates and sat down.

"Let's eat first," Eddie said. "We got some talking to do but that's hard on an empty stomach. You probably didn't eat last night, did you?"

Russell shook his head and tears welled in his eyes but he ate the breakfast. When they'd both finished, Eddie put down his fork and pushed his plate away. "Let's go outside so I can smoke," he said and they went out and sat across from each other on lawn chairs.

"So what happened?"

"He stuck my head in the toilet," Russell whispered. "Until…until I told him where you kept the key to it." He began crying so hard he was barely understandable. He gasped. "I'm sorry…I'm sorry…I'm sorry."

"It's not your fault," Eddie said. "I would have told him too. Take a breath."

Russell wiped his eyes and tried to breathe. "I told him where the keys were, but I didn't think it would start. I thought the switch would be on but it wasn't."

Eddie blew out a plume of smoke. "I must have left it off. I was tinkering on the car the other night and I must have just forgot. So then what happened?"

"When it started, I was like, *Oh no,* and then Curtis made me go with them so I would be blamed too. He drove out near the river and then we went downtown. Burny and Josh were in the back and Curtis was driving too fast and you said that the engine was old and needed to be driven slow. But Curtis wouldn't listen and then we came to that big intersection that has all those different lights and streets. We came to the middle of it and I reached down and hit the kill switch."

"You hit the kill switch?" Eddie said and laughed.

"I did," Russell said. " 'Cause you're my best friend."

"What happened?"

"Curtis knew I did something but he didn't know what. So he just started hitting me. He hit me over and over, and Burny and Josh were laughing and cars were honking. I guess there were cops nearby 'cause they came and saw Curtis hitting me and then Curtis tried to hit one of the cops and then they knew the car was stolen and they took us away. My mom came and got me, but she left Curtis there."

"All that really happened?"

"I'm not a liar anymore."

Eddie nodded.

"Do you want me to leave now?"

Eddie shook his head. "I can't believe you risked your life for a piece-of-shit old car."

"It's not a piece of shit," Russell said and wiped his eyes.

"So what are you doing today?" Eddie asked.

Russell shook his head.

"I just got a job doing a remodel on a house near the river. I don't start for a month but they just gutted the whole first floor and there's an old claw-foot tub they're throwing out. The head contractor said I could have it. I was thinking we pick it up and then I gotta do a bid in the hills and then we'll eat some lunch. After that we'll pick up a new toilet and sink. A friend of mine is coming tomorrow to tile the bathroom. I have to get the shower out and gut the bathroom tonight so he has room."

"You're redoing the bathroom?"

Eddie nodded.

"Does that mean Monica's coming back?"

"No," Eddie said and laughed. "I'm just getting old and my back hurts. I think sitting in the bath might help. Are you too beat up to help?"

Russell shook his head. "I can help," he said. "My face hurts but nothing else does. I told Curtis that he didn't have the guts to hit me in the face. I knew he'd hit me in the face then and when the cops and my mom saw how bad I looked, I knew they wouldn't let him come back."

"That's pretty smart thinking," Eddie said. "And just so you know, I'm pressing charges against Curtis for stealing the car. With all that and hitting the cop and his priors, he'll be in some shit for a while. But sooner or later, eventually, he'll be back."

"I know," Russell said. "But I'm going to start growing soon. I know I will."

THE PLEASURE OF GOD

by Luis Alberto Urrea

THE OLD MAN lurched over the pass under the brutal Mexican sun. Behind him, the ocean was dull and heavy as indigo felt, heaving slowly toward a shore hidden by cliffs. He didn't waste time staring at the sea. The sea was of interest to him only when his neighbors brought up abalones or langostinos. Tortillas and butter and beans. Not the fried shit from cans, either—beans, boiled and soupy with a chunk of fatty pork for flavor.

He was angry at the sun. It hammered so hard that he was bent under its blows, and his hair had stiffened with old sweat into a sculpture. He smiled once, in spite of the rotten molar in his mouth. He was as old as that useless sea, and his hair was still black. Even the hair on his balls. He had never been broken, and he intended to live forever. He was cursed with vitality.

He spit. He normally would save it in this heat, would suck a rock as he walked to make himself salivate. But he had two Pepsi bottles full of water strung across his shoulders on a rope. It was only twenty kilometers. He should have worn shoes for this hike, though. But he didn't have any good walking shoes. He wore his huaraches—and they made him furious. Leather straps and soles made of old tires. A cactus thorn had worked its way deep into his left foot, and he couldn't carve it out with his knife. He stomped harder with that foot, rubbing the pain into his flesh so the infection would swell and force the thorn out. He wasn't afraid of infections—the bad molar was leaking black-tasting poison into his mouth and swelling his cheek. When he got to town, he'd find some pliers. He'd show God and everyone else what he was made of.

He walked on. Not far now. He had walked out of Sal Si Puedes, his little blister of a fishing town hugging the cliffs, with one thing on his mind: revenge. Especially now—man, he was going to ride, but thanks to those *cabrones,* he had to walk. That he had to walk to Ensenada made him madder than he usually was. Life was generous: it gave a man a thousand things to be pissed off about. He was old, after all. Old men had the right to be mad all day. Just a kilometer to go till he reached Guadalupe, a small community on the outskirts of the city. There was a guy there with a wrecking yard. He could get pliers there. And the guy had a mule. The old man had a deal in mind. He was going to trade for that mule. And he was going to collect what he wanted.

"I get what I want," he said to the air. "When I want it."

He would have ridden his old moped up the highway, but those *narco* assholes had backed into it and broken the back wheel and fork. Well, he could have walked up the frontage road, nice and level, except they had hung naked bodies off the bridge after they crunched his moto. The *policías* had shut the whole road down. God damn them. Made him walk over the mountains and get thorns in his feet, and him with this rotten tooth leaking pus into his mouth.

He smiled again.

"We will see what we see," he said.

They had that yellow VW van, though, those *pinches narcos*. He liked that van. He was going to take it when he was done with them. He would shit in their mothers' milk first. Then park their van beside the sea.

His ridiculous mother came into his mind. She had named him Benigno, a stupid peasant name he never forgave her for giving him. But her sayings, her *dichos*, came back to him sometimes. Her tone came into his voice when he didn't want it. Usually advising a course of mayhem. She hadn't survived as a trash picker by being soft. He shook his head and grimaced at the memory of that little leather-faced demon. He saw a flash of her striking a pit bull over the head with a pipe. Today, Mother's voice said: *Vengeance is the pleasure of God.* Oh yes, he had heard that one before.

"Bueno, pues, Mama," he said out loud. "I must be God, then."

He descended.

He first saw that VW van at the prison.

Before Benigno got into the orphanage racket, marrying the widow Abigail in Tijuana and opening their house to street kids and abandoned waifs and attracting Baptist missionaries with their endless vanloads of food and clothes and toys and doughnuts—and cash—Benigno had been a guard at La Mesa. The penitentiary, that stink hole east of town. He'd been hired because he was good with guns and was meaner than any inmate. He met Abigail when she brought the *pinches* gringos there. Translating Bible stories for the scumbags inside. But she was just what he liked—a bustling fat woman with a big bottom. And a car.

"You cook?" he asked her. "I know you drive."

It was his idea of courtship.

He shacked up with her shortly after that. The Christians gave him a Bible and a cross he wore. He drank only when they weren't around. They feared him—he was smaller than the blond gringas with their folk guitars, but his red eyes and grimace repelled them like a force field. He sometimes sat outside the little house and listened to them all shrieking their hymns, and he'd smoke and watch the street. You couldn't own guns in Mexico, but he was a guard, and to hell with them all. He kept a Glock in the back of his pants, and if anyone did not return his smile, he thought: *I know what you would look like with your brains on the street,* chingado. Those were good afternoons. Plus doughnuts.

The yellow van had appeared at the prison in the midst of the uproar surrounding the capture of El Surfo. *Shit,* Benigno thought now. He had to spit every time he heard that stupid name: El Surfo. Jesus Christ, they had enough Mexican *narcos* and *sicarios,* but this red-haired asshole was raised in California and had come down here chopping heads. Big celebrity. American accent. Calling himself the Surfer.

Benigno liked walking guard duty on the wall. Nobody in his right mind went down into the yard or into the cell complexes. It was a den of monsters. There was nothing like it outside of Mexico. Gangsters with La-Z-Boy loungers and big-screen TVs. Transvestite hookers and children. Women washing laundry and doing chores and marrying and cooking and working as whores. Booths selling tacos and knives, and babies playing in the dirt. Smoke. Screams. Music. Barbers. They had their own little city in there, and the gangsters sliced up anybody they disliked. Guards got Christmas bonuses from the *narcos*. Life went on. Benigno stayed up above it— aside from the smell, it was all right. It was like watching TV.

Then that fat red-haired bastard was dragged in, wrapped in chains. Helicopters and TV news crews swarmed. He'd grinned as he was led in. Smug. Looking around like a big movie star. His chained hands out in front, his big body laid back against the cops. He started to laugh. *"¡Me vale madre!"* he called.

Benigno watched from atop his wall and held his ancient M1 to his chest and hoped for a chance to drill him through one of his eyes. He didn't care if they sold drugs, if they chopped off heads. He hated it that they were lazy and arrogant. These *narcos* thought they were tough. He, Benigno, was the one they should have feared. If the government gave him enough guns and bullets, he'd have every one of those fools cold and facedown in the street.

Later, when El Surfo strode around the crowded yard with his bodyguards and hookers and fans and, sometimes, gringo journalists, Benigno tracked him, keeping his melon head in the sights.

Who had bright yellow VW vans in Tijuana but surfers? Benigno understood that van was Surfo's. It was his trademark. That's why it was painted so brightly. Everybody knew who was in it, even if the windows were black. But nobody dared take a shot. They had seen pictures of skinned enemies, their terrifying grinning red skulls left on street corners.

Surfo's associates came every day as a form of *narco* theater. Showing off. Parking that famous VW in the lot.

People loved El Surfo as much as they feared him. In Mexico, death was philosophy, mysticism. And Surfo was its boy king. They thought he was some Pancho Villa figure, some hero of the poor. Shit. That van was there to accomplish one thing: feed the fear. They kept two brilliantly painted surfboards bungeed to the roof rack. If he hadn't wanted to steal it so badly, Benigno would have set it on fire.

The Surfer. What a fool. Looking at him, Benigno was sure he couldn't even swim. He'd sink like a hog. Well, Benigno himself couldn't swim. So what. He couldn't drive either. He had found out that he was a good father—father to about thirty stinky-butt street urchins and Abigail's three kids. Everyone knew not to mess with his kids. Even bullies were afraid to steal their shoes or schoolbooks. It took only two or three visits from Benigno to make their *colonia* a peaceful kingdom for the orphans. It was amazing what a broken leg and a bloodied parent could accomplish. He liked it. He even liked the Baptistas calling him Brother Benigno.

He was almost a Christian.

It had started to go sour when El Surfo beat a hooker with some rebar.

Benigno was on the go-team when the whistles started blowing. They charged into the stampede of running criminals, following the sound of screams. That fat bastard was standing over a sprawled woman with three feet of rebar in his hand. She was dead, they thought at first, but Benigno found a pulse. Her head was battered into a strange shape, and her eyes were rolling. Nobody knew her name.

They pointed their sidearms at him, but he just laughed and went back to his rooms. He didn't have a cell. He had rooms. His cartel had paid thousands of dollars. Inmates called it the Penthouse.

The guards carried her to a storehouse outside the walls and laid her on the floor. Nobody knew who would get in trouble. It was clear that word had come down from outside that her injuries could not be blamed on the cartel. Important men were arranging Surfo's fate, and nothing should stand in its way. Freedom. The officers and guards were told to go back to work. So the doors were closed and she was left there to dream her life away.

Benigno didn't like being told what to do. And he didn't care for Surfo's smirk when they'd suggested they were going to shoot him. Too bad about the woman, of course. Yes, that wasn't very good.

After dark, he checked on her—still breathing. "Damn, girl," he told her, "you're as hard as I am." He heaved her onto his shoulder. "You don't weigh a goddamned kilo!" he said. "That fat asshole had to use an iron rod to win a fight with you!" He smuggled her out during the evening Bible study and hid her in the Baptists' van. The pastor took one look at her when he was done and nodded to Benigno and threw a blanket over her and drove them out of the lot. They got her treated at a clinic outside of the city. Incredibly, she survived. He moved her into the orphanage. It took her months to stand, to eat. Benigno had surprised himself by feeding her baby food with a plastic spoon until she could do it on her own. He changed her diapers. It was all a mystery. He had cared for only one other creature like this—a goat, when he was small. Mother had cut off its head and cooked it.

Abigail was furious. She was sure Benigno nursed the prostitute only so he could see her naked when he bathed her. But he ignored his wife and refused to allow others to help him.

When the woman finally came around, she was like some ghost. Her head was all lumpy, bits of her hair missing forever. She stood silent in corners and covered her eyes with her hand. He called her Maria. When he said it, she laughed. She laughed when she saw him naked too. But she could not talk. If he gave her a broom, she swept. Otherwise, she covered her eyes. One morning, Maria woke him with her shoe, hammering his face with it until blood was flying.

"Maria," he said. "No! Bad!"

So at night, he tied her to her bed.

"The only good thing I ever did," he said to Abigail.

Of course, the prison discovered it was he who had stolen Maria, and of course this good deed had cost him his job. Bastards took away his *pistola* and badge.

Benigno limped into the village of Guadalupe in the afternoon. He'd been walking since dawn. He threw a couple of kicks at the street dogs threatening him in the dirt alley. He spied Wilo's *yonke* ahead. The old junkyard. Wrecked cars were stacked behind a rattling chainlike fence. In a shabby corral beside the main office hut, Panfilo the mule hung his boxy old head in boredom. One ear swiveled toward Benigno as he approached.

"*¿Qué onda, pinche mula?*" he called.

Panfilo lifted his head and peeled back his lip and waited for Benigno's carrots. Benigno always brought carrots from the damned Baptists' larder. He hated carrots. He patted the mule's neck and went inside the shack.

"*¿Qué onda, Wilo?*" he said.

"*¡Don Benigno! ¿Qué hay?*"

"*Aquí nomás.*"

Benigno sat down and picked up a Mexican magazine featuring vividly crimson dead bodies basted in their own blood. A poster of a topless woman was taped to the bathroom door.

"Got pliers I can borrow?" he said.

"Sure."

Wilo shuffled over to a workbench and rattled around. Guy looked like a vulture, Benigno thought. Wilo handed him the pliers.

"Thanks."

Benigno opened his mouth and reached in and clamped the molar.

"Oh Jesus," Wilo said.

Benigno used both hands to twist it. Tears fell from his eyes. He grunted. He ripped the tooth out of his head. Noxious fluids choked him. He hurried to the toilet and spit red globs into the bowl.

"Jesus!" Wilo cried.

When Benigno sat back down, he had wads of toilet paper stuffed in that side of his maw. He showed Wilo the dark tooth. He was very proud of himself. He had done that. Nobody else could do that. But he wasn't stupid or crazy. He also knew he had just terrified poor Wilo. Now he could negotiate. Wilo understood he would stop at nothing to get what he wanted.

"I want the mule," he said.

"My mule?"

"Sí."

"But that mule, *es muy caro.* I don't think you can afford him. No offense."

"I'll trade you a car engine for him."

Wilo stroked his chin.

"What kind of engine?"

Benigno had done his research. He wasn't much on beauty. Not interested in nature. But he loved machines. Machines he could understand. When he was a boy in the garbage dumps, he would pour ground glass into the fuel tanks of the big tractors and watch them die when their operators tried to start them.

Later, the gringo-skateboard Baptists brought him old car magazines. He couldn't read a word. But he laughed at Rat Fink cartoons and studied hot-rod flatheads and full-blown hemi engines as if the magazines were scriptures. In his spare time, he drew fantastic dragsters and Formula One cars on notebook paper he stole from the kids.

The only time Maria spoke to him was when he showed her a modified '36 Ford with chrome blowers and upswept pipes in a magazine centerfold.

"Muy bonito," she had said.

He lit a cigarette and said, "Ah, *cabrón!*"

Now he grinned at Wilo—something Wilo did not want to see, considering the grisly tooth on a rag on his bench.

"Porsche," Benigno said. "A 1986 Carrera, rebuilt, fuel-injected, geared to a VW transmission."

He had looked at the van many times out in the lot, chatted

with the *buchones* leaning on it with their stupid *narco* cowboy clothes, guarding it ostentatiously.

Wilo's eyes widened.

"Nice," he said.

"You can have the transmission too if you give me a few other things."

"Condition of the engine?" Wilo said.

"Better than new."

Wilo wasn't a fool either—that Porsche engine was worth ten mules. Twenty.

"Did you kill somebody?" he asked.

"Not yet, no."

Wilo laughed nervously.

"Decide," the old man said.

They shook on the deal. Wilo put the supplies Benigno requested into a paper bag.

Benigno told him he'd be back for the mule in three days. He hoisted the garden hose over his shoulder, took the sack Wilo handed him, and set off toward Ensenada. He kept laughing all the way down the alley. He had missionary money in his front pocket, and he had the bottle of codeine they had given him for his toothache in his ass pocket.

Life was fulsome and redolent.

Nobody would tell him where El Surfo hung out. That *culero* had served two years in La Mesa and had walked. They knew better than to rat him out to anyone. But Pemexes all along the main drag were full of bored men waiting between cars to pump gas. "Man," he said at each one. "Have you seen that yellow Volks van? It's a beauty."

Cowards looked at the ground and mumbled, "No, no."

But it didn't take long.

The tenth guy had seen it. He wore a baseball cap with a homemade logo inked on it. In Sharpie he had written *KISS in LIVE! Puro rocanrol.* The van? The Volkswagen with the loud engine? It was always parked at the Farolito, a cantina off the docks not far from the cannery.

"Just follow the gulls," he said. "And the stink."

Benigno gave him twenty dollars.

"I need you to meet me beside the cannery," he said. "At five in the morning. Yes. Five, *vato.* I need a can of gas. And you need to drive me to Wilo's *yonke.* I'll give you fifty more dollars and two new surfboards."

"*Órale.*"

They shook.

Benigno started to whistle.

He walked past the bar. Yeah, it all stank. Stank of bad old fish. Pelicans squatted on the pilings of the dock. Boats out there bobbing. Benigno thought Maria might have found this romantic once. Now, she'd just cover her eyes and chuckle. His *vieja* Abigail would just want to get some cheap fish. Why lie? He desired Maria, not Abigail. It made him hot. Maria was still young enough. He thought he might be able to teach her to talk again, though he preferred silence. He stuck his tongue in the wound in his jaw and jerked himself back into the day.

He had paid the Pemex guy back home to give Maria a ride. If it all worked out, and it would work out, he'd give her a big surprise. She couldn't be expected to walk or take part in this business. But he had plans. *Pinche* Pemex! He was spending so much on them, he should be made president of the company.

There it was, fat and yellow and beautiful, that *pinche* surfer van. Two tones of yellow, pearl-white flames painted down its sides. Tinted windows and little curtains. He'd peeked in when it was in the prison lot. He knew there was a bed back there. Phony-ass surfboards still tied to the luggage racks on top. He shook his head. If you're going to cut off heads, at least be a man. The first thing Benigno was going to do after he killed El Surfo was get rid of that garbage.

He kept walking. The *sicarios* standing guard watched him and sneered. Some of them had those long *narco* boots, with toes so extended that they curled upward for six extra inches and looked like genie slippers. Black cowboy hats. Gold belt buckles with AK-47 insignias. He nodded. They nodded back. Some old bastard hauling a hose down the street.

He coiled the hose in an alley when night fell and made a nest there and slept the sleep of the righteous with his head on the paper bag.

When he'd lost his job at La Mesa, he and Abigail were even more dependent on the Baptists. Word went out in the barrio that Benigno had a crazy woman in his house. Maria would step outside completely naked, and Abigail would chase her back in with the broom. Cops sometimes drove down the alley and paused outside the house. Benigno knew it was only a matter of time. Some bad men of one stripe or another would come along wanting to know who she was and where she'd come from. He was sure the cartel would want to finish the job of protecting Surfo from further hassles. When the Baptists told him they needed a new director for their Casa de Luz orphanage south of Ensenada, he immediately volunteered.

Abigail didn't fight him—a house near the beach? A paycheck and no rent? Away from Tijuana? In her mind, an endless supply of gringo Cristiano goods and utter cachet in her new village. She was delighted.

Aside from the Bible studies and no tequila, it was a good life.

Soon, though, Benigno started to chafe. All the hubbub, all the noise, the smell of kids. It made him mad. He was old now. He just wanted to sleep. He didn't need much. He needed a room to himself. No snoring Abigail. No six a.m. shouting kids. Well, maybe Maria laughing quietly.

When he was a boy, homesteading the garbage dump in Mexicali with his mother, he loved his small hut made of box slats and plastic sheets. A tidy den where he could hide and dream his days away. There was a spot behind the orphanage. Flat. About ten feet above the high-tide line. He imagined his little hideout there. Maybe get the missionaries to bring him some old American garage doors to hammer into an extra room—he could dig his own outhouse. It wouldn't be hard to do. Sit out there as long as he wanted, staring out at the waves. Yes.

It was more of his general bad luck when that damned yellow van showed up in Sal Si Puedes. Two years of peace and here was the *narco* again. He walked down the stony road and stared at the back end of the VW sitting beside the little cantina by the Pemex. There was a four-room motel behind it, and stooges could be seen carrying Surfo's gym bag to one of them.

Benigno rubbed his jaw and spit and cursed. He was startled when that redheaded asshole stepped out of the bar and waved at him. He was hitting a bottle of Carta Blanca pretty hard. Benigno realized that El Surfo had no idea who he was. He lifted one hand and nodded. Surfo urinated in the street.

The whole plan presented itself like a revelation from Jesus. Benigno slapped his own forehead.

Surfo zipped up and went back inside.

Yes. Benigno was a genius. He would hop on his little motor scooter and putt up to Wilo's first thing in the morning. The mule. The garden hose. He rushed back to the house and wheeled the little spindly bike over to the Pemex and put gas in its tank. He didn't have to drive a car to get around. It was like the super-bicycle. Pedal until you were up to speed and hit the little motor and fly. He didn't even wear a helmet, just chugged along at five miles an hour.

He put down the kickstand and left the bike chained to a short white steel pole behind the station. No need to wake Abigail pedaling it ten times to get it started in the morning. He'd sneak away and be back before lunch, he thought.

Morning.

He was so happy. He went to the bathroom, where ten pestilential stalls sat in open cubbies. A flimsy plywood wall whitewashed and nailed to uprights separated the boys from the girls. He had been having some problems with their filthy toilet habits lately. He took a small can of black paint and a narrow brush and painted directions on the wall above the sink:

DON'T SHIT ON THE FLOOR. DON'T WIPE
WITH YOUR FINGERS. DON'T
WIPE YOUR FINGERS ON THE WALL.

Maria followed him out of the orphanage building.

"Go home," he said.

She turned around and went back inside.

He walked down to the Pemex. His motorbike was crushed and bent against the pole. The pump attendant came out from the garage, wiping his hands on a blue windshield cloth. Benigno was speechless. He just pointed.

"The Volkswagen," the man said. "Backed out. They were laughing."

Benigno had taken the Pepsi bottles out of the trash and filled them and started walking. Dirty sons of whores. He saw it was his destiny now. It was always meant to be.

He'd walked up the frontage road, figuring he could trudge along beside the highway. It was fairly flat all the way to Ensenada. But he came up out of the Sal Si Puedes access road and realized why Surfo had come to town. The little cement bridge over the Baja California highway had three naked bodies hanging from it, dangling from nooses. Cops had shut down the roadway and stood atop the bridge staring stupidly at the dead men. That fat bastard had come into town and killed fishermen!

But the worst part was the highway being closed. That meant no Baptists. No clothes or toys or doughnuts. Who knew how long the highway would be closed. *Cabrones.*

The cops didn't care that he had been a prison guard. They wouldn't let him walk up the frontage road or cross the bridge. They made him run across the dead highway and climb the rocks on the other side.

Surfo, he thought. *Just wait.*

The next morning, Benigno awoke in his nest of rubber garden hose. He was stiff. His foot stung, but with a fierce prod from one fingernail, the red volcano of flesh burst and the cactus thorn popped out. The jaw was already better, though his breath was like some rotten beast beside the road. He pissed on the wall and stowed his bag and hose and trudged to the cantina.

Too early, even for degenerate fishermen or *buchones*. It was dark and abandoned. He grabbed one of the white plastic chairs on its shabby cement porch and sat in the sun, eyes closed like a lizard. The barkeep was the first to arrive, around noon.

"*Viejo*," he said. "You can't sit there."

"I have a hundred gringo dollars that say I can," he replied, not opening his eyes. The hole in his gums still dripped poison down his throat. "I want to drink it all."

Abigail would be furious when she discovered he had emptied her coffee can of missionary money.

He could feel the man standing there, staring down at him.

After a few moments, there came the rattling of keys and the crack of the door lock snapping open.

The *sicarios* came in a pickup and two Japanese motorcycles. They stomped up to the porch and stood before him in a semicircle.

"*¿Y tu?*" one of them said.

"Waiting for El Surfo," he said.

"Who's that?"

"Funny," he said.

"We don't know a Surfo."

"I knew him at La Mesa."

Silence.

"He was in cell block twenty. He had cells ten, eleven, and twelve. In the Penthouse. I was one block over. In a corner cell. I did him a favor once."

Silence.

"Stand," the same guy said. He stood, held out his arms. They frisked him. Took his knife. Felt the plastic bottle in his back pocket. The *sicario* pulled it out and inspected it.

"*¿Y esto?*" he said.

"A gift for El Surfo. Got it from the gringos. I can get more. Lots more. Try one. It's codeine. You'll love your fucking life."

The guy smiled and glanced at his associates.

"Look at this old guy," he said.

"*Viejo loco.*"

They laughed, with no trace of warmth at all.

"*Bueno,*" his interrogator said. "You can stay." He handed the plastic bottle back to Benigno.

They held open the door of the cantina.

"Sit in here. We'll be watching you."

Te vamos a wachar.

El Surfo was a bear-shaped bastard, all right. He was hilarious. He seemed to fill half of the bar. Chain-smoking and hugging his crew of killers and kissing his worshippers. Benigno watched him from a corner as he sipped a tepid beer. Damn, but that boy could eat. It was Ensenada—he had platters of shrimp tacos and fish tacos delivered to his corner booth. Women in tight dresses and piled-up dyed-blond hair ate bits of taco from his fingertips. He demonstrated the immense bad taste of displaying a gold-plated AK on the table beside his greasy wax-paper rubbish and empties. Benigno watched him squeeze *chi-chis* and tell jokes. You could almost forget good old Surfo liked to make videos of men getting their heads cut off with electric saws. That he once wrapped two teenage girls' heads in duct tape and then filmed them writhing on the ground as they died of suffocation. And then he had come to Sal Si Puedes and pissed all over everything. Benigno's eyes grew redder as he squinted.

Maria, he thought.

The first *sicario* gestured for him to stand. He stood. The thug leaned down and murmured in Surfo's ear. Surfo looked over at Benigno and jerked his head in the universal Mexican gesture meaning *What do you want?*

Benigno stepped forward. He felt the pus bubble in his foot leak. His huarache was slippery. The pain was a small lightning bolt up his ankle, dissipating in his calf. Clean pain. Focus. He smiled.

"Jefe," he said.

"Yeah?"

"I knew you back in the day."

"When?"

"When you were in La Mesa."

Everybody knew El Surfo didn't like to talk about prison.

"I don't remember you," he said.

"Why would you?" Benigno moved closer, went to sit. "May I?" he asked.

Surfo opened his hands like a king and nodded.

Benigno slid into the seat across from the great man. He was shorter than Surfo by a head at least. The *sicarios* all thought he looked like a monkey.

"Can I smoke?"

Surfo nodded. "Give me one."

Benigno had Dominos, the notoriously rough Mexican cigs. Real men sucked the corrosive smoke into their lungs and let it slither out of their noses and never coughed. He shook one out for the *narco* and lipped out one for himself and lit them both from the same match.

"It's like we're on a date," El Surfo said.

His men exploded in laughter.

"Not going to kiss you," Benigno said.

"Look at this guy!" Surfo shouted.

Benigno took a drag. "I did you a service back then," he said.

Instantly suspicious, Surfo crossed his arms and narrowed his eyes.

"And what was that?" he demanded.

Benigno made a show of discomfort. He glanced at the *sicarios* and smiled shyly.

"It was…delicate," he said.

"What. The fuck. Are you talking about?"

Surfo's meaty palm smacked the table.

"The girl," Benigno whispered. "The—you know—whore."

Surfo snapped his fingers. Two thugs swarmed the bench and held Benigno's shoulders so he couldn't move.

"Which whore, old man?"

"The one. The hurt one. I took her and buried her for you."

El Surfo stared at him. His brows knotted over his freakish pale blue eyes.

Benigno whispered, "I smothered her and carried her out. Buried her up in Colonia Obrera."

"How."

"They let me go when I volunteered to do it. For you. I was set free. It was a good trade."

A strange kind of sigh came through the room. Surfo nodded once, and his gunmen let go of Benigno.

"I just wanted you to know that's what happened. It was taken care of."

Surfo drank some beer and belched and grinned.

"You came to tell me that?"

Benigno nodded. Took his plastic pill bottle out and set it on the table.

"And for this."

"*¿Qué es?*"

"Codeine. From California. Medical missionaries. They want to sell."

Surfo rattled the pills in the bottle.

"I sell to them, they don't sell to me."

"Not codeine, jefe. Not the best codeine in the world. I thought a genius like you—millions."

Surfo grinned with one side of his mouth.

"Genius," he repeated. "Handsome too."

His men laughed.

Benigno kept his eyes down.

"It won't take you long," he said, "to own these *pinches* gringos. Do what you want with them. Make them your slaves."

"*Pinches* gringos."

Benigno nodded.

"How many pills?" Surfo said.

"How many do you want?"

The *sicarios* and the jefe laughed.

"Have some tacos," the big man said.

Benigno took a pill and held the bottle out to Surfo.

"Sample," he said.

Surfo stared at him.

"You first."

"Ah! Of course. Very wise, jefe."

Benigno bounced two capsules in his palm and downed them. Held out his tongue. After five minutes, Surfo swallowed a couple of pills and washed them down with beer.

He couldn't know that drugs had absolutely no effect on Benigno.

Benigno ordered two tequilas.

He had never been drunk a day in his life, no matter how much he drank.

"You like the van," Surfo said.

It was after midnight. Some of the *sicarios* were asleep; most were drunk. Two of them danced in slow motion with hookers. All was smoke and red lights.

"I love the van," said Benigno. They were five tequilas down and had drunk an equal number of beers. "I always saw it through the front gate of the prison."

"Stop saying that. Damn."

"What, prison?"

"Hey."

"Sorry, jefe."

"And now you want a ride in it."

"Is that too much to ask?"

Benigno popped another codeine and slid the bottle to Surfo.

"Keep it, jefe," he said.

Surfo took another.

"You're all right, old man," he said.

They stood up. Benigno was glad to see that Surfo was unsteady already. He snapped his fingers at the bartender.

"Una botella más," he called. He dropped dollars on the bar. "Drinks for the boys."

One of the ridiculously pointy-booted gunmen said, "Boss. You all right?"

"I do what I want."

His men looked at each other. Surfo was a notoriously difficult guy to control. The gods seemed to be smiling on Benigno.

"You all right to drive, jefe?"

"Around the block, *pendejos*! How hard is that."

"Drink," Benigno said. He had his arm around this murdering asshole's shoulders. Partially bracing him with his body. He had to get him out of there, get him in the van, get him to start it and drive away to his dark place.

"I know where there are some fresh *muchachas*," he whispered.

Surfo hugged him and slurred, *"¡Pinche viejo jodido!"*

He laughed all the way to the van.

Benigno snagged his hose and tossed it on the roof. Surfo didn't even notice. They climbed in.

Although Benigno didn't drive, he appreciated a good vehicle. El Surfo had the interior tricked out with plush leather seats. The bed was in the back. Everything was deep maroon in there. Frankly, it looked like a whorehouse. It smelled like incense and marijuana. He gazed all around. Roomy. He liked it. It would fit right in that slot above the waves. *My bedroom,* he thought.

He watched El Surfo start it. Fancy. There wasn't even a key. The redheaded bastard pressed the brake to the floor and pushed a button, and the creamy roar of that Porsche engine filled the van.

"Sweet!" Surfo said. "Right?"

"Right."

Benigno handed him the bottle. After Surfo swigged from it, Benigno took a sip too. To him, it was like water.

Surfo eased the van into gear and they rolled.

The engine purred and snarled.

Surfo punched a button and god-awful noise filled the cabin.

"Skrillex!" Surfo yelled. *"¡Está chingon el guey!"*

They were out of sight of the bar. Almost to the cannery. Out of reach of the one streetlight.

"Stop for a second," Benigno said. "Over there. I want to piss." He looked around as Surfo pulled over. He left the engine running—good. "Then we head back. You have already been too generous."

Surfo nodded, rubbed his eyes.

"What was her name?" Benigno asked.

"Who?"

"The woman. In prison. What was her name?"

Surfo blew air through his lips. He shrugged.

"You don't know?"

He lit another Domino and studied its bright red cherry of embers.

"Nah."

Benigno put the cigarette out in Surfo's right eye.

Surfo didn't scream—he roared, like some animal. They were at least a kilometer away from the bar—nobody was going to hear it. But Benigno was already hammering his face with his left elbow, striking heavy blows over and over until Surfo slumped with his head back and bubbles of blood inflating in his crumpled nostrils and popping in the air. The old man hopped out and retrieved the hose and paper bag from between the surfboards. He unrolled the hose and went to the back of the van. He had Jesus songs on his mind. Missionary songs. He sang them softly to himself as he got the duct-tape roll from the bag. He shoved the hose into the exhaust and used half the roll to make sure it was secure and not leaking fumes. He ran the hose down the side of the van and inserted it in the window and made sure the exhaust was flowing nicely.

"You like duct tape," he said to El Surfo as he turned off the lights and eased the door shut.

The gas had run out long before the Pemex kid in the Kiss hat showed up. By then, El Surfo was dead as a slaughtered pig. Gray-blue and foaming at the mouth. Benigno had hauled him well off the road, among scraggly weeds. He heaved a few cracked cement slabs onto the corpse and sat in the shadows until the kid showed up. All doors open to air out the van.

They filled the tank and they were pleased at the sound of that Porsche engine and they drove out of town, though the kid didn't understand why Benigno wouldn't let him turn on the headlights. At Wilo's, the kid took his fifty bucks and the two surfboards.

"Sell those," Benigno said. "Don't let the bad guys see you."

The kid was gone like smoke.

It took Wilo twenty minutes to rig the chains onto the engine, and it came out like a tooth. They tied heavy ropes to the front end and hooked them onto Panfilo the mule's harness.

"I want that harness back," Wilo said.

"You can have the mule too," Benigno said.

They headed down to the frontage road. The mule was a puller. It made Benigno happy as he walked beside the big brute. By now, the road would be cleared. Light like God's own fires was pouring over the dry gray peaks. Silver fish-belly clouds. Violet and orange streaks above him. Soon, he'd see the ocean again. Though he didn't care about it. He patted Panfilo as they walked. He fed him a carrot. Truckers honked and he waved at them. If the bad guys slept a little late, he'd make it home. If they came looking for him... well, it would be a bad day for them.

Benigno found Maria in the van, sitting in the driver's seat, her hands already on the wheel. She looked at him and laughed. She imagined hitting him with her shoe. Hammering his head with it. But she loved driving the van. She rested her elbow on the door frame and let the sea air coming through the open window lift her hair. She closed her eyes and remembered that her name was Veronica.

People in their cars, speeding to La Paz, laughed at the little old man and the mule and his daughter sitting in the broken-down old bus, the whole parade walking like some velvet painting you'd buy in a tourist shop. It was all so picturesque. So very simple.

ACKNOWLEDGMENTS

I'd like to offer my respect and gratitude to all the contributing authors, who took my vague guidelines and produced a remarkable batch of stories. Special thanks go to Josh Kendall, who believed in this project from the beginning and provided much-needed guidance. I'd also like to recognize the hard work of Pamela Marshall, Ashley Marudas, Maggie Southard, Pamela Brown, and the rest of the gang at Mulholland and Little, Brown. Copyeditor Tracy Roe's expert parsing and trimming improved the book immeasurably. Kari Stuart and Patrick Morley at ICM Partners provided invaluable assistance every step of the way. As always, I owe a tremendous debt to Barbara Peters, John Goodwin, and all of my peeps at the Poisoned Pen Bookstore. The music of Townes Van Zandt inspired the book's title and, in some ways, its theme. Gary Phillips gets a special mention for giving me the blessing to tweak his idea and run with it. My good friend Dennis McMillan deserves credit (blame?) for gifting me his 1960 Cadillac and helping to awaken my adult-onset mechanic's syndrome. Finally, deepest thanks go to my beautiful wife, Sandra, for her unconditional love and support and for tolerating my idiosyncrasies and obsessions.

CONTRIBUTORS

Ace Atkins is the *New York Times* bestselling author of nineteen books, including the Edgar-nominated Quinn Colson novels and five critically acclaimed continuations of Robert B. Parker's beloved Spenser series. A former newspaper reporter and SEC football player, Atkins also writes essays and investigative pieces for several national magazines, including *Outside* and *Men's Journal.* He lives in Oxford, Mississippi, with his family, where he's friend to many dogs and several bartenders. He drives a 2000 Ford F-150 with over 350,000 miles on the odometer.

C. J. Box is the bestselling author of twenty-one novels, including the Joe Pickett series. His latest, *Off the Grid,* debuted at number one on the *New York Times* bestseller list. Box's many awards include the Edgar Allan Poe Award for Best Novel (*Blue Heaven,* 2009), the Anthony Award, the Barry Award, the Macavity Award, and, most recently, the 2016 Western Heritage Award for Literature by the National Cowboy Museum. His books have been translated into twenty-seven languages, and over ten million copies of his novels have been sold in the United States alone. Box lives in Wyoming with his wife, Laurie, and he drives a Ford F-150 Lariat four-by-four truck. His first-ever auto was a classic '53 Chevy pickup.

Kelly Braffet is the author of the novels *Save Yourself, Last Seen Leaving,* and *Josie and Jack*. Her work has been published in the *Fairy Tale Review, Post Road,* and several anthologies. She currently lives in upstate New York with her husband, the author Owen King, and is at work on a new novel. Braffet drives a hybrid Toyota Camry, which she realizes is not that exciting, but since it's one of the models that have been known to accelerate uncontrollably occasionally, she still feels pretty dangerous.

Michael Connelly is the *New York Times*–bestselling author of twenty-one novels featuring LAPD detective Hieronymus "Harry" Bosch. He has also written six novels featuring LA defense attorney Mickey Haller (the first of which, *The Lincoln Lawyer,* was adapted into a feature film starring Matthew McConaughey) as well as several stand-alone crime thrillers. Sixty million copies of Connelly's books have sold worldwide and his work has been translated into thirty-nine languages. He has won the Edgar Award, the Anthony Award, the Macavity Award, the *Los Angeles Times* Best Mystery/Thriller Award, the Shamus Award, and many others. Connelly is also a producer and writer for *Bosch,* the Amazon Prime television show based on his work. Connelly lives with his family in Florida and California. Connelly's latest novel is *The Wrong Side of Good-Bye*. He currently drives a 2014 Chrysler 300 SRT8.

Diana Gabaldon is the author of the award-winning number-one *New York Times*–bestselling Outlander novels, described by *Salon* magazine as "the smartest historical sci-fi adventure-romance story ever written by a science PhD with a background in scripting 'Scrooge McDuck' comics." The series is published in forty-two countries and thirty-eight languages, with twenty-seven million copies in print worldwide. Gabaldon's current writing projects include the ninth major novel in the Outlander series, as yet untitled, and a collection of novellas. She is a coproducer and adviser for the *Outlander* TV series, produced by the Starz network and Tall Ship Productions, which is drawn from her novels. Gabaldon lives with her husband, Doug Watkins, in Scottsdale, Arizona. Watkins provided both the original suggestion for "Fogmeister" and the historical research on which the story is based, and he is a car enthusiast himself; at the moment, he's restoring/rebuilding a 1971 Firebird from the wheels up. (Diana drives an Audi S6.)

Sara Gran is the author of the novels *Dope, Come Closer, Saturn's Return to New York,* and the Claire DeWitt series. Her books have been published in over a dozen countries and as many languages. Sara Gran also writes for television and film and worked for two years with the Peabody-winning John Wells production *Southland.* Born and raised in Brooklyn, now living in California, Gran has worked with books as a writer, bookseller, and collector for most of her career. She currently drives a filthy Mini Cooper around Los Angeles.

Patterson Hood is a critically acclaimed singer-songwriter and a founding member of the Drive-By Truckers, whose latest recording, *American Band,* is set for a fall 2016 release. He has also done three solo albums, the most recent of which is *Heat Rumbles in the Distance* (2012). As an author, Hood has written a number of essays and articles that have appeared on NPR and in such publications as the *New York Times* and the *Oxford American*. Hood was born in Muscle Shoals, Alabama, where his father was bassist for the legendary Muscle Shoals Rhythm Section. He lives in Portland, Oregon. Hood's past cars have included a 1957 Dodge Custom Royal and a souped-up 1969 Chevy pickup, but now he just drives a Subaru Outback and a Honda minivan.

Joe R. Lansdale is the author of over forty novels, including the popular Hap and Leonard series, and numerous short stories. His work has been published in more than two dozen short-story collections, and he has edited or co-edited over a dozen anthologies. He has received many awards, including the Edgar Award, eight Bram Stoker Awards, the Horror Writers Association Lifetime Achievement Award, the British Fantasy Award, and, most recently, the Spur Award from the Western Writers of America for his novel *Paradise Sky*. His work has been adapted for film (*Bubba Ho-Tep, Cold in July*) and television (the Sundance Channel's *Hap and Leonard*). Lansdale lives in Nacogdoches, Texas, and he drives a Toyota Prius.

George Pelecanos is the bestselling author of nineteen novels set in and around Washington, DC, a recent collection of short fiction, *The Martini Shot: A Novella and Stories,* and the graphic novel *Six*. He has been the recipient of the Raymond Chandler Award in Italy, the Falcon Award in Japan, and the Grand Prix Du Roman Noir in France and is a two-time winner of the *Los Angeles Times* Book Prize. His credits as a television producer and writer include *The Wire, Treme,* and

The Pacific. He is currently at work on *The Deuce*, a new series for HBO. Pelecanos lives in Silver Spring, Maryland, and drives a Bullitt Mustang.

Gary Phillips is the author of more than a dozen novels, including *Bangers, The Jook, The Warlord of Willow Ridge*, and the popular Ivan Monk mysteries. He's edited numerous anthologies, published more than fifty short stories, and some of his work has been optioned for TV. In addition to being a longtime member of the Mystery Writers of America, Phillips chaired the Eleanor Taylor Bland Crime Fiction Writers of Color grant awarded by Sisters in Crime and served as president of the Private Eye Writers of America. When not sharing the oh-so-PC Prius with his wife, he puts the hammer down in his V-8 '92 Cadillac Eldorado. Maybe, he tells himself, one day he'll get that '58 Ford Fairlane he and his mechanic pops rebuilt many years ago running again.

James Sallis is the critically acclaimed author of numerous novels, including the Lew Griffin series, *The Killer Is Dying, Death Will Have Your Eyes, Drive*, and the recently released *Willnot*. He has also published multiple collections of poetry, essays, and short stories, a major biography of Chester Himes, and a translation of Raymond Queneau's *Saint Glinglin*. Sallis lives in Phoenix, Arizona, with his wife, Karyn. He drives a Nissan Frontier pickup but says that he is saving up for that pinnacle of modernity, a Hudson Terraplane.

Wallace Stroby is the author of seven novels, four of which feature professional thief Crissa Stone. An award-winning journalist, he was an editor for thirteen years at the *Newark Star-Ledger,* the state's largest newspaper. His first car was a jet-black 1967 Mustang convertible, which he bought in 1978 for five hundred dollars and wishes he still owned. These days, he drives a more sedate (but still jet-black) Toyota Scion TC.

Luis Alberto Urrea is the critically acclaimed and bestselling author of sixteen books, including *The Hummingbird's Daughter* and *Into the Beautiful North.* His most recent book, *The Water Museum,* a collection of short stories, was a finalist for the 2015 PEN/Faulkner Award and contains the Edgar Award–winning "Amapola." *The Devil's Highway,* his 2004 nonfiction account of a group of Mexican immigrants lost in the Arizona desert, won the Lannan Literary Award and was a finalist for the Pulitzer Prize. His work is taught in universities throughout the country. Urrea lives in Chicago with his wife, Cindy, and drives a Ford Escape but imagines he's driving a '67 Mustang fastback in metal-flake blue with mag wheels and glasspack mufflers.

Willy Vlautin is the author of four novels, *The Motel Life, Northline, Lean On Pete,* and *The Free.* In addition to being a writer, he is a musician, a singer-songwriter, and a founding member of Richmond Fontaine, whose latest album, *You Can't Go Back If There's Nothing to Go Back To,* was released in March of 2016. Vlautin also writes and records with the Delines, whose debut album, *Colfax,* has earned worldwide critical acclaim. *The Motel Life,* Vlautin's first novel, was adapted for the big screen in 2013. Vlautin lives in Portland, Oregon, and is at work on his fifth novel. Sadly, he says, he had to sell his prized derelict red 1968 Le Mans to a hesher. But even now he still dreams of her, and he rates the sale at number fourteen in his top one hundred biggest mistakes.

Ben H. Winters is the award-winning author of nine novels, most recently *Underground Airlines* (Mulholland, 2016). *World of Trouble* (Quirk), the concluding book in the Last Policeman trilogy, was nominated for the Edgar Award from the Mystery Writers of America. *Countdown City* was an NPR Best Book of 2013 and the winner of the Philip K. Dick Award for Distinguished Science Fiction. *The Last Policeman* was the recipient of the 2012 Edgar Award. Winters has also written extensively for the stage and has published several books for young readers. He recently moved to Los Angeles, where he drives his second Honda Odyssey in a row.

COPYRIGHT ACKNOWLEDGMENTS

ABOUT THE EDITOR

Patrick Millikin is a longtime bookseller at the Poisoned Pen Bookstore in Scottsdale, Arizona, and a freelance writer; his articles, interviews, and reviews have appeared in *Publishers Weekly*, the *Los Angeles Review of Books*, *True West*, and other publications. He is the editor of *Phoenix Noir* (Akashic Books, 2009), which contained the Edgar Award–winning story "Amapola" by Luis Alberto Urrea. Millikin lives with his wife, Sandra, in Phoenix. He currently drives a 1997 Chevrolet Cheyenne K2500 pickup and is slowly restoring a 1960 Cadillac Sedan DeVille.